SHTORM

NICOLÁS MARTÍNEZ

Shtorm

SHTORM
Nicolás Martínez

© Nicolás Martínez 2025

Published by The Little French eBooks

All rights reserved. No part of this book may be used or reproduced in any manner whatsoever without written permission, except in the case of brief quotations embodied in critical articles or reviews.

978-1-387-50363-6
Imprint: Lulu.com

"Never before, since the Second World War, has Europe been so necessary. And yet, it has never been so endangered"

Emmanuel Macron

PROLOGUE

Special forces from Belarus in their MI-8 helicopters and about three hundred Russian paratroopers in their IL-76 planes carried out aerial assault military exercises about fifteen kilometers from the border with Lithuania. Two Russian paratroopers died in the training. In turn, Lithuania, pro-Western, pro-NATO, and pro-US, has amassed troops at its border, while Poland, its neighboring ally, has gathered fifteen thousand soldiers and war material at the same border. Nearby, Russia has stockpiled 2S1 122mm anti-aircraft batteries, Buk-M3 anti-aircraft missiles, and other equipment from the 34th Motorized Infantry Brigade, moving all this personnel and material from its base in Kerch, Crimea (taken by Russia in 2014), to position it in Yelnya, about one hundred fifty kilometers from the border with Ukraine. Russian television and TikTok videos were in charge of spreading these movements and military practices along the border, generating fear and concern throughout Europe and the world about a possible Russian invasion of Ukraine.

Simultaneously, a pro-Russian Telegram channel in Belarus broadcasted videos of a train transporting American M109 Paladin artillery units as they crossed through Legnica, in Poland, announcing that the convoy was heading to the east of Belarus, when in fact, the convoy was heading west, towards Germany.

The aforementioned events are not advances of what Shtorm offers us in its pages, but real activities from the last months in a Central European scenario that includes Iraqi migrants, the Minsk II agreements, NATO, the EU, Brexit, the USA, Turkey, extremist groups from the Middle East, and naturally, Russia.

Putin's words: "Forget about the current map of Europe", weigh like a sentence on a continent that at times seems to have lost its way, with migrants, Islamists, secessionists, and revanchists everywhere. It's not the idyllic Europe that tourism taught us, but a multiform misunderstanding that seems to resurrect from the ashes of the second world war to bring down the foundations of the Judeo-Christian civilization of the West.

The plot with which the author delights us, sprinkled with artificial intelligence, hypersonic weapons, disinformation campaigns, cybercrime, a potential mutually assured destruction with tactical nuclear weapons, and of course, of rancor, hatred, envy, egos and ambitions, moves us restlessly between the main European capitals and terrorist camps lost in the middle of nowhere. A type of hybrid war not exempt from bombings, assassinations, missile attacks, and a tireless offensive of spies and intelligence specialists who move among renowned old continent and global information agencies. The narration is continuous, unstoppable, dramatic. The terms are precise without being complicated and accurate without being pedantic. The argument is more than relevant, worrisome.

In an interesting note from December 2021, the Spanish journalist Ricardo Angoso, seasonally residing in Colombia, poses the million-dollar question these days: "IS THERE A RISK OF A WAR BETWEEN RUSSIA AND UKRAINE?". And he answers himself: "It is evident that there is, but whoever triggers the conflict will put at risk the stability and security on the European continent for many years, leading us to a new cold war with unpredictable consequences for everyone." A systematic understanding of the dynamics that animate the situation in question helps to place on the situation map, the probabilities, the possibilities and the best of our reason and our perception in the hope that in 2024 Europe and the world will be a concert with less bluster and with few global survival challenges as the ones sketched in Shtorm.

Since his first texts as a writer, Nicolás Martínez demonstrates his great research capability, his intuitive way of linking facts, and his narrative skill. The leap from the Latin American jungle, from the Colombian-Venezuelan confrontation, from narcoterrorism activity to the "civilized" European political-military culture offers us a great opportunity to highlight his excellent conditions as a novelist.

That there is a Colombian involved in this whole complex scenario of escalation and eventual confrontation is novel, as intriguing as it is to delve into the bowels of the main protagonists of this narrative, who move between the excitement of tactical, detective-like research and the strategic transcendence of rational actors in action.

The invitation is to immerse yourself in this roller coaster of tensions, intrigue, and imagination based on true events that could, by the time you, dear reader, finish the story, have us subjected to a pre-war or even warlike situation of unsuspected consequences. Shtorm offers us a granular reading, worthy of one of Latin America's top military experts, paired with an expectant plot that involves serious geopolitical thoughts on the current European reality, and incidentally, the North American and Russian ones. With this novel, Martínez sets himself on the path of classic real-life based thriller narrators, like Follet, Collins, Clancy, Chandler, and others.

JOHN MARULANDA

FIRST PART

I

The subject entered the languid, whitish hospital room with a slow and stealthy step. It was spacious compared to those overcrowded with beds and numerous complaining sick people he remembered; few had access to so much space in a clinic in the Soviet Union. "No matter the size, there's nothing more depressing than a hospital room," he thought. The individual stopped, with a gesture of deep respect, and bowed his head; after lifting it again, he observed, at the end of the room, the patient who lay prostrate in bed. An officer with the rank of KGB major whispered something to the sick man, then Yuri Vladimirovich Andropov seemed to wake from the deep stupor he was in. Andropov lifted his trembling left hand with difficulty, signaling for the subject to come closer, who, as if propelled by a spring, immediately obeyed. The major quickly brought a chair to the edge of the sick bed, and the guest sat down with a somewhat puzzled face; with great effort, Andropov turned his head to indicate to the major, in a quiet voice: "Leave us alone, Vasili, make sure no one interrupts us." The major nodded and quickly left, carefully closing the pearled door.

Andropov shifted uncomfortably in his bed and then ordered: "Pass me the glasses, Vladimir Vladimirovich." He promptly took them from the table right beside, after putting them on, the yellowish face of the Soviet leader seemed to gain, for a moment, the vigor of previous years. "The brightness of the Rodina, like that of my existence, slowly fades," he complained, "my life has been marked by austerity, and always keeping a distance from the flatteries that power entails, both are dangerous companions, they cause us to lose our leadership's north in regard to the revolution's objectives." Andropov made a slight grimace of pain, after a few seconds, he continued his soliloquy: "Today, despite my efforts to cleanse it from so much garbage, the party's direction is in the hands of decrepit corrupts and vain with the power given by their positions, foolish mummies who in their blinded dissolute life do not see the apocalypse of the Soviet Union coming." A bout of coughing interrupted him, the subject, surprised by what he was hearing, saw a pitcher of water on the table, poured the liquid into a glass, and handed it to him.

After drinking a couple of sips and returning it, the dying leader continued: "We should have replaced Leonid Ilich years ago, his personality cult, accompanied by his addiction to alcohol, plunged the party's direction into years of inaction; while economic stagnation, like a lurking enemy, grew and was ignored, our country needed to accompany the changing times, instead, we turned our back on modernity, infatuated with feats of the past, locked in our comfortable dachas drinking vodka and eating caviar." Andropov's gaze remained fixed on the window, where one could see the fall of delicate flakes heralding the start of a snowstorm; the slow, fragile voice was heard again: "In circumstances like this, I don't know how to qualify fate. Is it an irony, do you know? I have clarity in my mind and enough power to change the course of this great nation, yet, the specter of death roams this room, my days, what am I saying, perhaps my hours, are numbered." The individual, who was sitting, perplexedly witnessing the final words of the most powerful man in the USSR, tried to say something. Andropov stopped him cold by slightly raising his hand: "No, my time in this life is scarce, I must finish what I want to say to you." The subject bowed his head in reverence, maintaining a prudent silence. "Five years, that was the time I required to straighten the course of this heavy ship called USSR, unfortunately, I will not have that time, what little is left of my life slips away like water through the fingers of my hands." Another gesture of suffering seemed to reflect on Andropov's face; it took him a few seconds to overcome it, then, after catching his breath, he expressed: "The youth must take the reins of our nation, Mikhail Sergeyevich is a hope for the prosperity of the nation, similarly Alexander Nikolaevich; however, I highly doubt that after these kidney ailments take me to the grave and I'm rendered all honors with the pomp characteristic of our party members, either of them will be chosen to succeed me. Sadly, the Politburo has already selected another mummy to ensure their privileges are preserved. Take it as a fact that Konstantin Ustinovich will be the next general secretary of the party, good news no doubt for those old-timers, but an ominous omen for the destinies of the Motherland."

Andropov continued. The cold, penetrating gaze of Yuri Andropov rested on his silent interlocutor for a few seconds, which to the young individual seemed like centuries. The Soviet leader scrutinized him with his unfathomable eyes; the young man shivered slightly. "Hand me that red folder at the bottom of the table," he directed. The person promptly placed it in his hands. After this, Andropov closed his eyes for a moment, appearing to lose consciousness; however, he was tapping his fingers slowly on the folder. The individual was about to stand up to notify the major that something bad could be happening when his weary voice was heard again: "Remain seated, I am merely organizing my thoughts; you must know that difficult times are approaching for our beloved nation, internally and also beyond our borders; the West will want to take advantage of our weaknesses, they will probably succeed. The folder you just handed me may contain a good part of the solution to prevent it, or... to take revenge, as the case may be; I want you to keep it." The individual's voice was heard for the first time: "Why are you entrusting me with this information, Comrade General Secretary?"

A faint smile could be observed on the face of the elderly leader: "Nothing in the Soviet Union escapes my scrutiny, I have followed your short career at the Center, you also made an interesting analysis of the United States' containment strategy against our interests in Africa, equally remarkable are your reports on the Americans' policy in Europe, they align with my thinking on how to confront them: diplomatic containment, military threat, and sabotage; the military solution must be the last alternative, however, we must make them know that we will not hesitate to use our military power if necessary —a short fit of coughing emerged again—. Time is of the essence, Vladimir Vladimirovich, it won't be long before I once again enter a period of uncertain unconsciousness; that final, catastrophic, and frustrating end, of our nation, I mentioned, will come inevitably; our homeland will change, the Motherland will no longer be as we have known it for decades; it could happen in a year or in ten, and we must be prepared; it's a direct order from me, keep, study, and analyze the right moment to implement what has been planned there; your obligation is to return the state of affairs to the course from which they should have never deviated." Andropov handed the gleaming red leather folder to the stunned young man, who was about to pose a final question when the elderly man lying in bed seemed to run out of air, the individual rushed to the door to alert the officer, who let out a loud cry for a doctor to come, then, a group of doctors and nurses rushed into the huge room; amidst the commotion that ensued, the flustered young man disappeared down the long hospital corridor, with the mysterious red portfolio in one of his hands.

II

areed Zakaria introduced, then extended his hand to greet the guest on his weekly analysis and opinion show, Fareed Zakaria GPS; Craig Eastman courteously returned the greeting with a smile. Zakaria then provided a brief description of Mr. Eastman's resume and experience. He had graduated from the faculty of international relations and political studies at the University of Cambridge, with a PhD in defense issues from King's College London. Mr. Eastman had also written two books on defense topics, and was a frequent contributor to articles on sensitive military matters for Jane's International Defense Review magazine. Zakaria commented, picking up a book from the coffee table, that Craig Eastman had just published his latest literary work, its title: Back to 1939? The New Military Challenges for A Europe in Crisis; the conversation that evening would revolve around his new book. Zakaria took his notebook, and after reviewing it for a couple of seconds, he said:

"Craig, without a doubt, your book contains important elements of analysis, as well as very worrying ones, on the current military reality of the European Union. How would you summarize this situation?"

"Let me begin at the moment where I believe the genesis of what we now call the European Union's identity crisis occurred. It happened on January 15, 2019, when the British parliament rejected the European Union exit agreement; this decision had a harmful consequence, the hard Brexit, which, in the following years, led to a chain reaction that ended in the political tensions we are living today within the EU."

"You talk about a chain reaction. What other events are part of this identity crisis that the European Union is experiencing today?"

"A first event, which happened at the beginning of 2020, brought our economies to a standstill. I refer to the coronavirus, or COVID-19. The management of the crisis within the EU was disastrous. The Schengen Area, which eliminated border controls and common borders, fell apart in March of that year. Several of the member countries, which were practically begging for medical material to stem the spread of the virus and to attend to the many serious cases they had, received a denial from the European leadership. The drama reached such a point that the Serbian president, with a broken voice, angrily expressed in a press conference that 'European solidarity does not exist... For the European Union, we are not good enough'. It is clear that countries had to prioritize the welfare of their nationals, however, the mismanagement of this crisis generated resentments in several union members, which could be taking their toll now; a second fact, unthinkable until a few years ago, is happening. We are on the verge of the dissolution of the United Kingdom; Scotland and Northern Ireland have initiated political processes to separate from England; this has reignited the independence flame in Catalonia, the consequences of which we still do not know today. Another unforeseen event happened: the victory, in 2022, of Marine Le Pen; her main campaign proposal, the French exit from the EU, or Frexit; Le Pen moved forward with holding a referendum to decide on this exit at the polls. This referendum will be held in the fall of this year, and it is worth noting that polls are predicting a victory for the 'yes' side; this was followed, like a domino effect, by decisions to carry out several referendums in countries that are part of the union; Italy, Belgium, Austria, Greece, and Hungary will also put to popular vote, in 2024, the possibility of leaving the EU. A bleak outlook looms over Europe."

"You mention in your book that Europe is on the brink of a military conflict. At what moment did the political crisis lead to the military tensions we perceive today among the EU partners?"

Craig Eastman grimaced uncomfortably before answering the question:

"Even worse, Fareed, we are not only facing worrying military tensions among European partners, but the current EU borders are under serious threat."

Zakaria narrowed his eyes, asking:

"Let's take this one step at a time, Craig. What are the tensions among EU partners today?"

"These tensions have their origin in the United States' decision to withdraw from NATO; as part of the isolationist process of the Trump government, the president promised, in his reelection campaign, to cut military spending; once reelected, Donald Trump threatened his partners, at the beginning of 2021, to withdraw from it if they did not increase their budgetary contribution to the organization's expenses; Germany and France understood the proposal as an ultimatum, and then proposed something that had already been suggested some years ago, the creation of a European army; annoyed, the North American president took the opportunity to order a staggered withdrawal of army and air force troops, this withdrawal should be completed by the end of 2024.

Zakaria expressed:

"I understand, Trump launched this ultimatum as a kind of bluff."

"Right, he never thought the German and French proposal was really serious; he used it to pressure an increase in European contributions."

"By the way, how is the idea of creating a European army going?"

"Not good."

"Why?"

"First, because amid severe fiscal restraint, it is not easy to replace the more than six hundred billion dollars that the United States contributes to NATO defense spending; although, to be fair, their real contribution to defense spending in Europe barely exceeds forty billion dollars. Even so, it is not easy to reach an agreement on how to finance the new European army; let's be clear, without the United States, NATO is doomed to disappear. Second, when it came time to develop the idea of the European army, the egos and interests of some member countries took precedence over the general interest of Europe. How would this be formed? Would the national armed forces be under a community authority? Or would it be a group of national armies grouped into battle groups, but subject to a common military command? Finally, are we talking about a single and community European army, placed parallel to the national armed forces? As if that were not enough, and in line with what I mentioned at the beginning, the strategic interests of each EU member are diverse, Poland does not have the same military priorities as Germany or France, just as the priorities of the Baltic countries are different from those of Spain or Portugal; it's clear that reaching a consensus on this has not been easy."

"So, is Europe far from having its own army?"

Skepticism took over Eastman's face.

"For now, I'm afraid so."

"Craig, you also mentioned that the current borders of the EU are at risk. Why?"

"Russia is today, although it always has been, a latent threat to the security of Europe. Winston Churchill once stated, referring to Russia, then the USSR, that it was a riddle wrapped in a mystery inside an enigma, and that, perhaps, the key to solving it could be found in its national interest; such strategic interest lies today in the gradual approach in the past by the EU and NATO to its borders, which has posed a direct threat to its national security, now that there are signs of weakness in both, that threat, which today becomes fragile, could turn into an opportunity for the Russians."

Zakaria furrowed his brow.

"I understand the issue with NATO, but why would the EU be a challenge for Russia?"

"The Russians have always considered the United States and Europe, and their vital values, democracy, human rights, economic liberalism, rule of law, among others, as a threat to their national interests; if we add to that the supposed humiliation suffered before a hypothetical deceit by the EU and NATO, regarding the non-expansion of their borders to the east, Russia's revisionist stance, translated into two aspects, military and energy, turns into a potential headache for the EU."

"How would you explain these two aspects, Craig? What would they consist of?"

"The unheeded warning by Russia, regarding the expansion of the EU's borders to the east, which also meant the expansion of NATO's influence limits, has generated a strategy on their part that consists of several elements: the first, to use all economic, political, and military tools to obstruct such expansion; the second, the beginning of a less noticeable war, but equally harmful, that consists of an information war, most of the time misinformation, which includes hacking, carrying out cyberattacks, and promoting extensive fake news networks; its purpose, to interfere in electoral processes to benefit political parties or candidates that denigrate the current international order, generally from the extreme right or left, who are anti-system; the 2016 elections in the United States demonstrate the power of this dangerous tool. Finally, in my opinion, the United States did Russia a favor by withdrawing from the INF Treaty in 2019, which then decided to deploy a series of actions aimed at eroding the main nuclear disarmament treaties, this poses a serious threat in the medium term to world peace, which we have enjoyed, relatively, since the end of World War II"And the matter related to energy? What is it about?"

"It is clear that, despite all the efforts by the EU to reduce energy dependence on Russia, it remains. This is a matter that generates concern among the union's authorities and its governments; Russia knows this and will not hesitate, if necessary, to use this tool to pressure Europe."

Zakaria shook his head a couple of times, a sign of concern.

"The title of your book mentions the year 1939. Why?"

Eastman took a breath to answer that question:

"Do you know something, Fareed? In my opinion, World War II did not end in 1945."

Zakaria made a face of strangeness.

"Sorry? If it didn't end that year, when did it end? Germany, history says, lost the war."

Craig Eastman outlined a smile on his lips.

"That's what historians say, Fareed. History, sometimes, is like a river, with deep underlying currents at its bottom."

Fareed Zakaria leaned forward, moving a few inches to the edge of the chair, with his eyes wide open.

"Let's see, Craig. How is that?"

"World War II actually ended on November 9, 1989, with the fall of the Berlin Wall. The Cold War was just a hidden extension of it; although Germany lost that first chapter, the real loser, in 1989, was the Soviet Union, now the Russian Federation." Eastman paused, then said: "which brings us back to 1939."

Zakaria couldn't help but show a look of surprise.

"- Wow, Craig, I ask you to help me with the development of that idea."

"The germ of World War II is related to the humiliation suffered by Germany in the Treaty of Versailles, signed in 1919, which ended the Great War."

"That's right, Craig. Sorry to interrupt, but let me pose another question. You propose, according to what was previously stated, that Russia is humiliated today. Is that really correct?"

"Absolutely, consider that territorially it lost more than six million square kilometers, around one hundred and forty million inhabitants left the USSR, it dropped from the third to the eleventh place in GDP size, its geopolitical influence was greatly diminished until recent years; an additional ingredient, the Warsaw Pact, a military counterweight to NATO, crumbled in 1991, this pact constituted its security zone, which was made up of the German Democratic Republic, Poland, Czechoslovakia, Hungary, Romania, and Bulgaria, that zone vanished, and with this also went more than a million and a half military personnel and weaponry; its nuclear arsenal dismantled, from thirty thousand nuclear warheads, in 1991, to just over seven thousand in 2018. Believe me, Fareed, there are strong arguments to think that the once powerful USSR, whose heir in world geopolitics is Russia, is wounded in its pride. Vladimir Putin has been determined for years to recover the luster of that lost pride."

"Does this, in your opinion, return us to a situation similar to that of 1939?"

"Worse yet, a combination of factors that occurred prior to the First and Second World Wars, the genesis of the Great War, in 1914, was due to the rivalries of European politics at the end of the nineteenth century, which were somehow contained by the agreements at the Congress of Vienna; those mechanisms to avoid conflicts were dead letters at the beginning of the twentieth century; it took thirty days, from the assassination of Archduke Franz Ferdinand, for the horror of war to return to Europe and erase the European spirit of concord signed in 1815; today's Europe in some way bears many similarities to the agitation of 1914, the chances of entering into conflict are based on the resurgence of nationalisms that promote rivalries between its states. If you combine the rise of nationalisms in Europe with Russian humiliation, whose outlet mechanism is the desire for revenge, like Germany in 1939, the situation becomes complicated; accompanied by another factor that should concern us."

Zakaria joked:

"Craig. Another one? Which would this be?"

"Like in 1939, populist candidates, in addition to nationalists, are taking power by storm, using democracies to get there, and could then remain in it indefinitely. Hopefully, this does not happen, it happened with Adolf Hitler in Germany, Benito Mussolini in Italy..."

"Undoubtedly alarming scenario."

Zakaria responded, then took the copy of Craig Eastman's book from the coffee table.

"So, Craig, according to your latest work, what happens?"

The interviewee smiled, then answered:

"I invite your audience to buy my book, to find the answer to your question."

Nodding his head several times, Zakaria pointed with his right hand at Eastman—You're absolutely right, Craig, however, everything you express puts us in a delicate situation. According to you, we're sitting on a powder keg. Isn't that right?

Craig Eastman's smile vanished, turning into grimness.

—Indeed, Fareed. Do you know what the worst part is? We don't know who, and when, will light the fuse to set it off.

INF Treaty: Intermediate-Range Nuclear Forces Treaty.

Valdas Skvernelis finished eating his toast, gazed distractedly at the garden from the small dining area in the kitchen, his mind was actually elsewhere; President Skvernelis was amidst the uproar of the campaign for presidential re-election in Lithuania, two particular issues concerned him about this campaign, issues that had become critical, and therefore, determinative in the upcoming presidential election results; the country's economy was not doing well, the last two years marked a significant decline in the growth of the Gross Domestic Product, it was 15% lower according to the latest report from the Ministry of Economy, this resulted in a significant increase in unemployment, which went from less than 4% to 17%, the fiscal deficit, consequently, grew to more than 16% in the same period, the reduced public spending caused general discontent among the population, which in recent months expressed it in increasingly frequent and vehement street protests; as if that were not enough, the defunct Lithuanian Democratic Labour Party, the LDDP, of the far left, was revived in response to the clamor of many Lithuanians dissatisfied with the economic crisis that their country was going through; former members of the banned Lithuanian communist party in 1991, led it, their main proposal, a rapprochement with Russia, which they considered should be, as in the past, Lithuania's great protector, the LDDP was growing in the polls; the re-election, which a few months earlier seemed guaranteed, was in jeopardy. Skvernelis listlessly finished the rest of his breakfast; after finishing getting ready, he took one of the ties from the closet and tied it in front of the bathroom mirror, then, the President of Lithuania quickly went down the stairs of his luxurious property on the banks of the Neris River, in the exclusive residential area of Valakupiai, downstairs smilingly waiting in the living room was Ugné Fomina, his wife, and the presidential driver with the briefcase; Skvernelis gave her a warm kiss and went out after the man to the parking lot, the Mercedes Benz started, a few seconds later it passed through the metal gate of the residence to turn left onto Vaidilutés street, escorted by two policemen on motorcycles; a few meters further, the convoy crossed paths with a man who was leisurely walking a German shepherd, the man bent down to pick up, with a plastic bag, the waste it had just deposited on the grass, the vehicle and its escorts soon disappeared into the distance; the man with the dog momentarily left the bag on the ground, pulled out his mobile phone from the jacket and made a short call.

The director of the DGSE (General Directorate for External Security), Pierre Cousseran, closed, with some unease, the folder containing the intelligence report, it mentioned an operation against terrorism in the Parisian suburb of Saint Denis; two days earlier, the GIGN (National Gendarmerie Intervention Group) raided a small apartment, just above a bakery, on Rue Gabriel Péri. In the operation, three subjects of Algerian origin had been taken down, the initial objective was their arrest for interrogation; however, they responded with gunfire and their elimination was inevitable, the operation could have had a disastrous consequence for the GIGN men, since one of the terrorists almost activated an explosive vest; inside, in addition to a complete arsenal of weaponry and explosives, maps of the Paris metro with two stations circled in red, La Défense and Nation, were found, two potential deadly attacks had been, fortunately, deactivated; but that was not what was worrying Cousseran that misty winter afternoon; an email file had been found on a laptop, its sender identified with the alias Valiant, the text was written in Dariya, a Moroccan dialect, there it spoke of a special event which the sender called Naqma, whose meaning in this dialect was revenge, the short message ended stating that "Allah is great, the world will soon know his power."The director stood up from his chair, thoughtful, walked towards the thick window of his office, inserted his hands into his pants pockets with concern, several questions began to shoot through his mind: Who sent this message? What the hell are those ISIS lunatics scheming? An attack? Where do they plan to do it? Thoughtful, Cousseran took a couple of steps back and took the phone from his desk, dialed the number of an extension.

Air France flight AF429 from Bogotá gently landed on runway 09R of Charles de Gaulle airport, after taxiing for a few minutes, it stopped at one of the sleeves of terminal 2E. Tomás Cruz took the opportunity to get up from the comfortable executive class seat and stretched his legs while the plane's door opened, then took his backpack from the overhead compartment and patiently waited for the flight attendant's instruction to exit; it had been a long flight, however, Cruz felt happy, his long-awaited vacation was beginning, after four long years without enjoying a break. He would spend two months in Pa'Is, a city where he felt at home and Ih he decided would be the base from where he would'visit several countries in Europe; In addition, he would stay in the apartment of his old friend, Jean Claude Lebel, whom he had met a few years back in a cyber intelligence course of the IHEDN (Institut des Hautes Études de Défense Nationale), from the beginning of the course, there was chemistry between them, Lebel practically adopted Cruz for those eight weeks; with a vocation as tour guides, he and Carole, his beautiful wife, dedicated themselves, several weekends, to showing him Paris and the French countryside, Cruz pulled from his memory some images of the fantastic apartment that his friends had in a Hausmannian building on Ile de la Cité, his memories were interrupted when the delicate voice of the slender flight attendant indicated he could now exit the Boeing 787; after the tedious immigration procedure, Cruz picked up his suitcase and completed the last customs procedure, upon leaving he recognized from afar the smiling face of his French friend.

The BMW braked to turn right and take Prospekt Leninsky, fifty meters ahead, the vehicle crossed the bridge over the Pregolya

River, advanced about four hundred meters; on the left hand, the occupants of the car observed a museum, a huge banner announced the art exhibition of a young Russian painter; the BMW sped up fifty meters, then, a tremendous explosion shook the tranquility of that afternoon, pieces of the vehicle, and of its occupants, were scattered around, even remains were found in the peaceful park adjacent to the avenue, a hundred meters away.

The individual heard the calm voice of the television presenter; the Al Jazeera television channel was broadcasting a breaking news story; the woman narrated, in English, with a grave face, the occurrence of an attack in Vilnius, the capital of Lithuania, against its president, Valdas Skvernelis; the car in which the Lithuanian head of state was traveling was hit by a high-powered explosive projectile, apparently fired from a rocket launcher, the vehicle was destroyed, its occupants had died, among them, the Lithuanian president; two suspects were detained minutes later a few blocks from the site of the attack and were being interrogated under strict security measures. At the official residence of the Lithuanian prime minister, a security council was being held at that time to assess the delicate situation the country was going through at those moments, the presenter made a connection via Skype with an English political analyst, she asked a question about who could be involved in the execution of this attack, her guest replied that it was still too early to determine the perpetrators, but, without a doubt, he added, the eyes were on Russia; the individual watching the news lowered the volume, then smiled.

"Salut, Tom, good to see you!"

Lebel approached Cruz to give him the customary greeting kisses, a thing to which Tomás still hadn't fully gotten used to; his French friend noticed the look of astonishment, smiling, exclaimed:

"Come on, Tom. I know you prefer this type of greetings with women!"

Cruz nodded, responding:

"Especially if it is a beautiful Parisian blonde, monsieur Clouseau."—Cruz sometimes jokingly referred to his friend as inspector Jacques Clouseau, a fictional character, created for the Pink Panther by Blake Edwards.

Lebel took him by the shoulder and invited him to walk to the parking lot where he had his car, raising his arm in a sign of complicity.

"And Tom? How did the mess of your adventures with Venezuela and the Colombian guerrillas end?"

"It's a long story, my friend, it merits opening a bottle of wine to have enough energy to tell it to you." "We'll have time, Tom, I'm dying of curiosity to hear what happened," Jean Claude changed the subject. "By the way, you'll see Carole's beautiful friend that we have to introduce you to, I'm sure you're going to love her! Welcome to Paris, my friend!

"Thank you very much. And how is Carole?"

Lebel replied enthusiastically:

"She's happy. Next week she's opening her exhibition of the latest sculpture collection she's been working on for almost a year. Of course, you'll be the main guest."

"Magnificent! And you? How is your mission to liberate France from foreign enemies going?"

Lebel frowned.

"Complicated, there's a case I'd like to talk to you about, but today is my day off and I don't want to think about anything that has to do with saving my country. Let's go to the apartment, you drop off your things and with Carole we're going to Le Climats, the trout there is a delight and the Chablis I've reserved. I know you're going to love it!"

"Welcome to this special broadcast, a serious incident adds to the critical situation in the Baltic countries; Anton Dyumin, the young governor of the Kaliningrad province, was assassinated today as he was heading to an art exhibition opening. A powerful bomb exploded as the vehicle that was transporting him drove down the access avenue to the museum where the art exhibition was to open. Our correspondent in Moscow, Fritz Lichtenberg, has more details on this brutal attack. Go ahead, Fritz."

Lichtenberg's image at the Red Square appeared next, the CNN journalist greeted Pauline Allen, presenter of CNN Newsroom. At the bottom of the TV screen, a "breaking news" sign warned viewers that it was a piece of breaking news. He narrated the details of the attack; two suspects had been detained a couple of hours later, belonging to an extremist group of Lithuanian nationalists, the Lithuanian Popular Front (FPL), which promoted rejection of any Russian interference in their country. Allen asked a question:

"Fritz. Do we know the motivation of the FPL for carrying out this cruel action?"

"Pauline, the Russian authorities are evaluating the possible causes of this assassination. However, unofficial sources have given us a possible motive that must be confirmed; apparently, this act was retaliation against Russia for an attack carried out weeks ago that cost the life of the Lithuanian president, Valdas Skvernelis."

"Besides the issue of nationalism resurgence, analyzed in previous chapters, another factor has gained unexpected, yet worrisome weight. This refers to an essential element of the nuclear arms control mechanism, which prevented their proliferation not only between the United States and Russia but also served as a persuasive factor for other countries that had a nuclear arsenal. This mechanism ceased to exist in February 2019; the United States, after a sixty-day moratorium in which they had given the Russians time to save the INF, withdrew, initially temporarily, and then definitively at the beginning of 2020; Russia did the same. At that time, both countries saw China, which was not part of the agreement, as a threat to their nuclear dominance. This strategic vision remains almost five years later; from there, North Korea and Iran, along with the rest of the nations that make up the nuclear club, started a dangerous buildup of intermediate-range weapons, nuclear or not, between five hundred and five thousand five hundred kilometers; Europe is the main affected party in this new arms race. Dangerously, Russia has significantly increased its atomic inventory, also placing S400 missile batteries and SSC-8, with a range of five hundred kilometers, in Kaliningrad and along its extensive border with Europe, from Finland to the Black Sea, fifty kilometers within its territory; another serious threat to European security is the modified Kalibr ground-based missile system, whose launch platform is the same used for the Iskander M, but with a range starting from five hundred to two thousand six hundred kilometers. The Russian Ministry of Defense indicated that this spring it will begin to place more than four hundred R500 and R500E Kalibr launch systems, putting almost the entire European territory within the reach of the Russian defense system, including areas east of Great Britain. To this disturbing element, a growing unpopularity of the President of the

Russian Federation, Vladimir Putin, is added, unpopularity that could lead to political instability, which in turn might be the genesis of a military adventure by the Russians; "The best way to avoid a revolution is to win a small war," this phrase, once suggested by Viacheslav K"Von Plehve to Tsar Nicholas II, is today, dangerously, more relevant than ever. Will President Putin, under current circumstances, yield to the temptation of a small war, pressured by the internal problems facing the Russian Federation?" (Back to 1939? The new military challenges for a Europe in crisis [Craig Eastman]).

The subject paused, took a breath, and then closed the book, slowly placed it on the small table next to the armchair in which he was seated, reclined again, observed the name of the work in detail, Back to 1939? The new military challenges for a Europe in crisis, reflected for a few seconds, the work, undoubtedly, offered a detailed analysis of the geopolitical reality of Europe, and of course, provided multiple scenarios that placed it in serious danger.

President Putin walked decisively to the lectern, where the shield on its front, with the golden double-headed eagle, and imperial crowns on each of its heads, represented the power of the Russian state; Putin, after observing the group of journalists attending the press conference, opened the folder and began to read the content of the statement: "Yesterday, a young promise of Russian politics was sacrificed by the blind and irrational terrorism, our esteemed governor of Kaliningrad, Anton Dyumin, lost his life at the hands of the cruelty of his assassins, several other lives were, equally, atrociously taken; their families and the Russian people mourn today for this cowardly attack on our nation, an aggression that the Russian Federation will know how to respond to in kind; our intelligence services have determined, with certainty and promptly, the material and intellectual authors of this heinous crime, the FPL, in connection with authorities of the highest level of the Lithuanian Land Forces, conceived and perpetrated the despicable attack; they should not now deny everything, we have the confessions of the arrested assassins and interceptions of communications after its occurrence that incriminate two colonels and a general. In the coming hours, in the Security Council, this government will determine the response actions to this disloyal attack to our nation, the Russian people only seek peace, but know how to respond to injustice and undue provocation; I swear, for the pain of the wives and mothers who today suffer for the loss of their loved ones, that the deaths of these innocent Russian citizens will be vindicated."

The background music that could be heard in the Georges Pompidou art center's hall where that night the opening of the sculpture collection of Carole Perier was being held, could not be more appropriate for the occasion, Claude Bolling performed the Suite for Flute and Jazz Piano; the guests began to arrive, some, like Tomás Cruz, opted to take an initial tour and observe part of the sculptures that were part of the exhibition; Cruz approached a voluptuous woman, at least two meters in length, sculpted in bronze, she ecstatically raised her arms, between her hands she held a baby who seemed in turn to fly with arms open, her head, without a defined face, seemed to fix her absorbed gaze towards the infinite sky. "That, I believe, is at least what Carole seems to express," Cruz thought out loud, then read the title of the work, Mother and Little Child; he walked a few steps, observed the next sculpture, a female figure, more than three meters tall, was standing with her legs together, the woman, immobile and with a huge belly, indicating the advanced state of pregnancy in which she was, directed her head downwards, as if wanting to signify the tender contemplation of her son, soon to arrive; the work was called Sweet Maternity. A sudden flurry, right at the entrance of the hall, interrupted the tranquility of his tour, Cruz quickly directed his gaze there.

On the television screen could be seen Vigaudas Paksas, Lithuanian Prime Minister, offering an informal press conference at the exit of the security council held on the occasion of the assassination of President Skvernelis. "The evidence was irrefutable," affirmed the Prime Minister, in response to one of the many questions that the journalists surrounding him shouted; "the subjects detained were of Russian nationality, active members of the political party United Russia (Yedinaya Rossiya, in Russian), whose leader was the president of Russia, Vladimir Putin; authorities had in their possession two short videos where they met a few days before the attack with members of the Lithuanian Democratic Labour Party, the LDDP."Another question, posed by an English journalist, was heard; the Lithuanian leader responded with a grave voice:

"This cruel and contemptible murder is of absolute seriousness, it is of course an inexcusable Russian affront to the peace and political stability in Lithuania, certainly the result of the old ambition of the Russian Federation to regain dominance over our country, as well as over Estonia and Latvia. What will come next? A military invasion of our countries? President Putin should know that we will not stand idly by waiting for what we already know will happen; I have requested an immediate meeting with the North Atlantic Council, through the Secretary General of NATO, George Carington, to assess the protection mechanisms for our territory and those of our Estonian and Latvian brothers."

The France 24 presenter announced breaking news, military sources confirmed that the Supreme Headquarters Allied Powers in Europe, SHAPE, had ordered, through the Supreme Allied Commander Europe, SACEUR, to place NATO forces in Lertcon 3, that is, in simple alert, a condition in which the level of readiness of land, sea, and air troops is increased.

"The Lithuanian crisis becomes more complicated day by day, with the determination of Lertcon 3, all EU intelligence agencies are on maximum alert, it is a priority to anticipate what could happen, especially because, having the British and ourselves nuclear deterrence capability, we must assume that they would attack us, at the beginning of any invasion, to a NATO member country, this also applies to partners like Belgium or Italy, which still have nuclear weapons given by SHAPE. Any news, gentlemen?" inquired Pierre Cousseran, director of the DGSE.

An officer, with the rank of colonel, who was the liaison between the French Army and the DGSE, offered Cousseran, and the rest of the people present at the meeting, details of the latest events.

"Our Russian friends have started a campaign similar to the one carried out years ago in Crimea, calling for the uprising of the Russian minorities in the Baltic countries, with this they seek a pretext, as they had then, to intervene in their protection and achieve stabilization of the area; likewise, our information sources in Minsk have informed us that there have been meetings at the highest level between the Russian Ministry of Defense and its Belarusian counterparts, they are, apparently, agreeing on the plan that allows the Russian army to use the geographic corridor to the east of the Lithuanian and Latvian borders, this would connect Russia with what they call the 'Kaliningrad Corridor', and would also seek to preserve the stability and security of this Russian enclave; we know that there was a previous conversation on this matter between Putin and Aleksandr Lukashenko, the latter agreed to support said humanitarian corridor."

"Concerning developments, indeed. Do we know if a general mobilization of Russian forces has already been ordered?" asked the director.

"Not yet, however, we do know that both the Russian army and air force have been placed on a high degree of readiness. The Americans have shared satellite images with us where it is clearly seen that they are clearing highways and secondary roads in preparation for a general mobilization."

"Speaking of the Americans. What has been their reaction to the Russian threat?"

"Minimal, remember that in mid-2019 the United States had about seventy thousand men in European territory, today, after the sudden decision in 2020 to stop being a NATO partner, this number has been reduced to less than half; from thirty-nine military bases, today they keep twelve, mainly air bases with nuclear response capability in Germany, Italy, Belgium, Turkey, and England. The Russians are aware of the weak American military presence, this encourages them to take the initiative in a potential conflict."

"And our armed forces? How are they being mobilized?"

"Too slowly. From our point of view, Europe does not have a rapid deployment force, we still have, in addition, infrastructure problems in Eastern Europe, the roads are too narrow and moving our tanks and heavy military equipment under those conditions is very complicated."

The voice of Jean Claude Lebel was heard:

"Colonel, I have a hypothetical question: what would happen if the Russians decide to invade the Baltic countries tonight?"

"Have you heard of the Crimea Effect?"

"Yes," Lebel replied tersely, "Europe and NATO could do little in 2014 in the face of the Russian invasion in Crimea."

"Exactly, between the cost of losing Crimea and the risk of losing Ukraine, NATO, and us, preferred to sacrifice Crimea."

Cousseran, showing his discomfort, scratched his chin. "Do you suggest then that this time, as in 2014, we would have to sacrifice the Baltic countries?"

The colonel, slightly annoyed, nodded; then he affirmed with resignation:

"If we don't, gentlemen, we can forget about the current map of Europe."

On the monitor screen, Nick Robertson, CNN's senior reporter, was seen reporting from the Šiauliai Air Base, in northern Lithuania. Behind Robertson, four Eurofighter jets from the Spanish Air Force could be made out, the journalist showed to his right, on the runway, how, successively, Rafale fighter jets from the French Air Force were landing, mentioning that a total of eight of these aircraft would reinforce NATO's presence at this base, four more Eurofighters would arrive from the Torrejón Air Base, near Madrid; similarly, Robertson reported, it was informed by the NATO Secretary General, in an early morning press conference, that the presence of fighter jets, helicopters, and transport aircraft would be reinforced at the Powidz Air Base, NATO would not allow, by any means, an adventure by the Russian armed forces. Sixty kilometers to the west of the site from where Nick Robertson narrated the arrival of fighter jets, at thirty-nine thousand feet above the ground, a Boeing E3C Sentry early warning aircraft from NATO was monitoring; it was monitoring the airspace within a range of three hundred and seventy-five kilometers around it, any movement of Russian fighter jets would be immediately warned of.

"The European Union is a vulgar chimera, it's nothing more than a trinket with the appearance of a refined jewel; a trifle with which the French and Germans deceived us to satisfy their own interests, especially the latter, who, despite losing World War II, won everything in the supposed peace resulting from the setting up of that trap called the Maastricht Treaty; the only ones who have benefited from this assault on our countries are the German banks, the only beneficiaries of this scam called the Euro, to benefit the monetary unit, are located in Frankfurt; with the fraud of this union, we lost sovereignty in all aspects, a simple decision, for example, to increase the salary of our teachers or to improve the equipment of our police must go through the supervision of a foreign and distant bureaucracy, resident in Brussels; bureaucrats who, by the way, are very generous, excessively generous with immigrants; it's an undeniable reality that migrants contribute little to that mirage that the European Commission calls, with some pomposity, Europe; they, those arriving from Africa and the Middle East, do not generate wealth, much less work, nor do they add culture; this scourge called immigration has only brought to our nations, insecurity, terrorism, poverty, and unemployment; yes, unemployment, by plucking the work of our fellow countrymen to give it to an uneducated but cheap workforce; what happened recently in Hungary, Poland, and Italy should fill us with optimism and enthusiasm, with Brexit, finally our peoples begin to understand that the path laid out to lead us to that fantasy of a single Europe is nothing but a dead end; finally, the citizens of each of our nations understand that the way is the recovery of territorial, fiscal, and monetary sovereignty; enough of cheap politicking and of deceptive words like globalization or Europeanization, which seek to standardize to steal, which only intend to cover our eyes to sow the bloodless seed of a Shangri-La, and then continue stealing our fair aspirations to regulate our own destiny; we are more than the blind and docile flock that they have cleverly led along the path of abuse for two decades; the time has come, dear citizens, to raise our voice against disorderly immigration, against a subdued cultural and religious invasion that seeks, from the mosques, to erase our ancestral Western principles and values. The liberation from this burden called the European Union is just around the corner, we cannot lose faith and motivation to achieve it, we owe it to our children, the real future of the Netherlands, the only hope for the nations of Europe" (Back to 1939? The new military challenges for a Europe in crisis [Craig Eastman]).

In Dam Square, Amsterdam, an excited crowd applauded and shouted slogans, for several minutes, in favor of the Netherlands and against the Union of Europe; Gerrit Bolkestein raised his arms exultantly with the V for victory; one week later the general elections would take place and his party was leading in the polls.—

General, how is it possible for the Russians to have a photograph of one of the terrorists sitting having coffee with you on the terrace of a restaurant on the outskirts of Vilnius?

General Gintaras Grazulis, as pale as the wall of the Lithuanian Prime Minister's office, replied:

"It's clear I fell into a trap, Mr. Prime Minister. I attended that meeting because this individual claimed to have information about a potential attack on our military facilities".

The Prime Minister, Paksas, shook his head from right to left in a sign of annoyance.

"General, you are the head of the intelligence services. Couldn't you delegate that meeting to a subordinate?"

"The man only wanted to talk to me. I considered, naively, I accept, that what he had to tell me was worth attending the meeting" —the general answered with resignation.

"Who chose the meeting location? You?"

"No, Mr. Prime Minister, one of his contacts provided us with the place and the date".

"Did you get any relevant information from that meeting?"

"No, Mr. Prime Minister, only vagueness".

"You definitely fell into a trap. Going to a meeting in a restaurant full of tourists in front of Trakai Castle? Without getting any information in return? Why didn't you report this meeting to your superiors? —The Prime Minister tried to hide the enormous annoyance affecting him at that moment—. General, with all the affection I have for you, you've made a beginner's mistake. I don't doubt your loyalty to Lithuania, however, naively, yet irresponsibly, you have served on a silver platter an excuse to the Russian government to carry out a plan similar to the annexation of Crimea, and we already know how those kinds of plans end".— Paksas paused to catch his breath, then looked at the Defense

Minister, Valdas Karbauskis, and General Rolandas Adamkus, commander in chief of the Lithuanian defense forces—. "Please, let's be alone, Gintaras, I need to review this matter with your superiors".

As if walking to the gallows upon heading towards the exit of the Prime Minister's office, General Gintaras Grazulis left the room with his head bowed and shoulders drooped.

Jean Claude Lebel didn't seem like a citizen of the 21st century; with a fine mustache, he always wore elegant dark suits with a vest, as well as discreetly colored ties with a perfect Windsor knot. He also never abandoned his Billiard pipe made of briar wood; jokingly, his colleagues in the DGSE called him Maigret, the famous commissioner created by Georges Simenon, unlike Tomás Cruz, who mockingly nicknamed him Clouseau; on several of his birthdays, they had gifted him, as a joke, a Fedora hat, a heavy black trench coat, and some pipes; they would also leave different types of pipe tobacco and magnifying glasses of various sizes in his office, it is worth highlighting the loud laughter that was heard on the floor where his office was located, once he discovered the hilarious gifts. That morning, Lebel was using one of those magnifying glasses, bringing it closer and then farther from a blurry photograph that rested on the desk, two brief knocks on the door woke Inspector Lebel from the task he was involved in.

"I should record this scene on my cell phone, mon cher Maigret, it would further enlarge your legend in the world of espionage. What are you looking at so intently, Jean Claude?" — mentioned with sarcasm one of his colleagues from the Operations Directorate.

Startled, Lebel replied:

"Come in, Bernard, I'm examining this troublesome portrait. Do you remember the ISIS terrorists we took down recently? In the files of the computer we seized, several photos were found, in some, Yassine Abdalla appears, the recipient of the enigmatic email written in Darija, the Moroccan dialect, I was analyzing the other photos, in two of them he appears alongside Abdelkrim Buazaui, the leader in Morocco of the Salafiya Jihadiya."

Bernard Dumont, responsible for the Special Actions Division, furrowed his brow.

"I don't understand, Maigret. Weren't we talking about ISIS? What on earth is the leader of Al Qaeda in Morocco doing next to an Islamic State soldier in a photograph? They can't stand each other."

Lebel, resigned, set aside the photograph and placed the magnifying glass on the desk.

"That's the very question I asked myself, dear Bernard. ISIS and Al Qaeda together? However, this photo is what kept me awake last night."

Lebel took the portrait and handed it to Dumont. In the image, Buazaui could be seen sitting on a thick ochre blanket. The man was sitting sideways, seeming to point at something in front of him; however, he was looking to the right side. A subject wearing glasses was accompanying him, also seated and with his back to the person who had taken the photograph. The companion appeared to be wearing a white robe or tunic and a turban of the same color, a bushy beard stood out on the individual, who was looking at what seemed to be a piece of paper in the same direction Buazaui was pointing with one of his hands; the image of the companion was cut off at the edge of the photograph, which seemed to have been taken from stairs leading to the area where they were seated. Between them, at the edge of the staircase railing, could be seen, in a very blurred manner, the barrel and muzzle of an assault rifle; Dumont leaned in closer to this part of the image, then asked Lebel to hand him the magnifying glass. After a few seconds, he said:

"I think I know what you were looking at with such interest and concentration, Jean Claude..."

"That's right, Bernard, that blessed assault rifle."

"Without a doubt, it's a Kalashnikov, similar to the one that appears in the videos of Ayman al-Zawahiri. Could this be the individual in the photograph?"

Lebel raised his hands in a sign of uncertainty.

"Who knows, but we must assume initially that it is, he has the same beard; besides, he wears a similar turban and robe."

"Do you have confirmation of what date this photograph could be from?"

Jean Claude Lebel made a face of discomfort.

"No, however, the file indicates that it was uploaded to the computer six months ago."

Dumont scratched his head nervously.

"What the heck were these couple of cherubs talking about?"

"We must assume it's the same matter mentioned in the email received by Yassine Abdalla."

"Do you think this guy is Valiente? If so, they were planning another attack in the West, to finish us off, the infidels."

"It could be Valiente, and by the text of the e-mail, we would be talking about the mother of all attacks."

"Mmm..., quite a puzzle we're getting ourselves into, we need to solve it quickly, we're already quite tangled up with this issue between the Russians and the Lithuanians."

Lebel picked up the magnifying glass again to store it in the drawer, then said to his companion:

"That's right, Bernard, for now, I'll ask for help from our Moroccan friends of the DGSN (General Directorate of National Security) and from our friends in MOSSAD, in Israel, to verify the movements in the last two years of Abdelkrim Buazaui; maybe we

Shtorm

can get a better perspective of if he actually met with Al-Zawahiri and when their meeting happened."

IV

Craig Eastman's cellphone rang, he was busy with his seven-year-old daughter, finishing giving her breakfast; the school bus that would pick up his two kids was due to pass by in a few minutes and today they were somewhat short on time, since the battle to wake them up that morning, both Diane, his wife, and he, had lost. Diane, who was hurriedly feeding the boy, and much more agile than her husband, answered the device as best she could, listened for a few seconds to reply, then, with a face of evident perplexity, plus a short yes; looked at Eastman, with her eyes wide open, and said:

"Darling, you have a call from Downing Street."

Eastman made the same gesture of surprise, left the small spoon and the dish with lukewarm egg, which he was giving to his little one, and took the cellphone. His wife, jokingly, whispered:

"What trouble did you get yourself into, 007?" He returned a sarcastic smile.

"Hello? Yes, Craig Eastman speaking." - The man listened attentively, then replied - "I understand, no problem. How soon? " - He went silent - "But I can't make it." - He looked at his watch - "that's in less than an hour." - Eastman widened his eyes, seconds later, looked at the cellphone screen and touched the hang-up icon.

"And? What did they want you for at Downing Street?"

"For what they want, you mean, I have to be there in forty minutes."

Diane gestured skeptically.

"Forty minutes? Forget it, at this hour by car from Weybridge, with the traffic jams entering London, you'll get there, at best, in an hour and a half."

Eastman, with an enigmatic smile, and in the best James Bond style, crossed one leg over the other and bent one of his arms, his left hand simulating a pistol.

"Don't worry, dear Moneypenny, in five minutes, a Royal Air Force helicopter will come for me."

"Mr. Eastman, a pleasure to have you with us, first of all, I apologize for the abrupt way we made you come to this meeting."

"Don't worry, Prime Minister, I assume that the reason I'm here warrants it."The English Prime Minister, Harold Callaghan, pointed out a comfortable sofa in the Terracotta Drawing Room, one of the splendid lounges at 10 Downing Street; after ordering tea for those present, he said:

"Allow me to introduce you to the Secretary of Defense, Nick Fallon, and one of our defense advisors, Mr. Liam Davis; I want to also tell you that I am a fan of your books, you are a dedicated and profound analyst of military affairs; always so complex and challenging, ultimately, we are talking, essentially, about human lives, committed in any armed conflict. Do you know something? It's shocking to conclude that we allocate large amounts of economic resources to improving technology to destroy lives; let's hope that humanity understands, at some point, that this money, and the advanced technologies we develop, can be invested in improving the quality of life in our societies.

Craig Eastman cleared his throat a couple of times, before responding:

"It is clear, Prime Minister, that we will be a fully intelligent civilization when we discard the use of weapons; the challenge for humanity is in advancing to determine when we will reach that point. Our understanding of war is based on the belief, in my opinion erroneous, that we are doomed, by our own history, to resolve our conflicts through violence derived from the use of war.

"War is the continuation of politics by other means, there is no better summary of what you have mentioned than this emphatic statement by Carl Von Clausewitz; anyway, Craig. May I call you by your name?"

Eastman nodded.

"As I was saying, returning to our matters, I have read with interest your last book; tomorrow we will have a meeting in Brussels and I wanted to have an informal chat about some topics you raise in it that will undoubtedly be the subject of analysis and discussion in this meeting. I want to be direct, since time is short and pressing, under the hypothesis, increasingly likely, that Russia decided to carry out a military action in the Baltic countries. Could we repel this attack?"

Eastman took out a pen from his jacket and then took a napkin and made a small drawing, at one point of it, he detailed a narrow strip.

"My apologies for the low quality of this map, I'm a poor draftsman; this is the so-called Suwalki Gap, which I'm sure you have heard of many times. To the right of this strip, are the Baltic countries, in particular, the border between Poland and Lithuania; at the top, the Russian enclave in Kaliningrad; further to the right, Belarus, an ally of the Russian Federation; in essence, everything depends on whether NATO can defend this strip I mentioned earlier, this is a low-lying geographical corridor, with a length of ninety-six kilometers, located right between Kaliningrad and Belarus; these ninety-six kilometers are the border line between Lithuania and Poland, that is to say, the umbilical cord between the Baltic countries and NATO. If the Russians take it, Lithuania, Estonia, and Latvia will be, in practice, left to fend for themselves.

Somewhat uneasy, the English Prime Minister pointed to the strip drawn on the napkin.

"How long would it take for the Russians to take over this strip?"

Eastman did not hesitate to answer:

"Sixty hours, if the strip falls, twenty-four hours later, Russian troops could be entering Vilnius, Tallinn, and Riga."

"In that case. Could we retake the Baltic countries by launching a naval operation?" inquired Liam Davis, the defense secretary's advisor.

"That would be very complicated, Liam, they have a strong naval presence in the Baltic; plus, there are the Iskander missiles they have in Kaliningrad."

Eastman and Davis knew each other, having participated in the past in informal meetings of the Defence Council of the United Kingdom as advisors to the members of the Defence Committee, where strategic direction issues were discussed and defense matters internal and those related to the United States and Europe were reviewed. The Secretary of Defense pointed his right index finger at the napkin, with his left hand he took his pen and drew a circle around Kaliningrad.

"The Iskanders pose a serious threat to European capitals such as Berlin, Stockholm, and Copenhagen, to that we must add Warsaw, which was already in the sights of the Russians with the S-400 Triumph missiles."

Eastman added:

"Not to mention the P-800, they are supersonic anti-ship missiles, can be launched from submarines or from trucks with launchers; they would do a lot of damage to any NATO naval unit trying to approach Kaliningrad or the coasts of the Baltic countries."Eastman took a breath before exhaling forcefully; "Moreover, gentlemen, our own weaknesses play against us."

The Secretary of Defense made a gesture of helplessness"I know them, yet it wouldn't hurt to analyze them again, Craig. What are these, in your opinion?"

"The first is the narrowness of the road system to reach the border with the Baltic countries. In the multiple drills, we have experienced traffic jams that, if their consequences weren't so serious, would be laughable; this problem, which has yet to be resolved, prevents an immediate response to any Russian action in the Baltic countries. This is a difficult dilemma to solve, if we send troops in advance, the Russians will almost certainly respond immediately by attacking the Suwalki Corridor; however, in my opinion, the worst weakness lies in the bureaucracy, one has to fill out dozens of forms to be able to circulate, mainly in Germany and Poland"—Eastman let out a light laugh—. Liam knows about this case, which is, to say the least, pathetic; in one exercise, it was planned for these permits to take two weeks, in reality, they were obtained in four months."

"Two weeks is an eternity in a war as it is, we're talking about the Russians being able to take Lithuania, Estonia, and Latvia in four days," grumbled Calaghan.

The Secretary of Defense posed one of those questions that none of those present would want to face.

"Craig, if the Russians take the Suwalki Corridor, what would be your recommendation for a response by NATO?"

Eastman pursed his lips for a couple of seconds.

"Do you play chess, Mr. Secretary?"

"Yes," he replied.

"Well, let's suppose for a moment that the Baltic countries are one of our bishops, the opponent in the game moves one of theirs and could take our queen, the only way to save her is to place that bishop in the midst. What would you do?"

"The answer is obvious. We would have to sacrifice them."

"It's regrettable, but, in my opinion, NATO, and Europe in general, would have no other alternative; if we don't do it, the next bishop that we would have to hand over would be Poland, and who knows, maybe other countries could fall again under the Russian sphere."

The Sukhoi Su-27 took off, with the first light of the morning, from the Russian Air Force base in Baranavichy, Republic of Belarus, the base, inaugurated in 2016, was part of a mutual defense agreement between the two countries; once in the air, the fighter jet immediately headed to the assigned patrol area, near the border with Poland, in a sector almost three hundred kilometers long, between Grodno and Brest. The mission, to patrol the border for a couple of hours and send a strong message to its counterpart on the other side, the firm Russian decision to defend its ally. Throughout the day, various planes would take the same route to ensure that the Poles and their NATO partners received the message clearly. The pilot looked at his helmet for the elapsed mission time, about fifteen minutes to completion, he was about to make a slight turn to the southeast of his position when suddenly, a strong intermittent noise started to be heard in the headphones, the alert system in the helmet showed a couple of small lights headed towards his plane, instinctively, the pilot initiated evasive actions while launching chaff and other electronic countermeasures; seconds later, the man sighed with relief when he checked that the missiles had lost their track and were following a different course; however, in a matter of moments, a third missile hit the fighter jet in the tail, the strong explosion caused a bright fireball, fragments of it fell to the ground chaotically. The radar system of the airbase, which received real-time data from the Kontéiner, a new generation early warning radar located near Smolensk, a Russian city a few kilometers from the border with Belarus, registered the impact, as well as the origin of the missiles; the three had been launched from Polish territory, south of a small town called Grabarka-Klasztor, a little less than five kilometers from the Belarusian border. An alert message was immediately transmitted to the Russian Ministry of Defense and the Air Force command in Moscow.

At thirty-eight thousand feet, one thousand five hundred kilometers inside Russia, the cruise missile J101 detached and seemingly slowly dropped from the Russian Bear H, then, its ignition system launched a small flare, the J101 slightly jumped forward, simultaneously its small fins opened and it descended to begin its low-level flight towards the target. About fifty kilometers from the border between Poland and Belarus, flying at forty thousand feet, the E3 Sentry detected the entry, into Polish airspace, of the J101; however, it was useless, seconds later, a strong explosion shook the base of the 18th.Reconnaissance brigade in Bialystok, Poland; twenty soldiers lost their lives that rainy afternoon and more than two hundred were seriously injured, much of their facilities were destroyed completely or partially. Skirmishes between troops of the 6th Polish Airborne Brigade and the Belarusian special forces brigade occurred in the hours following the attack on the base facilities in Bialystok; the alert level of NATO forces was raised to Lertcon 2; meanwhile, unexpectedly, in the Kremlin, the red phone rang for the first time in many years.

"Is that confirmed, Jean Claude?"

"Yes, sir. Both Mossad and the Moroccan DGSN confirmed that Abdelkrim Buazaui traveled twice, under two different identities, to Islamabad, in Pakistan."

"Do we know where he went from there?"

"No, sir, only that, during one of those visits, he stayed at a small hotel, the Laraib Inn, and the next day, he vanished."

Pierre Cousseran, the director of the French DGSE, thoughtfully tapped his desk with his pen several times.

"Mmm, we have the photograph and now the confirmation of these two visits, it's clear that Ayman al-Zawahiri is hiding somewhere in Pakistan, these events don't seem to be coincidental. How long ago did the two trips occur?"

"The first trip, eleven months ago; the second, two months later."

"That coincides with the date of the email sent to the terrorist we neutralized in Paris, something is being plotted by Al-Qaeda. Any suspicion of what atrocity they are scheming?"

"No, sir."

"And Buazaui? Do we know where he is?"

"The DGSN informed us that he was seen less than a month ago in Rabat."

Cousseran, absorbed for a moment, scratched his forehead several times, then looked at Lebel.

"Jean Claude, coordinate with our Moroccan friends for a lengthy meeting with Mr. Abdelkrim Buazaui, we need to ask him some questions."

V

The torrential rain allowed no visibility despite being the early hours of the morning; intermittent flashes of light, followed by a deep rumble that made the ground vibrate, showed the thick drops of water falling on the swampy and narrow path where one could barely walk in the midst of dense vegetation. A powerful lightning bolt illuminated, once again in the distance, the dense foliage, accompanied by a rough and vibrant sound; Tomás Cruz, surprised, felt a painful blow to his legs that immediately threw him into the mud. Immobilized and about to faint from the intense pain, he felt the tremendous and oppressive weight of a bundle that was leaving him without air, he removed, with one hand, the water falling over his eyes to see more clearly what it was, it was the lifeless body of his communications officer, he shook him without getting any response, then, he took the soldier's head with his other hand to shout his name when, stunned, he realized it was... Cruz opened his eyes alarmed;

petrified and in the silence, the faint light that filtered through the curtain brought him back to the peaceful reality of his friend's apartment in Paris. Relieved, he breathed deeply; it was the recurring nightmare that frequently tormented him at night; once again, the slow-motion film of the ambush that, years ago, the Colombian guerrilla had set for him, returned; however, this time the face of the soldier on top was that of his friend Jean Claude Lebel. Cruz, who since the first time he had suffered that tormenting and distressing dream, analyzed every detail of it, took a while to fall back asleep, questioning in his mind, several times, the reason why Lebel appeared this time as one of the victims of the ambush. Could it be because of dinner? Perhaps the meat sauce, delicious by the way, was heavy. The wine maybe? After these questions, a tingling sensation took over his body in a pleasant way. Cruz turned over in his bed, then, fell back into a deep sleep.

The next morning, Tomás Cruz decided to get up early to join his hosts during breakfast; while showering, he went over his dream from the previous night, in fact it had been abundant in memories; apart from the recurring nightmare of the ambush, he remembered fragments of a dream with his ex-wife, both were in the living room of a house, she, who was wearing a flowing pajama, placed a vinyl record on the turntable, the song that followed was "Olvídame Tú" by Miguel Bosé, it had turned into one of those songs that, incomprehensibly, reminded him of Marta, that was her name; the woman approached him and whispered the lyrics, dedicating the song to him, the woman's lips approached his and at the moment of the kiss, the dream ended abruptly. Cruz reflected about the relevance of the message contained in the lyrics of this melody and the reality of what had happened between them, "after so many years, to be honest, the one who forgot me was you, meanwhile, as it seems, I have not been able to do the same," he said quietly. Sometimes, he learned through mutual friends that she was happily living with her husband, whom she had married a few years after the divorce, and two children had followed; her life seemed fulfilling, while his continued amidst loneliness and unrest. With the shower water falling on his neck, Cruz sang—or lamented?: "Respond to my name if they whisper it to you, completely tear off my skin which is so yours, let my body burn if you're not with me, love, forget me not..."; later, at the dining room, with Carole and Jean Claude, Cruz mentioned to his friend about the novelty in his nightly nightmare.

"Did you dream about me? Wow, Tom, I hope I didn't do any indecency in your delirious companion of every night."

Carole let out a small laugh. Tomas then shared the strange episode of his friend's face in the fallen soldier in the trap set up by the guerrillas, Lebel and his wife looked at each other oddly.

"It reassures me, at least, I didn't put on a striptease show or anything of the sort."

They all laughed, Carole put a hand to her forehead, got up instantly to bring the coffeepot, which she had forgotten in the kitchen, Cruz took the opportunity to ask his friend:

"By the way, Clouseau. How is the case going, the one you wanted to consult me about some doubts that have been on your mind?"

"It's getting more complicated," Lebel briefly explained the background. "You know what, Tom? I have a crazy hypothesis that has been spinning in my mind these last few days, I must confess it seems less far-fetched every time, it's about..."

Carole's voice was heard from the kitchen, asking her husband to help her bring the toasts, which she had also forgotten, Lebel raised his hands in a gesture of helplessness, then pushed his chair back to stand up and, obligingly, walked to the kitchen to perform the task entrusted. Back at the table, Carole wanted to know more about Cruz's nightmare, the topic again led to her husband's jokes about his indecent acts in it; after finishing breakfast, Lebel checked his watch, exclaimed in French, dashed out, he was late and time was pressing. Cruz, later on, would remember that he was tempted to ask his friend again about the outlandish hypothesis in the case he was working on, he refrained from doing so due to the urgency Lebel showed, after all, he thought at that moment, they would have a chance to talk about it, he would see him that night at Carole's sculpture exhibition.

"Hello."

"Nick?"

"The same speaking. Who's calling?"

"Bob Brown, a pleasure to greet you, Nick. Can you talk?"

"Sure, I have a few minutes, tell me."

"Perfect, Nick. Can we switch to secure mode?"

"I understand, give me a couple of minutes."

The line went silent for a while, then, Robert Brown, the Deputy Secretary of Defense of the United States, heard the ringtone of his phone, then heard, from the other end of the line, the voice of Nick Fallon, Secretary of Defense of the United Kingdom, it now sounded a bit distant.

"Hello, Bob, I'm all ears."

"I wanted to ask you something important, Nick, something that's probably related to the mess brewing in the Baltic and Poland. Have you heard about Zapad 2.0?"

"Zapad 2.0? I believe that's what the Russians call their military exercises with Belarus, but I haven't heard anything about it. Is it about military exercises, Bob?"

Inquired, in a deep voice, the British Secretary of Defense, Nick Fallon.

"That's right, our intelligence folks just found out something about it, so we decided then to take a look at the area with a couple of our satellites, things are getting, apparently, heated there, Nick."

"Heated? What do you mean?"

"The Russians have mobilized more than eighty combat aircraft and other transport aircraft to airbases close to the border with Poland and the Baltic countries, we have seen additionally much activity of tanks and troops near Saint Petersburg, Pskov, Novosokólniki, and Kaliningrad."

"Definitely, concerning. How many tanks and troops are we talking about, Bob?"

"More than seven hundred tanks; the Russians are moving between ten and twelve infantry divisions to the region."

Fallon's voice, until then calm, expressed some discomfort.

"Right now, the missile directed at the Polish military base was an unnecessary provocation, this is, undoubtedly, an even more defiant maneuver by the Russians, it means moving more than a hundred thousand men to the NATO borders.""As you know, we are on our way out of NATO, it wouldn't hurt for the SACEUR, who is now French, to ask, rather demand, the Russians for a better explanation of these exercises," Brown paused. "Do you know the report from the Rand Corporation regarding the various scenarios of a Russian attack on the Baltic countries? It was published in 2016."

After a few seconds, Fallon replied:

"Uh..., I vaguely remember it, Bob."

"OK, it indicated, among other equally alarming things, that NATO would only have a six-day warning of a potential Russian attack on the Baltic region."

"I remember now, Bob, that didn't give us much time to prepare a counteroffensive."

"Nick, according to this report, with which I agree, there would be no way to prepare a counteroffensive. I don't want to be a fatalist; however, anything related to our Russian friends is worth extreme caution. The satellite images are from yesterday; this can mean that we are on the fifth day before the invasion, and the countdown continues, my friend."

Youssoufia is a modest neighborhood in the suburbs of Rabat, that hot morning, a street vendor was offering fish in a small park; not far away, an old Renault van was parked, with a sign advertising plumbing services. Inside, in the back part, Major Ahmed Hajjar of the DGSN, who was commanding the operation to capture Abdelkrim Buazaui, waited for the confirmation from his field agent to give the green light to execute the operation. Two days before, his last known location had been identified in a small house. The night before, Buazuai had entered his residence and had not left since then. The fish vendor pretended to be scaling a shad, then took the opportunity to write the keyword, "Alosa," on WhatsApp. Moments later, the same word appeared on Hajjar's phone screen; he took the walkie-talkie and said, "Our fish has bitten the hook, good fishing." Two blocks away, another van, with the special operations team, headed towards the small house, located next to a furniture upholstery; the vehicle stopped a few meters before the entrance, the group of men got out of the van and quickly approached the door to break it down in seconds, once inside, they searched the living room and the dining room without success, as well as in the kitchen; then, two agents entered the only room, the man was not there, both looked at each other and automatically positioned themselves by the bathroom door, one of them silently counted to three with his hand, the other agent entered, saw nothing on the floor, looked towards the shower curtain, then saw the dark outline of a figure, slowly, he moved the curtain, he made a grimace of disgust, the bloodied body of Abdelkrim Buazuai lay inert on the floor.

"Was he murdered? How did those fools let this happen? Weren't they watching him? One of the purposes of watching him was to prevent them from killing him!"

Lebel tried to control his anger, took a deep breath, then asked:

"Did they find anything interesting in the house?"

The voice was heard on the other end of the line:

"Yes, sir, something quite interesting, in a small notebook. Buazuai wrote a date and the name of a person, Vasiliy Kozlov."

Lebel, surprised, furrowed his brow.

"The man had scheduled a meeting with a Russian?"

"No, sir, it seems they had already met, there's also a date, it's from a week ago."

"Have they identified the Russian?"

"No, sir, our friends from the DGSN are working on it, as well as our people from the DGSE."

"Perfect, keep me updated once they identify him."

Jean Claude Lebel hung up, and sighing, looked at his watch, he was just in time to leave; outside, he walked the block that separated the DGSE building from the Piscine des Tourelles complex, early in the morning, having decided to park his car there to make it easier to leave for the Centre Georges Pompidou; Lebel mapped out in his mind the route he would take once he left the complex's parking lot, the best option was Avenue Gambetta and then continue on Avenue de la République, in thirty minutes he could be arriving at the Pompidou. The man sighed, in just over an hour, the ceremony to present Carole's sculpture exhibition would start; Lebel was happy and looking forward to it, it was a very important event for his wife, he wouldn't miss it for the world, he wanted to be there for her in this special moment for both of them. The man crossed Rue des Tourelles, walking briskly to the entrance of the complex, in his mind came the conversation he had just had with his DGSE assistant: "A Russian was going to meet with Buazuai...""What the hell can a Russian and an ISIS terrorist talk about? This case gets more and more tangled as days go by...

I think the theory I've been thinking about might not be so far-fetched. What if...? On the glass door, Lebel noticed in his reflection that in the corner, a person seemed to be watching him, intrigued, he quickly turned around, the person had disappeared. "This case is making me paranoid," he thought; Jean Claude Lebel took the elevator down to the basement where he had parked his car, walked to his gray Peugeot 508, from a distance, he deactivated the alarm, he was about to open the door when he again saw a shadow that seemed to be lurking in the distance. This time, he didn't stop, he opened it and started the car, drove a few meters towards the exit when suddenly, an individual appeared from behind a column, blocking his way; Lebel stepped on the brake, the car stopped abruptly, the person was about four meters away, he detailed his face, the light from the front lamps, which were on, allowed him to see clearly, it was not the man he had seen outside, in the glass door reflection, this one had no beard; the individual in front of his car was dark-skinned, wearing a long black coat, had his hands in his pockets, showed him a wide smile, closed his eyes and took his hands out to open it, subsequently, slowly, Lebel realized, horrified, that the subject was wearing an explosive vest. "My God, this madman is going to blow up the complex!" Instinctively, he decided to reverse.

The autumn of 2024 did not bring good news for the unit of Europe, between September 29 and November 27, referendums were held in Italy, Belgium, Austria, Greece, and Hungary, after a vigorous campaign, in all these countries, the popular decision to leave the EU was imposed; a year earlier, the Frexit had overcome by more than ten points those in favor of staying in the European Union, this victory exacerbated the spirits of the eurosceptics, who, appealing to nationalism and anti-immigration, convinced the electorate that the costs outweighed the benefits regarding the stay of their countries in the European Union. Nicola Sturgeon, Scottish Prime Minister, called, in October of that year, for the consummation of independence. "England is no longer a reliable partner, Great Britain is a sinking ship; all this mess in which Europe finds itself today is caused by its own arrogance," she said at a rally, outside of Edinburgh. Carles Puigdemont, leader of the Catalan European Democratic Party, PDeCAT, expressed in a speech in Barcelona, before the members of the Parliament, that "the time for Catalonia has come, we have gone from suffering the indifference of a disdainful, indolent Europe to the right we Catalans have to govern our own destiny, to have, unfortunately, a Europe victim of its obtuse mistakes, deaf to the clamor of the just claim of our people to obtain their freedom, compatriots, in today's Europe, Catalonia does not fit in Spain." As if it were gunpowder, nationalisms exploded soon after in Belgium, the Basque Country, Northern Ireland, and Brittany, a region located in the north of France; Europe thus reached a deep identity crisis that also generated secessionist attempts by Poland, the Czech Republic, and Austria. The dish of discordant nationalisms was served; the individual, reading the latest news, confirmed it with a smile of satisfaction.

VI

Tomás Cruz would keep that moment engraved in his memory. He observed, as if in a scene in slow motion, the gesture of anguish that Carole expressed in front of the Police Nationale officer right in front of her; the strident noise of a wine glass shattering as it hit the floor had previously caught his attention. As he directed his gaze towards the origin of such a clamor, he saw the distorted face of his friend; as if in a telepathic trance, the glances of Carole and Tomás crossed for an instant, which seemed, moreover, eternal; a grimace of deep sadness and unfathomable powerlessness preceded the tears that, stained with the dark color of the eyeliner, rolled down the cheeks of the beautiful woman; Cruz, without thinking, ran towards her.

In the waiting room of the emergency area of Saint-Antoine Hospital, where his friend had been referred, Cruz listened with interest to the latest news on television, at five and eighteen in the afternoon, a powerful explosion had shaken the Piscine des Tourelles aquatic complex. The place had been cordoned off by the authorities. The reporter, who was narrating from a location one block away from the site of the explosion, indicated that members of the police and emergency services had arrived at the scene to assist the injured; a woman, fortunately unharmed, evacuated a few minutes earlier, had expressed to him, horrified, that there were numerous lifeless bodies, as well as injured ones. The image on the TV changed, now another journalist was interviewing an officer of the French National Police, the former inquired whether it was an attack, the officer responded that although a final confirmation was missing, everything suggested that it was a terrorist act, the interviewer asked if there was already information on the perpetrators, the officer indicated with a head movement that it was not yet possible to confirm who could be linked to the possible attack. Cruz observed from the corner of his eye the silhouette of Carole approaching, he stood up from the chair to ask if she had any news on the state of Jean Claude.

"Nothing yet, Tom, J.C. is still in surgery," she said with a downcast face, then extended her hand towards him—"This anguish is killing me, I decided to go grab something to drink, here, I brought you a coffee."

Cruz received it with a small smile.

"Merci, mon amie. You know, from what they say on the news, everything seems to indicate that it's a terrorist attack."

Carole shook her head indignantly, then let out a sigh and spoke in a reflective tone, glancing sideways at her friend.

"I was raised in a conservative family, Tom, I often hear my parents complain about the violent, chaotic present that France and Europe are experiencing," Carole took a breath to say. "They often claim: 'when did we lose France?' They live in the nostalgia of a better past; although I had leftist flings in my youth, sooner rather than later, I decided that the center was the best option, I am convinced that the extremes do not help at all the future of our country." The woman looked through the huge window of the waiting room; "I have always thought that supporting migration, provided that it is sustainable and regulated, prevents a greater evil, by integrating into our societies people who otherwise would have no future at all, something that, by the way, the crazies who commit these deranged acts of terrorism do not understand." She sighed again. "You know something, Tom? J.C. always teases me about my centrist stance, in his opinion, the lukewarmness, as well as the tolerance to migration, at the levels accepted by the European Union, through the system of quotas for each of the member countries, are a double-edged sword; today, when thanks to the madness of some fanatics, my husband's life hangs in the balance, I question whether, perhaps, he was completely right."

Cruz sipped a little coffee, then looked at his friend and affirmed:

"Carole, as you know, I live in a country that has suffered too much from the cancer of chaos and violence generated by terrorism, a disease caused by drug trafficking. I consider that it is not easy there, as here, in these circumstances, to be centrist; we did not understand it at the time, but our nation required, for a time, the exercise of authority, to achieve control of such a amount of confusion, which is what terrorism feeds on; this requested the unanimous support of society, however, far from achieving it, we were divided, or allowed ourselves to be divided. I lived tragedies, shared the suffering of mothers, wives, and children, of friends and subordinates, of lives lost due to the madness of a perverse enemy; to my surprise, the interpretation that was given in each of the sides, into which we allowed ourselves to be separated, was different in its entirety, while some lamented it, advocating for the decisive response of the State, others validated it by persisting in the search for a negotiated peace; according to them, that was the price to pay for a country that would soon be free of violence if we managed to negotiate it.

"A few took advantage of the divorce they generated in Colombian society; my friend, I believe that this evil, surreptitious, covered and dangerous, threatens today your beautiful country and all of Europe, nationalisms are, in my opinion, the consequence of those dark interests."

Carole stared intently at her friend.

"Speaking of dark interests, Jean Claude mentioned something about it to me recently, before you arrived."

Cruz asked curiously:

"Oh, really? What did he tell you?"

Suddenly the sound of the emergency room door opening was heard, a doctor pronounced Carole's full name; she, as if propelled by a spring, stood up from the chair, and walked quickly towards him, the doctor's grim face seemed not to bring good news.The decision for the mobilization of the USS Abraham Lincoln carrier strike group arrived early in the morning at the office of its commander, Captain Amy Stedding, in San Diego, California. The mission was to reinforce the scant naval presence of the United States in the Mediterranean Sea. A few months earlier, contrary to the recommendations of the Secretary of Defense and the Joint Chiefs of Staff, the President of the United States had ordered the relocation of the Sixth Fleet, whose headquarters was located in Naples, Italy. Now, an operation for rapid deployment to Europe was practically started in a rush, including ships, aircraft, and troops from the U.S. armed forces to support their former NATO partners and deter Russians from starting a conflict. Trump had addressed his fellow citizens in a national television broadcast the previous night, announcing the sending of military reinforcements to Europe. However, he harshly criticized the EU, especially Emmanuel Macron, the former President of France, of whom he said: "His ego, and of course, his weakness in the polls, led him to embark on the adventure of not paying his contributions to NATO and creating a small army that cannot even save the French from Germany." He also spared no criticism for Germany, a country he rebuked for not fulfilling commitments to increase their contributions to the NATO budget. "Weakening NATO to satisfy their own interests?" he asked; he also indicated that the Germans were complicit in the Russian war adventure in the Baltic by promoting the creation of a European army, which he called "failed delirium of a declining continent" and a "fatal mistake of a declining power headed for disaster because of its gross errors." The response from European institutions was not long in coming. The presidents of the European Commission and Council described President Trump's words as unacceptable and offensive. "We have been loyal partners of the United States for many decades. This bewildering message from the president of the Americans seems more like that of a Russian ally than the words of a state until recently allied with the European Union," Juncker replied harshly. On the other hand, German Chancellor Annegret Kramp-Karrenbauer stated, "Europe is not one of your nation's states, President Trump. We do not have to beg for protection from your armies, nor do we have to ask for your authorization to define how to shape ours." The British, French, and Italians reproached the German Chancellor for the terms of the response. Germany appeared to be alone in defending European unity and defense.

"How the hell could this attack happen right under our noses?" The question, fired point-blank by the director of the DGSE, and which burned like a hot coal, made everyone present shift nervously in the conference room. After an uncomfortable moment of silence, Bernard Dumont, colleague, and friend of Lebel, spoke:

"The ISIS folks cleverly played by planting a false threat, Mr. Director."

"Are you referring to the message shared with us by the English MI6? It spoke of a potential threat to Notre Dame Cathedral."

"That's right, Mr. Director. We focused all our intelligence and police security efforts on that area of Paris; frankly, we did not see it coming. There was never any alert in that regard, neither from our sources nor from our partners abroad."

Cousseran let out a sort of snort.

"Gentlemen, this is a slap in our capacity to anticipate a terrorist attack, the only thing missing was for them to leave a car loaded with explosives in our parking lot; on top of that, because of this attack, one of our best men is fighting for his life in a hospital; the pressure I am getting from above is huge. By the way, does anyone know why Jean Claude left his car parked in the aquatic complex?"

Dumont stepped forward to indicate:

"I understand, from what he expressed to me in the morning when we had coffee, that since he is a member of the complex, he parked his car there because it was easier for him to leave from there to the Pompidou, where Carole, his wife, had, that night, the beginning of her sculpture exhibition."

"Hmm..., it's still a fatal coincidence," Cousseran thought aloud.

"Do you think he was the target?"

This time Dumont's question made Cousseran shift uncomfortably in his chair. "Frankly, I don't believe so; however, no hypothesis can be discarded. The truth, gentlemen, is that we suffered an attack that leaves us in a bad position. I have a question, given this cowardly attack, can we rule out the potential attack on Notre Dame?"

A sepulchral silence once again took over the room."We are blind, gentlemen, we need to determine the timing, size, and location of new threats by ISIS or Al Qaeda. This, added to the powder keg that is forming in Poland and the Baltic countries, poses a huge challenge for us, we don't have much margin for error."

Annegret Kramp-Karrenbauer, or AKK, as she was commonly known, was born on August 9, 1962, in Völklingen, then West Germany, in a small town along the Saar River, very close to the border with France. Annegret grew up in a typical German middle-class Catholic household; although she was tempted to follow in her father's footsteps as an educator, she preferred to study law and political science, which she did at the universities of Trier and the Saar. From a young age, Kramp-Karrenbauer dedicated herself to politics, as a militant of the Christian Democratic Union, CDU since 1981. In 1984 she obtained her first elected office, councilwoman of Püttlingen's City Council, and shortly after, entered the regional executive of the youth branch of her party. After a brief stint in German federal politics, due to the end of Helmut Kohl's era of government, at the end of 1998, she returned to regional political activity in the Saar, to reappear in the national scene, twenty years later, as Angela Merkel's heir to the leadership of the CDU. Like her mentor, Kramp-Karrenbauer felt more comfortable in the center of the political spectrum; she was also a pro-European, convinced that after the United Kingdom's exit from the EU, Germany, hand in hand with France, had to lead

European unity. "A strong Europe is the guarantee of a peaceful Europe," she stated in her campaign for the general elections at the end of 2021, which she won by a wide margin and which led her to succeed Merkel as Federal Chancellor of Germany. The Franco-German collaboration lasted only a few months that remained of Emmanuel Macron as president of the French, he lost the presidential elections in May 2022; his successor, Marine Le Pen, came to power to fulfill her campaign promises; to hold a referendum on France's membership in the EU, review her country's continuity in NATO, as well as to stop what she called: "A pernicious migration that damages the foundations of French nationality." Kramp-Karrenbauer lost, gradually in the months following Le Pen's possession, the dialogue with France, "I will never be the vice chancellor of Annegret Kramp-Karrenbauer," she stated repeatedly in her campaign, and there was no doubt that Marine Le Pen was fulfilling this promise to the letter. By the end of 2022, a stunned Germany only had the support of a weakened Spain, battered by the Catalan and Basque issues, and the timid backing of a few countries located on the periphery of the EU, to defend European unity; it was just the beginning of the ordeal, the worst was yet to come for Germany and its chancellor at the end of 2024.

The medical report about the condition of Jean Claude Lebel left more shadows than lights; due to the severe blow received to his head, as a result of the powerful explosion, a board of doctors decided to induce a coma to reduce blood flow and thus allow the reduction in brain swelling, the doctor indicated that recovery could take days or, in the worst case, months; Carole, with teary eyes, inquired about the possible consequences of the induced coma, the doctor pursed his lips to answer: "Well, as the days go by, as your husband comes out of the coma, we will evaluate the neurological sequelae; however, the final state of the patient will largely depend on the primary damage he has suffered, let's hope that this is minor, so that his recovery can be complete." Carole observed Tomás Cruz, he made a gesture of helplessness, while he thought about the doctor's response, it was as vague as the dense fogs in the early mornings of the Sabana de Bogotá. Two days later, already in the apartment of Carole and Jean Claude, while she and Tomás were having breakfast, the woman abruptly stood up, her friend, surprised, saw her return, after a while, to the small auxiliary dining room of the kitchen, with a thin stack of papers, Carole sat down and then handed it to her friend.

"Last night I was looking for a lost payment receipt that I thought was on J.C.'s desk, rummaging through the drawer, I found these papers, they were inside a manila envelope, there was this sticky note with your name."

Cruz, taken aback, looked at the yellow sticky note, read the words written by his friend, "For Tom," then he opened the envelope and began to leaf through the group of papers, its contents would disturb him even more.

The USS Abraham Lincoln carrier task force was joined in the Mediterranean by the USS John C. Stennis, with more than nine thousand men and Marines, fourteen ships, and one hundred thirty fighter planes, the message from the United States to Russia was clear and strong. Its ambassador in Russia, Joseph Simkins, claimed that their sending meant the deployment of "two hundred thousand-ton diplomacy, necessary to preserve the peace of our allies in Europe." To the two American task groups were joined British, French, and Spanish ships. The Russian response was swift; the Black Sea Fleet was reinforced with the presence of the nuclear cruisers Peter the Great and Marshal Ushakov, also accompanied by two Slava-class cruisers, the Variag and the Sevastopol; likewise, the air presence in the area was increased with the transfer of several squadrons of the Air Force and Naval Aviation from the Central Military District and the Pacific Fleet. "We are not afraid of the diplomacy of violence, if this is to be the way of communicating, we have the capacity to respond with as many or more tons of diplomacy," stated sternly, in a press conference, the Russian Defense Minister, Army General, Sergey Serdyukov.

More Russian shows of strength occurred in the following weeks in the Baltic region; progressively, and alarmingly, tensions between the United States, NATO, on one side, and Russia, on the other, were increasing.

The subject asked:

"Is our Sayida ready?"

"Yes, alqayidal'aelaa."

"Very well. When is her appearance scheduled?"

"We leave it to the discretion of our mujahideen, this will allow us to maintain confidentiality and the element of surprise."

The man sketched a malevolent smile.

"Damn infidels... they don't know the suffering that awaits them."

After the results of the referendums carried out in the fall of 2024, a myriad of internal divisions and the advent of small groups with different positions emerged within the EU; this affliction also spread to NATO, the factions were organized around three different positions, the first supported, unreservedly, the permanence of the EU, and of course, the existence of NATO; a second stance outright rejected the unity of Europe and the conservation of NATO; while a final group advocated for the existence of a common market, without a single currency, while defending the validity of the military alliance. The first group included countries like Germany, Spain, or Poland; the second, by France, Italy, Hungary, or Austria; the final group, by nations like the United Kingdom, Sweden, Denmark, or Greece. These deep disagreements were aired, in mid-December of that same year, in two meetings of Heads of State and Government, which took two days, at the headquarters of the European Council, and NATO, in Brussels.

"Sergey, there is no phrase that better describes our secular attitude towards Europe and the circumstances that today confront us with it than that once expressed by the Empress Catherine, 'The only way to defend my borders is by expanding them'; it is true that we have not fostered or sought to foster the events that have affected our security, neither am I today one hundred percent convinced that the EU is aiding them; however, we have not had in years a better opportunity than this, to defend our borders in the best style of our great Catherine." - Vladimir Putin observed firmly, with the icy gaze that characterized him, to his Minister of Defense, then looked at the map to indicate afterward: "For decades, since the end of the First World War, Europe, and now the European Union, became an uncomfortable tool of American foreign policy, later, with the advent of NATO, Europeans allowed the Americans to use them as a tool of military deterrence, they surrendered their leadership in exchange for security at their borders." - The Russian president let out a slight laugh -, "then came Donald Trump, to give us the best gift, the one we did not expect, the political and military divorce of the United States and our annoying neighbor." - Vladimir Putin looked at the red folder, which showed on its top part the hammer and sickle, over these, the red star with a golden border, symbol of the once powerful Union of Soviet Socialist Republics, slowly he opened it, a word appeared in big black letters, SHTORM, then he focused his gaze on the map, later encircled a location on it with his ballpoint pen. "The time has come, Sergey Nikolayevich, to recover what we lost due to the ineptitude of Mikhail Sergeyevich, let the storm fall upon Europe..."

SECOND PART

I

"Europe's security and prosperity lie in its unity"

Winston Churchill

The memory of Ayman al-Zawahiri was suddenly flooded with a particular date, May 2, 2011. He was sleeping in his refuge when one of his closest personal guard members woke him up. Al-Zawahiri shuddered as he remembered the moment he saw the President of the United States, Barack Obama, walking confidently along a long corridor of the White House, to announce, with a clear and strong voice, that Osama Bin Laden had been killed that dawn in the house that served him as a refuge on the outskirts of Abbottabad, in Pakistan; his eyes filled with tears, amidst sobs, another guard member asked: "What do we do now, sir?". Al-Zawahiri cleared his throat a couple of times before responding: "Avenge his death, the West will pay dearly for this cowardly murder." Things had not been easy since then for Osama Bin Laden's successor in leading Al-Qaeda, the process of cementing his leadership faced several obstacles. At the beginning of 2014, Al-Zawahiri, now the leader of The Base, decided to split from the Al-Qaeda operation in Iraq. The reason for such a decision? Abu Bakr al-Baghdadi, its chief, changed the group's name in 2013. From that moment on, it would be called the Islamic State of Iraq and Syria, or ISIS, by its acronym in English, which also absorbed Al-Qaeda's operation in Syria; months of fruitless negotiation led Al-Zawahiri to break ties with ISIS, realizing that the latter operated independently. The differences between the two were evident, ISIS's radicalism, as well as the cruelty of many of its actions, shocked the Al-Qaeda leader; it was indisputable that while the Islamic State gained popularity and followers due to its barbarism levels, Al-Qaeda lost prominence. Regardless of the territorial loss suffered in Iraq and Syria, ISIS continued to score points among young Muslims, thanks to the media effectiveness of its terrorist acts. A new schism seemed to loom in Al-Qaeda, this potential split once again tested Ayman al-Zawahiri's leadership; the reason for the breakdown of the precarious unity in Al-Qaeda had a name, Amer Bin Laden, Osama Bin Laden's son, who was with him when he was killed in 2011. Amer, now thirty-four years old, promised to avenge his father's death, for this it was necessary to regain the lost prominence, it was necessary to strike the West, carrying out terrorist attacks very much in the style of ISIS, something with which Al-Zawahiri disagreed. This divergence of criteria gradually generated a fracture in the organization, more and more saw a change of leadership in Al-Qaeda in a positive light, and a son of Bin Laden was, for many of its members, good news to forcefully retake vengeance against the Western enemy. Al-Zawahiri urgently needed a strategy to attack the West while retaining the reins of Al-Qaeda, in addition, there was the secret, that compromising and confidential event...; he thought about this as he started the program he was looking forward to watching that night, on his CNN program, Fareed Zakaria introduced his guest, defense analyst Craig Eastman.

Craig Eastman closed the book and placed it on the sofa, the cover showed a map of Europe, it had several tears, in the background, a photo of Vladimir Putin smiling, winking, in his open eye you could notice the European Union flag replacing the cornea; briefly observing the cover, Eastman remembered the moment when he first had the idea to write his book Back to 1939? The new military challenges for a Europe in crisis, it was June 23,

2016, he remembered Nigel Farage delivering the victory speech for the Brexit win in the referendum held that day, "The genie of Euroscepticism has been let out of the bottle," he exclaimed exultantly. A few weeks later, David Cameron, the Conservative Prime Minister, resigned, Theresa May was chosen by the Conservatives to succeed him; then began a long and difficult negotiation with the EU, to negotiate the terms of the United Kingdom's exit from the EU, three years later May resigned, failing to achieve the approval of the exit agreement with the European Union in the British Parliament, again the Tories had to choose a successor, then came Boris Johnson, and the hard Brexit, equivalent to a non-negotiated exit from the EU, arrived on January 31, 2020, that day destiny began to mark the tortuous path that from then on, Europe would have to tread.

Thousands of kilometers away from London, Ayman al-Zawahiri was also finishing a book. In his mind, the last words of the epilogue echoed incessantly, "I once read in a book by Henry Kissinger that history is like a river, its waters always changing; however, it is curious that different waters, at different times, generate the same floods and therefore, cause harmful consequences; we are on the verge of a severe overflow of events, one of those that despite having developed slowly and progressively, will paradoxically take us all by surprise, especially our leaders. Those who handle the destinies of the European Union, and each of its member countries, should take into account the symptoms of several radical changes that are already happening without anyone noticing. War, and I am not referring to one that has the characteristics of the Cold War, but to a conflict loaded with chaos, violence, and death, could be just around the corner."

The HMS Daring entered the Gulf of Oman at a speed of twenty-five knots. Its destination was Bahrain, where the United States Fifth Fleet is stationed. The Daring was returning to base after several days of patrolling, supporting the Americans in controlling the exit of oil tankers to the Arabian Sea. The normality of the mission was interrupted by an irritating alarm. On the bridge, its commander, Captain Tony Hine, concerned, inquired of his executive officer, what was happening.

"What is it, Patrick?"

"It seems like a weak signal, sir, on the starboard side."

"Distance?"

"Forty miles."

"Send a Wildcat immediately."

"Sir, that thing is heading towards us!" exclaimed the sonar officer from the CIC*.

"Damn, evasive maneuvers! Tell our Wildcat to launch several sonobuoys. Is it a torpedo? Are they Iranians? We need to know where those bastards fired it from!"

"Sir, if that thing is a torpedo, it's huge! Depth, one hundred twenty feet and rising," affirmed Jack Wedell, the helicopter commander.

"Rising? Damn! I don't understand, Jack, if it's a torpedo, it should be at periscope depth. And the Nixie? Is it operational?" Hine was referring to the torpedo decoy.

"Yes, sir, we're already towing them," responded the executive officer.

"Sir, I see it!" yelled the duty officer. "Bearing, three, five, zero!"

"Full left rudder, increase speed to 30 knots!" Hine gave the order.

"Whatever is approaching us bypassed the Nixie, sir!" shouted the sonar officer from the CIC again.

"Sir, that thing is going to hit us, it's less than 300 meters from us," exclaimed the executive officer resignedly.

Hine grabbed onto a bulkhead and could only manage to shout through the intercom:

"HMS Daring crew, brace for impact, I repeat, brace for impact!"

*CIC: (Combat Information Center).

A strong explosion occurred seconds later in the middle of the warship, right on the beam. Water began to pour in through the keel, which had a hole of more than four meters; minutes later, the water was already overpowering the engine room, and the Daring began to sink by the stern. The pressure from the weight of the water caused it to break in two abruptly, the stern was almost immediately lost in the waters of the Gulf; soon after, the bow took the same fate. Some sailors swam helplessly, yet surprised, in the sea; one hundred sixty-five sailors accompanied the remains of the HMS Daring to the bottom of the Gulf of Oman.

"Tom, if you are reading this document, I am either out of this world or about to leave it; you might wonder why leave you a letter that contains my conjectures about all the madness that these days surround and threaten us instead of telling you in person or sharing it with my people at the DGSE; first, I believe I will not have enough time to do so; second, it is so far-fetched that at The Pool they would decide to send me to a mental asylum, so I have no other option but to write it to you, my friend. I also don't know what you can do with this information that I am going to share with you, however, I know that you will come up with something to find answers to the multiple riddles that this case poses. Just before you came to visit us, an issue arose that caught our attention, it was about..."

Carole entered the room with coffee and cookies, gently, she placed the tray on the large center table.

"And well, Tom, what strange thing have you been able to find in that letter?"

Tomás Cruz took a breath to answer:

"I was just starting to read it, I am really surprised that he decided to write and leave this letter for me." Did you notice anything strange about him in the days leading up to the attack?

—The usual, you know, there are cases that make you, those who live in the world of blessed intelligence, into automatons; in these last days, J.C. spoke little and thought a lot, a symptom that he was in the midst of a case that was worrying him.

Tomás Cruz took a sip of coffee, then asked:

—Did he mention anything about it to you?

Carole looked thoughtfully at the ceiling of the room.

—Hmm, let me remember... yes, I think a couple of days before the stupid attack he said something related to a threat...

—A threat? Against whom? Did he mention if it was directed at him?

The woman shook her head and shrugged her shoulders, indicating she didn't know the answer.

—I wouldn't be able to say exactly, honestly, I was so wrapped up in my own problems with my sculpture exhibition... He mentioned something about a book, a matter that could be related to the terrorists of Al Qaeda; but I'm not clear what he meant to tell me, I repeat, I didn't pay it much mind at that moment.

—A book? Do you remember if he mentioned the title?

—Hmm..., I think he mentioned it to me, but I can't remember it.

—Anyway, if you happen to remember it, it would help me a lot, perhaps by reading it I can tie up more loose ends of this mess your beloved husband left us.

Carole nodded with a resigned smile, stood up from the couch, picking up the tray, and asked Tomás Cruz:

—I'm going to the clinic. Will you accompany me?

Tomás Cruz looked at her, then picked up the sheets and the manila envelope containing the letter from his friend.

—Of course! I'll take the opportunity to finish reading the letter and we can discuss it on the way to the clinic.

—What the hell sunk our destroyer? —asked Nick Fallon, the British Secretary of Defense, visibly irritated.

—Sir Secretary, its name is Poseidon, it's the latest in submarine drone technology —answered Admiral Jerry Cunningham, First Sea Lord, the title given to the commander of the Royal Navy.

—My God! Do they already have that thing, Jerry? Wasn't it supposed to start operating in 2027?—asked Sir Barry Dalton, the Royal Air Force Chief of Staff, horrified.

—Unfortunately for us Barry, they brought forward its service entry by more than three years.

—This places our naval fleet, as well as our naval facilities, in serious danger —observed, with concern, the commander of the Royal Air Force.

—And who produces that blessed thing, Jerry?

—The Russian military industry, Sevmash, to be precise, is the naval industry that belongs to the Russian Ministry of Defense, Mr. Secretary.

Fallon shook his head several times in frustration.

—The blessed Russians are still intent on provoking a war, Jerry, this is, frankly, unacceptable. Is it as serious a concern as Barry mentions? How could we not detect this attack?

—It's not for nothing that Poseidon is called "the doomsday weapon", Mr. Secretary, its autonomy is very broad, more than ten thousand kilometers; plus, there's the depth at which it can operate, more than a kilometer, which makes it nearly undetectable.

—Where was it launched from?

—That's another recent technology developed by their military industry, they already have four submarines of this project they called 09852, the Belgorod and the Khabarovsk were launched at the end of 2019 and mid-2020, respectively, military intelligence informed us that six months ago two more submarines left the shipyards of Severodvinsk, which have already been assigned to their fleet in the Pacific.

—Mmm..., so, from one of these new submarines, they launched their new toy.

—It seems so, Mr. Secretary.

Nick Fallon frowned, then leaned back in his chair.

—Things are getting complicated, Jerry, the United States and NATO are pressing us to give an equivalent response in retaliation; the Russians deny having given any order in this regard, the prime minister gave the Russian government twenty-four hours to provide a satisfactory explanation, meanwhile, despite not being very happy with the decision, we must prepare an attack proportional to the damage they have caused us. Any suggestions?

Without thinking too much, Admiral Cunningham gave an answer:

—I don't buy that the Russians have nothing to do with it, it's simply a dilatory maneuver; we should hit them where it hurts most these days, Mr. Secretary.

—And where is that, Jerry?

Cunningham showed the Secretary of Defense the screen of his laptop.

—Here, Mr. Secretary. —His finger pointed on a map of the Crimean peninsula, towards its lower part, the city of Sevastopol—, there is the Russian base of the Black Sea Fleet.

II

By the middle of 2024, Europe was a sinking ship, with the once European unity breaking into pieces, generating strong tensions among EU members. Regarding Scotland, despite the British government's refusal, Nicola Sturgeon, supported by the Scottish Parliament, carried out a referendum to decide on the separation from the United Kingdom. Once the 'yes' vote for independence triumphed, Sturgeon promptly began the legal process to formalize the divorce from the United Kingdom. Then, among other things, the Scots claimed that more than eighty percent of the oil reserves belonged to them, which led to bitter discussions. England, of course, was not willing to give in on this issue. Internally, on the external front, the formal request made by Sturgeon to the EU to become part of this organization, a few weeks after the triumph of independence, caused strong friction within the Union. Spain, Belgium, Italy, and also France, due to the Breton issue, opposed even accepting such a request. Processing it was, in the opinion of their governments, a step towards the dissolution of their own nations. This resulted in fierce reactions from Catalans, Basques, and northern Italians, or Padania; protests full of unprecedented violence broke out in these countries in the following months, revolts that far from subsiding, grew and became more frequent. These economic, social, and political tensions also affected the cohesion of NATO member countries. Scotland's independence implied, among other things, the decision by the English on where to relocate their nuclear submarine base. Scotland also determined the creation of its own armed forces, which included, as a consequence, its request to become a member of this organization, which it effectively made a month after the 'yes' victory. NATO, under tremendous pressure from its member countries, outright refused any action related to its processing for the Scots; the humiliation suffered within two institutions that represented Europeanism par excellence led Sturgeon to declare in the Parliament that "Scotland has defended the idea of a strong Europe tooth and nail, what we have received in the last few weeks is a slap in the face to our loyalty. Well, if we don't deserve to be Europeans, then Europe doesn't deserve our oil." This statement sparked an endless series of applause and cheers among the members of the Parliament and Government present at the Parliament in Holyrood, Edinburgh. The confusion in Europe was of such magnitude that the former French president, Emmanuel Macron, stated, with a downcast face, in an interview for Christiane Amanpour's program on CNN, that "what we are experiencing today in Europe is very serious. It's an issue that shakes the very foundations of Europeanism. If a Catalan doesn't feel Spanish or a Basque doesn't see himself as part of Spain; if a Scot doesn't see a common destiny with the English and Irish, if a Fleming doesn't share a country vision with his Walloon brothers, if the Lombards think the same about Italy. How on earth can we have a strong and permanent conviction over time about being Europeans?"

"Is that fully confirmed, Sergey?"

Russian Defense Minister, Sergey Shoygu, responded with a frown: "Absolutely, Mr. President."

Vladimir Putin seemed to glower at Alexandr Chemezov, the CEO of Rosoboronexport, the state-owned company that controls Russian military equipment exports.

"How could this happen, Alexandr?"

Chemezov squirmed uncomfortably in his seat, then glanced sideways at his colleague next to him as if asking for an apology.

"Mr. President, we have conducted a detailed investigation of this regrettable incident, which I must inform you occurred much before the Poseidon could reach our hands."

"I don't understand, Alexandr, explain yourself better," Putin replied, annoyed.

"Mr. President," Dmitry Nikolaevich, the CEO of Sevmash, the Russian naval manufacturer, interrupted, "the terrible loss of the Poseidon actually happened in our factory."

"An inexcusable mistake, I assume you agree with me. Don't you, Dmitry?" Putin struggled to keep control amidst his boundless anger. The President of the Russian Federation took a sip of water and placed the glass back on the table, his hand trembling slightly. "The responsible parties must be punished. Have they been identified?"

"We are working on that, Mr. President."

Vladimir Putin's eyes were fiery.

"Make the investigation quick, Dmitry. Ineptitude and lack of control are synonymous with complicity to me, and... I don't forgive complicity either." "Is that clear?"

"Completely, Mr. President, you will soon have the results of the investigation," Dmitry Nikolaevich replied with a trembling voice. "The meaning of the word 'soon' is similar to another term, extremely disappointing for me, it is the term 'eternal', honestly, that tells me nothing, Dmitry; you have two weeks to discover and bring me those responsible," Putin subtly observed his Minister of Defense, "rely on the FSB for this, without a doubt, they will accelerate the results of the investigation."

Nikolaevich timidly nodded; the voice of Dmitry Medvedev, Prime Minister, was heard:

"Vladimir, in the meantime, how do we handle the matter with the Europeans? To them, we are the ones responsible for this escalation in tensions, unfortunately, everything points to us having sunk the English destroyer."

Vladimir Putin slightly scratched his chin for a few seconds, his gaze, momentarily lost, was directed upwards.

"Dmitry, there are actually two issues we must immediately address," Putin paused briefly and noted something in his notebook; "the first is to identify who is behind the theft of Poseidon, the responsible ones you," Putin stared again at Dmitry Nikolaevich, "manage to find will have to tell us to whom or to whom they handed it over, we need to find them quickly, as it's clear they have an interest in putting us on a collision course with Europe."

"Without a doubt, a point to consider, Vladimir. And the Europeans? How do we deal with them?"

Putin raised his eyebrows and slightly waved his hands.

"Simple, Dmitry, we will have to accept our responsibility in the sinking of the English destroyer."

Medvedev, visibly surprised, widened his eyes.

"But... Vladimir, this will undoubtedly exacerbate tensions with the EU and NATO. Isn't this a very high risk?"

Putin shrugged his shoulders a couple of times.

"It's worse and riskier for us to come off as a group of incompetents who don't control their military arsenal, no, Dmitry, I will never give that pleasure to the West."

"And what will we tell them then? The English have given us until tomorrow to explain what happened."

"We will respond, through a statement from the Ministry of Defense, that an internal investigation indicates that it was a regrettable error by one of our operators during a combat exercise in one of our submarines, we will send our sincere condolences to the British people and to the families of the deceased," Putin glanced sideways at his Minister of Defense. "What do you think about this, Sergey?"

"I agree, Mr. President, we have no alternative but to assume responsibility as if it were a mistake of ours."

Putin waved his hands again.

"It's inevitable, the English and the NATO folks will take retaliatory measures, we need to be prepared, Sergey." The Russian president pointed to Medvedev. "Dmitry, let's meet with Viktor." He was referring to the director of the FSB, the Russian secret service, "we need to know what the next steps the Europeans and their American friends plan to take are." Putin let a slight smile of satisfaction show, "I can't figure out what those causing this uproar intend, but, gentlemen, it may bring us some... unexpected benefits."

Craig Eastman was reading the news about the Russian response to the British request regarding the sinking of HMS Daring in The Times when a breaking news alert on CNN interrupted his reading; the naval base of the Black Sea Fleet had been attacked, a destroyer, the Smetlivy, was seriously damaged, the presenter added that there was not yet a report of casualties, however, unofficial sources claimed that dead and multiple injured could be seen; the explosion had apparently also reached a nearby fuel depot, multiplying the damage from the attack; the image changed and now appeared a defense expert contributor, to the interviewer's question about where this attack on the base could have come from, he opined that it was most likely a military response from the English, proportional to the damage caused to their destroyer in the Gulf of Oman; quickly the image changed again, in a room full of reporters in Portsmouth, a spokesperson for the Royal Navy outlined the details of the operation; from an unidentified point in the Mediterranean Sea, the launch of a

Tomahawk cruise missile was carried out with a positive impact result at 03:37 London time, the spokesperson regretted the sacrifice of human lives in said attack, however, the cowardly Russian action in the Gulf of Oman could not go unanswered, then began a round of questions from the journalists present there. Eastman lowered the volume on the television with the remote control. "Why didn't the Russians detect the Tomahawk? It's strange that it entered Russian airspace like he owned the place, an expression that in English means 'as if it was his own house,' they have everything from the S400, with a maximum range of four hundred kilometers, to the Pantsir, whose protection range is twenty kilometers. Did they not see it coming?" He pondered, when his cell phone rang, Eastman answered.

"Mr. Eastman?"

"Indeed, I am Mr. Eastman. Who's calling?"

"John Mansfield, the Prime Minister recommended that, given the recent events, I should have a chat with you."

For a moment, Craig Eastman didn't know what to say; the very director of MI6 was on the other line.

"Sir John, good morning, my apologies, you've caught me by surprise."

"No worries, Craig. I can call you that, right?"

"Of course, Sir John."

"Very well, Craig. Would it be convenient for you to have tea in my office this afternoon? How about 3 p.m., what do you think?"

Craig Eastman said yes, the MI6 director hung up immediately, surprised, Eastman said aloud: "My God, things must be getting more complicated than I think. Why on earth does the man who runs British intelligence want to talk to me?"

The phrase echoed over and over in Tomás Cruz's mind, he then decided to make himself a coffee, to help his confused brain make some sense of it, while the water boiled in the kettle, the words bubbled up again in his memory: "I think everything is connected, Tom, I don't know how, now you're reading these words and you must know how much I regret not having been able to talk to you about it, mon ami, you must find out what it's about and, believe me, time is of the essence..." "What the hell is Jean Claude talking about? What the hell does he want me to investigate?" pondered a distracted Cruz; the kettle began to whistle, he momentarily ignored its whistling, he was busy dealing with another unfinished phrase, to top it all off, it could facilitate his investigation: "I found something that might be useful, it was launched recently, and led me directly to a conclusion, at first, outrageous; however, every time I connect the dots, I end up at the same result, linking the terrorist attacks by Al Qaeda, or ISIS?, or both? with the issue that is heating up the atmosphere in Europe. Tom, you must talk to him, it's about..." his friend's letter ended there, for some reason, Jean Claude hadn't finished the sentence; the kettle's whistle was unbearable, in the midst of his reflections, Cruz felt something shaking him; alarmed, he turned his head to see what it was.

"Tom. Where is your head at? The kettle has been whistling for minutes," said Carole turning off the burner.

"Oh, forgive me, Carole! Your husband's damn letter has me completely baffled."

His friend then began to prepare the coffee, afterward shaking her head several times.

"What's crazy is this world, Tom. Did you see the news about the attack on the British warship? What were the Russians thinking to carry out such madness?"

Tomás Cruz looked at her perplexed.

"No, I haven't seen the news. When did it happen?"

"A couple of hours ago, at noon local time in the Gulf of Oman, CNN reports that unconfirmed sources point to the Russians."

"My God, this just keeps getting worse."

Carole served two cups of coffee and handed one to her friend.

"So, why does J.C.'s letter drive you to the brink of madness?"

Cruz drank eagerly, like an addict, a good gulp from the cup, after a long sigh, he replied:

"Jean Claude mentions a connection between Al Qaeda, maybe ISIS, assuming it has to do with all this mess that's complicating things in Europe, but I can't figure out what it is, the worst part is he left the letter unfinished, mentions something about a recent launch. What the heck is it about? A missile? And he indicates I need to talk to someone. But he doesn't mention who!"

Carole raised her eyebrows, then abruptly put down her coffee cup.

"Damn! Remember your question a few days ago? Tom, I think I know what launch my husband was talking about!"

III

"Craig, I would like you to take a look at this intelligence report we received yesterday from our people in Moscow."

Eastman took the report and read it carefully for a few minutes, then, somewhat astonished, looked at the director of MI6.

"No way... So, the Russians weren't the ones who launched Poseidon?"

"Everything seems to indicate that they weren't."

"And then who was?"

"They have no slightest idea, which puts us in the same position."

The look of surprise on Eastman's face grew.

"And why assume such a huge responsibility if they didn't carry out the attack?"

Mansfield pointed with his index finger at Eastman.

"That is the exact question we have all been asking ourselves since yesterday, Craig, including the Prime Minister."

Craig Eastman outlined a faint smile. "And that's the reason for inviting me to have tea this afternoon."

The MI6 director nodded.

"What ideas do you have about this, Craig?"

Eastman, thoughtful, took a sip of the tea, allowing the MI6 director to pose an initial question.

"A disinformation campaign, perhaps? It generates confusion within our intelligence sources, however, in the end, it was indeed them who were responsible."

A look of uncertainty crossed Craig Eastman's face.

"The Russians, normally, don't act like this, sir, especially if it shows a weakness. Is the source of this information credible?"

Without hesitation, Mansfield immediately replied:

"Absolutely."

"Sir..., then it's most likely that the Russians want to use this circumstance and take it as a pretext to recover what they believe they lost with the fall of the Berlin Wall."

"Mmm, one can expect anything from Mr. Putin, without a doubt, a concerning scenario, it puts us in an even worse predicament."

"That's right, sir, we have to deal with the Russians on one hand and... Holy God. Who is behind this?"

"That's the problem, Craig, in that regard, today, we are as blind as the Russians."

Eastman, for a moment, scratched the tip of his nose.

"With the difference that the Russians seem to enjoy the dance proposed by our hidden enemy."

"I agree with you, Craig. Suggestions?"

Craig Eastman wrote some words in his notebook, then showed it to the MI6 director.

"Prepare as best as we can for the storm that's coming and..., sir, find our hidden enemy, and besides capturing them, do all of this immediately, we have no other choice."

"Islam only knows two types of societies, there are no middle grounds in this: the Muslim or the Jahiliyah. The Muslim society is one where Islam is applied through faith, worship, legislation, social organization, the concept of the creation of our world, and the way of behaving; the Jahiliyah society is one where Islam is not applied: it is not governed by its beliefs, nor by the Islamic concept of the world, much less by its values, its legislation, and its customs. My disciple... a society where legislation is not supported by divine law is not Muslim, no matter how much its members proclaim themselves to be Muslims. Ayman, you must fight against tyranny, the one that usurps our faith, that threatens divine law... Any system disguised as what the West calls democracy or this system now called communism that denies our faith, that intends to demolish its foundations, must be fought and exterminated. Ayman, you must fight. You must practice and multiply Jihad..."

Al-Zawahiri opened his eyes, took a deep breath, the one speaking to him in the dream was Said Qutb, his ideological mentor; the Al Qaeda leader stirred on the hard bed, then, like a wave of cool breeze, the day he met Osama Bin Laden came to his memory, a slight smile drew on his face; it was a sunny afternoon, in the summer of 1980, in a field hospital attending fighters resisting the Soviet invasion, on the outskirts of Peshawar, in Pakistan, immediately there was empathy between them, for Bin Laden, Al-Zawahiri was an influential and recognized leader of radical Islam, the Saudi billionaire was fascinated by his revolutionary ideas, so he invited him the next night to dinner at the mujahideen training camp he funded, Majtab al-Jidamat, that evening would certainly change the lives of both of them and those of their mutual Western enemies.

"How did you reach such a level of inspiration, of knowledge and clear definition, so revitalizing of the jihad, dear Ayman?"

Al-Zawahiri took a sip of gahwa before answering the question:

"My country, Egypt, and many others, including yours, unfortunately fell into the clutches of secularism, a dangerous vision that has led to the harmful Westernization of our societies, which strays our minds and hearts from the truth of Islam, from the message of Allah and from His only envoy to this world, Muhammad. It is our sacred duty to restore the reign of faith in our disoriented societies."

Bin Laden interrupted him:

"A subject which I fully agree with you on, however, in your opinion" "How should this fight be carried out?"

—My source of inspiration, the great Said Qtub, who, by the way, is a martyr, no doubt, a brilliant mind and a faithful guardian of Islam, failed in his attempt at a peaceful search for the prevalence of the faith in Allah within our societies. His life was ended by the cowardly order of a dictator, Gamal Abdel Nasser; then another coward, Mohamed Anwar el-Sadat, betrayed the faith of Islam by making a pact with our most bitter enemies, with those who would happily see the day of the extermination from the face of the earth, of the bright light of our deep beliefs in the truth proclaimed by Allah, I refer to the Israeli infidels. It is our sacred mission to carry, through armed struggle, the truth of our God to our countries and to the very heart of the West.

—Is there then no other way than that of the radical search for faith, dear Ayman?

—That's right, the vulgar secular regimes in our troubled nations must fall by the force of the strike, with the sacrifice of our martyrs, just as must suffer the wrath of Allah their wicked sponsors in Europe and the United States.

Bin Laden offered a tray with Kofta to Al-Zawahiri, then took one and tasted it slowly, then inquired:

—How and where to start this struggle?

Al-Zawahiri replied with some difficulty, still eating a piece of Kofta.

—We should start in Egypt, Hosni Mubarak and his government of perjurers should be the first to pay the price of their betrayal... Then will come other attacks to the infidels in...

The sound of the footsteps of one of their bodyguards approaching took Al-Zawahiri out of his memories, something important had happened, and he had to learn of its details.

"Bonjour, Pierre, we are very sorry about the attack that affected Jean Claude. By the way, how is he doing? —asked Meir

Hofi, director of the Mossad, the legendary Israeli intelligence service".

"Nice to greet you, Meir—answered Pierre Cousseran, director of the DGSE—. Jean Claude remains in a medically induced coma, my friend, his condition is still uncertain, thank you for asking".

"It's a real pity, Pierre, you know how much we value Jean Claude".

"I know, and believe me, we miss him much more than you do, with this world getting crazier, we need his analytical ability, mm... however, I don't think you just called to inquire about the health status of Jean Claude. Am I mistaken?"

A slight laugh was heard from the other side of the phone.

"You are correct, my friend, actually take what I am about to tell you as a small gift for La France in retaliation for the cowardly attack by our common enemy, Arab terrorism".

The tone of the voice of the DGSE director showed curiosity.

"What gift are you talking about, my friend?"

"I knew it was going to catch your attention. Are you in secure mode?"

"I'm always in secure mode, mon ami".

A long and loud laugh was heard from the other side.

"Suspicious as always, that's why I value you, dear Pierre, in this world of intelligence, if you don't distrust, you die".

"That's right, damn, Meir, you're killing me with curiosity. What the hell is it about? Tell me".

"Let's get back to our business then, a couple of days ago, our people from the Shabak –the Israeli Security Agency— arrested, in an operation, three members of Hamas, well, actually two, as they were trying to enter through a tunnel into Gaza".

"Two or three terrorists? —Cousseran inquired".

"Three, the third we initially thought was from Hamas, the surprise for us is that the man belongs to Hezbollah".

"Hezbollah? No doubt that's not usual, but I don't understand the reason for the surprise, they eventually coordinate activities or exchange information".

"Okay, mon ami, the surprise has to do with the information that was carried on a small computer that the terrorist had with him, we found something that might be of interest to you".

"Come on, Meir, you're going to cause me a heart attack with so much anticipation. What surprise are we talking about?"

"Does the word "Valiente" ring a bell?"

The Foreign Intelligence Service of the Russian Federation, SVR, is located in Yasenevo, more specifically in the Southwest administrative district, in Moscow, its capital; surrounded by a huge forest, from there, Russia's intelligence and counterintelligence in the world are coordinated. Early in the morning, Mikhail Primakov stepped out of his Audi A4, after parking in the area reserved for department heads. He was in charge of Office X, the department responsible for developing everything related to scientific intelligence. Primakov heard someone calling him, turned his head towards where the voice came from, recognized the person, and raised his hand to greet him. It was Yevgeny Litvinenko, the director of Office R, which was in charge of controlling all the SVR's foreign operations. Litvinenko gestured for him to wait, and seconds later, they shook hands. Litvinenko then asked:

"Mikhail. Is our Chernobog ready?"

Primakov replied with caution:

"We shouldn't talk about this topic in a parking lot, lower your voice."

Litvinenko looked at him somewhat mockingly.

"Don't worry, 'Mr. Secrets,' there's no one here. I have to report to our director general about this matter today; our dear president is pressing to put it into operation."

Primakov looked around to make sure there was no one nearby; indeed, they were completely alone.

"Yevgeny, you can confirm to our director that it's available."

"Excellent! When can we send our worm?"

In a low voice, Primakov practically whispered to his colleague.

"We're in the final evaluations, we can have it ready for next week."

"Marvelous!" Litvinenko lowered his voice. "The surprise our English friends are going to get is indescribable; I wish I could be there to see their faces when they receive it."

The two walked slowly towards the elevator, a few meters away from where they were chatting, skillfully, Yevgeny Litvinenko changed the subject of the conversation, then asked about the weekend party he was invited to for the fifth birthday of Primakov's son. When both entered the elevator, those present had no idea of the destructive power of what they had been discussing minutes before in the parking lot.

"Sergei, what's the final report of human losses and damage?"

"Mr. President, thirty-one fatalities, including three civilians due to the explosion at the fuel depot; fifty-seven injured, nine of them in critical condition. Several facilities destroyed by the shockwave from the conflagration; the Smetlivy will require a few months of work in our shipyards for its recovery."

Vladimir Putin slightly rubbed his forehead with a hand.

"The collateral damage is regrettable indeed."

The Defense Minister stated firmly:

"It's now important to take retaliatory measures, Mr. President; we have several alternatives that we would like to propose this afternoon."

Putin drummed on the meeting table for a few seconds, then fixed his gaze on the director of the SVR, Vyacheslav Berezovsky, also present in the meeting.

"Vyacheslav Berezovsky. Is our project ready?"

The director, promptly, nodded with a slight bow.

"Yes, Mr. President."

"And the campaign against those who ordered the attack on our base?"

"That is also ready, Mr. President, we are just waiting for your orders to set both projects in motion."

The president of the Russian Federation sketched a smirk, then looked at his Defense Minister.

"We will take revenge, certainly we need to; however, this time, Sergei Serdyukov, the vengeance for the deaths and destruction caused by the British to our naval base in Sevastopol will be less noisy, more subtle... but much more lethal and damaging."

IV

Cruz spent a good while browsing the library of his friends' apartment, the book that Carole had mentioned was nowhere to be found. He then decided to walk to the nearest bookstore, Shakespeare and Company. After about ten minutes of walking, crossing the Pont des Coeurs, he entered the traditional Parisian bookstore via Rue de la Boucherie; he inquired about the book, one of the young attendants showed him the work he was looking for. Did he want it in English or French? Cruz immediately replied that he wanted it in French, to better practice the language. After paying the nineteen euros and asking for the famous stamp that certified his book had been purchased there, he decided to have a coffee and enjoy a lemon pie; "coming to Shakespeare and Company and not eating a lemon pie is like being in Paris and not going to the Eiffel Tower," he thought to himself; now at the table, and after observing for a moment people walking in René Viviani park, he took a long sip of coffee and looked at the cover of the book that had brought him there, its title, Back to

1939? The new military challenges for a Europe in crisis, its author, Craig Eastman. Tomás read Eastman's biography, "Hmm... the man is undoubtedly an expert on defense issues, but what the hell does his book have to do with the mess that got him tangled up in his investigation? We shall see," he replied with some resignation. The man opened the book; Michael Martin, Secretary of Defense for David Cameron, had written the preface. He read it carefully; the last paragraph caught his attention, "Europe's unity faces enormous challenges, just when we thought it was already consolidated. On one hand, Brexit has led to the resurgence of nationalisms we thought were extinct, the possible victory of Frexit in the next referendum, and the new Italian government's bid to leave the EU show dark clouds on the horizon; this has also motivated regimes within the EU, such as in Bulgaria and Poland, to be inclined to systematically weaken the rule of law, a fundamental principle of our social and political cohesion; corruption eats away at the Czech Republic and threatens to spread to neighboring countries; migration, let's be clear, far from being a unifying factor, to address it and find community solutions, has divided us, has fragmented our will to handle this factor which is determinant for the lives of millions of victims of the horrors of war, this has undoubtedly weakened the very fabric of the EU, today, thanks to this tension generated by the migration phenomenon, Europe and its institutions look confused and without a clear path to take, it is necessary to control migration flows, for this, better coordination with the countries of origin of these flows in Africa is required, in that sense the old dream of a European border police remains unfulfilled, in short, national selfishness, doubts about how to confront together the arrival of migrants have led to the growth of xenophobic nationalism, and the solution, far from being foreseen, looks uncertain; two additional issues pose challenges for European leadership, terrorism, and the monetary union, in them, we will also have to work together to consolidate our currency and minimize the harmful effects of terror and religious fanaticism, which among other things exacerbate xenophobia and fuel nationalisms. Finally, there's a factor that has always weighed on the stability of Europe, its name, Russia, its historic expansionist ambitions have struck and modified our borders and threaten to do so again in the short to medium term. In what form will these challenges come? In many and varied ways, from cyberattacks to military harassment and incitement of Russian nationalism in countries with ethnic minorities linked by the course of history to Russia. Is Europe prepared for this enormous challenge posed by the Russians? What consequences will the decline of NATO without the United States have for Europe? How is the project of a European army progressing? All these considerations are analyzed by Craig Eastman in this masterful book, which undoubtedly must be mandatory reading material for our European leadership. Wars are formed like storms, both inadvertently nourished by a dangerous combination of opposing forces that originate their disastrous consequences, well, a storm may be forming in the skies of Europe, and Craig Eastman warns us in an intelligent, yet worrisome manner, of this."

"Jean Claude mentions in the letter that he considered in some way his investigation of the terrorist attack was connected to this book. How are they related?" Tomás took a piece of lemon pie with his spoon; he was about to devour it when he remained motionless for a moment with a furrowed brow.

"Could it be... Could it possibly be what I am thinking?" Quickly, Tomás ate the piece of pie and wrote down his idea on a napkin. He was about to continue reading the book when the voices from a table nearby caught his attention; among laughter and exclamations, those sitting there were talking about a sexual scandal shaking politics in the United Kingdom.

More fuel would fall from the sky to fan the fire threatening Europe. An inexplicable error in issuing an attack order to a group of Israeli Air Force fighter jets ended in the bombing of a Russian military aviation base in Khmeimim, which caused severe damage to its facilities, three dead, and a dozen injured were the result of this terrible mistake. The Russian Defense Minister promised a proportional response, despite the apologies presented by the Defense Minister, Moshe Sharon, for the Russian government, far from an error, it was another provocation against the patience and peace-loving nature of the Russian people. Just a few hours later, an Israeli air base in Hatzerim, located in the south of the country on the outskirts of Beer Sheba, would be attacked by four Iskander missiles, two of which were neutralized; however, a pair of missiles managed to significantly damage radar installations and barracks housing soldiers, with five military personnel dead and more than fifteen wounded reported; both Israeli Prime Minister Benjamin Netanyahu and President Trump responded with outrage to this retaliation, with the President of the United States launching several threatening tweets, in one of which he stated that "our country will defend Israel, an unconditional ally, Putin and his gang of murderers will feel the fury of American military power".

Meanwhile, in the north of Pakistan, in a mountainous and inhospitable area near the border with Afghanistan, Ayman al-Zawahiri looked on with interest at the news of the tense moment between Russians and Americans.

"So, the Russian military exercises are confirmed?" —The German Minister of Defense could not help but show a grimace of deep displeasure.

"Zapad 2.0 is a dangerous reality, dear Andrea," said British Defense Secretary Nick Fallon; Andrea Trauernicht complained.

"This cannot be happening, Nick. Do you think it's a prelude to an invasion of the Baltic countries?"

Fallon looked at the general of the French Army, Bertrand Lavigne, the current SACEUR, and gestured with one of his hands to give him the floor.

"In light of everything that is happening, these seem to be the preliminary moves to an invasion."

"Why call it Zapad 2.0? I still don't understand that 2.0 part," the Minister of Defense indicated, puzzled.

"We also haven't been able to determine the reason for adding the 2.0; however, such denomination makes us think that the invasion thing is serious," replied General Lavigne.

"Nick, did anyone talk to the Russians about this?" Trauernicht asked again.

"I had a teleconference with their Minister of Defense, they insist it's just an exercise.

The truth is, it doesn't seem like that; they are additionally affecting communication systems of both NATO and the defense forces in Estonia, Lithuania, Latvia, and, furthermore, Poland.

"Are you referring to a cyber attack?"

"Yes, the Russians, in recent weeks, have launched a cyber offensive of rarely observed dimensions, targeting strategic objectives in each of these countries, from military installations to power plants, government offices, among others."

Nick Fallon then commented somewhat resignedly.

"Last week, a wave of cyber attacks rendered six of our nuclear power plants inoperative for several hours, two of them are still out of operation; likewise our computer brain that controls the air defense system was infected with a powerful virus, it was out of operation for twenty-four hours."

"Good Lord, Nick! What did you do? Were you exposed to an air attack?" exclaimed the German Minister of Defense, alarmed.

"No, fortunately, we reacted well and were able to implement the plan B we have in place for these circumstances; but, on another occasion, we may not be so efficient in reacting. We had a space of about two or three hours of chaos and confusion where anything could have happened, not to mention all the barrage of fake news or sexual gossip rumors they let loose on social networks and sent to The Sun...

"Do you think all this is related to the attack on their Black Sea naval base?" Trauernicht inquired.

A gesture of skepticism took over Nick Fallon's face.

"Andrea, I believe all this goes beyond the attack on their Sebastopol naval base, I fear it's part of a more structured, broader and more ambitious plan, which seeks to alter not only our institutions and personal honors... There is a clear Russian territorial ambition in all this."

General Lavigne opened a folder, then handed a sheet to each of them.

"I'm very good friends with Pierre Cousseran, director of the DGSE, he sent me a copy of a report originating from a call from his counterpart at Mossad, our Israeli friends encountered a Hezbollah terrorist, from there arose a line of investigation of a contact between Al Qaeda and ISIS, his alias, Brave, they are working on it."

"I don't understand, Bertrand. What does this have to do with the matter at hand?"

"For now, little or nothing, what did catch our attention from the report is a mention of the incident a few days ago between them and the Russians. Do you remember?" Both nodded with curiosity Initially, it was believed that there was a communication error between the airbase and the group of F16 planes, a mistake that generated the entire mess between them and the Russians. Well, subsequent investigations revealed that a "hacker" broke the security of the communication system and sent the order to launch the attack.

"Oh, my God," Fallon said. "Was it the Russians themselves?"

"Everything initially pointed to them, but when they traced the IP, which is the code that identifies the computer from where the attack originated, it indeed reached St. Petersburg; however, the search didn't end there, it went beyond, ending up in a small town in Jordan, about fifty kilometers from Amman, its name, Qasral-Hallabat.

Fallon tilted his head skeptically.

"Strange, definitely. Don't you think the Russians are playing with us and trying to set us up in Jordan?"

"We are working on it in coordination with our friends from the Mossad; we've also asked Jordanian intelligence to investigate the matter."

The German Minister of Defense nervously moved a lock of hair from her forehead.

"This puzzle becomes more complicated by the minute, far from getting out of the maze of confusion we find ourselves in, it seems we're diving deeper into it. How will all this mess end, gentlemen?"

V

Carole and Tomás Cruz were back in the apartment, having spent the afternoon in the hospital. The latest medical report was not very encouraging; Jean Claude was still not showing signs of recovery. The induced coma remained just that, a dark, deep state of unconsciousness, and from this opaque world, it seemed, for now, their good friend would not emerge. Time, merciless, passed, and the aftermath of the coma was not positive at all, threatening with total or partial paralysis of his body or mild to severe muscle injuries, not to mention memory problems, loss of speech ability, and a permanent impairment of swallowing capacity; Cruz, during the ride home, had suggested going to a restaurant for dinner to momentarily ease the bad news of Jean Claude's scarce recovery progress. Carole refused; she wasn't in the mood to go to a place full of people. He then suggested buying a couple of bottles of wine, to which she agreed and proposed instead to buy bread and make pasta at home.

"I've always thought that in difficult times, it's best to meditate on the problems in the peaceful solitude of home. Don't you think?" she said. He, nodding and with a resigned look, replied, "And a good pair of Pinot Noir bottles from Burgundy, accompanied by your unparalleled pasta, indeed make the hard times more bearable, my friend."

While Carole heated the pasta and organized the sauce, Cruz cut the baguette and decanted one of the bottles. After chatting for a while about inconsequential topics, Cruz spoke to his friend thoughtfully.

"I think I know what Jean Claude's message is about." Then he poured a couple of glasses of red wine.

"Oh, yes? Tell me." Carole immediately took a seat at the kitchen bar, where she was preparing pasta with a fragrant sauce.

"Please, don't neglect the pasta; it would be an unforgivable sin not to have it to enjoy with this sauce; the smell is killing me." Cruz watched her with a sardonic look.

"Don't worry, everything is under control. The one you're going to kill with curiosity is me, come on, tell me, what is it?"

"Do you remember that Jean Claude in the note mentions a conjecture? He believes there is a relationship between what is happening and people from Al-Qaeda or ISIS. I bought the book from the author you told me about, Craig Eastman..."

"And does he mention them?" His friend inquired, widening her eyes.

"No, the book is actually an interesting analysis, from a military perspective, of the current reality of Europe and all the challenges it must face amidst all the dangers that threaten it, especially those related to nationalisms, which can weaken it, at the same time leading it to a collision course with what he calls an always uncomfortable neighbor, Russia... And there, I believe, lies the crux of the issue Jean Claude proposes."

"I don't see how the Arab terrorists relate to Russia..." observed Carole skeptically. "The Russians are doing everything to lead us into a war and, well, the Ukrainians aren't helping much, to say the least, having shot down a Russian plane, the same with the Lithuanians, who apparently killed the Russian governor in Kaliningrad. What in the world Al-Qaeda or ISIS would have to do with this?"

"That's the part I still don't understand," Cruz lifted his shoulders in a sign of helplessness, "but I suspect that the path suggested by Jean Claude is that; somehow Islamic terrorism would be related to this."

"Bah, let me focus on the pasta." My friend, I think you're going down the wrong path," Carole grumbled, taking some wine and holding the pot where the delicious sauce was, to mix it with the fusilli. She looked at him with an ironic face. "Let's see if the pasta reactivates your neurons." Cruz returned her mock gesture with a grimace.

"Seriously, my friend, your husband was suggesting that possibility."

"Alright. And what do you think we should do?"

"I think we should talk to someone from the DGSE."

Carole finished serving the pasta on the plates and looked at him skeptically.

"For now, refill the glasses and let's get rid of this pasta. I think I know who you should talk to; however, I believe that the world of intelligence and counter-terrorism can wait until tomorrow. Now let's enjoy this dinner in the name of J.C."

Major Muhammad al-Shubaki, from Jordanian intelligence, patiently waited for the green light from his forward team. He was located outside Qasral-Hallabat, the small town where the computer that launched the worm virus infecting the Israeli Air Force's communication system had been identified. When the team leader confirmed that everyone was in position, al-Shubaki ordered to enter the small house next to a gas station. The team moved quickly and silently through a group of small bushes surrounding the house; once near the front door, its leader, a sergeant from the Royal Jordanian Ground Force, signaled to a soldier with his hand to break it down. The door shattered with the impact of the ram, and seconds later, four men from the General Directorate of Intelligence, including the sergeant, were inside. The house wasn't any bigger than fifty square meters. The first thing they inspected was the small living-dining room, a rustic kitchen adjacent to it was checked, then the two tiny bedrooms, two soldiers entered these. They were empty; the house was uninhabited; the sergeant then ordered to check inside the bedroom closets, they only found clothes and shoes, they didn't find anything under the beds either; while a soldier checked the messy toilet and two others searched the living room and dining furniture, the sergeant headed with the rest of the men to the kitchen, then he noticed one of the bottom cabinets was slightly open, he stopped and crouched to slowly open it, he saw at the back a black device with wires of different colors and a blinking red light, the man just managed to open his eyes wide, the light suddenly switched to green. Al-Shubaki, who was already heading to the location in a Jeep, felt the power of the explosion, the conflagration reached the gas station, generating a yellowish fire mushroom that rose more than thirty meters high, houses, within a hundred meters radius, were seriously affected; the powerful blast claimed the lives of several civilians and soldiers that hot afternoon, in addition to numerous wounded.

Craig Eastman was dismayed reading The Times, one of the main news was related to the harmful cyber-attacks received by the United Kingdom in recent days, several nuclear plants and Royal Air Force bases had been strongly struck, the damage to their systems had been considerable; a series of fake news about sexual scandals, as well as corruption by high government officials, ran endlessly on social media and were of course being published by tabloid newspapers, this inevitably put the prime minister, and the officials involved, in a difficult position, forcing them to give explanations about said scandals. Another disturbing piece of news, at the bottom of the page, caught his attention, the latest incident between Russia and Israel was turning the Mediterranean Sea into the most recent scenario of confrontation in which the navies of the Russian Federation and NATO were baring their teeth; in the United States, through a direct order from President Donald Trump, the news mentioned that the Secretary of Defense ordered to reinforce their presence there with an additional fleet, that of the aircraft carrier Dwight D. Eisenhower, additionally, the USCENTCOM, Central Command of the Armed Forces, ordered the deployment to its withdrawing bases in England, Spain, and Italy of army and navy special forces. "We will not leave our allies alone in this misguided and delusional military adventure that Russia intends to carry out," stated the Secretary of Defense in Berlin during a whirlwind visit to several member countries of the Atlantic alliance; a photograph showed two Russian Bear Tu-95s, escorted by three F15s of the United States Navy very close to the island of Crete, in the Mediterranean, right on the entry and exit route of the warships of the Russian Black Sea Fleet; the end of the news was not at all encouraging, "Everything seems to indicate that we are on the path of an inevitable military confrontation with Russia; if miracles exist, it is time to pray for one to appear, and soon, before it is too late and regretting is no longer enough." My God. Who or who are behind this? Is Putin so deranged to want to stir up trouble of these proportions?, Eastman wondered. As he pondered the answers to this question, his cell phone rang, he looked at the number on the screen, with a look of surprise he just managed to express in a low voice:—It's a long-distance call... France? Who the hell is calling me from Paris?

"Do we know who owned the computer remains they found in the house at Qasr al-Hallabat?"

"Not yet, sir, however, we recovered several emails between him and an individual whose name is Vasili Koslov."

"Vasili Koslov? That name rings a bell..."

"Sir, it's the name of the Russian we found in Abdelkrim Buazuai's notebook."

"Of course, that's him, Bernard, briefly remind me who we are talking about," said Pierre Cousseran, the director of the DGSE."

"Koslov is an active GRU agent, we tracked his activities with our friends from the CIA, MI6, and Mossad."

"So in the computer files we managed to recover, there appear a couple of emails between him and our enigmatic Valient. What date are the emails?" —Cousseran inquired.

"The emails are dated two months ago," answered Bernard Dumont.

"Mmm. We found Buazuai dead shortly after. Would that confirm that he could be the so-called Valient we've been tracking?"

Dumont frowned, what followed was a gesture of doubt.

"It could be, however, there is something that makes me suspicious."

"What is it, Bernard?"

"In one of the emails sent by the mysterious terrorist owner of the computer." —Dumont handed a sheet to his boss—, there appear a couple of brief paragraphs. —He read it carefully—: "V would like to meet with you. What date would be best?" —Below was a brief response in Arabic—: "V will send envoy, Damascus 23-10." —The translation indicated—: "V will send envoy, Damascus 23-10."

Now, who made gestures of uncertainty was Cousseran.

"Hell. Is V Valient?"

"We all ask ourselves the same question."

"10-23 seems to indicate a date. Could they be talking about October 23rd?"

"That seems to be the case, sir director."

The director of the DGSE took a calendar from the desk.

"That date is next week, if that's the case, a possible envoy from our enigmatic Valient will meet that day in Damascus with the also mysterious subject of the email, the problem is we do not have their photo IDs and the meeting place."

Dumont cracked a slight smile.

"Our friends from the Mossad are very efficient, they tracked the hard drive's memory and found the face of the mysterious sender of the email on Facebook, they are identifying who it is, although we do not have the place, we can recognize him, we have already instructed our people in Syria, our friends from the Spanish CNI, the CIA, and the MI6 did the same thing.

"Wonderful!" —said Cousseran, raising his right hand—, hopefully, we can locate them, it's imperative we reach the so-called Valient."

Bernard Dumont nodded.

"Sir, next week, Damascus will be a hive of spies searching for a needle in a haystack, let's hope that this time luck is on our side."

*GRU: Main Intelligence Directorate of the General Staff of the Armed Forces of the Russian Federation.

*CNI: National Intelligence Center.

VI

Tomás Cruz entered the main offices of the DGSE, after finishing the tedious security checks, an army sergeant guided him to the office of the director general, immediately Cousseran ordered him to go to the meeting room next to his office, a few minutes later the director came in accompanied by Bernard Dumont. After a brief greeting, Pierre Cousseran launched a chilly phrase that took Cruz by surprise.

"May I know why an officer from Colombian intelligence has privileged information exclusively for the use of the French state?"

Cruz replied with a phrase as cold as the one just expressed by the director of the DGSE. "As far as I know, the books published by Craig Eastman are not owned by La France, Mr. Director."

Cousseran glanced at Bernard Dumont, one of the men accompanying him, then smiled in affirmation.

"I like this man, Bernard, he's not easily intimidated. I thought my legendary intimidating look would break him." —The director's eyes remained fixed on those of Tomás Cruz, who held the gaze without blinking. Cousseran nodded his head up and down and then smiled slowly— "Very well... very well, Mr. Cruz, Carole briefly mentioned Jean Claude's message for you and your theory about this whole mess we find ourselves in. What the hell is it all about?"

Once Cruz finished explaining his hypothesis, Cousseran, after scratching his chin, indicated.

"So, according to your conjectures, the Arabs would be behind all this. Is that so?"

"I believe that is precisely what Jean Claude wanted to point out in his message, Mr. Director."

Dumont, with a wrinkled brow, said.

"Could it not rather be that the Russians are using Arab factions from ISIS or AL QAEDA?"

"That is a possibility." —Cruz shrugged in a gesture of helplessness— "To be honest, Jean Claude's message is, unfortunately, quite vague."

"Did Jean Claude mention anything else in the message?" — Cousseran inquired.

Tomás Cruz pulled out a sheet from his sports jacket, then showed the director the entirety of his friend's message, who read it carefully for a few seconds.

"Jean Claude mentions in the note something about a launch, also, that you should talk to someone... Carole told me that you have a guess about who it might be. Is that so?"

"True, when we talked about it, she mentioned the name of a writer, Craig Eastman. I read his last book and I think it is the basis of Jean Claude's theory."

The head of the DGSE made a gesture of helplessness, as if to suggest he was unfamiliar with whom they were referring to.

"Craig Eastman? I don't recall him. What's the name of the book?"

Cruz mentioned with a firm voice the title of the work.

"Back to 1939? The New Military Challenges for a Europe in Crisis."

Dumont, who was leaning back in his chair, made a quick movement forward.

"Wait, I think I've seen that book on Jean Claude's desk one of the last times we talked about the Buazaui case and our mysterious Valiant."

The director turned his face towards Dumont.

"Bernard, I think we should immediately check Jean Claude's desk."

The three men quickly headed to the office of Jean Claude Lebel, after entering, they searched the desk, the book was not there; then Dumont opened several of his drawers without success. Cruz, who was standing next to the director of the DGSE, noticed something immediately caught his attention at the back of the office, in the middle of a small cabinet containing some folders, the man walked over there, the spine of the book was unmistakable, after picking it up, he expressed satisfied:

"We've found what we were looking for, gentlemen." —Cruz noticed that a green bookmark seemed to mark a page in the book, he opened it to see what it was about, Cousseran and Dumont approached him, the director then commented.

"Bernard, let's get Mr. Eastman's phone number, we need to meet with him."

Tomás Cruz made a satisfied grimace.

"That's not necessary, gentlemen, Jean Claude has already done that task for us." —The man showed them the page, at the end of the book a phrase was circled with a ballpoint pen—, "War, and I'm not talking about one with the characteristics of the Cold War, but a conflict full of chaos, violence, and death, could be just around the corner." —An arrow pointed to a name and a telephone number in Paris, written by Lebel's hand, "C. Eastman, 447 987562143."

"BREAKING NEWS: Prime Minister of England has an affair with the Secretary of Defense! The security of the United Kingdom is at stake." An anonymous news network, ACB News, released the false news, it reached more than three hundred fifty thousand retweets and around two million interactions on another social network; although both later shut down the portal on their networks, the damage was already done, the news, based on a lie, ended up being the opening story on television newscasts and front page of newspapers. A series of falsehoods were issued in the United Kingdom, France, and Germany by other anonymous portals, all of them aimed at inflaming nationalist sentiments, amidst the highest tension in decades within the European Union. Who was behind this disinformation campaign? European intelligence agencies were on the trail of those responsible, the results so far were quite precarious, however, everything always led to the same place, Russia.

"Mr. Eastman?"

"Yes, that's my name. Who am I speaking with?"

"A pleasure to greet you, Mr. Eastman, this is Pierre Cousseran, director of the DGSE of the French Republic."

Eastman narrowed his eyes.

"French DGSE? My apologies, Mr. Cousseran, but you take me by surprise, I believe there must be a mistake. What is the reason for your call?"

"I understand your astonishment, Mr. Eastman, however, we would like to talk with you about your latest book."

Craig Eastman, uncomfortable, shook his head several times.

"Mr. Cousseran, I must confess that now I am not only surprised but seriously concerned."

A slight laugh was heard on the other end of the line.

"I perfectly understand, Mr. Eastman, however, I insist that I must ask you some questions about your last book. Can we meet tomorrow at a place of your choosing in London?"

"Look, sir, I don't want to be rude to you, but I must decline your kind invitation; if you like, I can give you the phone number of the people from MI6, with whom I think you should talk to first."

"Honestly, I apologize to you, Mr. Eastman, I thought that the MI6 people had already contacted you."

"No, I haven't received any call whatsoever, which leads me to think that I should hang up this instant, if you excuse me, good day…"

A slight buzzing sound was heard in the background of the conversation, Eastman looked at the screen of the cell phone; it was a local number, at the same time, the house's landline rang.

"Mr. Cousseran, I must hang up, goodbye."

The man hung up, remained still for several seconds, the landline kept ringing insistently; him, confused, then answered the call.

"Yes?"

"Craig?"

"That's me."

"John Mansfield."

"Sir John, what a pleasure to greet you!"

"The pleasure is mine, Craig, I apologize for not notifying earlier, the people from the French DGSE will contact you, or have they already called?"

Eastman closed his eyes.

"Sir John, I just abruptly hung up on the director of the DGSE, I must admit."

A slight exclamation was heard from the head of MI6.

"Hmm, well, no matter, it was my fault, Craig, don't worry, the DGSE people want to talk to you about some of the hypotheses you propose in your most recent book."

Relieved, Eastman said:

"No problem on my part, I think at some point the phone will ring again to agree on the meeting place for tomorrow."

"Don't worry, Craig, as compensation for the bad moment we've made you go through, I'll take care of arranging with Pierre the time and place. Does tomorrow, at eight in the morning, at the White Gentlemen's Club work for you?"

Shtorm

VII

The subject left the migration area of the Damascus International Airport, carrying a small black suitcase; the man walked directly to the international flights exit, where he quickly took a taxi. Right in front of the passenger exit, in the parking lot, one could observe, among the parked cars, a burgundy van, on its sides had the logo of a catering company, the hidden cameras, in various parts of the body, recorded the man's exit, a few seconds later, the images were sent to the Mossad's central offices, located a few kilometers from Tel Aviv; fifteen minutes later, the confirmation of the identity of Vasili Kozlov was sent to several allied intelligence agencies, including the French DGSE.

The television image showed the interviewer from Televisión Española asking a question to Inés Arrimadas, leader of Ciudadanos, a center-right party of this country, the inquiry was related to the recent pro-independence marches developed in Pamplona, capital of the Chartered Community of Navarre; similar marches had been carried out in Palma de Mallorca, Valencia, Bilbao, and Vitoria, some of them had ended in violent incidents against the police and some public buildings. Arrimadas responded firmly to the question:

"María, thank you very much, firstly, for your kind invitation to your program La Mañana. Your disturbing question about these recent protests has, without a doubt, a name of its own. It is a well-orchestrated operation to destroy the unity of Spain, a plan that did not start yesterday. Albert Rivera and I said this some years ago. Ciudadanos knows what this whole mess is about, which we have denounced for a long time. This was born in Catalonia more than thirty-five years ago and has been incubating, with the collaboration of Catalan independence movements, in the Basque Country, Navarra, the Valencian Community, and the Balearic Islands for just over two decades. I insist, what we are witnessing today is the final phase of a plan intended to break Spain into pieces.

"Is Catalan nationalism, according to you, behind this plan?"

"But of course. Who benefits the most from all this atmosphere of confusion and chaos other than Mr. Puigdemont, Torra, and their insane followers of this crazy adventure? In your opinion, what follows after these violent days of protest?"

"We are paying for the inaction, the negligence that both PP, due to simple neglect, and PSOE, complicitly, had by irresponsibly negotiating with Catalan nationalism; both parties ignored our warnings about the dangers contained in the attack on the Spanish Constitution by secessionism in Catalonia. We find ourselves amid the social fracture that these independence movements have promoted, dangerously pitting Spaniards against other Spanish brothers; here, either we stop this immediately, using the resources that the Constitution itself grants us, or we will be forced to face a challenge of incalculable dimensions to return normality to our country.

The subject, satisfied, finished recording the interview, hours later, it would be analyzed somewhere in the inhospitable mountains of Pakistan.

Craig Eastman arrived punctually at eight in the morning at White's, located on St. James Street, after announcing himself, a concierge accompanied him to the elegant private room where John Mansfield, who was accompanied by his French colleagues from the DGSE, was already waiting; after the introductions, Mansfield gave the floor to Pierre Cousseran.

"Well, Pierre, I believe what you have to tell us is very important, we are all ears."

The director of the DGSE took a sip of tea, then expressed in English with a strong French accent:

"Thank you, John, Mr. Eastman, I would like to share with you a theory that at first sounds a bit far-fetched..."

Cousseran laid out the hypothesis that he had discussed with Tomás Cruz just two days ago in Paris.

"What do you think, Mr. Eastman?"

Craig Eastman made a face of skepticism and responded to the director of the DGSE:

"I agree with you, sir, that the theory sounds quite far-fetched. Does this have to do with my most recent book? Are you saying that a member of your team suggested it?"

"Well, actually, the conjecture was suggested by a good friend of Jean Claude, our director of the Operations Division, who is on vacation in Paris."

"Frankly, sir, I don't understand." —Eastman's gesture denoted confusion.

Cousseran then detailed the attack against Lebel and Tomás Cruz's role in the development of the recently proposed theory. Mansfield again posed the question to Eastman:

"What do you think of everything you've heard, Craig? Does it still sound far-fetched to you?"

Eastman's response was short and direct:

"Honestly with you, I don't see the Arab terrorist groups behind this."

Mansfield looked at his colleague from the DGSE, who gave him a slight nod, the director of MI6 opened a folder and pulled out a photograph, then showed it to Eastman.

"Craig, this photo corresponds to an agent of the Russian GRU, his name, Vasili Koslov, the photograph was taken yesterday in a hotel in Damascus."

Eastman shrugged, then said:

"Syria is a close ally of the Russians, for now, I see nothing strange in that."

Now it was Cousseran who spoke:

"Mr. Eastman, we have been working with our friends from Mossad on a case of local terrorism that arose a few months ago in Paris." —The director of the DGSE tried to be brief in the details of this investigation, when he concluded, Eastman indicated intrigued.

"Valiente... So our Russian agent apparently plans to meet with this enigmatic character; if we get to him, we might unravel things."

Bernard Dumont, who was accompanying Cousseran, added something that caught the attention of the English defense analyst:

"Sir, we must not forget the apparent relationship between Valiente and Ayman al-Zawahiri."

"Oh, yes, Bernard, I was overlooking this matter, thanks for reminding me." Mr. Eastman, we obtained, from the computer archives of the seized computer, a photo containing an image that leads us to believe that Al-Zawahiri could somehow be involved, though we do not know how. In my opinion, it's likely that Valiente is either him or someone working for him.

"Mmm..." expressed Eastman, "according to what I've been told, in the intercepted email, Valiente indicated he wanted to meet with the Russian. Al-Zawahiri wouldn't be so crazy as to travel to Damascus."

"A subsequent email addressed to Koslov indicates that Valiente will send an emissary to Damascus to meet him. I think it's not far-fetched to consider Al-Zawahiri as our mysterious subject."

Craig Eastman, slightly uneasy, scratched his head.

"Gentlemen, what a puzzle we are facing, whether the Russians are using the Arabs, or they are using us all, my goodness, how do we verify this? Still, I fail to see why my book is of any use in this mess."

Pierre Cousseran was precise in his response:

"Jean Claude's friend believes that someone, that someone for him is within Islamic terrorism, wants to set us on a collision course with the Russians."

Craig Eastman widened his eyes then stared intently at the Frenchman.

"Wow, Mr. Cousseran, that's quite a bold theory. Is this gentleman on hallucinogens? What's his name?"

A few light laughs were heard in the room, but Mansfield, however, kept a stern face, looking towards the ceiling of the room, he commented:

"Craig, as illogical as it may seem, we must consider this scenario; the friend of Jean Claude Lebel is called Tomás Cruz, that's the lunatic we are discussing."

"Wait a moment... Tomás Cruz? The intelligence man who handled the incident between Colombia and Venezuela?"

"The same," Mansfield replied.

Cousseran added:

"Exactly, years ago, in an intelligence course in Paris, Lebel and he met and became close friends."

"Then we must take his hunch seriously; the man saw the attack on Colombia coming. Now, I have a question, how can I help in this matter? Frankly, I don't see how."

Mansfield outlined a slight smile.

"Simple, Craig, by working in coordination with our people and the good friends of the DGSE, you are one of Europe's best Defense analysts, we need your valuable perspective in this quagmire, especially if the Russians are involved in this mess."

Eastman shrugged in a gesture of helplessness.

"I suppose given the circumstances I have no choice. When do we start?"

Mansfield smiled again.

"We started forty minutes ago, Craig. Tell me, what do you need to help us?"

Eastman set his gaze on the director of MI6.

"For now, I need Tomás Cruz; if the man orchestrated this entire mess, it's imperative that he helps us to unravel it."

VIII

A white car parked in the alley separating Ufundí House from the United States embassy in Nairobi, Kenya. Two young women, who were about to enter the embassy building, unwittingly watched the driver as he slowly maneuvered to park the car, it was the last thing they saw, seconds later, the vehicle exploded, the powerful blast heard kilometers away, pulverizing everything within a radius of three hundred meters and claiming the lives of seventy people, among them, eight embassy officials. He watched the horrific explosion from the rooftop of a building, several blocks away. The chilling image on CNN shows a plane crashing at full speed into the south tower of the World Trade Center in New York; eighteen minutes earlier, a Boeing 767 had crashed into the north tower, which at the time was smoking in the middle of the sunny morning, like a house of cards, the two towers collapsed, shortly after. Another plane fell from the sky onto the Pentagon in Washington, on its western facade; a short message, in an email sent by him stated that "it was all done for the glory of Allah... Three thousand infidels eliminated, Ayman. Our brave martyrs have avenged, in Washington and New York, the exploitation and humiliation that for centuries has systematically been carried out by the West on the Arab nation. They, with the sacrifice of their lives, have purified it, freeing it from the disgrace of unworthy, disloyal leaders..., as well as their cowardly followers. May Allah reward them and fill them with glory!" The voice of his assistant awakened Al-Zawahiri from his disparate memories.

"Sir, he has arrived."

Calmly and softly, Al-Zawahiri replied:

"Very well, have him wait in the small room near this one, I'll be out in a few minutes." Al-Zawahiri thought to himself, "the meeting must be carefully prepared, it is essential that everything goes perfectly in ash-Shām"; as he slung his Kalashnikov over his shoulder, another thought came to him, "besides, there's the secret... That damned secret... Anyway, each day brings its own worry, we'll see in due course how I handle it." The man walked slowly out of his modest room, he was expected.

"Mr. President, the attack should start in these two zones."

The Russian Minister of Defense pointed with a long pointer at the extensive map on the meeting table.

"Mmm. And then, Sergey? What would be our next moves?"

The minister replied firmly:

"To enter Estonia without delay, within the next few hours, then Lithuania."

"Very well. How many men are we talking about?"

"Seventy divisions, plus air and naval support, Mr. President."

"Total time of the operation?"

"Sixty hours."

A hesitant Putin drummed on the meeting table.

"When would the operation begin?"

"We are finishing refining some final movements, Mr. President, everything will be ready to start in forty-eight hours."

Vladimir Putin sat down, unbuttoned his shirt collar, then loosened his tie knot, drummed his fingers on the table again for a moment.

"Are we prepared for a nuclear response, Sergey?"

"Both tactical and strategic weapons are available and at maximum alert, Mr. President."

"And cyber warfare? Is our entire arsenal available?"

"Completely, Mr. President."

Putin put a hand to his forehead, rubbed his eyes for a few seconds.

"Seventy-two hours, Sergey, when I give the order in that time, it will start...," Vladimir Vladimirovich Putin's memory briefly returned to the red folder that a dying old man had handed him many years ago, the first page of which indicated a name, Shtorm. After remaining silent for a few seconds, the President of the Russian Federation looked squarely at his Minister of Defense. "As I was saying, Sergey, in seventy-two hours, the 'Operation Storm' will begin. It will lead to the final recovery of the greatness of our

Motherland. Is there a god, Sergey? Christianity is the cornerstone on which Russia was built, so if God exists, we're going to need his help."

Vasili Koslov walked firmly through the spacious lobby of the Sheraton Hotel in Damascus, dressed in a blue shirt, dark khaki pants, and a blue blazer; in reality, Koslov had registered as Pavel Baranovich, his cover indicating that he was the CEO of a Russian chemical company, visiting the country to meet with several of his most important clients. In one of the reception rooms, a group of tourists was chatting, laughing and joking, Koslov, with an uninterested face, walked very close to them, then walked about twenty meters more before taking the door that led, through some stairs, to the splendid pool, once there, he took a seat. The man raised his hand and signaled to call a waiter, ordered something to drink. That beautiful morning, from his walk through the lobby to the pool, Koslov was the subject of furtive visual tracking by several people, a beautiful receptionist was the first to identify him, of course the cheerful group of tourists and finally one of the young men serving guests at the pool; several Western intelligence services, including the DGSE, received confirmation of Koslov's movements minutes later. For over half an hour, the Russian agent drank a local beer and distractedly read a book, after ordering another bottle of Arados. A woman wearing a turquoise shayla sat at a table near the Russian, with her back to him, after calling another waiter, she looked at the menu, then ordered a kahwa with dates, the woman took out a small object from her little purse, a light scarf then slid out of it and fell to the ground. The Russian noticed that the woman had not realized it had fallen, stood up from his seat to pick it up and hand it to her, she, tilting her head, thanked him, after a brief exchange of words, the Russian returned to his table. The waiter carrying a tray at the other end of the pool exclaimed quietly through his intercom: "Hawk made a possible contact"; seconds later, the information reached the Mossad's headquarters, and from there it was shared with the CIA, MI6, and their French colleagues. Koslov's move was also perceived from a room that had both a privileged and discreet view of the Sheraton hotel pool; he had been watching, for several minutes, with small binoculars, all the movements at the pool, including, of course, those of Koslov. Everything happened overwhelmingly quickly. By the time Tomás Cruz realized it, he was sitting on a Falcon7X of the French Air Force, taking off from a base southwest of Paris, heading to London. Bernard Dumont, his travel companion, shortly after takeoff, brought them both on a tray, water, coffee, and transparent plastic bags containing ham and cheese sandwiches. "Courtesy of the l'Armée de l'air," he indicated with a smile, after opening one of the packages and taking a huge bite of the sandwich, Dumont managed to express, despite the considerable piece of food he had in his mouth:

"The boss says you are held in high esteem at the Ministry of Defense of your country; he had to press, and a lot, for them to allow 'the loan 'of you for this mission."

Drinking a sip of coffee, Cruz grimaced in displeasure.

"There are still many things to resolve with Venezuela."

"I imagine, one day you'll have to tell me the whole story of that mess."

Cruz looked at the landscape through the airplane window, expressed disheartened:

"Gladly, Bernard. You know, I also owe that story to my friend J.C."

Dumont frowned.

"My friend, let's then hope that once we get out of this fine mess we're in, you'll tell us about it with a good bottle of wine."

"May it be so, Bernard, for the recovery of our good friend." Both toasted with their coffee cups.

"Changing the subject, Tomás. Do you really think J.C.'s hunch about the Arabs being involved in this mess is serious?"

"I consider, from what he mentions in the message, that there is a high probability of it being so, if you add to his suspicions the premonition regarding Craig Eastman's book, the possibilities increase; anyway, we have to wait and see how the whole issue of the enigmatic Valiant develops. By the way, what is known about him?"

Dumont arched his eyebrows, then brought his right hand to his chin.

"I can tell you that Damascus is, at this hour, a swarm of intelligence agents after him, if we catch him, as you rightly say, this puzzle could be solved soon."

"Then let's hope that Valiant is captured alive, it's essential that we can get from him all the possible information about who is behind this plot."

The Falcon reached its maximum flight altitude, in the distance, through the window, the French coast could already be seen. In little more than half an hour, Cruz and Dumont would be landing at Northolt, the RAF airbase, located in the outskirts of London; they just had to wait for the results of the crucial hunt in Damascus, however, other surprises awaited them upon their arrival in the United Kingdom.

IX

"What do you think of these photographs, Mark?"

General Mark Sullivan, director of INSCOM —the United States Army Intelligence and Security Command—, took the set of images received from the spy satellite, looked at them for a few seconds, and then looked at his interlocutor.

"My God, Pete, Ivan is moving everything he has towards the Baltic countries."

Peter Toland, director of the CIA, nodded with a noticeable gesture of concern.

"That seems to be the case, Mark, I wanted to share them first with you because you come from the Cavalry and what is seen in the images are many tanks. What do you think they're up to?"

Sullivan rubbed the back of his neck for a moment.

"Without a doubt, for me, invade. The movements of the Russians, the previous weeks, are child's play compared to what they are doing now, Pete. In this respect, the RAND Corporation* conducted a war simulation years ago, they update it every year, according to this, it would take less than three days for the Russian forces to control Latvia, Estonia and Lithuania." The director of INSCOM paused. "We developed another war game a couple of years ago, we called it Crusader, we estimate like RAND what NATO's movements would be to repel the invasion, believe me, they are more optimistic than the results of Crusader."

"I don't understand, explain it to me a bit more."

"During the Cold War the Soviets had just across the border Germans, Austrians, or Italians; with the fall of the wall, their 'security cushion 'also fell, democratic Germany, Poland, Czechoslovakia, etc." Sullivan made a grimace to imply he was not going to mention the rest of the countries of the Iron Curtain, then raised his right index finger, expressing: "and the Baltic countries."

"I still don't get the message, Mark…"

"Let me finish, in Crusader we assumed a series of scenarios, the least harmful contemplates that the Russians only take the Baltic countries..."

"OK, I understand now, another scenario supposes that they will want to go further, right?"

"Exactly, if they are already involved in the mess, given the little or no reaction of NATO, why not continue?"

"That scenario is very very complicated, Mark." "How far do you think they would get?"

"Poland? Hungary? Romania? Slovakia? It's hard to predict, but what I can assure you is that Ukraine and Moldova would be invaded. The priority for the Russians is to again have a territory that allows them an attack, whether tactical or strategic, on the Europeans."

"Good Lord, Mark. Are you saying that NATO can do little to neutralize the Russian attack?"

Sullivan's skeptical grimace said it all.

"Little, or rather nothing. In all the scenarios we considered, the defeat of NATO forces is the general rule, except..."

"I imagine, a nuclear response. Am I right?"

"Affirmative, Pete, but we already know what comes after that."

The CIA director rubbed his shiny bald head and then leaned back in his chair.

"The Russians respond, we respond likewise... the apocalypse... So, what do we do then?"

"Does the president know about this?"

"Not yet, Mark, as I mentioned, I wanted to discuss it first with you."

"What about the British?"

"Neither, I prefer the Secretary of Defense to handle that."

Sullivan placed both elbows on the table.

"Do you believe in God, Pete?"

The CIA director burst into laughter.

"Of course!"

"Then you must pray." —Sullivan gave a malicious smile.

"OK, and after entrusting ourselves to the Lord. What else should I suggest to our Secretary of Defense?"

"You know? After leaving NATO, even before, the leeway we had was, and still is, very limited; in my opinion, maybe we should massively mobilize our diplomacy, Pete; and except for moving a rapid deployment force to Germany or the Czech Republic, as a symbolic response expressing our commitment to Europe, or keeping the couple of aircraft carriers we have in the Mediterranean, there's little we can do."

"Can't we send more planes, bombers perhaps? That might help."

General Sullivan showed a gesture of disapproval.

"Don't bother suggesting it, Pete. Our entire air force would be insufficient to contain the Russian attack."

Mohammad Raza finished excitedly, programming the malware, which, a worm type, promised to be very harmful. Raza pondered for a few seconds about the name he was going to give his new toy, one came swiftly to his memory, Zaida, that was his girlfriend's name. "Why not? She is impetuous, besides this means 'the one who grows' in Arabic, as this fantastic worm will grow," he said to himself; a loud notification indicated that a message had arrived on WhatsApp.

"Is the package ready?"

Raza replied:

"Yes."

"Perfect. When is it sent?"

"End of the day."

"Ready."

Raza decided to go to sleep for a while, there were still a few hours to midnight, he was exhausted, set the alarm on his cell phone for eleven forty-five at night, then got into bed, a few minutes later, he was sleeping soundly. Nothing suggested that, in a few hours, from a suburb of Karachi, a dangerous malicious computer program that would wreak havoc, especially in Europe, was about to spread.

"Any news, Adil?"

"No news, sir, Falcon remains in place."

"And the woman?"

"She continues at her table as well."

"Hmm... Did the man come to Damascus to sit and read a book by a pool? I'll be awaiting any news, Adil."

For about an hour more, Koslov ordered something for lunch, had coffee, and read his book, a few minutes later, he closed it and asked for the bill.

"Boss, Falcon is leaving the nest," —the agent reported in a low voice, from a table where he was collecting glasses and plates.

"Understood. And the woman?"

"She's still there, checking something on her cellphone."

"Hafid, follow him, do not lose sight of him." —Another agent, who was having a beer on the other end of the pool, replied by bending down to pick up the napkin he purposely threw to the ground.

"Understood."

After paying, Koslov got up from his seat and walked back to the reception of the hotel, without looking at the woman, he climbed the stairs swiftly and entered it.

"Hafid. Where is our Falcon?"

"He is heading to the entrance of the hotel, sir, he asked for a taxi."

"Understood, give me the license plate number so our people can follow him."

"Understood, sir."

"And the woman? What is she doing, Adil?"

"She requested the bill, sir."

"Fadhila... Don't lose sight of her."

"Don't worry, sir," —replied the young girl who was offering desserts to the diners.

"The car's license plate is SYR 305347..."

"Did you get the license number, Gamal?"

"Affirmative."

"Yasser?"

"I have it too, sir."

"Don't lose him, I need to know where he's going and who he's meeting."

The radio remained silent for a couple of minutes, a short click on the communication devices broke it.

"What happened with the woman, Fadhila?"

"Sir, she headed to the lobby."

"Understood, Tahira." —She was the agent at the reception desk attending guests—, check if she's a guest and give me her name. —The woman replied shortly after:

"Agreed." The voice of the man who was managing the tracking operation of Koslov was heard again:

"Who is behind the woman?"

"I am, sir," Hafid replied.

"Where is she?"

"Taking the elevator, sir."

"Go up with her, don't lose her."

"Understood, sir."

The man discreetly took a tray of coffee and snacks at the reception, then quickly walked to the elevator and asked the woman to wait for him, she, without looking, stopped the door. Three minutes, which seemed like an eternity, Hafid's voice was heard:

"She entered her room, sir."

"Did you manage to identify which one it is?"

"Yes, sir, fourth floor, room 4070."

"Tahira, room 4070, give me her name."

"ZhalehBahaduryan... She has an Iranian passport, sir."

"Mmm..." A slight snort was heard. "An Iranian woman and a Russian agent... Nice combination..."

"What do I do, sir?" Fahid inquired.

"Can you hide somewhere?"

"Yes, sir, from the emergency door that leads to the staircase, I can observe her room."

"Stay there."

"And what about us, sir? What do we do?" asked Adil.

"Wait, damn it... what else can we do, wait."

X

cyber attack was carried out in the early hours of yesterday, affecting the entire metropolitan area of Moscow, as well as extensive areas to the west and southwest of the Russian capital; likewise, Minsk and the central region of Belarus were affected by this blackout caused by the devastating "effects of a worm," indicated the spokesperson of the Russian Ministry of Defense, who also expressed that "we are evaluating with our specialists where this cowardly attack came from. The disruption of the electrical service also affected bases and military facilities in other regions of Russia; after about five hours without electrical supply, the service has begun to be gradually restored in the affected areas. Once we identify those responsible, we will take the corresponding retaliatory actions, we will not allow the security and well-being of the citizens of the Russian Federation to be put into question," he assured, visibly upset. Craig Eastman, thoughtful, turned down the volume of the television, the door of the meeting room was opened by an assistant to the director of MI6, the man expressed a brief greeting, behind him Bernard Dumont and Tomás Cruz entered, who was now temporarily assigned to the French DGSE, then followed the standard introductions, everyone sat down, Cruz observed the television screen which, without sound, showed the CNN presenter interviewing someone about the news of the day, the blackout in Russia; Eastman commented:

"Did you hear about this electronic attack in Russia?"

Cruz replied:

"I read something on my phone about it."

Dumont also nodded, mentioning that Cruz had told him something related to this incident.

"Do you think it is related to our matter?" asked Cruz.

"It's quite likely, if your theory is correct, Tomás, someone wants to enrage the Russians, and vice versa, and lead us into an inevitable conflict." Eastman made a slight pause. "These types of attacks are precisely seeking that."

Dumont asked:

"Do we already know who were responsible?"

"No," Eastman replied.

Cruz made a sarcastic grimace.

"Let me guess, Bernard, I dare to propose a hypothesis, the Russians will say that the United States, or some European country, are responsible."

"Or both, maybe, they also blame NATO," Eastman added laconically.

Dumont opened his briefcase and took out a computer, then said, opening his eyes.

"Gentlemen, time, and the Russians, press us, we must solve this puzzle as soon as possible. What should we do?"

"That's a good question, Mr. Dumont." Eastman looked at Tomás Cruz for a moment. "Tomás, you brought the Arabs into the equation, what do you suggest? Where should we start?"

Tomás Cruz, absorbed, briefly glanced at the television screen, then, as if waking from a short sleep, shook his head, indicating.

"We should focus on our mysterious Brave, for now it's all we have." Cruz fell silent for a moment again. "We would have to investigate everything around him, everything we do to find him, and know who are behind this and what their motivations are, will probably lead us to solve this puzzle."

The screen showed the spokesperson of the Russian Ministry of Defense again, Eastman took the remote control, the sound returned. "This unacceptable attack on our country, arbitrary and unfair, was launched from two cities, one in Germany and the other in Poland. Once again, the enemies of peace in Europe want to promote a conflict in which we do not want to see ourselves involved. Russia is a peaceful country but does not fear war if it is forced to defend its sovereignty and peace; we warn those irresponsible individuals who carried out this vile provocation that we will know how to take, in the coming hours, the necessary measures to compensate the Russian people for this reckless and thoughtless incitement."

A transport paralysis surprised, at the beginning of the next day, Germany and Poland, all their radar and communication systems were attacked with a powerful computer virus, the same fate befell the reservation and operations systems of all German and Polish airlines, as well as the railway and bus transport systems; this paralysis extended to the subway systems of Berlin and Warsaw. The transport chaos, which effectively paralyzed both countries, lasted more than twelve hours, causing also a deep feeling of fear and vulnerability in the population; the German and Polish governments were at that time meeting evaluating the situation and possible retaliations; General Klaus Steinhoff, president of the NATO Military Committee, called an urgent meeting in Brussels, the aim of the meeting, to deliver options for defense and military response, as well as cybernetic, to its Secretary-General and the Defense Ministers or Secretaries of the member countries. On social media, nationalist proclamations laden with fake news began to circulate almost simultaneously, urging Catalans, Basques, Scots, Walloons, and Northern Italians to undertake an independence crusade; the streets of Barcelona, Bilbao, Vitoria, Edinburgh, Glasgow, Aberdeen, Brussels, Liege, and Milan, among other cities, began to fill with pro-independence demonstrators, many of which ended in chaos and vandalism; a growing wave of discontent filled with nationalism began to dangerously take over a large part of Europe.

An elderly man walks slowly down Eisenbahnstrasse, a street in Neustadt, a suburb of the German city of Leipzig, from his thin and wrinkled neck hangs a sign that exhorts: "Brothers, the end of the world is near... Are you prepared?", the old man, with his wavering step, watches smiling, without taking his eyes off the person approaching in the opposite direction. Walther Stoph had to change course to avoid colliding with the lean old man, glanced sidelong at the sign, thinking to himself, "the poor old geezer isn't so deranged, that's where we're headed," Stoph sped up, crossed Hildegardstrasse and entered, right on the corner, the Bruder´s Bäckerei, the sixth bakery in the area in three years. "Oh well, the coffee is terrible, but this one, however, sells better bread," he said to himself somewhat resignedly. Once seated, he ordered a coffee with milk, to mitigate its poor quality, with some toast, then opened the Leipziger Volkszeitung, the local newspaper; the news was not encouraging, to the unemployment rate, which was already around fifteen percent, was added a critical panorama of low wages in this German region, which at that time was located about fifty percent below the average income in Germany; the economic depression had led many to enlist in gangs that were dedicated to drug trafficking, one of the news precisely mentioned that, the previous night there had been a shootout between two groups disputing control of this area of the city;

Leipzig, the article mentioned, suffered from growing poverty, whose threshold had already reached levels higher than twenty-eight percent, unlike Munich, the city in Germany with the lowest unemployment, which proudly showed levels below five percent the journalist concluded the information with a gloomy question: "Are we still the other Germany? The forgotten and poor one?" Walther Stoph closed the newspaper and drank a sip from the coffee cup absently, the man had been born fifty-three years ago, he was the favorite grandson of a high official of the extinct German Democratic Republic, GDR, his name, Hans Stoph; Hans held, between 1958 and 1962, the position of Minister of Defense, he fell into disgrace once the Berlin Wall fell, being accused of manslaughter due to the multiple deaths of those East Germans who tried to flee to the Federal Republic of Germany; more than a hundred deaths were attributed to him "My grandfather was punished for defending the greatness of communism, while other members of the so-called Council of State and the party, who claimed to be his friends, turned their back on him to sell out to capitalist Germany... Traitors, weathervanes of ideology, mere political peddlers who sold themselves to the highest bidder... All of this will be avenged, the humiliation my grandfather suffered will finally be vindicated; soon it will come; the revenge against the insatiable European capitalism will arrive to reset things to their natural state, to the rise of the people and the proletariat under the aegis of a glorious superpower that should never have disappeared, the Union of Soviet Socialist Republics; times of glory are coming," Walther Stoph outlined a smile, finished his coffee. "The good news received from Erich is comforting, it's time to initiate his plan..." The radiant man stood up and paid directly at the register, when he went out to the street, a heavy rain began to fall, accompanied by a blizzard, in the distance the rumble of powerful thunders could be heard, the man raised his jacket collar to protect himself from the storm; a strong storm, furious and threatening, was approaching.

Two soldiers from the United States Navy's special operations force entered the room, a faint light was projected from outside of it, one of them saw at the window a woman, the soldier, instinctively, crouched down pointing his weapon at her, his companion was already aiming at her with his HK416 assault rifle, a long shadow was projected behind her, the subject, observed the soldier, was holding a weapon in his right hand. "Surrender, it's useless, it's all over," expressed the Navy SEAL in Arabic, the subject raised his weapon to shoot, then a short burst came from the assault rifle of the soldier who was aiming from the door; a long, powerful scream was heard, the woman, on the edge of hysteria, was screaming incoherences in an Arabic dialect, Hijazi, the body of the subject fell to the floor causing a strong sound as it hit a nightstand. Everything was chaos in the house as they organized, in a room, the children and women who were inside; after a few minutes, the face of the killed terrorist leader was sent to Washington, then the President of the United States stated: "We got him, however, we have to wait for the definite confirmation of the DNA analysis." Once this was carried out, Barack Obama addressed the nation, with a stern face, he assured: "Good evening, today I can report to the American people and to the world that the United States has conducted an operation to take down..." The memories of that day came back to Ayman al-Zawahiri, one of his trusted men, with his eyes filled with tears, interrupted the prayer that he was making at that moment, between sobs, the man managed to stutter, with a face full of anger, "Sir, our beloved leader has been killed by the infidels," Osama Bin Laden, the leader of Al Qaeda, had died. It took some time for al-Zawahiri to recover from the loss of his leader and friend, a few weeks later he began to plan the revenge for his sacrifice; "the United States will pay for the affront they have committed against the Arab people, we will know to wait patiently for the moment to make amends... This will, sooner or later, come"; fourteen years later, that moment had arrived.

"I don't understand, with all this mess and such a barrage of attacks and incidents from both the Russian side and ours. How the hell are we not already at war?" Bernard Dumont asked, with a look of perplexity.

"Have you read Tom Clancy, Bernard?" asked Tomás Cruz.

"Mmm..., let me think, I think I read a book of his... The Hunt for Red October?"

"Good book, no doubt," commented Craig Eastman.

"I agree with you, Craig, excellent novel, it was also made into a movie." Cruz tilted his head.

"Going back to our matters, in another magnificent novel by Clancy, Red Rabbit Operaion, one of his characters expresses a phrase that fits well as an answer to your question, Bernard, 'We must never forget that wars are started by frightened men. They are men who fear war, but more than that, they fear what will happen if they don't start one.' Fear..." Cruz reflected for a few seconds with his gaze lost on the TV screen. "Fear might be what has so far saved us from war."

Eastman added:

"Very true, Tomás, there is nothing more uncertain than war, however well the battles are planned, no matter the degree of strategy design, everything can go awry because of a human error, an unexpected rain, the lack of commitment of a platoon of soldiers... or because of the ego of those who lead them; despite this, regardless of that fear of war...

"Sooner or later it begins," added Cruz. Dumont made a gesture of displeasure.

"It remains paradoxical, gentlemen, that being in Europe's prime, we find ourselves on the verge of going back decades, returning to times when our differences were only resolved through arms."

"You should read Mr. Eastman's book, Bernard, it will certainly clarify many of the questions you rightly raise."

Craig Eastman thanked Tomás Cruz with a nod and a slight smile.

"First off, I'd like to ask you a favor, Tomás, let's address each other informally, I feel more comfortable speaking that way among us, so I propose we switch to English." —Eastman smiled, and Cruz returned the gesture, nodding; then, the Englishman resumed the matter at hand—. "A few years ago, when he was still president of France, Emmanuel Macron expressed, in my opinion with some foresight, that seventy years ago, at that moment, 'we achieved a small geopolitical, historical, and civilizational miracle: a political equation without hegemony that brought peace. But today, there are a series of phenomena that put us on the brink of the precipice.' Macron also indicated that NATO was experiencing, at that time, a 'brain death,' reflected in a total disconnection of its members, another symptom, in his view, of Europe's path towards the precipice he mentioned."

"Wow, Craig. Why do you think Europe reached this level of disconnection?" Dumont threw out the question.

"For several reasons, the first, brilliantly put by Macron, the European Union, inexplicably lost focus on its origin, prioritizing the economy over politics, instead of working to strengthen the bonds of the EU as a community, we focused on the economy, we preferred to bolster the concept of an economic market, this undermined political unity, we began to look at ourselves, oh the irony, remember that the EU still —Eastman made a short gesture of irony— has a common currency, it's like a club of friends where some have more power and money than others, resentments soon emerged, providing arguments and propaganda tools to the enemies of European unity.

"In other words, we went back many decades, indeed, like in 1914, when we looked at each other more as rivals than as friends.

"Indeed, today we are no longer part of the unity, everyone wants the biggest piece of the pie and resents not having it if they fail to achieve it.

"And the second reason?" asked Cruz.

"The United States stopped being our ally, it prioritized its own problems, in addition to focusing on its commercial and political relationship with China, this opened Pandora's box, in my opinion.

"Pandora's box? In what sense?" Bernard Dumont inquired.

"This is the third reason, two elements emerged from that box, China and Russia, in addition to the emergence of an unexpected geostrategic element that got out of control, Turkey.

"Too many issues at play," Cruz interjected, "let's take it step by step. I understand, and you affirm it in your book, that Europe was left alone, the United States, its natural ally for a long time, abandoned it, and, to make matters worse, nationalisms arose, leading to a dangerous conflict among brothers. Am I right?"

"That's right, Tomás, alone, without political unity and even worse, without military unity; which made us more vulnerable against our natural geostrategic rivals, mainly the Russians and the Chinese.

"Didn't we react in time to this threat?" asked Dumont.

"No," Eastman replied with a resigned gesture. "We underestimated the risks of that vulnerability, we let nationalism grow, we also lost the global influence we had gained with the EU; the most regrettable thing about all this is that we are losing, if we haven't already lost, control of our own destiny, what is happening now, and what keeps us busy in preventing it, is a palpable example of this.

"And the Turks? What role do they play in this story?" Cruz asked again.

Eastman stood up from his seat to pour himself water in a glass, after leaving the pitcher on a side table by the conference table, he commented:

"Do you remember the Turkish incursion into northern Syria? Erdoğan carried out this military operation aimed at attacking the Kurds in that region, this happened in October 2019. Many criticized the United States for abandoning, in a surprising and abrupt manner, its former allies in the fight against ISIS; among the surprised were NATO and its partners; Turkey, a member country of this organization, acted against NATO's own policy on the matter, even defying the EU's own interests in the region. From then on, the Turks acted more in coordination with the Russians than with their European partners and the United States, let's say this was one of the symptoms of weakness both for Europe and NATO, we have not been able to recover from the Turkish syndrome "The worrying thing is that, in practice, today the Turks are an ally of Russia, which complicates the situation in the face of the threat we face," Dumont added.

"We should also mention that, with the closeness between Russians and Turks, it complicates our control over the exit of the Russian fleet from the Black Sea to the Mediterranean Sea, which, without a doubt, gives us an additional headache to the one we already have in Ukraine and the Baltic countries."

"What a complicated situation we are facing." Dumont rubbed his head several times. Tomás Cruz poured himself coffee, offered some to his colleagues, Dumont accepted, after serving him, he commented:

"By the way. Do we know anything about Valiente?"

"For now, nothing. Koslov, under the guise of the executive director of a Russian chemical products company, met with a local distributor."

"Could the distributor be a deception?" Cruz inquired.

"It could be; all our intelligence friends are working on it."

"And the woman? Was anything else known about her?" Cruz inquired again.

"There are also no new developments regarding her; she went up to her room, didn't leave until the next day, the woman had breakfast, paid her bill, and took a taxi to the airport, from there she flew to Tehran."

"And Koslov?" expressed Eastman.

"He remains in Damascus but has stayed in the hotel."

"What do you think, Tomás? Could this be a diversionary maneuver?" asked Eastman.

Tomás Cruz took a deep breath, drank a sip from his coffee cup.

"It could be... Bernard. Is there a way to obtain videos of Koslov and the woman in the pool? Also, of the woman's movements in the hotel those two days?"

Dumont furrowed his brow.

"We could try to get them, but... do you think it will be useful? Aren't we wasting our time?"

Cruz thought for a few seconds, then, scratching his chin, expressed:

"We need to know why the hell Koslov went to Damascus, we have to press our friends from Mossad and the other agencies to determine if something happened at that chemical products distributor where the Russian was; the encounter with that woman might have been coincidental, although I don't believe it; however, we need to rule it out." Cruz fell silent for a while, then commented: "Gentlemen, these encounters in Damascus are all we have for now, this is also the only lead that might help us find out who Valiente is and if Al-Zawahiri is behind all this mess. We solve it, or..."

The ring of the telephone on the table interrupted the conversation, Eastman took the call, seconds later he handed the handset to Bernard Dumont, who, after listening for a while, slowly hung up, his face changing to a ghostly pallor.

"Did something happen, Bernard?" inquired a worried Tomás Cruz.

"My God, my God... Gentlemen, things are getting worse at an unsuspected speed."

XI

Walther Sthop reminisced about that day, November 9, 1989, a woeful day for him, sad for his country, the German Democratic Republic. Two months earlier, thousands of compatriots —unworthy in Sthop's eyes— had left the GDR heading for Hungary; shortly thereafter, massive demonstrations by East Germans, capitalist scum —as he called them—, protests that brought to an unsustainable point of governability Erich Honecker, who resigned in mid-October of that same year; Egon Krenz, Honecker's successor —an inept and treacherous pig for Sthop—, then decides to issue a series of decrees regulating the exit of East Germans from the country, to top it all, the idiot Schabowski makes that damn mistake... Sthop referred to a press conference in which Günter Schabowski, spokesman of the German government, announced these measures; a journalist asked Schabowski, who was still unclear on how the new exit policies would be implemented, when they would take effect. "Ab sofort, immediately," the spokesman replied, his colleagues present looked at him in horror, in reality, the next page of the statement indicated that this decision would apply from the following day. The media in Germany and West Berlin then broadcasted the news, "The Wall is open!", a flood of East Berliners immediately headed to the checkpoints of the wall that divided the city. "I still remember the time," Sthop thought sadly, "I was there and looked at my watch at that moment, it was eleven o'clock at night, the guards opened the control post at Bornholmerstraße, we ran towards the western side, I looked, astonished, as my compatriots embraced warmly with the Westerners, I couldn't believe it, the endless flow of people crossing to the other side... In a nearby bar, they gave me free beer, surprised, I took it and started to drink, through the television I could see how thousands of compatriots climbed the wall and began to sing and shout, their faces reflected joy, quite the contrary, my soul felt nostalgia and pain." "Afterward, there were other matters; the following day, the crowd crossing into West Germany was much larger, that night Sthop watched in horror as men and women, the young and the middle-aged took whatever they had at hand, picks, hammers, even kitchen knives, to tear down the wall; everything that happened thereafter occurred too quickly, little more than a month later the government fell, the following year unified elections were held with the Westerners; within four months, the GDR ceased to exist to make way for a unified Germany, 'to our shame, we lost our country, today we continue to be pariahs in a nation that is not ours, we are simply second-class citizens,' Sthop's thoughts were interrupted by a brief sound from his cell phone; the man checked the device's screen, it was Erich, who sent him a message via WhatsApp, moments later Walther Sthop read it: 'The appointment time is at 09:00 today in three days. Otvazhny has already coordinated the meeting, the assignment will be delivered to you tomorrow, then I will send you the pickup address,' this message meant that the mission now had a set date; the time to avenge the shame of 1989 had come. 'The glorious return of communism is now an evident reality, and I will be part of its necessary return. Nothing can make me prouder than contributing to it!' he reflected; Stoph didn't even have a clue what it was about, but it didn't matter, he looked radiant, whatever it was, it was going to be decisive in changing the state of things. His eyes shone with happiness, they had, by a twist of fate, the same radiance of the moment that would happen seventy-two hours later.

"As we were informed yesterday by the DGSE, the Americans sent satellite photos showing what we fear most, the Russians are moving everything they have to the borders with the Baltic countries and Poland."

Bernard Dumont's face showed worry.

"Is an attack imminent, Craig? asked Tomás Cruz."

"Everything seems to indicate that yes, people from MI6 told me early this morning that our secretary of Defense was alerted a short time ago about Russian movements in Belarus towards the northwest."

Cruz squinted and clicked his tongue.

"You warned of these movements in your book, with these movements the Russians are taking position towards the Suwalki Corridor."

"And if they take this strip..."

"Goodbye to the Baltic countries." —Dumont expressed in advance.

"I know, from your book, that we have no way to react" —Cruz commented.

Craig Eastman slowly shook his head from side to side.

"No... You know what? I'm even more worried about what could happen to Poland and Ukraine."

"Do you think they dare to invade them too?"

"Why not? Without a NATO response capability and without sufficient rapid reaction forces both from the United States and ours. —Craig raised both arms—, If I were Putin, I would not hesitate to do it."

"Damn, we need to uncover who is behind all this" —said Cruz.

"That's precisely what the DGSE director mentioned to me last night" —Dumont sighed resignedly.

"By the way. How's the Russian in Syria going?" —asked Eastman.

Dumont replied skeptically:

"Koslov left Damascus this morning, had a couple of meetings at the hotel last night."

"Do we know who they were with?" —Inquired Cruz

"Two more clients, nothing out of the ordinary."

"It's curious —commented Eastman—. Koslov went on a business trip to Syria? The pieces of the puzzle don't fit. Am I right?"

"Totally agree with you —added Cruz—; however, we need to know for sure what the hell he went to Damascus for. Bernard, do we know anything about the videos?"

"That's what I'm working on, my people told me they had news for us today."

"We need it, and urgently."

"You know, gentlemen? Recently, in an interview with Fareed Zakaria, from CNN, I expressed that this whole mess was like sitting on a powder keg, at that moment I indicated that the worst part was that we didn't know who, and when, was going to light the fuse that would make it explode.

"What a comparison, Craig —commented Dumont—. Then we have to prevent them from lighting the fuse."

Eastman frowned.

"No, Bernard, we're facing something worse, that 'someone' has already lit the fuse, now what we have to avoid is the spark reaching the barrel of powder."

Bodo Fischer and his wife Hanna were happy together with their two young children; they had participated, months ago, in a raffle held in their neighborhood to raise funds for an immigrant shelter in their hometown, Schwerin, in the northeast of Germany. The Fischers were on the penultimate day of the grand prize they had won, which consisted of a five-day, four-night, all-expenses-paid trip to the beautiful city of Mannheim, at the opposite end of their country, in the southwest, less than ninety kilometers from the border with France. The city offered different tourist attractions, museums, the National Theater, the Bertha Benz Memorial Route, which runs from Mannheim to Pforzheim, squares, beautiful parks, shopping centers. That sunny spring morning, they were heading to Nanstein Castle, about fifty kilometers from Mannstein, but first they decided to stop to take some pictures in the wooded area on the way there. Erich Blecher, the tour guide accompanying them—courtesy of the travel agency that donated the prize—took a series of photos of the beautiful family, first with his professional camera, then from Hanna and Bodo's cell phones. Erich promised to send them, during the day, the images taken from his camera via WhatsApp; had the Fischers had the chance to look at them all, in several of them, Erich was not actually focusing on the family. In them, one could see a huge hangar, several C-17 Globemaster IIIs, a C-5 Galaxy, two Hercules C-130s, and a Boeing C-40 Clipper. A last photo showed a huge red brick wall that said "Welcome to Ramstein Air Base." Erich invited them to get into the minivan, the beautiful castle of Nanstein awaited them; "for lunch," Erich Blecher suggested, "I have a magnificent Thai restaurant for you, Khao Thai Cuisine, the Pad Thai is top-notch." Blecher sent a short message via WhatsApp before getting into the minivan—the pictures of the family turned out wonderful—thousands of kilometers away, the recipient of this smiled satisfied.

Eastman and Cruz were coming out with a look of exhaustion from the small room where they had worked all day, it was late, almost eleven at night; they had received, during the entire day, a tremendous amount of information from Israeli and American intelligence services; however, nothing new emerged from this, besides exhaustion, frustration overwhelmed them. Cruz pressed the elevator's down button, its bell rang indicating it had arrived at the floor, both were about to enter when a shout, from the end of the hallway, caught their attention.

"Tom, Craig. Wait! Something came in from our friends at the Mossad."

The two walked back toward Bernard Dumont, Cruz yawned before saying:

"Buddy, we're walking on autopilot, I hope what they sent us is worth it."

Dumont made a gesture of slyness.

"Tom, this is going to keep you awake, I assure you. Remember we asked for the hotel videos in Damascus? Voilà!"

Cruz's eyes widened in sign of interest.

"That's good news, Bernard. Who said we were tired?"

"Now I'll need a cup of coffee, Tom," expressed Eastman, laughing.

"Make it three! I'll go get them, you guys start reviewing the videos."

Three hours later, and several coffees in, the videos showed nothing abnormal, guests in the pool, at the reception, waiters serving in the restaurants; Dumont stood up and did several stretches.

"My friends, I suggest we continue watching the rest of the videos tomorrow."

"That's the smartest thing I've heard all day, gentlemen," observed Craig Eastman, with reddened eyes.

Cruz nodded smiling, he was finishing watching a short video, it showed the interior of one of the elevators, the door opened, a woman entered, there was a person inside, the camera only showed the back of his head, the woman slightly tilted hers in a greeting, the man returned the gesture; then she turned her back to him, the elevator door closed, Cruz observed the image, it was just them in the lift, a few seconds passed, the woman's figure became blurry, however, Tomás noticed a slight backward movement of her right arm, he decided to rewind the video to watch that part again, Cruz squinted and paused the same. He looked at Dumont to indicate:

"Gentlemen, I think I've found something"

XII

Walther Sthop arrived at the address indicated in the WhatsApp note, having left early in the morning from Leipzig heading to Dresden, a little over an hour's journey. He parked his old but well-kept Lada Niva, and after walking a few meters, he found himself in front of a gate. The address on the white mansion read "1-20 Tannenstrasse"; his phone rang, a message had just arrived on WhatsApp: "Enter, slide the latch on the small gate, go in through the first white door on the right-hand side, go up the stairs, then knock three times on the door marked with the number 102." Sthop followed the instructions to the letter. After knocking three times, a person wearing a wig and mask similar to those in the movie V for Vendetta opened the door; this person bowed slightly and gestured for him to enter. Surprised, Sthop entered; the masked figure, without uttering a word, pointed him to the living room where he, obligingly, took a seat. The mysterious host disappeared for a moment only to reappear with a tray carrying a teapot, two cups, two plates, cutlery, and an apple pie.

"Risky activities make me hungry," a raspy, deep voice was heard behind the mask.

Sthop could only manage a slight smile, preferring for the moment to remain silent.

"Worry not, Walther, the mask only serves to keep my identity a secret; at the same time..., it's much better for you not to be able to identify me."

A shiver ran down Sthop's spine; the thought of whether his life was in danger during this mission crossed his mind, yet again, he opted not to speak, simply nodding with some nervousness.

"Come on, come on, Walther..., relax, everything is going to be fine," the masked one cut two pieces of the pie, handed one to his shivering guest, and then poured two cups of tea. "Let's eat this delicious cake, the time to talk about the revenge will come..."

After eating and drinking in silence for a moment, Walther decided to ask: "Can I know what the mission is about now?"

The mask shook from side to side, indicating no.

"No, dear Walther, first we must talk about the motivations that lead both you and me to carry it out."

Sthop placed the cup on the coffee table.

"Mine are clear, to avenge the disappearance of my country, the poverty that my compatriots, who were sold a capitalist utopia, live in today, it's necessary to redeem it and also restore the former glory to the former Soviet Union. Perhaps yours are not the same?"

A hoarse laugh was heard.

"Why do we believe that we all have the same motives when carrying out an action? We seek the same end, Walther, you can be sure of that."

"I insist, you already know the reason why I want to carry out this mission, which, by the way, I still don't know about."

"Calm, calm, Walther, you will get to know the details of this operation, you see…, my motives are similar to yours… Did you know I was born in a small town in our GDR called Wittstock Dosse? My parents were state employees, my mother, a primary school teacher, and my father, a post office worker, both died not long ago, first my father from a heart attack, a few months later my mother from depression due to his loss. When the unfortunate reunification came, our town had around twenty thousand inhabitants, it was never an industrial center, but we lived well, we received a lot of tourism thanks to our beautiful historic center; after it, a great number, especially the youth, preferred to migrate to the more promising West in terms of jobs and opportunities, due to this, today we are less than thirteen thousand and the chances that in a few years fewer than ten thousand people will live in Wittstock Dosse are very high, we are on our way to becoming a ghost town, our GDR is heading there too." A sigh was heard from the mysterious figure, "my parents, dear Walther, retired in conditions far inferior to those who retired in the West, then came the euro and finished impoverishing them..." The masked figure seemed to have their voice break, waited a moment before continuing, "Do you remember that famous phrase by Helmut Kohl shortly after the fall of the Berlin Wall? 'No one will be worse off than before, but many will be much better off.' "The masked one complained, "mere cheap rhetoric." He pointed his hand at Sthop, "you, millions of East Germans, myself included, feel today like second-class citizens, a few have become millionaires with the reunification, while the great majority is today worse off than in 1990, it is our obligation, Walther, history calls us to it, to reverse the mistake of reunification, for this unavoidable duty to our past we find ourselves together today."

Sthop observed the man behind the mask for a moment. "Do you know something? There's a part of me that wants to run out of your apartment."

The raspy, deep voice was heard again, the masked subject then stood up from the sofa.

"You can do so if you deem it appropriate."

"You haven't let me finish. We have, for different reasons, the interest in avenging what was taken from us, but let's get to the point, explain to me how the operation we are going to carry out will be."

"Before I must reconfirm that you are committed to completing this mission. Are you?"

"Absolutely." The man in the mask stood up, gestured for his guest to do the same, then led him through a narrow and short corridor to a small room, Sthop could see two wooden boxes on a cot, the mysterious host opened them, the first, surprised, expressed:

"Wine bottles? Is this what I must carry? I don't understand anything!"

"Frankly, I see nothing abnormal, Tom," Dumont observed.

"Don't you see? The woman moves her arm backward, it seems she hands something to the subject."

"Mmm..., it could be," said Eastman, not very convinced. "Do we have subsequent images? From when the woman leaves the elevator? Of the subject leaving?"

Cruz advanced the video, the first image was of the woman leaving, nothing odd could be observed in the images, Cruz let the image play, focused his attention on the reflection of the elevator mirror.

"Gentlemen. Are you seeing the same thing I am?"

"Yes, Tom, you were right," expressed Eastman, "the subject puts something in one of his trouser pockets."

"Maybe the woman passed him her cell phone number? Perhaps a fling in Damascus," joked Dumont, all laughed.

The next shot of the video showed the subject leaving the elevator, walks toward the street, then signals a taxi, now more relaxed, the man gets into it, there the image captures his face perfectly. Tomás Cruz seemed to express his thoughts out loud:

"Bernard... Could we send the image of the subject's face to our friends in the Mossad, MI6, CIA, and DGSE?"

"Your wish is my command, mon ami."

Dumont sent an encrypted message with the image and the request, then looked at the clock.

"My God, it's past three in the morning, let's get some sleep, in the morning, probably, we'll have an answer about the identity of the subject."

Cruz yawned.

"We must also determine the role of the woman in all this, in short, we will continue watching videos tomorrow."

"And Koslov? How does the Russian fit into this puzzle?"

"Many questions for this hour of the night, gentlemen," replied Dumont complainingly, "tomorrow we will focus on solving them."

The three left the office, the answers they were looking for would come at the right time. In what way? Only time-and Valiente-would determine.

XII

Ayman al-Zawahiri felt a sharp pain in one of his knees, rubbed it for a moment, it was slightly swollen, in addition to warm; that sharp and intense pain took him back in time to the isolation prison of al-Khalaf; he remembered the tortures, his jailers had different techniques to prevent him from feeling comfortable there; sometimes he remained hanging from some ropes for several days, other times he was subjected to immersion for more than a minute, the terrible sensation of drowning assaulted him, they did it in large and filthy containers with water, many times accompanied by his own excrement, then came the electric shocks; hits, punches, whipping on the back, extraction of toenails and fingernails, among other indescribable sufferings; one night, during one of these painful and endless interrogation sessions, a sergeant from the Egyptian Army intelligence kicked the flimsy chair on which Al-Zawahiri was sitting, he fell to the ground, the sergeant and several of his men kicked him until he was unconscious, since then his right knee remembers, quite frequently, the rigor and harshness of the blows received that stormy morning. "Three years later, a regime judge declared him not guilty," reflected Al-Zawahiri. "The day I finally saw the path to freedom, that hot morning, in which I finally stepped on the street freed, I swore I would avenge the death and the torture of dear friends, of innocent believers in the faith of Islam, that I lost in al-Khalaf... Vengeance came on September 11th, but the vindication and compensation for our people, suffered and subjected to the violence of the West, has not yet ended, their leaders, their people, must pay for the war and oppression that they have arbitrarily and unjustly imposed on us," the man continued in his musings when one of his assistants spoke to him:

"Sir, he requests your final authorization for the development of the operation."

"Which one is it? The one in Germany?"

"That's right, sir." Al-Zawahiri once again rubbed the knee that reminded him of his days in prison, took a breath, for a few seconds kept his gaze lost in the dark stone wall he had in front of him, then, slowly, turned his gaze towards the assistant.

"Go ahead, you have my authorization."

Without enough rest, but a bit more rested, Eastman and Cruz reviewed intelligence information. Eastman analyzed the latest movements of the Russian troops; satellite images showed they were amassing a large number of tanks and men in Belarus. In the past twenty-four hours, seventeen tank divisions and another fifteen infantry divisions had entered through two points of the border between both countries and were rapidly heading northwest. "Just what I feared," he said to himself, "they are headed to the Suwalki Gap, they'll be there in a matter of hours." The reports he was reviewing that morning also mentioned that multiple cyberattacks were being carried out against state entities, banks, and news media; finally, the report mentioned that a feverish activity of the Russian Air Force was unfolding in recent hours on the border with the Baltic countries. "God... we are in the prelude to a large-scale invasion... It's no longer a matter of days, we're talking about hours," Eastman was about to share his conclusions with Tomás, however, he was preempted:

"Damn it, Craig, the woman in the elevator gave something to Koslov."

"Really? Where?"

"At the pool, she pretends to drop something, he kindly gets up from a nearby table and hands it to her."

Eastman stood up to look at the computer screen.

"Clear as day, she makes the delivery at that moment."

"Do you see how he then hides what she handed him under the book?"

"Mmm, no, Tom, I don't see it."

Cruz put the video in slow motion, Eastman shook his head in disbelief.

"You have the eyes of a lynx, my friend, now well, we have an Iranian envoy delivering in Damascus (Syria) we don't know what to a mysterious individual in the elevator and to a Russian spy in the same hotel pool. What the hell is this about?"

"Good question, Craig, I guarantee they are not postcards of Syrian tourist sites. Do you want to be more surprised this morning?"

Cruz played another video, in this one, Koslov could be seen leaving the hotel and getting a taxi, the image showed the driver, Tomás paused the video; Eastman exclaimed a curse under his breath:

"May the damn devil take us. It's the guy from the elevator!"

"I knew this would fully wake you up."

For a few minutes, Eastman and Cruz threw around guesses about what this non-coincidental meeting between the woman, the Russian, and the mysterious individual from the elevator could be about, when Bernard Dumont entered, with a radiant face, into the small room.

"My friends, we've got him! We've managed to identify the guy from the elevator."

Both informed Dumont of the latest developments, Tomás observed the Frenchman.

"So, Bernard. Who is it?"

"Said al-Hamzi, he's a young militant from Al Qaeda."

"We've got him, Bernard, this connects the people from Al Qaeda with this whole mess, now we must not let the trail go cold," Cruz expressed with satisfaction.

Dumont made a skeptical face.

"However, there's something that puzzles me in this matter, gentlemen."

Cruz and Eastman looked at him intrigued, the latter asked:

"What is it, Bernard?"

"Al-Hamzi was the right hand of Amer Bin Laden..."

Cruz scratched his chin, apparently not understanding where Dumont's reasoning was going.

"Amer Bin Laden? The son of Osama Bin Laden who was taken down a few years ago?"

"Yes, the same."

"And? What's puzzling to you?"

Eastman preempted Dumont to respond:

"Before Amer's death, and even more so after his death, two groups had formed within Al Qaeda, a majority, with Al-Zawahiri, another smaller one, but with huge influence because Amer was the son of Osama Bin Laden, they followed him; there are speculations in the intelligence world, in the sense that this minority group blamed Al-Zawahiri for Amer's death, according to them, to get rid of his main rival within the organization. It seems they could never reconcile, they are, in essence, enemies."

"Now I understand," commented Cruz.

"If a faction of Al Qaeda definitively separated and they can't even see each other, what the hell was Amer Bin Laden's right-hand man doing in Damascus?"

"And at a meeting with a Russian agent who is essentially quite related to the people from Al Qaeda," Cruz added.

"At least that's what we supposed until today," Dumont remarked. "And the Iranian, what role does she play in this festivity?"

The look among the three was of absolute powerlessness.

"Far from giving us clarity, this makes the panorama even murkier, gentlemen," Eastman indicated with resignation.

Tomás gave a couple of claps on the table. "Come on, let's not get discouraged, gentlemen, regardless of how confusing this may seem, we've entered the game, now we have to play our cards carefully, we can't lose track of al-Hamzi. Do we know what happened to him, Bernard?"

"No, we're already working on it."

Cruz looked at Craig Eastman.

"Craig, you were going to tell me something when I interrupted you with the Damascus hotel issue. What was it about?"

Craig Eastman's face darkened.

"Gentlemen, the Russian invasion of the Baltic countries is imminent."

XIV

The mission was a simple one, the masked man had explained. The elegant boxes of French wine, each containing twelve bottles, contained a low-powered explosive; the goal of the mission, to sow chaos at a US military base, was an act of protest that would trigger a series of terrorist acts aimed at claiming equal treatment for East Germans. "Everything will be different from the day after tomorrow, Walther, we will fight for equality, for freedom, that is, to return things to how they were before that fateful November 9, when we lost our homeland and, at the same time, our dignity," Sthop remembered the man's words. "It really doesn't sound that complex," he thought as he drove the van the man had told him to take to the outskirts of the military base, it was parked in the building where the mysterious man lived, before leaving he had given him the keys. "After finishing your mission, return, I will be waiting for you with a good bottle of wine." Sthop wondered what the mission would be like, he told him that he should drive the vehicle, which had a logo of a well-known local liquor distributor on each side, to the base's service entrance. "You just have to indicate that you are there to deliver an order made by the base's administrative management," the masked man then gave him a folder, which contained the order form, the delivery note, and an invoice. "This will give total credibility to the delivery," he said. "And how do I get the boxes inside? And my exit from there? How will it be?" the questions still echoed in Walther's mind. "Simple," the man immediately responded, "in reality, the service entrance of the base does not allow vehicles to enter for security reasons, there is an external parking lot for that purpose, there they will order you to park the van, later will come the inspection and delivery of the boxes; you will have to park and leave as soon as possible." "And how do I get out of there? The vehicle I assume will explode shortly afterwards." The masked man was silent for a moment. "No, the inspection will be done, there will be no novelty in it and you will return calmly." Sthop remembered that he had insisted on knowing how it was possible that the boxes would pass the inspection without any problem. "How in the world will they not realize it?" "You can be calm, it is a new type of liquid explosive, it is undetectable to any inspection, any, to that of explosive-detection dogs, machines, etc." Sthop saw the highway sign, there were still about fifty kilometers to reach his final destination, the US Air Base in Ramstein, then he looked at his clock, "I'm a bit early, I can't arrive so early," the man saw that a kilometer ahead there was a stop with restaurants and cafes, "I'll have something warm, bah, stop worrying, Walther," he told himself, Sthop felt encouraged, after parking, he entered the restaurant and ordered something to drink and a cake, everything was going according to plan; in fact, most of the explanations the masked man had given him were true, except for a small couple of details that Walther was unaware of.

"What the hell did Koslov travel to Damascus for? What is that thing the Iranian woman gave him? And the guy in the elevator...?" Cruz, excited, clapped a couple of times. "Damn it! And if the Iranian only served as a link between the Russian and the elevator guy? Did she deliver what Koslov was sending him?"

Dumont rushed into the room.

"Tom, good news, we identified the Iranian."

"Bernard, that's very good news. You know? I think the woman served as a link between Koslov and al-Hamzi."

"Really? You'll have to explain that to me, this information will surprise you, the woman's real name is Behnaz Sherkat. Do you want to know where she works?"

Tomas Cruz frowned, replying almost immediately:

"Let's see... In the VEVAK, the Iranian secret service?"

Bernard shook his head in frustration.

"You got it wrong, Tom, it's something even more surprising, she is an assistant engineer at the Busher nuclear plant."

Cruz replied startled:

"Wow, Bernard, this is indeed disturbing. The woman works in the Iranian nuclear program?"

"Worse yet, according to our friends from Mossad, according to their source, a couple of months ago, she was assigned to a special program" —Special program? What is it about?

"For now, we don't know; both they and we are currently pursuing the woman to find out what the special program is."

The tension was rising. Sthop had arrived at the service entrance of the airbase, where a long line of vans and other vehicles was visible; on his way to this entrance, he also noticed that a long queue of cars was forming at the main entrance. Sthop felt his heart might jump out of his chest, his heartbeat increasing. He decided to turn on the radio and listen to music to try to calm down; instead of the usual music, the voice of the local news presenter was heard, mentioning the results of a soccer match played the previous night. He was about to change the station when the serious male voice announced that an important event would take place that afternoon at Ramstein Air Base, attended by, in addition to local authorities, the German Minister of Defense, the United States Secretary of Defense, and... "We will also be honored by the visit of the Vice President of the United States, Mike Pence. This will undoubtedly be an occasion to strengthen the ties between both nations." A cold sensation of panic whipped up from Walther Sthop's feet to his head. "Shit... this bastard doesn't just want to give the Americans a small lesson... How could I have overlooked this... I saw something in the news, but my careless memory couldn't connect it... What other little lie did the masked man tell me?" The thought of opening the car door and fleeing came to Sthop, tormented by fear, a terrible image came to him, "what if this fool really wants to...?" the sound of knuckles knocking on his window pulled him out of his abstraction; Sthop, as best he could, disguised the terror that overwhelmed him and rolled down the window.

"Good afternoon, your documents, please."

Sthop concealed the tremor in his right hand, took out his identification document, and handed it to the sergeant, who made a face of displeasure.

"Sir, I meant the documents for the product you're carrying."

The man smiled nervously, then took the documents from the folder, extended his arm, and gave them to him; the sergeant closely scrutinized them for a moment, then with a firm voice, said:

"Please, show me the boxes."

Sthop got out of the van, then walked with some hesitation towards the rear door; the man inserted the key to open it, at that moment his cell phone, which he carried in one of his jacket pockets, rang, he didn't manage to pick it up to answer, a booming noise was heard, then everything turned dark, as if a TV screen had been turned off.

Late at night, back in his hotel room, Tomás Cruz decided to watch the last group of videos they had received; before doing so, he opened a bottle of red wine and poured himself a glass, then began to analyze the videos; forty minutes later and with two more glasses of wine consumed, Cruz watched the remaining video, the timestamp indicated around nine o'clock at night, the figure of a woman appeared walking slowly down the corridor, she was heading towards the elevator, pressed the button, and waited, after a couple of minutes the elevator door opened, she, seemingly distracted, did not notice the arrival of the elevator, the door began to close, however, it reopened and she entered, a shadow inside the elevator indicated that someone was there, the door closed again, the video was cut off there; Cruz prayed that the next image would show the interior of the elevator, the man sighed in relief, indeed, the next recording showed the woman, Cruz opened his eyes, "in the elevator again?" he joked; it was the Iranian woman, the person inside pressed the button to prevent the door from closing, she entered, smiling at him gratefully, both went down to the hotel lobby and headed to the restaurant; a final part of the recording showed them both sitting at separate tables, after dinner, she left and he stayed there for a while longer, apparently nothing happened that caught the attention. Cruz gave a long yawn, drank the last sip of his glass, closed the computer, and looked at the clock, it was quite late, time to sleep.

Tomás Cruz and Craig Eastman alighted from the car in the MI6 parking lot, heading towards the entrance when a loud whistle caught their attention, they immediately looked towards where it came from, it was Bernard Dumont, he signaled for them to wait for him, he hurried over, when close to them, he commented:

"This news will brighten your morning, we finally found al-Hamzi." Craig and Cruz nodded joyfully to affirm in unison:

—"What great news, Bernard!"

Cruz added:

—"Where did they locate him?"

As Eastman pressed the elevator button, Dumont answered:

"The Israelis have developed a sophisticated facial recognition program, they identified him at Amman airport catching a flight to Karachi."

Eastman shrugged his shoulders.

"Pakistan... It makes sense, there is a feverish movement of Al Qaeda and other Islamic terrorist movements there."

Tomás Cruz made a skeptical gesture.

"Mmm, if al-Hamzi was close to Bin Laden's son, it doesn't sound logical that he would go to meet with Al-Zawahiri. So, who is he going to meet?"

Bernard Dumont slowly nodded his head several times.

"That same question was raised by our friends at Mossad, Tom, their people are on his trail to determine who or whom."

The elevator door opened, inside was a woman and a man, officials from MI6, the former had a face of consternation, both were looking at her cell phone; Eastman, curious, asked them:

"Excuse me. Did something happen? I notice some concern on your face."

Both looked at them with a face of incredulity, the blonde woman indicated:

"How? You don't know about what happened in Germany?"

THIRD PART

I

"If there ever is another war in Europe, it will be the result of some damned foolishness in the Balkans."

Otto Von Bismarck

The three men, with faces of dejection, stood watching the TV screen on the wall, the CNN news showed a thick and dense column of smoke. At the bottom, a headline informed of an attack on the American airbase in Ramstein; the reporter commented that there were still no preliminary data on deaths or injuries; however, he added that the damage to the base was significant, unofficial sources spoke of several deaths and screams of people calling for help; the bewilderment was total, a deafening noise of sirens, people running, and soldiers giving way to ambulances and fire trucks was what surrounded the journalist, who as he could, spoke, almost shouting. Cruz turned down the volume of the device a bit.

"You say the Defense Secretary was on the base, Bernard?"

"Yes, the Vice President was saved by a whisker, the bad weather in Paris prevented him from reaching the base."

Craig Eastman took a seat.

"Is there any news on the condition of the Defense Secretary?"

"Not so far, it's only been just over half an hour since the attack."

Cruz let out a long exhale.

"Do we know anything about the perpetrators? Has anyone claimed the attack?"

"Not yet," Dumont replied; then Eastman pointed, with his right index finger, toward the screen.

"Whatever they used must have been very powerful, look at the size of the black smoke cloud coming out of the base."

"True," Dumont expressed, "local police reports indicate that the explosion was of such magnitude that it was felt many kilometers away."

A breaking news alert appeared on the screen, Cruz took the remote and turned the volume of the TV back up; the news anchor referenced a video that was circulating on social media, apparently a terrorist group had already claimed responsibility for the attack.

Avigdor Lapid was about to finish his shift in the Mossad Research Department, the man looked at his watch, "forty minutes and I'm done," then he sighed, a smile outlined his lips, for a few seconds he imagined the romantic dinner that night with Ayeled, his young and beautiful girlfriend, that day they were celebrating one year of dating, he had invited her to dinner at one of the best restaurants in Tel Aviv, Lumina, the man smiled again, he said to himself, "Avigord, what you will experience tonight will be epic, a good dinner, a good wine, and then, a romantic night..." The noise coming from the computer brought him back to reality, subconsciously, he understood that what the analysis system was looking for had been found, immediately he looked at the monitor, read aloud the received message, "Behnaz Sherkat, previous assignment, nuclear plant Busher, last assignment..." "What the hell? Shit," Lapid expressed in a contained voice, "my boss needs to know about this." The man jumped from his seat and started running towards the office of his director down the hallway.

The languid face of Gamal Abdel Nasser on the black and white TV screen said it all, the young Al-Zawahiri, about fifteen years old, heard his parents lament, he then understood, helplessly, that Egypt and the Arab coalition created to defeat the enemy of Israel had been defeated. "That ominous day, the day we lost the June 1967 war, I understood that Sayyid Qutb was right," he thought. "The reason for our defeat was simple," he reminded himself, "we lost because we renounced our legacy, we abandoned Islam, without it, our hearts do not beat, warriors become automatons devoid of will and courage, we can send a hundred thousand, a million men to battle, and it will be useless, it's faith that moves our souls and hearts, it was necessary then, and it still is now, to give it back to our troubled people, this is a long-term task, we will not falter in achieving revenge on the audacity of our enemies, we cannot do it, we will never stop fighting." The hurried steps of someone approaching pulled Al-Zawahiri from his thoughts, a shadow appeared in the dimness, with an exalted voice said: "Sir, the mission has been completed." Al-Zawahiri's eyes turned to the shadow in the dimness: "And what has been the result?" The shadow, startled by the emotion, responded: "For the glory of Allah, it has been a success, sir."

"The day of final vengeance has finally arrived, the useless sacrifice of our nation, carried out by the savage capitalism of the West Germans, has begun to be reclaimed; the greed of the banks and companies from the western side has done nothing but bring misery, abandonment, to millions of East Germans, poor those who migrated to that land of exploitation, they are, painfully, unjustly, seen in a different way, they are treated as inferior beings, while their wages are lower than the perfect race, which, according to them, has only seen the light in West Germany; their wicked accomplices have also profited from our land, the Americans have promoted the merciless plundering that the German Democratic Republic and its citizens have been subjected to; well, they and the other capitalist trash will receive their punishment, yesterday we started with the Americans, but new battles will come to reclaim our right to be an independent nation again under the guidance of the eternal principles of communism." On the TV screen, a hooded figure could be seen, their hood was red, this person raised their hand and shouted: "Glory to the German Democratic Republic, glory to the new Socialist Unity Party of Germany!" Behind him, a banner could be seen with the acronyms NSED and some hands joined with a red flag and the hammer and sickle in the center of it; the image was cut off, a black background took over the monitor, Bernard Dumont turned off the TV.

"This is quite strange, isn't it?" Dumont inquired.

"Do we have any indications of the existence of this group?" Cruz replied.

"No, I checked with my people and at least, in the DGSE, this is a surprising novelty. Does this group sound familiar to you, Craig?"

"We didn't have information about their existence either, I asked my contacts in MI6 and they are equally baffled."

Dumont looked at his computer screen, the sound that announced the arrival of an encrypted message was heard, the man opened the message and followed the protocol to read it, then he looked at it for a few seconds, slightly tilted his head back, and opened his eyes wide.

"My friends, the thing about the Iranian woman is getting interesting."

"In what sense?" asked Eastman with a curious gesture.

"The Mossad managed to identify where she was transferred, she is now assigned to the Lashkar Abad plant."

Eastman and Cruz looked at each other, showing they didn't understand, Dumont made the typical gesture of a teacher who realizes his students are not following him.

"Let's rewind then, gentlemen, this plant is listed in the reports given to the International Atomic Energy Agency as a plant closed by Iran in 2005, it was a pilot plant dedicated to isotope separation."

Eastman interrupted him:

"Wait, Bernard, that means they were producing uranium to make nuclear weapons there."

"That's right, Craig, the IAEA report indicates that the Iranians closed it since it was not their intention to produce nuclear weapons."

Tomás Cruz stood up from his seat, walked to the coffee maker, poured himself a cup, and took a long drink.

"Gentlemen, I think better when I have coffee. Let me understand, Bernard, the Iranians closed the Lashkar Abad plant in 2005, it was a pilot plant for producing nuclear weapons... and now, our Iranian lady is transferred to a plant that was supposed to have been shut down nineteen years ago... Strange, without a doubt, isn't it?"

"They are resuming the production of uranium and, for that, gentlemen, we are talking about a plant that is not a project for tests... and the Russians..."

"Our friends from Russia are, in some way, supporting them."

"What the hell are they planning?" expressed Cruz.

The image of the President of the United States, Donald Trump, appeared on the screen, this time Tomás Cruz took control to turn up the volume, next to him were the Secretary of State, the Director of the CIA, the NSA, and the Joint Chiefs of Staff; the three looked at each other with some curiosity, it was not normal for all of them to appear in a press conference of the US president, Trump's face showed a huge annoyance, he approached the microphone at the podium and stated: "Good afternoon everyone, today has been a sad day for the American people and for its armed forces, a cowardly and cruel attack was carried out against our base in Ramstein, Germany, senselessly causing the death of hundreds of our brave soldiers and officers. "I must also communicate, with deep sorrow, that in this brutal attack, our Secretary of Defense has also perished, as well as members of his team who were accompanying him on the visit to our base," the president paused, his hands trembling, his reddened face showing restrained fury. After clearing his voice a bit, he continued: "Innocent German citizens have also fallen, the life of Defense Minister Andrea Trauernicht was likewise taken; from the depths of my heart, I send a message of condolences to all their families, to their loved ones, all these valuable lives lost plunge our two nations into deep sadness," Trump fell silent for a moment, took a sip from the glass of water he had on the podium, "America will prevail, as it has prevailed before when facing terrorism, or attacks disguised as such; I must affirm that intelligence sources have informed us that this unjustified aggression was planned from Russia and executed by mercenaries in their service, we are making a final reconfirmation of our sources, if this is corroborated, we will take the appropriate retaliatory actions, we will not allow foul play in international politics, nor will we let pass without vengeance the lives lost today. My dear fellow citizens, difficult times loom ahead, but we will know how to face and manage them for the good of the civilized world, God bless us and bless America." The three men were absorbed for a moment, the phone at the head of the table rang, pulling them out of their abstraction, Dumont picked up the handset, after two or three words, nodded, after hanging up and with a stricken face, said:

"Gentlemen, NATO troops have been moved to Lertcon 2, the President of the United States has also ordered DEFCON 2."

Craig Eastman slowly covered his head with his hands.

"My God, this is the prelude to war, gentlemen, it's also the step before a nuclear conflict. What in the devil are we getting into."

II

Vladimir Putin watched the television screen impassively, once President Trump's address had finished, he turned it off, and, looking at his Minister of Defense, posed the question:

"Is the Americans' alert condition confirmed, Sergey?"

"Yes, Mr. President."

Putin rubbed his nose for a couple of seconds, then said:

"In reality, we've been in a condition similar to theirs for weeks, but it wouldn't hurt to make public our maximum readiness condition this evening, in the sense that today, in response to the American escalation, we must respond in the same manner; we will also indicate that we are forced to make this decision despite being a people of peace, and that we do it to protect the people of Russia."

The Russian Minister of Defense nodded, then said:

"Will this affect our plans in the Baltic, Mr. President? Do you think we should postpone the start of this operation in light of the new events?"

Putin, with his gaze fixed on the conference table, replied:

"No, Sergey, our plans continue, I don't know who or what is behind this." - Putin tapped his fingers for a few seconds - "we'll find out, however, we will take advantage of it, it is an unbeatable situation to proceed with our storm, which will soon fall mercilessly on Europe."

The Leopard 2 tanks were stuck on route 61 in northeast Poland, right where route 63 ended, at a roundabout, from there the dual lane became a narrow road with one lane in each direction, the commander of one of the tank platoons, an officer with the rank of lieutenant, got out of the tank leading the column, lit a cigarette and, walking slowly, approached another officer friend, who was reading a map on the hood of a transport truck.

"Hey, Hans. Couldn't you find a better route to bring us?" - he joked.

The officer, who was concentrated looking at the map, turned with a bad-tempered face, but smiled when he saw it was his friend.

"Hey, Klaus! Damn the hour they cancelled the expansion of these shitty roads! Our politicians seem to live in Narnia, they want to go to war and they have no fucking idea of the messes they make when they only look at the money when it comes to cutting expenses. How the hell are we supposed to defend Europe from the Ruskies if they don't invest in strategic defense issues? You know something? Ten kilometers ahead the soldiers aren't patrolling, they're herding some cows, and big ones at that. What the hell are we supposed to do? Milk cows?"

Klaus burst into laughter, looked around, then spoke in a low voice:

"Don't let our commander hear you, dear Hans, you could end up changing the oil of the logistics support trucks at our base in Bergen."

Hans raised a hand in protest. —Bah! No way, good thing he's not here, he would be throwing a damn curse a thousand times bigger than mine at everyone! For eight years now, hear me well, eight fucking years, he has been warning about this damn mess of the road expansions towards the Baltic countries. And what did we do? Lower the budget to allocate it to health and education of migrants. Can you understand it? We are not only miserly inept, but we are also naive sissies!

—Calm down, calm down, Hans, the damage is done, no way around it, speaking of more pressing matters. How far are we from the Lithuanian border?

The man looked at the map.

"Hmm, about a hundred and sixty kilometers, our assignment is further north, at a point called Podwojponie."

Klaus took one last puff and threw the cigarette on the pavement, stamping it out with his combat boot.

"How soon do you think we'll get there?"

His friend shrugged in a sign of helplessness.

"I have no fucking idea, they say we'll start moving in a couple of hours, but, at the rate we're going, the Russians are going to get here first. And surely we'll have to run so they don't kick our asses!

"So the Russians are involved in this?"

"Yes, Mr. President."

Mark Esper, the acting Secretary of Defense, directly answered the question of the President of the United States, Donald Trump; gesturally, as was his characteristic, Trump made one of his typical gestures of displeasure, with a look of boredom, he said:

"So, Mark. How should we respond? I am for bombing one of their bases, it would be a response proportional to the damage they caused us, don't you think?"

Esper glanced at General James Gilday, Chairman of the Joint Chiefs of Staff, the select group of high-level officials, high-ranking military officers and government advisors was in the White House crisis room, the latter made a slight gesture that meant no, the secretary then responded:

"Mr. President, given the current circumstances in the Baltic countries, and the movement of Russian troops in the area, we consider it prudent to wait before taking a retaliatory action."

Trump moved his arms in a sign of discomfort.

"Let's see, Mark. What's that about?"

"Mr. President, while we assess the appropriate response to the Russians 'movements, we can carry out a strong diplomatic response, this would also give us time to finish coordinating the transfer of our troops and those of NATO to the potential conflict point."

"Without an immediate response, Mark? Aren't we giving in to Russian aggression? Our people would not forgive us for staying still in the face of this."

General Gilday intervened:

"Mr. President, we could maneuver our fighter jets near their border, perhaps further north, in the Baltic Sea, to send the message of our displeasure, while we finish positioning our troops better in Poland."

Trump shook his head several times in disagreement.

"This doesn't convince me, gentlemen, Vladimir Putin mocks us in our faces and we're flying planes in the Baltic Sea?"

Esper added:

"In parallel, with our air activity in the Baltic, we could conduct a cyber attack on key military facilities for them and their infrastructure, for example, nuclear plants, ministries..."

Trump interrupted him:

"Mark, tell me something, CNN, even other outlets, do they broadcast news that it is not known if it happened? Do you think the Russians would let us know about such attacks? If they attacked me like that here, I wouldn't let the media publish it. — Trump clapped softly on the table—. No, gentlemen, the retaliation has to be proportional, public, and notorious, so that the media broadcasts it, so that the American people know and feel protected by their Government and armed forces, I do not admit delays in this matter. Do you have any targets to propose to me?"

Esper and General Gilday looked at each other again, the former nodded slightly with his head.

"We do not have them at this moment, Mr. President, but we can have them ready for your approval in an hour."

Trump pursed his lips and nodded his head up and down several times, showing obvious satisfaction.

"Very well, gentlemen, I'll wait for you in an hour, we need the Russians to understand that you do not mess with America... without facing consequences."

III

The videos analyzed on the highway and in the streets near Ramstein Air Base showed the face of the man driving the van, a couple of hours later he was identified, his name, Walther Sthop; immediately, his residence was located, a small apartment in a dilapidated building in Neustadt, on the outskirts of Leipzig The videos recovered from the cameras at the service entrance of the base showed the subject waiting for more than half an hour, a non-commissioned officer approached the driver's door, he got out and headed to the van's rear door, before opening it, he stopped and looked towards one of the pockets, then the screen went white; the perspective from another video camera showed the scale of the explosion, a close-up indicated the same movement of the driver before opening the rear door, everything exploded afterward. The raid on Sthop's apartment shed little light, a personal computer that was seized and was being analyzed, in a small notebook, kept inside the drawer of a bedside table, a short phrase was scribbled: «22-07-24 contact Otvazhnyy

1-20 Tannenstrasse...», this material had been sent to all European intelligence agencies and to the CIA in the United States; a small private room, which had a terrace overlooking the Thames, had been granted to Eastman, Dumont, and Cruz, that day the meeting room was occupied by their director; that hot afternoon they were analyzing the information received from Germany, Dumont was the first to speak:

"How did the van explode? Did the driver activate the bomb?"

Everyone watched the video on the monitor attached to the wall, Tomás Cruz commented:

"I don't think so, Bernard, rewind the footage. —Dumont rewound that part of the video, everyone watched again, Cruz pointed to the television—. Look, the subject stops before opening the rear door. Do you see how the man leans his head towards one of the pockets?"

"True, Tom" — added Eastman—. "The ring of a cellphone, perhaps?"

"Exactly!" —replied Cruz.

"Mmm..., I see what you mean, Tom." —Dumont spoke softly—, "those bastards activated the bomb remotely."

"That's right, Bernard, and I believe, from the surprised look on the individual's face, that the poor man did not know."

Eastman focused his gaze on his computer screen.

"The note found shows what seems to be a date, July 22nd, that was four days ago... Is what follows an address?"

"And the name of a contact" —added Dumont—. "Is it a Russian surname? I think so."

"It seems so, Bernard" —responded Cruz— "The address, where could it be?"

Dumont responded:

"Good question, I was researching on Google maps and there are several cities that have a street with that name, it's the same in my country, if you search, for example, Rue de l'université, at least five cities appear with that street name."

"Then we'll have to start eliminating" —said Cruz— "Another issue. Does it appear that he met with someone there?"

"It's a possibility, the other option is that he picked up the bomb there —expressed Eastman."

"Good point, Craig" — indicated Dumont. The sound of the arrival of a new message on the latter's computer was heard, the man read it carefully, then said to his companions— "They found in the subject's email two emails where the surname from the note is mentioned, in one of them he wrote that he will meet the contact from the so-called Otvazhnyy soon."

Cruz scratched his head a couple of times.

"What's the date of the email, Bernard?"

"It was sent on July 20th to a certain Richard Stage, they are also investigating him —indicated Dumont."

"So, the Russian friend has a contact who met with Sthop" — added Eastman—, "this would lead us to believe that the Russians are behind all this."

Cruz had a hunch, he was about to use Google search when the ringtone of Eastman's cell phone was heard, he answered, a message arrived at the same time on Dumont's computer, after listening for a few seconds, the former hung up; Dumont and he looked at each other.

"Damn it, gentlemen, what the hell is happening" —Cruz complained.

Eastman replied:

"The Russian Air Force transport base in Shchólkovo, which is very close to Moscow, was attacked, a few minutes later President Trump, through a tweet, communicated that he had ordered this attack in retaliation, allow me to quote the reason: for the cowardly and unjustified Russian aggression against the United States of America."

In the quiet city of Narva, in Estonia, with fifty-seven thousand inhabitants, nothing foreshadowed that soon the peace would be replaced by chaos. From the other side of the Narva River, which the city owes its name to, lies Russia; that summer afternoon, many residents from a building complex on Albert-August Timani Street were walking around peacefully, many children were playing soccer among the rows of parked cars, one of the balls lightly hit a sedan, one of the kids, acting as a goalkeeper, went for the ball, the little boy, while picking it up, noticed that there were wires of different colors visible at the back of the car, he was about to peek through the window when one of his teammates called him to continue the game, the boy returned running, throwing the ball to one of the defenders, the game continued; two minutes later a powerful explosion interrupted the peaceful and warm afternoon.

Gennadiy Borisov took a long drag from his cigarette, it was just after ten at night, Borisov was the commander of a platoon of self-propelled howitzers 2S35, the five tracked vehicles were camouflaged and in position, each one twenty meters apart; boredom had been taking over the artillery group, they had been in the area for just over seventy-two hours. Captain Borisov looked into the distance to the north, just over six hundred meters separated his group from the nearest platoon, the same was true to the south, his group was part of the 45th artillery brigade of the

Russian Army. The hurried pace of his communications officer shook him from his boredom.

"We have the green light to start the operation, sir," said the soldier with an altered voice.

Borisov, without looking at him, replied after taking another long drag:

"What time are we to start?"

"At zero three hundred hours, sir."

"Do we already have the targets assigned?"

"Yes, sir, an area covering about two kilometers in length, near a small town called Berezniki, the Poles have both infantry and artillery there."

"Distance to the target?"

"About twenty-two kilometers, sir, the plan is to saturate the area and then sweep every two kilometers from there to the border, which, as we know, is about five kilometers from where we are."

Borisov exhaled a slow puff of smoke, then threw the cigarette butt into the small water reservoir in front of him, looked at his subordinate, and walked back to one of the 2S35s.

"Very well, Sergey, let's prepare for the start of the dance."

The assigned saturation area included a key sector of the entrance of the Russian cavalry and infantry to the Suwalki Gap, the mission of the 45th brigade would consist in battering with their artillery a strip of twelve kilometers from the Belarusian border with Lithuania to a point called zero, to the south of the Augustowski Canal. The units of the 45th were located about five kilometers inside Belarusian territory; ten kilometers further back, there were five 2S7 Malka howitzer units with a firing range of forty kilometers, and ten kilometers from the 2S7, five platoons of the BM30 Smerch and five of the Tornado S, the most modern multiple rocket launcher of the Russian artillery, would subject to their firepower an entire sector of ten kilometers wide up to the Polish border with Kaliningrad. A real hell would begin on the border with Poland in less than five hours, after the intense fire punishment, a small softening by the air force would allow the arrival of airborne troops to secure the area, then the cavalry and infantry would enter, watching the rear. Lithuania would be dissuaded from defending this strip, half an hour after the start of the Russian artillery attack, three fronts of attack would open from Belarus, the main target, Vilnius, its capital. NATO troops and the Polish army would also receive an unpleasant surprise that dawn.

The column of armored transport vehicles crossed the narrow iron bridge, at the front of the caravan two of them carried huge flags of the Union of Soviet Socialist Republics, the last of the transport vehicles displayed the standard of the Soviet Army with the red star and the hammer and sickle in the center; Mi-24 helicopters escorted the Soviet withdrawal from Afghanistan. "That day was February 15, 1989, I remember it with emotion as if it were today," reflected Al-Zawahirí. The Soviet invasion of this country had started at the end of 1979. "Ten years of death, oppression, and persecution of all those who professed our faith," Al-Zawahirí took off his glasses to clean them, took out his handkerchief and did so, then put them back on. "Ten years... A million brothers killed and the faith of Islam offended, the Soviets before, and now the Russians, have used our peoples in the same way that the Americans used us at their time; both killing our brothers in Syria, they use us, they divide us to move us like chess pieces... The Russians take advantage of our people in Syria, there they have their puppet, and at the same time they kill us in

Chechnya, they play with us, they kill our women, youth, children, elderly if necessary... they pretend for us to be their disposable marionettes; the West, its arrogance, its enormous existential void, ruled by its only god, money, is the greatest threat for Islam, it is the monster to be defeated," Al-Zawahiri rubbed his beard for a moment, then shook his head in discomfort. "As our great teacher Sayyid Qutb said, the taghut, that abominable tyranny represented in communism or in that monstrosity they call democracy keeps its victims in ignorance, in paganism... All of them will pay for their audacity; the time has come, thanks to Allah, to take revenge, Russia will also pay for its crude materialism, they will be condemned for defying Allah," Al-Zawahiri's face lit up, a smile hinted at his lips, he made a bow to the ground then stated, "fortunately, my God, vengeance is near."

Half an hour after Gennadiy Borisov received the alert in the cold night of the beginning of hostilities, the Baltic countries began to suffer interruptions of internet services, mobile telephony, television, and electricity supply; gradually and intermittently, Tallinn, Riga, and Vilnius experienced the blocking of these services, gradually extending to the rest of the territories of the respective nations. An alert was issued after midnight, it was sent to the central command of NATO in Brussels and to the headquarters of the European Parliament, as well as to the presidents of the Council and the Commission of the EU. "Is this the beginning of the plan to take over the Baltic countries?" inquired a still sleepy President of the European Council. "It's quite likely, Charles, it's part of the exercises that the Russians have been carrying out for years, the risk of the beginning of the attack is imminent," replied the NATO Secretary General with an uneasy voice. A warning was also sent simultaneously to the headquarters of the Department of Defense in Washington, both the United States Armed Forces and its intelligence services were alerted, fifteen minutes after receiving the warning, a call was made to the White House; the night would be long and tense on both sides of the Atlantic.

IV

Narva was one of the cities in Estonia with a large population of Russian descent, particularly the area where the bomb exploded was one of those with the highest concentration of pro-Russian population. The cruel attack generated strong outrage among the population in the Baltic countries that had ties with the Motherland; the Russian government strongly condemned the attack, more than fifty dead and nearly a hundred injured was the toll of the explosion; in a press conference, the Russian Foreign Minister, Sergei Lavrov, indicated that all alternatives to protect the Russian-origin population in the Baltic countries would be analyzed; a keen BBC journalist then inquired about a possible military escalation in the Baltic; Lavrov firmly responded that no option would be discarded, which undoubtedly included, a preventive military action. Protests by the Russian minorities in the three Baltic countries started a few hours after the explosion of the device, in them they asked the Government of Vladimir Putin for protection, for them it was the beginning of a systematic extermination campaign. Social networks began to show brutal videos and photographs of the lifeless bodies of the elderly, youth, and children scattered in a parking lot; lootings, fires, and confrontations with the public force were experienced during the following days, a regrettable incident would end up aggravating the already tumultuous situation. In Riga, the Latvian capital, a massive demonstration ended with the death of three young people who were protesting against the Government, more than a dozen people suffered injuries that took them to the hospital, the outrage grew and the pleas for help addressed to the Government of Russia also increased.

"How many casualties are we talking about, Sergey?"

The Russian Defense Minister replied with a grave voice:

"Fifty-seven dead and more than a hundred injured, Mr. President, we still have ten people missing."

President Putin took a small sip from his bottle of water.

"This is regrettable, Sergey, totally unacceptable also. How could this happen? Weren't we prepared?"

The Defense Minister handed him a folder. "Mr. President, someone disabled our defense systems during those minutes we were in the dark, we were attacked by the Americans."

"Someone? Are we not sure that it was perpetrated by the Americans?"

The minister replied with a gesture of helplessness:

"No, Mr. President."

Putin blinked several times, he seemed not to understand.

"I don't understand, Sergey. Did the Americans take advantage of a cyberattack to bomb our base? How did they find out about it?"

"A reliable source informed us that seconds before our defense systems went dark, they received an anonymous alert that this was going to happen."

Without losing his composure, Putin indicated:

"This is inconceivable, Sergey. Did they hire hackers for this? Don't they have the capability to do it themselves?"

"We are working on that, sir, it's a possibility."

"No, I don't believe it, Sergey, I would dismiss it. I have the feeling that it's the same people who have been manipulating us, and them, of course, so we go to war." Putin moved one of his hands aside. "Anyway, we will talk with Viktor to clear up this doubt." The Russian president was referring to Viktor Kovaliov, the Director-General of the FSB, the Russian Federal Security Service. "Report on the damages at the base, Sergey?"

"At least ten transport planes destroyed, fifteen helicopters suffered the same fate, others were severely damaged and will require a maintenance process to recover, several hangars and lodging barracks destroyed."

Vladimir Putin gave a strong punch to the meeting table.

"We must retaliate, Sergey."

"We are contemplating several targets, sir. May I mention them to you?"

The Russian president rubbed his forehead several times, then looked at his Defense Minister.

"No, Sergey, let's be more subtle but relentless, in the military we already have enough to deal with the Baltic issue." Putin made a mischievous grimace. "Don't we have recent information on the love affairs of the Secretary of State? We can also use the corruption scandals in Defense contracts... and, of course, that case of the stripper with the president; there are no better news than those with sexual content and corruption..."

Five groups from the KSK, Kommando Spezialkräfte, special forces of the German Army, were deployed in the cities that were most likely to be the place mentioned in the note found in Walther Sthop's notebook; the third group, consisting of twelve men, approached the indicated address, 1-20 Tannenstrasse in Dresden; two blocks around it, a cordon guarded by the local police was created, nothing and no one entered or left. Four snipers watched from the terrace of a building that conveniently had an excellent perspective of the entrance and exit of the white house with several apartments; the lieutenant in charge of the group of soldiers divided the group into two, some would enter through the main door, others would take control of the exit and a long side garden, to prevent the escape of any possible occupants inside the apartment; in addition, two of them would descend from the roof of small gray tiles to enter through the window that seemed to lead to a living room. A soldier slid a cable with a small camera under the door, and on the screen of the small tablet, the officer saw some furniture in addition to a small table; there was no one there. Then, the lieutenant quietly asked a sergeant leading the second group, "Heinz, are you in position?" Through the lieutenant's headphones, confirmation was heard. Next, the officer asked about the soldiers who would descend from the roof, "Are both of you in position, Fred?" A "Yes, sir" was heard a few seconds later; the lieutenant gave a thumbs-up to everyone to indicate they were ready, then gave the order to enter. As the door was thin and somewhat frail, a burly soldier only had to kick it hard to knock it down. It swung wide open, and the men quickly entered the apartment, checking all the spaces, the two bathrooms, the two small bedrooms, and the living-dining room; the apartment was uninhabited. From one of the rooms, the lieutenant heard one of the soldiers call out. The officer headed there, where in one of the closets there was a computer. The lieutenant opened it; a white light blinked on the screen, he hesitated for a few seconds, however, he pressed the black button on the upper left of the device to turn it on. The men standing next to the officer were surprised, on the screen appeared the image of a person, who was wearing a black hood, wearing dark glasses to prevent his eyes from being seen. For a few seconds, the hooded figure watched the camera in silence, then a distorted voice could be heard, the man used a device for it, "Congratulations, you are very skilled, you have found the computer, under normal circumstances I should acknowledge that this could have valuable information to determine my identity, indeed it had," the hooded figure tilted his head then looked back at the camera, a slight laugh was heard, "I must congratulate you, you've reached your highest moment of fame, right now my image, and yours, thanks to your curiosity, is viral on social media, Facebook, Twitter," the person made a brief pause, "Well, as I was saying, the evidence was on this computer, fingerprints, emails, photos... It's a shame, for you I mean, but in an act of selfishness, I confess, I am very bad, I deleted everything," the individual stopped talking for a few seconds, looked at his watch, then showed it to the camera, "It's incredible how time flies, gentlemen, I must say goodbye to you, oh, by the way, that time, as always, scarce and volatile... is also running out for you. In the name of a free East Germany, I bid you farewell, dear gentlemen." The screen suddenly turned black, the officer looked at his soldiers, he just managed to say, "Shit, how stupid I was! This is a damned trap! Let's get out of...!"

Millions of people watched live on social media as the hooded figure addressed the group of German special forces men, in the images, they could be seen running away from the camera; while this occurred, the video stopped, then, reappeared with the hooded individual seated in front of a table with a red tablecloth, in the background a huge black banner with the initials NSED in red. He called for the vindication of the German Democratic Republic, the resurgence of Russian power, and the right of the people of East Germany to live under its aegis. The individual indicated, raising his hand, that more acts of revenge were to come. Although Twitter deleted the video, the damage was already done, a feeling of unease and fear spread throughout Europe; amongst the German population, it went from fear to indignation, isolated protests in Berlin, Bonn, Cologne, and Stuttgart, among other cities, were held to protest what they called the cowardly Russian aggression; interestingly, in cities of the former GDR, marches also took place, but demanding the return to communism and the separation from what they called the "inhumane capitalist exploitation of West Germany"; CNN showed a huge banner in a protest held in Magdeburg, it read, "Better a physical wall than the invisible barriers of exploitation, discrimination, and inequality between first and second-class Germans"; the protests in the following days, far from diminishing, were worryingly increasing, an urgent meeting of the European Parliament was called in Brussels to study this and other critical situations that the continent was experiencing.

V

Tomás Cruz preferred that tense morning to be alone, he decided to take advantage of the bright sun and pleasant temperature to sit under a parasol on one of the small terraces of the MI6 building, he needed tranquility to review a matter that had been on his mind since the day before. He watched the video of the hooded figure for the fifth time, feeling that something had caught his attention from the first moment he saw it, but he still couldn't determine what it was, he lowered the volume to better concentrate on the images, the subject tilted his head towards the wrist where he had the watch, then showed it to the camera, the special forces team members ran towards the door and the screen went dark... Cruz closed his eyes and replayed the video in his mind, then opened his eyes wide to state out loud, "Damn, I've got it! It's about his hand!" Cruz hurried to rewind the video to that part, with the wireless mouse he moved the cursor to the pause symbol, after clicking it, the image froze, that was it, what had caught his attention was that the hooded man had a tattoo on the hand where he wore the watch; right on the outer edge of the back, above the thumb, one could see a scimitar descending to the start of the middle finger; Cruz furrowed his brow, why had the tattoo caught his attention? Something told him he had seen it before, but where? Countless images appeared in his memory, nothing seemed to relate to what he was looking for, he got up from the table and walked to the edge of the terrace, from there he watched the Thames, a boat sailed slowly, on board were tourists taking a river cruise, an alert immediately went off in his mind, Tourists... "Of course, that was it!" he affirmed out loud again, he knew at that moment what it was about, then his memory took him to Damascus, he rewound in his mind the elevator scene at the hotel, the woman was entering it, the doors were about to close, the man inside prevented it by pressing the button with his left hand and there, the scimitar appeared. "Good God! It's the same person!" Cruz looked up, rubbed his head several times, then another memory emerged suddenly in his mind, as if it were a lightning bolt, it lit up; at that moment Cruz, instinctively, ran towards his computer, a word had also been echoing in his head since yesterday. What was it? For a few seconds, he closed his eyes again, shortly after, it emerged from the darkness of his memories, "Otvazhnyy", but why did that word catch his attention? Cruz rubbed his forehead several times again, helplessly, he thought: "what the hell! Let's search it on Google." He typed the words on the keyboard, the search results appeared, the first said it was a Soviet destroyer from the 60s, "no, this isn't what I'm looking for," he stated, then he looked at the second possibility, it posed the question, "What does Otvazhnyy mean in Russian?", Cruz pressed the enter key, the result in English appeared... Brave, his brain immediately translated the word to Spanish, it meant 'Valiente'. Tomás Cruz closed the computer violently, walked briskly to the door, and ran into the building.

The mayor of Palm Beach, with a face full of concern, announced in the press conference that all the municipality's computing systems, as well as the one controlling the county's traffic lights, had been victims of a cyber attack. "All our citizen support systems, as well as emergency lines, transit system, and collection in public services, such as power, water, and taxes, have collapsed —Mike Coniglio took a brief pause to drink from a Coca Cola bottle—. Other counties have suffered these attacks, among them West Palm Beach, Boca Raton, Pompano Beach, and Fort Lauderdale, also the electronic toll systems on the Turnpike have stopped working, we are working with our people and the FBI to investigate who is responsible and return to normality as soon as possible. In that sense, I ask for patience from all our citizens."

Then came the time for questions from the media, a journalist from the Miami Herald inquired, "Mayor, is it true that Mar-a-Lago was also hacked?" The mayor responded affirmatively, stating that they were evaluating the extent of the damages with the club's administration; a reporter from a local TV news program raised her hand, "Were other Trump group facilities attacked?" The mayor nodded and indicated that authorities in the locations where the attacks had occurred were also assessing the scale of the attacks; finally, a journalist from The Palm Beach Post posed the question the mayor did not want to answer, "Mayor, what information is there regarding the photos of the stripper with the President of the United States?" Coniglio couldn't help showing a look of disapproval before giving his response, "Tom..., I'm not going to refer to that deplorable matter, it is simply fake news, a dirty smear campaign against our president," the mayor left the room with visible annoyance after answering the question. Similar attacks were carried out on the Hoover, Shasta, Seminoe, and Calderwood dams, affecting the electricity supply in Arizona, California, Wyoming, and Tennessee and other states; two nuclear power plants, with their two reactors, Braidwood 1 and 2 in Illinois, and Calvert Cliffs 1 and 2 in Maryland, were also affected, the blackout lasted several hours, and in some areas, the electricity had not yet been restored. The culprits? The director of the FBI stated that they were investigating, however, everything pointed to a Russian retaliation for the attack on their airbase outside of Moscow.

CNN broadcasted live images of the Russian invasion of the Suwalki Strip, in the darkness of the night, the self-propelled howitzers 2S35 spat fire incessantly, then were seen flames that briefly lit up the darkness as they were rapidly launched at different angles from the multiple rocket launchers BM30 Smerch and Saturno S. Between three and six in the morning, the punishment of the Russian artillery on the strip was ruthless, this accompanied by strategic movements of the air force to the south on the border between Belarus and Poland, a series of preemptive strikes were carried out on air bases, military facilities, bridges, and roads that connected central Poland with the east of the country, then the 4th Guard Tank Division and the 3rd Motor Rifle Division menacingly approached the Polish border, in this way the Russian attack forces forced the Polish defense forces to reserve troops and equipment to defend themselves from a potential invasion; the NATO immediate response force, composed of about eight thousand men, entered to cover the flank opened by the Russians to the north of Poland, supported by a division of

Leopard 2 tanks and Gazelle and Apache attack helicopters. A reporter sent specially to the border between Poland and Lithuania, who was on the Lithuanian side, outside a small village called Seirijai, about twenty kilometers from it, described the movements of the Russians and NATO in the combat area, the images showed convoys of troops moving along a narrow road towards the border with Poland. Cruz entered the room where Eastman and Dumont were, both observed worried the information that the reporter shared with the audience, they were so focused that they did not notice the presence of their friend, Cruz cleared his throat to get their attention, both, still absorbed in the news, glanced at him and continued watching CNN; Cruz expressed loudly:

"Gentlemen, excuse me for interrupting your news program, but it's important that I mention this, Valiente is the man in the video."

Both continued like automatons watching the reporter, a few seconds later, Dumont slowly turned his head towards Cruz.

"What the hell are you talking about, Tom?"

"Just as you heard, it's the same man from the elevator in the Damascus hotel, it's Valiente."

This time, it was Eastman who looked at Cruz.

"Tom. How the hell did you come to that conclusion? That video was of no significance, you yourself dismissed it."

Cruz opened his laptop screen and explained the reasons, those he had discovered minutes earlier on the terrace, when he finished the explanation, Eastman commented:

"So the man was in Damascus, this only raises more questions. Did he deliver something to the Iranian scientist? She is part of Iran's nuclear program; then he appears in Dresden (Germany), planning an attack on an American airbase. What role does Valiente play in all this?"

Cruz pointed his hand at Eastman. —Don't forget about Koslov... What the hell did he go to Damascus for? Did he give something to the woman in the pool? Or was the woman the contact for the delivery to our cherished Valiente?

"Calm down..., we don't know if he indeed gave something to the woman, unlike al-Hamzi, who definitely hands over something."

Dumont indicated:

"And on top of that, we have al-Hamzi!"

Cruz complained, then Craig Eastman inquired in a thoughtful tone:

"What a mess, things are not so clear for us, we have many characters in this novel, now, the underlying question, gentlemen, is: are the Russians involved in this?"

Without hesitation, Dumont immediately answered:

"But of course they are! Aren't you seeing it on the television, gentlemen? What a mess they are creating in the Baltic countries."

Cruz nervously scratched his chin for a moment.

"You know, Bernard? Craig is right. To what extent could the Russians be involved in this matter?"

Dumont answered:

"In my opinion, Koslov met with the three in Damascus, or used them to triangulate the information. What is it about? It's not clear, but it definitely has to do with the Iranian nuclear program and what is happening today in the Baltic."

Eastman, sitting, with crossed arms and legs stretched one over the other, made a face of doubt.

"Or... that's what they want us to believe."

"Who? Koslov, the Iranian, al-Hamzi or Valiente?" —Dumont sarcastically remarked—. "Come on, gentlemen, they are all in the same party."

Cruz stood up from the chair, after stretching and yawning, he said:

"You know, Bernard? Craig's theory isn't so far-fetched, speaking in theatrical terms, I think that Valiente is not part of the first scene."

Dumont narrowed his eyes, leaned back in the chair, then in a low voice said:

"Then what scene does he belong to? Wasn't he in Damascus? At the same time with the others?"

"It's a good point, Bernard, however, I agree with you, Tom, it's very likely we are dealing with two separate cases... The thing is that we can't prove it" —Craig Eastman indicated.

"And how the hell do we prove it? Europe is about to explode and we need answers, our bosses are already asking for them, and we know their lack of patience. —Dumont asked, widening his eyes."

Cruz drummed on the table.

"I think we would have to prioritize the door that was opened to us with the mysterious Valiente in the Germany attack."

"Tom, they'll kill us if we propose to set aside the issue with the Iranian woman and al-Hamzi."

Eastman glanced at Cruz for a moment, then asked:

"What do you propose, Tom?"

Cruz touched the back of his neck, wincing in pain, his muscles there were too tense.

"Let's work on the two scenarios in parallel, after all, we still don't know for sure if we are talking about different cases, but let's handle this with two teams, since Craig is the military expert, he, and one of us, should focus on Valiente and Koslov, the other would work on the issue with the woman and al-Hamzi."

"Two teams? We are the three musketeers, remember?" — joked Dumont.

Eastman smiled slightly.

"I think what Tom is saying is that we have to bring someone else in."

"In that case, Craig, we should think of someone from MI6" — added Dumont.

Eastman responded by nodding twice with his head, then affirmed:

"No problem. How do we split up?"

"Gentlemen, for that, there's nothing better than the coin flip, heads or tails" —Dumont indicated.

Luck decided that Eastman and Cruz would form the group to analyze the case of Valiente and Koslov; Dumont and his not yet selected group partner would take care of the woman and al-Hamzi. Eastman turned on the television again, on the screen, a destroyed Leopard 2 could be seen, the news apparently was not good, the CNN anchor was reporting significant losses in NATO's defense forces. The phone in the room rang, Craig Eastman answered, certainly by his face, the news was not encouraging.

VI

The Boeing BBJ3 of the Secretary of Defense of the United States was flying at an altitude of twelve thousand meters, its destination, Brussels, the reason, an urgent meeting of the North Atlantic Council; although his country was leaving this organization, he was invited, the situation warranted a joint review of the challenge that the Russian attack had imposed, looking through the window at the sunset colors, Mark Esper spoke on the secure line to his British colleague:

"Nick, a pleasure to greet you, before we see each other in Brussels I wanted to mention something that worries us, our satellites have also detected a strong increase in the activity of the Northern and Baltic Fleets."

The acting Secretary of Defense of the United States was referring to Nick Fallon, the Secretary of Defense of the United Kingdom, a brief silence took over the phone line.

"Are we in secure mode, Mark?"

"Yes, don't worry, there's nothing to worry about —replied the American Secretary of Defense. "Do you think their movements indicate they are after something more than the Baltic countries?"

"We are not sure yet, it could be a distraction maneuver, the truth is that from Kaliningrad they are launching strong artillery attacks on the Suwalki strip."

"Don't even say it, they are also intensely harassing a thirty-kilometer strip between the border with Lithuania and a point called Kumiecie Male, we assume it's the prelude to a ground invasion to the south."

"The movements of their naval fleet worry us, and a lot, Nick, you must already know, less than two hours ago, they attacked the NATO radar station in Bornholm, nothing good can follow that."

"I agree with you, Mark, the satellite images they shared with us also concern us, they are moving a large part of their submarine fleet from their base in Zapadnaya Litsa, to add to that, the aircraft carrier Kuznetsov, the nuclear cruiser Peter the Great, several of their destroyers and frigates have already set sail from Severomorsk."

"Mmm..., they are moving everything they have. Why on earth? Another issue that concerns us is related to the satellite photographs they shared with us, it concerns seven warships leaving Polyarny. Why?"

"It is very concerning, if you noticed, there is an aircraft carrier, and it's not the Kuznetsov, it appears they have already launched the first of their new aircraft carriers as part of the 23000e Shtorm project, it has a displacement of a hundred thousand tons and would carry ninety birds on board." —A long exclamation was heard on the other side of the line—. "The other three, we still do not know exactly what they are about, Nick, we believe they are the new destroyers of the Leader class, which, according to the preliminary information we have, have a displacement of twenty thousand tons, plus a cutting-edge combat team not to be underestimated, the rest of the ships, we suspect, are new helicopter carriers of a project they have called 'Avalanche'."

"Does the aircraft carrier and the helicopter carriers carry equipment on board?" —Inquired an intrigued Nick Fallon.

"Yes, according to our analysts, they are fully equipped and armed to the teeth, apparently they want to test them in this mess; in short, whether it's a distraction maneuver or not, things do not look good, I just wanted to warn you before our meeting, it's a topic we will have to figure out how to deal with." —A brief silence was heard on the line—. "I'll see you in Brussels!"

The individual, dressed in a dark blue jacket and jeans, was drinking coffee and eating a sandwich in a small restaurant in the city of Brno, in the southeast of the Czech Republic; the couple at the table next to him, apparently lovers, who had sat down there minutes earlier, argued for some reason, the individual tried to concentrate on his own business, to avoid trouble, the argument gradually escalated, diners from other tables began to watch concerned the heated conversation of the couple, seconds later the furious woman threw the contents of the cup she was drinking at her companion at the table, the liquid primarily hit the man's face, he screamed in pain, apparently the drink was very hot, without thinking, he got up and slapped the woman hard, she fell to the floor from such force, the man then delivered a violent kick, a howl came from the girl's mouth; the subject, out of control, was about to punch her when the individual from the table next to him pulled him by the shirt and hit him in the face, right in the nose, he fell to the floor, like a bag of potatoes, blood began to flow profusely from the place of the blow, soon dyeing his face and the floor red. The stranger extended his hand to the girl to lift her, after helping her to sit down and amid the applause of some of those present, he smiled walked to the cashier and paid in cash for both tables, walked to the narrow door of the place and disappeared.

The owner of the place immediately called the local police, who arrived minutes later, the boyfriend was still asleep from the blow when the officers arrived, who threw cold water on him to wake him up, one of the officers asked the young woman if she wanted to file a complaint for the blows received, she indignantly nodded her head, the officer looked at his colleague, who proceeded to handcuff the attacker, for now, he had to be taken to the station, so that both could give their respective statements. A curiosity arose in this, both the young woman and the owner of the restaurant mentioned in their testimonies that the anonymous hero who defended the offended girlfriend had a tattoo on his left hand.

Bernard Dumont's face didn't need to say anything; a broad smile accompanied him as he entered, along with the beautiful woman, into the meeting room where Eastman and Cruz were, who looked at each other intrigued; the woman wore an elegant and tight-fitting dark grey suit, her long blonde hair was tied up into a large bun at the top of her head. Cruz tried to decipher the color of her large, well-defined eyes, which seemed to have an exotic mix between blue and green; the suit she was wearing reached just above her knees, showing well-shaped legs that Craig Eastman couldn't help but look at. She was definitely tall, with the elegant high-heeled shoes she was wearing, she reached the height of Dumont, who was around one meter eighty-two centimeters tall, the thin heels matched the color of her dress. Exultant, Dumont introduced his beautiful companion:

"Tom, Craig, it's a pleasure to introduce you to Rosamund Frost, she has been assigned by MI6 to accompany us in the search for al-Hamzi and to resolve the matter of the Iranian woman."

Both, with a cordial smile, extended their hands to greet her, Cruz could feel the softness of the woman's long, delicate hand, the sweet voice of Rosamund Frost was heard returning the greeting; Dumont winked his right eye without her noticing, then expressed:

"My friends, could we provide Miss Frost with some background on our affairs?"

They both nodded, the presentation of the details began, after about forty minutes of conversation regarding the details of the two cases that occupied them, the woman asked:

"What makes you think that this guy, al-Hamzi, and the Iranian woman, aren't related to Valiente and the Russians?"

Eastman and Dumont looked at Tomas Cruz, after all, he was the one who had proposed that theory. Dumont commented:

"I believe Tom is the best person to answer your question."

Cruz looked at his friends with a slight gesture of reproach, then he began his explanation:

"I see," he paused, looked at his friends sarcastically, "Sorry. We understand that it does not make sense that on one hand, work is being done on the Iranian nuclear project, in which the Russians are very likely involved. Meanwhile, this matter of the bombings in recent weeks has, apart from other motivations, different timings."

The woman made a gesture of doubt.

"Sorry, Tomas, I understand the different motivation, according to you, someone else, Valiente, who would not be connected with the Russians, is behind the bombings, but I don't understand the timings. Why are they different?"

"The Iranian matter is medium or long-term, it is unlikely, if not impossible, that Iran has a nuclear weapon, even if low power; in contrast, the bombings aim to generate, or rather, they already started, a conflict between the Russians and Europe; that's why, in my opinion, we are talking about two cases."

The woman leaned towards Cruz.

"And what if that is precisely what the Russians want? To make us believe that these are separate cases and they want to place a nuclear device on our territory to make us believe it's the Iranians?"

Dumont intervened in the conversation:

"That's precisely our task, to make sure they are not, or in fact, are related."

Craig Eastman added with a worried face:

"Time is running and we have less and less of it, my friends, we need to urgently determine what we are facing."

VII

The huge circular table with the four-pointed star on a yellow and partially blue background, symbolizing the former strength and unity of NATO, was already fully occupied by the Defense and Foreign Ministers of its member countries. The Secretary-General, George Carington, who was chairing the meeting, formally began the extraordinary meeting of the North Atlantic Council; General Klaus Steinhoff, president of the Military Committee of the organization, and all members of this committee were also present. After a short introduction, Carington gave the floor to General Steinhoff, before doing so, he commented:

"General, please, we need to understand the magnitude of the challenge posed by the Russians, for this it is essential that you be completely clear about what is happening now in the Suwalki Gap, we want your description of the good, the bad, and the ugly; similarly, we want to receive from the Military Committee all the alternatives, also good or less good, to respond in the best way to the Russian aggression." The Foreign Affairs and Defense representatives of the Baltic countries and Poland raised their hand, Carington looked at General Steinhoff signaling to ask for a few minutes for them to intervene, the general nodded, the Secretary-General gave the floor to the Lithuanian Defense Minister, Valdas Karbauskis, who, with an annoyed expression, stated:

"We are concerned, Mr. Secretary, and in this I believe I also represent the feelings of my colleagues from Latvia and Estonia, by the words you mentioned regarding evaluating also the less favorable options. We ask this Council and the Military Committee for an explanation regarding this matter. We have practically on our noses soldiers, tanks, and Russian planes."

A slight murmur arose in the room, Carington raised his hand, to ask everyone for silence, then with a loud and clear voice indicated:

"Gentlemen, calm down, calm down, I understand the concern of both you and your colleagues from Latvia and Estonia." —The voice of the Polish Defense Minister, Andrzej Macierewicz, interrupted the Secretary-General— "My apologies for the interruption, Mr. Secretary, Poland also needs to know what the level of NATO's involvement in the defense of our sovereignty will be, today the entire eastern border of our country is under Russian attack."

Carington took a deep breath, then replied calmly:

"We understand the problem, Andrzej, we are currently supporting with the resources available in the theater of operations and, without a doubt, we maintain a strong commitment to the Baltic countries and Poland. This has been a cowardly attack on all NATO member countries and will be responded to accordingly; however, I think it is important for the members of the Committee to present their assessment and alternatives to define the best possible response strategy." —He directed his gaze at General Steinhoff— "Now, General, please, proceed with the Committee's conclusions."

Steinhoff first developed the presentation on the current state of the Russian combat and invasion zones, things were not going well; the map, on the huge digital screen, showed the extent of the attack, the Russian onslaught compromised ten tank divisions of which four were already pressing from the south through the Suwalki corridor, from Kaliningrad strong attacks by Russian artillery and aviation were pressing south through this corridor;

likewise, two armored infantry divisions were trying to penetrate south at the Lithuanian border, amphibious assault troops were dangerously approaching the Latvian border, Steinhoff indicated that their clear objective was to take Riga, its capital. Further north, near the Estonian border, four tank divisions were heading at full speed to penetrate from Russia into their territory, the attacks by aviation and artillery were intense; the same situation was occurring at the Lithuanian border, four divisions were seeking entry from two points into their territory. The situation on the border between Poland and Belarus was equally complex, airfields, roads, and bridges in the eastern region of Polish territory had been mercilessly bombed by Russian artillery and aviation, four tank divisions and at least three armored infantry divisions were positioned just three kilometers from their border. The situation in the Baltic Sea also presented huge challenges, at least fifteen Russian warships were making their presence felt in strategic naval corridors, some of them were already harassing positions on the Latvian coast as well as NATO radar stations, their intention was clear, to block the entry to the Baltic to any warship of the organization. Steinhoff concluded his presentation and paused, Carington interrupted him to inquire about a topic that worried everyone in the meeting.

"General, you and I have previously discussed this, but it's important for the Council to know. What has been our response? Where are our men located? Have we suffered casualties?"

Steinhoff displayed on the screen the movements of NATO forces, also of the Polish army troops.

"Let's go by parts. Regarding the Suwalki corridor, the Russians managed to break our defense lines, they entered from the southeast on both sides of the border between Poland and Lithuania, they have already advanced about eleven kilometers from the Belarusian border, we have managed to stop their advance at an undetermined point we have called defense point number 1, defending this point has cost us a lot, we have lost men and equipment there, we have also evacuated more than a hundred wounded soldiers."

"How many casualties are we talking about?" —interrupted Carington "Just over a hundred men, mainly infantry, although some tank operators and artillery positions have also lost their lives, have destroyed nine tanks and some transport vehicles; undoubtedly with these movements they seek to gain control of a space between Kalvarija in Lithuania and the start of the corridor in the south, some forty kilometers from there. This area is perfect as a resupply and rest point for their troops."

"And in the north from Kaliningrad? How have we resisted the attack?" asked the British Defense Secretary.

"First, I must also report that in Lithuanian territory from the south the Russians have made greater progress, having penetrated almost twenty-five kilometers. Our troops there are resisting in an area less than two kilometers away from a place called 'Estankunai'. Regarding our front in the north, we have stopped the advance less than ten kilometers from the border, where they also entered through the Polish border, coming straight through route 651 and are a little more than three kilometers from a point called Potopy." The general pointed with a laser pointer on the map. "The Russians made another point of penetration, through Lithuanian territory, one kilometer north of Vištytis Lake." The red dot of the pointer indicated the area of the attack, "they have covered a good distance through route 200; we have been able to prevent the advance from continuing more than fifteen kilometers from the border, in Gražiškiai, it's clear they also intend to close the encirclement in Kalvarija."

"Casualties?" asked Nick Fallon again.

The general Steihoff replied:

"About two hundred men, plus several artillery positions, ten tanks, and armored troop transport."

The NATO Secretary-General asked about the situation on the Polish eastern border, Steinhoff replied:

"Bridges and roads have been bombed, as well as bases and positions of NATO and Polish forces, the Russians try to cut us off from the Belarusian border and Suwalki. So far, we have resisted better there, although so far the attacks have been more about softening our positions, they have not yet penetrated this border, although they have already moved two tank divisions to less than three kilometers from this, and the artillery continues to saturate it with intense bombardments." Steinhoff paused, "fortunately, we have had few casualties, less than ten men."

The French Defense Minister raised his hand to say:

"An important question, general. Do you believe the Russians intend to invade Poland?"

"Not for now, Mr. Minister," the Chairman of the NATO Military Committee immediately responded.

The Frenchman looked at him in surprise.

"I don't understand, General. Why do you say for now?"

"It is clear to us so far, I insist, that the Russians seek to isolate the Baltic countries, we do not see as their priority to also invade Poland, we consider they would reconsider if they see their position in the Suwalki corridor at risk, in that case, they could start an invasion of the Poles to force us to defend them and relieve the pressure on the corridor."

"In conclusion. How are we?" inquired Nick Fallon.

"The Suwalki corridor is in serious danger of being lost, we are fifty kilometers from it."

"That is not good news, General," exclaimed the Polish Defense Minister.

"Certainly not, we knew the Russians would employ all human and military resources to achieve it."

"What alternatives do we have?" posed Carington.

Steinhoff outlined the possible responses that were already being carried out. After just over half an hour, he finished; the atmosphere did not show much optimism among those present at the meeting. The French Defense Minister, Gerard Debré, directed his gaze at the Secretary-General.

"George, what about Ukraine? Is it possible that the Russians take advantage of the situation to invade?"

Carington, glancing sideways at Steinhoff, replied:

"Certainly a possibility, Hervé."

Steinhoff added:

"We have not observed movements there yet, which is also not reassuring. They have placed everything they need for the invasion there and in Crimea; it's just a matter of receiving the order for it to begin."

With concern, Longuet expressed:

Shtorm

"Gentlemen, if our forces do not neutralize this Russian attack, we would face a scenario where we lose our Baltic allies and surely an additional headache in Ukraine and... who knows what other headaches, that's a luxury we cannot afford."

VIII

The aircraft carrier Admiral Kuznetsov arrived imposingly at the assigned position, located between the Faroe Islands and the Shetland, about three hundred and fifty kilometers north of the latter. The Kuznetsov was escorted by several warships, including three destroyers, several frigates, and Oscar II class submarines, as well as a couple of Akulas and three Borei class submarines armed with cruise missiles. The mission of the group of warships was to ensure control of the entrance and exit of the Baltic Sea; declared obsolete several times, the Kuznetsov resisted being taken out of service, undergoing a deep modernization between 2018 and 2021, this aircraft carrier had become a powerful air deterrence factor, the modifications had turned it into an impregnable combat platform, in addition to retaining all its air offensive power, it also carried the fearsome Kalibr, anti-ship missiles with a range of more than two thousand five hundred kilometers; above, at thirty-seven thousand kilometers in height, a reconnaissance satellite of the United

States National Reconnaissance Office (NRO), sent a series of photographs of the combat group, soon these would be distributed among the various government agencies interested in this information.

Rosamund Frost had joined MI6 five years ago, spending the last two in the counterterrorism department, specifically she was part of a group of agents focused on investigating the reactivation of IRA (Irish Republican Army) terrorist cells, which had gained strength since the consolidation of Brexit in 2020; her work was widely valued by her superiors, who from the beginning understood that her elegance and beauty were directly proportional to the keen intelligence that accompanied her, Frost additionally had an innate ability to break down a seemingly unsolvable problem into different parts and solve each of them until reaching the answer or answers that allowed a good conclusion; a tireless and obsessive worker, she did not rest until the case occupying her was resolved. The woman slept little the previous night, devouring all the available information on the Valiente case and the Iranian nuclear program, upon entering the MI6 building in Vauxhall Cross that rainy morning, the woman had a better understanding of both cases. None of the three men in the room could avoid looking at her as she entered the meeting room, the woman wore her blonde hair again gathered in a black bun, a short suit and pants also of the same color, as well as the belt, and a fine white shirt that contrasted in a magnificent way. Cruz, who among his many obsessions had one for footwear, glanced at the elegant high-heeled shoes the woman was wearing that morning, "what this girl is wearing today is as expensive and elegant as what she wore yesterday... Does she have a husband with money?", he wondered; his conscience punished him seconds later with a thought that invited him to stop having so many sexist thoughts; the woman greeted everyone with a wide smile, then in her direct style, she said:

"Gentlemen, I have worked most of the night on the material you provided, the approach you have given to this pair of issues is correct, but the approach to their solutions is totally wrong."

With some incredulity, they looked at her. Bernard Dumont replied:

"Good morning, Rosamund," he said ironically. "In what have we succeeded and in what are we mistaken?"

The woman wrote on the electronic board.

"Let's go in parts, yes, we are indeed talking about two problems." Frost wrote the word Valiente and circled it, then, on the other end, she wrote the name al-Hamzi; however, two more variables need to be added to the problem. The woman scribbled at the bottom the word Russia, then did the same on the opposite side, when she finished writing, everyone could read the word Al Qaeda.

"And Koslov? And the Iranian? Where do you place them?" Dumont asked.

The woman's deep green eyes briefly looked at the Frenchman, she wrote again on the board.

"Koslov, for obvious reasons, goes with the Russian issue, the Iranian, in my opinion, should go with Al Qaeda."

Cruz, with a tone of skepticism, commented:

"However, the woman exchanged something, we don't know what, with Koslov."

Frost connected with a line the words Valiente and Russia.

"True, however, what I'm suggesting is that, for the purposes of our work, everything that has to do with Germany must now be related to the Russians, whether directly or indirectly."

"And Al Qaeda? It's clear Valiente works for them," Dumont questioned.

The woman drew another line, now connecting al-Hamzi with Al Qaeda. "I like your proposal, Rosamund," Tomás Cruz confirmed with interest, "it is the application of the Cartesian method to our case; we start with a couple of hypotheses, from which we go, through the scientific method, discarding options or adding alternatives. I agree."

"I feel the same," added Eastman, nodding his head up and down several times.

"In that case, I have no choice but to surrender to your method, dear Rosamund," joked Dumont, making a slight bow; "although I must insist. What about Al Qaeda?"

Craig Eastman took over:

"Bernard, what Rosamund proposes is simple, divide the problem without excluding any possibility. It is likely that Al Qaeda is related to both cases, however, with the framework she presents to us, each team that was formed can focus more on the case corresponding to them. Along the way, we will modify what needs to be changed."

Dumont stood up from his seat.

"No more to be said, let's go after them then."

Eastman, looking at Tomás Cruz, showed a grimace of uncertainty.

"And how do we locate Valiente?"

Frost and Cruz, almost at the same time, answered:

"Sooner or later the prey..." Cruz smiled, giving the woman the chance to finish the phrase. Frost outlined a smile at the corners of her lips, then affirmed:

"...Makes a mistake, from there the opportunity is ours."

The Su-57 stabilized its flight altitude, the stealth-capable combat aircraft was conducting a breathtaking low-altitude flight over the rugged surface, already near the border between Belarus and Poland; its commander, Lieutenant Colonel Pyotr Upenskoy, located the targets on the radar system. Seconds later, he released a couple of Kh-59 Ovod-MK2 missiles, which smoothly detached from the plane to reach their targets. Minutes later, the Kh-59s hit their targets, anti-aircraft artillery batteries of the United States Army assigned to defend NATO positions near the Suwalki Gap.

That afternoon, defense points of the Americans were hit, at least fifteen of their soldiers died in the attacks, in addition to about fifty wounded; a proportional retaliation measure against the Russians was taken in the coming hours by the Americans, close to fifteen missiles were launched from three B-52H bombers assigned to airbases in the United Kingdom, three of them hit the designated targets, one caused minor damage on the Russian aircraft carrier Kuznetsov, the other two caused the destruction of a radar station and an anti-aircraft defense system in the Russian enclave of Kaliningrad, as well as the loss of twenty of their operators and more than forty injured.

"Mr. President, our satellites have located the North American aircraft carrier."

Vladimir Putin looked at the image, it was the USS Eisenhower, sailing accompanied by its escort fleet in the Mediterranean Sea, one hundred thirty kilometers southwest of the island of Crete.

"Good, Sergei, order it to be attacked."

"It will be done, Mr. President." Sergei, the Russian Defense Minister, nodded with a martial gesture.

Putin glared powerfully at General Sergei Serdiukov.

"Sergei, the order is clear, let the damages to the American aircraft carrier be minor, for now, they are only measures of retaliation."

IX

Sergeant Ales Zeman, a non-commissioned officer of the Police of the Czech Republic, checked the email he had just received from his superior, the district commander of Stred, in the city of Brno. An alert had arrived half an hour earlier; that day, Interpol had issued to its member countries in Europe an orange circular that alerted of a potential threat. It was related to the individual who had ordered and orchestrated the terrorist attack on the American air base in Ramstein, he was probably fleeing towards southeastern Europe, Turkey, or Greece. Zeman continued reading the contents of the circular, a photograph of the subject was not yet available, however, he had a tattoo that could help locate him, it was a scimitar, a type of curved saber, used in the East and by Muslims. Zeman immediately remembered the incident in the restaurant a few blocks from the station and began searching for the file, after finding it he read it carefully, two witnesses in the report made reference to an individual who had a curved sword, as both referred to it, Zeman looked for the date of the occurrence of the fact, it had occurred just under forty-eight hours before. "Could it be the same subject?" he wondered. He decided that in any case, it was worth reporting it; the man stood up and walked, with determined steps, towards the office of the district station commander of Stred.

The seven Tu-22M flew level at forty-three thousand feet over the Russian city of Krasnodar, the mission commander observed on the screen the distance to the target, just over one thousand eight hundred kilometers. "It's time," he communicated to his companions, the respective weapons officers of each of the strategic bombers carried out the launch procedure, minutes later the KH-47M2 were launched, in total twenty-eight missiles were fired; these swiftly headed at mach 10 towards their goal, the Kinzhals leveled their altitude to forty thousand feet, once they left Turkish airspace they would take a sea-skimming flight mode at about five hundred meters in altitude. "Are the dogs already after the prey, Boris?" the commander inquired. "Yes, sir, they are level and heading towards our target." The commander then indicated, "Very well, gentlemen, let's get out of here as soon as possible." The Backfires turned to return to their base in Diáguilevo, eleven kilometers east of Ryazan.

Aboard the USS Eisenhower, the voice of the officer in charge of the CIC was heard:

"Sir, we are detecting multiple signals of electronic interference!"

Captain Conner responded with a hoarse voice:

"Source, Mike?"

"Undefined, sir, the signals are coming from multiple places."

"Positive identification of missiles?"

"Not yet, sir."

"Damn it. Everyone to combat positions!"

"Sir, we have identified several missiles heading towards us!" indicated the CIC officer of the USS Higgins that was part of the combat group.

"Free fire!" ordered the group's anti-aircraft combat officer, immediately deploying the AEGIS system of all the ships in automatic, the sophisticated equipment that involves the joint work of radar systems and their computers began to identify the enemy missiles and assigned each one a priority for its destruction.

"Are the Sparrows activated?" Inquired Captain Conner with a worried voice.

"Affirmative, sir, as are the RAMs."

Conner was referring to the intermediate and short-range missiles that served as protection against a potential missile attack. The voice of the Eisenhower's CIC was heard again:

"Damn, sir, the missiles are very close!"

The AEGIS could never identify the origin of the attack, the powerless computer system decided to order the launch of the escort ships' missiles, as well as its own Sparrows towards points where there was nothing. Seconds later three explosions shook the Eisenhower and two of its escort ships also received impacts, the USS Higgins being the most damaged. The first Dagger — NATO's designation for this type of Russian missiles— hit the deck of the aircraft carrier, many of the F/A 18s that were on deck were blown into the air, as well as a Prowler and a Hawkeye that were about to take off; most of the auxiliaries and mechanics who were on deck at that moment died instantly. Less than a second later a missile exploded at the bow of the Eisenhower, on the port side; almost simultaneously, the third missile hit the lower part of the flight deck, almost in the middle of the aircraft carrier, between its bow and stern. In the CIC, this last explosion threw Captain Conner to the ground, disoriented by the strong fall, he heard the cries for help from several of those who were there, the man felt a sharp pain in his forehead, touched it and felt the moisture of blood on his fingers, in the midst of the dimness he squinted his eyes, to observe how his left hand had a red coloration; as best as he could, Conner stood up and, leaning on a console, observed that part of the CIC was no longer there, several of his men were unconscious on the floor, a sailor entered and helped him out to the corridor leading to the flight deck.

"Damn it, sailor, the CIC practically disappeared!"

"By a miracle, we all didn't vanish, sir! There's fire in several parts of the aircraft carrier!"

Already on deck and still supported by the sailor, Conner, astonished, could not believe what he saw, charred pieces of combat aircraft burning, as well as chunks of human bodies scattered across the deck, many men screaming pleading for help; in the background, the commander of the Eisenhower observed one of the escort ships wrapped in a thick, black column of smoke that rose uncontrollably towards the blue and sunny sky. "My God! —he thought to himself—, they also hit the Higgins!"

"Bingo! We found the bastard!"

Cruz and Craig Eastman watched with interest as Dumont, the former inquired:

"Which bastard are you referring to, Bernard?"

"Your damn Valiente! The Czech police identified him, the news came to us via Interpol a few minutes ago." —Dumont told them about the police report and the restaurant incident.

"Magnificent!" —Eastman replied excitedly.

"Czech Republic?" —asked Frost.

"That's right" —affirmed Dumont. Then he looked at Cruz— Everything seems to indicate that your hunch about Valiente's escape route was correct, it goes south.

Cruz searched for a map of Europe on his computer, soon it appeared on the screen.

"Bernard, where do you say they located him?"

"In Brno, a small city in the Czech Republic."

Cruz looked at the map again, zoomed in to see the detail of the country's borders.

"Brno is to the southeast, I bet a hundred dollars the man is heading to Slovakia. Does the report mention when the incident occurred?"

Dumont checked the email again containing the information sent by the Czech police.

"Forty-eight hours."

Cruz looked at the map again, after observing it for a few seconds, he decided to project the image of it, then stood up and walked towards the screen where the projection appeared.

"Rosamund and dear friends, the man has already crossed the Slovak border, I would dare to think he has also crossed the Hungarian one and is heading to Serbia or Croatia."

Rosamund Frost stood up to point at the image.

"And what about Austria? From there, one can also get to Croatia, crossing Slovenia."

"Good point, Rosamund, we should alert all the authorities in the countries we've mentioned, plus Slovenia."

Craig Eastman scratched a cheek, then expressed:

"After all this, do we have any picture of Valiente?"

Everyone simultaneously looked at Bernard Dumont, who returned them a mischievous gaze.

"I thought you'd never ask."

Dumont projected the man's face, all observed it in silence for a moment.

"How is Jean Claude, Carole?"

Tomás Cruz had just arrived at the hotel, before having dinner he decided to call his good friend Carole in Paris to inquire about Lebel's health status, every other day he communicated to follow his progress, optimism could be noticed in the woman's tone of voice.

"Today I'm happy, yesterday, as you know, they brought J.C. out of the induced coma, the specialist managing his recovery told me he's responding favorably, even today he recognized my voice, squeezed my hand when he heard me."

"What great news, Carole! Did the doctor give you any estimation of the time his recovery will take?"

The woman's voice seemed to return to a state of nostalgia and unease:

"You know doctors, Tom, they are like lawyers, they never commit to give a date or a precise answer about times or consequences in the case of a legal or medical issue, the only thing he answered was: 'There are encouraging signs, Carole, but we must wait patiently the next days, even the following two weeks, to have a clearer picture of your husband's state; if you are Catholic, you must pray a lot'. I got nothing!"

Tomás Cruz lamented on the other side of the line:

"I understand, that and nothing is the same."

The woman asked:

"And you, how are your attempts to save this world going?"

Cruz let out an exclamation, he responded with general information, giving her a small summary of how things were going, he heard a slight laugh.

"You know something, Tom? You are worse than the blessed doctor at the clinic, but, from what I understand, you are as tangled up as my husband's recovery."

Tomás Cruz chuckled.

"You are completely right, Carole, despite certain hints, we continue to be blind."

"You know? My husband says that you are like a hunting dog, you feel better in the field chasing prey, I think you should get out of that office and chase it on the ground, if you are as good as J.C. says, and I'm sure you are, that's the solution, think about it, my friend."

After talking a few more minutes, they hung up, the words about the hunting dog kept echoing in Cruz's mind.

*AEGIS system: a naval weapons system developed in the United States.

X

raig Eastman, still surprised, entered the room at Downing Street where the crisis cabinet—COBRA—called by the English Prime Minister was meeting. Harold Callaghan raised his hand to greet him and invite him to sit in a chair close to him.

"Welcome, Craig, I always have you running to join us in these meetings, my apologies."

"Don't worry, Prime Minister, it's a pleasure for me to be here."

After taking a seat, Nick Fallon, the Secretary of Defense, extended his hand as a gesture of welcome, the latter took the opportunity to comment:

"What a response from the Russians in the Mediterranean, Craig."

"That's right, sir, the strike was forceful and, I must say, loaded with disturbing news."

Fallon expressed a question:

"Do you refer to the Daggers?"

Eastman was about to answer when the Prime Minister interrupted him:

"Excuse me, Craig, we will have the opportunity to discuss that issue in the meeting, I would like to take advantage of your company to also review several issues, matters that we had already had the opportunity to discuss before all this madness started." Callaghan took a brief pause to organize his thoughts, then checked his notebook to make some verifications; the first question was fired as quickly as a missile.

"How far do the Russians intend to go with this adventure, Craig?"

Eastman shifted in his chair before answering the question:

"In my opinion, this is a matter that is yet to be determined; however, I believe that initially they aim to take the Baltic countries, without discarding that they might intend something in Poland and Ukraine."

"Concerning, without a doubt, the matter of Poland and Ukraine would push their borders westward, we would have the Russians less than a hundred kilometers from Berlin. In your opinion, is this matter already defined?"

Eastman frowned and slightly tilted his head.

"Excuse me, I didn't understand the question, Prime Minister."

"I mean if we already lost them, I am referring to the Baltic countries, in the last conversation, you did not show much optimism regarding being able to keep them."

"In my opinion, we can forget about them, the Russians are about to close the Suwalki gap, and if they got themselves into this mess, it's hard for things to return to the state before the conflict began."

"A conflict that, by the way, we did not start," added the Prime Minister, "but we will return to that matter, on a scale of one to ten, how likely do you see the invasion of Poland and Ukraine?"

Eastman thought for a moment before answering.

"I would give it an eight, I insist, the Russians have already gotten into the mess; they will undoubtedly want to take advantage of the circumstances, in fact, we all know what they have mobilized in terms of troops and military equipment to both borders.

"Suppose for a moment we conclude the Baltic issue and accept that they take it. What should we do to avoid losing Poland and Ukraine?"

Eastman, after a brief moment, took a pen and wrote a word in his notebook, then showed it to those present; on the page, everyone observed the word "Deterrence".

"Deterrence? Could you be more specific, Craig?" indicated Callaghan.

"Well, sir, there are two alternatives, the first, to immediately mobilize more troops and equipment, mainly tanks, and anti-tank equipment, to both countries, in this, we would have to count on additional help from the Americans, their deterrent power is greater than ours. The Russians must receive a clear message from our side that Europe and the United States are not willing to allow things to go back to the Cold War era; as for the second alternative, it is the least desirable...

Fallon interrupted him:

"Are we talking about the nuclear option?"

"That's right, Mr. Secretary."

With Craig Eastman urgently summoned to Downing Street and Bernard Dumont called by the director of the DGSE for a last-minute meeting in Paris, Tomas Cruz took advantage of the warm summer afternoon to review on the terrace the recent developments from the discovery in the south of the Czech Republic. Cruz was sitting in front of his computer, wearing headphones, his Spotify playlist playing Billy Joel singing "Zanzibar"... "But the waitress always serves a secret smile...", shortly after, the saxophone followed Joel's voice; Tomas Cruz got distracted for a moment from what he was working on, the man thought of the song's name, "anyone would think that Billy Joel is referring to the archipelago in Tanzania, that would be logical, but it's not the case, Joel actually means to show the routine of a sports bar with that name, it's curious that he describes the day-to-day of a bar just as he does in Piano Man... it seems like his artistic career might have started in a tavern... Could it be? I don't think so, from what I know of his biography, he...", a soft touch on his right shoulder brought him out of his abstraction, Cruz reacted startled.

"Excuse me, Tomas. Am I interrupting anything?"

Cruz answered:

"Not at all, Rosamund. What's up? Any news?"

A slight smile appeared on the woman's lips.

"You can call me Ross, I feel like I'm being scolded, I remember my parents calling me that when they were about to reprimand me."

"Well, if we think about it more carefully, I think I could be your father's age," pointed out Cruz with some humor.

The woman let out a light laugh.

"My father is approaching seventy years, Tomas, unless you are following some geriatric treatment to stop aging, I don't think you are that age."

Now it was Cruz who laughed.

"That does not change the fact that you are much younger than I am, Rosam... sorry, Ross, and, please, then call me Tom."

"OK, Tom, we will have time to talk about our ages. Don't you think?"

"I hope so. Can I, before you tell me what you want to say, ask why Ross? Wouldn't, for example, Rose, be better?"

"Good question, it turns out I'm a fan and faithful reader of a very good crime novelist, Ross Macdonald." "What a coincidence! I am an avid reader of Macdonald and his novels 'protagonist, the detective Lew Archer."

"Without a doubt, a great writer, who also inherited from Raymond Chandler, one of the fathers of the noir novel."

"Interesting, we will also have time to discuss the noir novel, a literary genre that I find fascinating, okay? And now, yes. What did you want to mention to me?"

The woman's smile disappeared.

"I wanted to discuss something related to al-Hamzi."

"What would the consequences of entering a limited nuclear war be?" asked the British Prime Minister, his face showing concern.

"It is, definitely, the worst alternative; a study from a few years ago, developed by Princeton University, indicated that, in a limited nuclear conflict, Europe, in the first forty-five minutes, would lose at least thirty-five million lives and more than fifty-five million would be injured, not to mention the potential for escalation, the worst would come in the following hours. With entire cities destroyed, how would those injured be cared for? The deaths would increase, not to mention the aftermath of the subsequent radioactivity. It is curious, but I believe things got worse when the United States left the INF, signed by Reagan and Gorbachev in 1987; this, as we know, removed the possibility of a limited nuclear war in Europe from European territory by removing missiles with a range of five hundred to five thousand five hundred kilometers from the inventory of nuclear weapons.

Nick Fallon lamented:

"Certainly, this complicated things for us, this, added to the fact that in 2002 the Americans left the ABM treaty, the Russians argued that this gave them the prerogative to withdraw from the INF."

"Which complicated the ratification of START III, signed in 2010," added Eastman.

"Something we are aware of," the prime minister said with some sarcasm. "Conclusions regarding this issue, Craig?"

Eastman took a deep breath before answering:

"I would tend to think that the Russians will not use short or medium-range nuclear weapons, they will use the entire arsenal of conventional warfare, which is undoubtedly numerous; their nuclear inventory is, for now, deterrent."

Callaghan grunted:

"Which is the same as being robbed by having things taken from my pockets with a gun pointed directly at my head, it seems we don't have many alternatives, Craig. Should we, in your opinion, yield the Baltic countries and try to defend Poland and Ukraine?"

Rear Admiral Nicholas Utley, from the British Royal Navy staff, clearly annoyed, replied to Eastman:

"Excuse me, Prime Minister, I must tell Mr. Eastman that this is clearly a defeatist position. What do you know, sir, about what a soldier should do on the battlefield?"

Eastman kept his composure, calmly responding to Utley:

"Beyond what I have mentioned about the Russian nuclear arsenal, their army has twenty-five thousand tanks, one thousand five hundred light tanks, eighteen thousand infantry fighting vehicles, more than sixty thousand armoured transport vehicles; seven Russian armored divisions are today cutting off contact between NATO and the Baltic countries, more than fifteen divisions are today a few kilometers from the Polish and Ukrainian borders." —The man paused—. "Meanwhile, how many tanks do we have in NATO? Eleven thousand, I misspoke, we had that number, we must subtract the three thousand five hundred from Turkey, which denounced the treaty by which it was a part of NATO, leaving us with less than eight thousand, add to that the five hundred tanks that the United States still has in Europe, it means they outnumber us, they also nearly double us in infantry transport and fighting vehicles. As we could, we placed five tank divisions to support both the Baltic border and Poland and Ukraine." — Eastman stared at the rear admiral—. "A soldier must offer his life to defend the land of his ancestors, but would you calmly send your soldiers to an operation theatre where the enemy practically outnumbers us more than two to one in everything? Even in men?"

An uncomfortable silence took over the room, Utley was speechless, Callaghan broke it, stating:

"An undoubtedly disturbing balance that you present us with, Craig."

Eastman tried to soften what was said:

"Sir, I know my answer is not politically correct, I apologize, but Europe is paying today the cost of what it did not do for years to, if the time came, successfully defend the Baltic countries and avoid the consequences of this Russian invasion in Poland and Ukraine."

*START III: Strategic Arms Reduction Treaty

Shtorm

XI

"What's happening with al-Hamzi?"

Cruz asked, his investigative instinct brought him back to reality, curiosity prevailed over the sensation of the good moment he had just had with Rosamund Frost. The woman took a photo from a Manila envelope and showed it to him, Cruz identified the figure of al-Hamzi, who was walking down a dusty street without sidewalks.

"Where is this, Ross?"

"Mirpur Khas."

They both spoke in French, Frost had requested Cruz to converse in that language, she liked to practice it; the woman outlined a smile, Cruz opened his eyes in a gesture of helplessness.

"And... where is that?"

"Pakistan, it's a town just over two hundred kilometers from Karachi."

"When was al-Hamzi photographed?"

"Forty-eight hours ago, the curious thing is that he wandered around Mirpur Khas all morning without a clear direction, ate something at noon, and then took a bus back to Karachi."

"Maybe the man was very stressed and wanted to take a walk" —joked Cruz.

"I would be too, in his place." —She paused briefly—, "I know you are involved in the Valiente affair, but I would like you to help me with this for a few minutes."

"No problem. What do we have? Reports, photos, videos?"

"All three."

Cruz rose from his seat to serve himself a cup of coffee, the dispenser was a few meters from the table where they were sitting, while getting up, he indicated to the woman:

"Can we watch the videos? A coffee?"

Rosamund nodded, she prepared, meanwhile, the three videos she had received, once he returned with two cups of coffee, Cruz sat back next to the woman to watch them, after a few minutes they ended, nothing seemingly relevant; Frost then placed on the table, one by one, the nine photos the file had; Cruz took his time to observe them, he was on the penultimate image, about to continue to the next, when he instinctively stopped, after a couple of seconds he revisited the photo he had just reviewed, glanced at his partner to say:

"A favor, Ross. Can you play the videos again?"

The woman nodded, the first video appeared on the computer screen, shortly after the second one started, Tomas Cruz said:

"Ross, stop it, backtrack a bit."

Frost backtracked, Cruz then asked her to pause at a point in the video, a subject walked in front of al-Hamzi; the man went back to scrutinizing the photograph, in it, the Arab was drinking something in a small café, something had caught his attention in that photo. What was it? Tomas stopped focusing his gaze on him, a little higher up, in the background of the image, something caught his attention.

"Bingo."

Frost intrigued, looked at him, then asked:

"What did you see?"

Tomas looked at her intently for a moment.

"Can we address each other informally? I feel like I'm talking to my grandmother, she used to address me formally."

The woman let out a loud, short laugh.

"In that case, your grandmother must have loved you a lot, I still can't say the same, we barely know each other."

Cruz made a face and shrugged as if he didn't care, then he would be surprised by what he said next:

"Let's skip the step where we don't know each other yet, I know that over time you might come to like me."

The woman apparently didn't expect the comment, smiled, her face slowly turned crimson.

"Alright, let's address each other informally. In my experience, men always disappoint, anyway, I'll give you a chance, which doesn't mean anything different from addressing each other informally" —she clarified emphatically.

"That's fine by me, for now..."

She observed him silently for a while, then nodded, returning to smile, that last comment would also surprise him hours later, when he replayed the scene in his mind.

"Back to our matters" —said Cruz, pointing at the frozen image on the computer screen—, "the shirt of this guy in the video is the same as the one in the photo, if you look closely, it seems like it's the same man."

The woman looked at both images for a while, then nodded in amazement.

"Wow, Tomas, you have eagle eyes, I would never have connected the video with the photo."

"Thanks, Ross, one question. Where was photo number 7 taken?"

"Let me take a look at the report." —Seconds later Frost said—:" In a small café in the city center, its name, Shimla Sweets and Bakers."

"And where was the video recorded?"

Frost checked the report, there weren't many details about the locations of the recordings.

"No, there's no information about that."

Cruz scratched his chin.

"Where did we get this from?"

"It was shared with us by our friends from the Mossad. Would you like me to ask for more details?"

"Yes, Ross, please, and now that we have the photo of the subject, let's verify internally at MI6 and with them, maybe they have his identification and we can find out who he is." Rosamund

Frost watched him for a moment, then after softly clapping her hands on the table, she stood up to head inside the building.

"Perfect, dear Sherlock," she joked, "I'll also ask Bernard and our people to check it with the CIA."

Not far from the Kremlin is the National Defense Center, from there the Russian government and military high command control and track the main activities related to defense or attack control and monitoring, such as the campaigns carried out in Crimea or Syria. The building was imposing, under it, more than twenty meters deep, was the Crisis Room, which actually looked like a huge three-story theater, similar to NASA's Mission Control Center in Houston; on the first floor, rows of officers and technicians monitored the huge screens of their computers, on the second and third floors there seemed to be what looked like boxes forming a prolonged U, on the second level sat the commanders of the different forces, in the center, Vladimir Putin, accompanied by his Minister of Defense, watched the enormous fourteen meter wide by seven meter tall screen, which was accompanied by at least eight seventy-inch screens. The image of the giant central screen showed numerous Russian war tanks speeding through a green meadow, on the left side the screens showed the faces of various generals, on the right satellite images and flying Backfires; Putin looked at General Sergei Serdyukov.

"So we are close to concluding phase 1, Sergei?"

"Affirmative, Mr. President, the pincer our forces have put together between Kaliningrad and the penetration of the Suwalki strip is about to close."

Putin's inscrutable, icy face, true to his style, showed no emotion, with slight reluctance his lips barely moved to say:

"How close are we to closing it?"

"Just under fifteen kilometers, Mr. President."

"Do you have an estimate of when this stage will be concluded?"

"Less than twenty-four hours."

Putin looked in his notepad, his lips moved slightly again.

"Just over the sixty hours estimated, not bad, although it's not cause for celebration, Sergei."

"The enemy gave us a tougher response than we expected, sir."

"That was already accounted for within the sixty hours, anyway, what's important is to complete the encirclement and isolate the Baltic countries, a zone that should never have ceased to be ours."

The Minister of Defense nodded, returning a nervous smile to him; Putin scratched his cheek a couple of times, then said:

"When is the second phase expected to start?"

"Ten hours after closing the pincer."

"Very well."

The colossal central screen showed something that immediately caught the attention of the Russian president, he leaned forward visibly interested, leaning on the table with his elbows, it was the new SHTORM type aircraft carrier, sailing escorted by several warships, the trails of all the ships at sea could be seen with total clarity, a side screen showed its location, the combat group was about a thousand kilometers north of Iceland.

XII

The rumble of explosions approached and increased, the rough and intermittent noise of the rotors of several helicopters was heard among the pauses of the bomb blasts; it was a squadron of Ka-52 Alligators, both they and several squadrons of Ka-50 Hokum-A, or Black Sharks, had attacked this area located between two small towns, Trakènai and a point marked on the map as Zelionka, mercilessly. The distance separating them barely exceeded ten kilometers, Captain Bertrand Thoret, commander of the first artillery regiment, felt the powerful shaking of the earth before a nearby explosion, as best as he could he shouted to his communications assistant:

"Damn it, Maurice, the Russians are literally massacring us! The situation is already unsustainable!"

"Sir, the latest information we receive from the regiment command indicates that the Russians are less than five kilometers from where we are!"

Three successive explosions were heard, fragments of earth and small pebbles hit the ground, the uniforms and helmets of the soldiers who, lying on the ground, accompanied the multiple rocket launcher battery. Thoret took the communications device from his assistant, called the command, located thirty kilometers inside Polish territory.

"Here B1, here B1, we request instructions, we are under intense enemy fire!"

A sepulchral silence was the only response. After a few inexplicably calm seconds, the Russian artillery began to saturate the area where the first French artillery regiment was located. This time, the intensity and proximity of the explosions made the group of men jump several centimeters; the rough noise of a voice on the communication equipment was heard:

"B1 to BC, B1 to BC. Get out of there as you can!"

Thoret roared:

"Now we're really screwed, gentlemen." —The man took a map out of his knapsack, and after checking it for a few seconds, he saw a group of trees about two hundred meters away, leading to a relatively wooded area—. "Follow me and run for your lives!"

Like the first French regiment, many NATO men covered the few kilometers that separated them from Polish soil that afternoon, as the Russian encirclement of the Baltic countries was about to close.

Craig Eastman was preparing to leave Downing Street. It was already late at night, and the day there had been long and exhausting. "What a relief, I need to get home and have a double shot of whisky," he thought. He was about to cross the threshold of the shining black door marked with a 10 in the center when a security officer called him, he looked back.

"Mr. Eastman, my apologies, the Prime Minister wishes to speak with you for a few minutes."

Eastman, between puzzled and annoyed, nodded. The officer directed him to a small private room where he indicated that Callaghan would join him shortly, offered him tea, and served it.

After about ten minutes, which felt like an eternity to him, the British Prime Minister entered, followed by the Defense Secretary.

"I express my sincerest apologies again, Craig; we really have troubled you today."

"Don't worry, Prime Minister, these days are hectic for everyone."

The Prime Minister ordered more tea and some sandwiches; Eastman thought to himself, "from what I'm seeing, this won't be a matter of a few minutes, I think I'll leave the whisky for another day." After the officer had left, Callaghan said:

"Sadly, events seem to be precipitating in the direction you pointed out, Craig. It's a matter of hours before Lithuania, and therefore Latvia and Estonia, become isolated from their NATO partners... and the rest of Europe. —The man paused—. Our troops are retreating in Lithuania, plus we are taking defensive positions inside Poland; the same thing is happening in Ukraine, where we are sending troop reinforcements and military equipment. It is to be expected that, as you also expressed, the Russians will soon begin invasion operations in these two countries."

Craig Eastman lamented:

"I regret not having been able to bring better forecasts, Prime Minister."

Callaghan stared at him for a few moments.

"You know what? You were right."

Eastman returned the gaze, intrigued.

"In what sense, Prime Minister?"

"We did nothing for years to improve our response capability in the hypothetical case of a Russian invasion, and we had time, since before Donald Trump's arrival, we should have implemented those capacities." —Callaghan scratched his chin—. "Nationalisms sprouted like a bad symptom of what was coming, then came the Crimea warning, then Trump's threats to leave NATO, a warning he later fulfilled, all of which encouraged the Russians. It's a pity, Craig, but I think Europe is paying the consequences of its inaction, and finally, your predictive book came."

"Prime Minister, I believe all I did was piece together the puzzle."

The Prime Minister chuckled softly.

"Something politicians apparently don't do! Anyway, Craig, that's not what I wanted to talk to you about. There are two issues I want to discuss privately with Nick and you."

"With pleasure. What is it about, Prime Minister?"

As Callaghan was about to answer, two light knocks were heard on the private room door, then an officer opened it and a maid entered with the sandwiches and tea. After she placed them on a nearby table, she hurried out, and the British Prime Minister resumed the conversation:

"Firstly, one issue worries us, Craig, it's about the recent Russian attack on the Eisenhower aircraft carrier, the speed with which the missiles arrived gave no time for the defense systems of the escorting strike group to respond. I understand the Russians have developed a technology that today gives them a strategic advantage over NATO and the Americans."

"From the moment I saw the news, I imagined they had used hypersonic missiles."

The Prime Minister looked at his Defense Secretary.

"Nick mentioned something about it to me, I understand it also renders the United States' missile defense system somewhat ineffective."

"Absolutely, sir, hypersonic missiles develop speeds twenty times the speed of sound, that is, in fifteen minutes they can attack targets in the United States."

"My God, that means that any target in Europe could be reached in..."

Eastman interrupted him:

"A missile launched six and a half minutes ago, from its base in the Ural Mountains, would be falling right on top of us in London... now."

An exclamation came from the mouth of the prime minister, Nick Fallon added:

"And practically, we wouldn't have a way to know, there isn't yet an early warning system that allows us to detect an object at that speed."

"Even worse, the Avangard, as they have named the missile, carries several conventional or nuclear warheads that can take various directions and randomly change course before reaching their targets, which makes it impossible for current defense systems to react."

Callaghan launched a question, although the tone gave it more the character of a lament than a question:

"Do we have the technology to develop a defense system against this?"

Eastman's response also sounded like a complaint:

"No sir, something more serious, neither the Americans, nor us, nor even the Chinese, have been able to develop a missile of these characteristics, progress has been made, but I fear that it will take us several more years."

"In conclusion, we are defenseless today, they have an advantage over us."

"That's right, prime minister, without considering the other "toys" they already have and we are barely working on models and, in the best case, prototypes."

"What are you referring to, Craig?"

Nick Fallon answered that question:

"Craig is referring to a nuclear-powered underwater drone, it's a missile launch platform, we've already seen the capability of the hypersonic missiles launched from the Backfires; they also have the new SARMAT, another high-speed intercontinental ballistic missile that will allow them to attack targets traversing the North or South Pole."

"And... the laser, everything seems to indicate that they have a weapon of these characteristics."

Callaghan raised his hands, as if to signify impotence.

"All the more reason to be cautious in the military response we give to the challenge they pose. You know what? I'm very afraid we find ourselves in the middle of a labyrinth."

Eastman and the Defense Secretary nodded, everyone took a pause to attack the sandwiches, after finishing, Callaghan indicated:

"I understand that you are supporting people from MI6 and the DGSE in a case involving Arab terrorist groups."

Eastman responded with a nod, the prime minister commented:

"Can I learn more details about that case, Craig?"

The man gave him a summary of the case and the progress it had made, a look of skepticism was noted on Callaghan.

"I have a doubt, Craig. Are we not wasting our time on it? At least for now, it is clear that the Russians are behind all this mess we find ourselves in."

"It's possible, sir, however, it could also be a masquerade by Al Qaeda to bring us to the point of conflict we find ourselves in; if we manage to unmask this plot, perhaps we can defuse the dangerous conflict we have at hand."

Callaghan looked up at the ceiling, maintaining a skeptical face, pressed his lips together for a moment, then said, glancing at his Defense Secretary:

"I wouldn't want to waste time embarking on endless conspiracy theories or unclear purposes, Craig." —The British prime minister looked at him intently, then said—: "A week, Craig, if by then we haven't returned to the Stone Age; let's take that time to determine if the case has merit, I don't want a valuable resource playing guessing games. Understood?"

Eastman nodded, then the prime minister's eyes lit up for a moment.

"The day has been very long, gentlemen. Do you fancy a single malt? I have a good reserve of sixteen-year-old Lagavulin that, I am sure, will go down very well at this hour."

Fallon and Eastman nodded in good spirits.

"Well, God is good and just, at least I didn't miss out on a good whisky tonight," the latter thought.

XIII

The lady in charge of selling tickets at the train station in Subotica, a town a few kilometers from the Serbian border with Hungary, served the next person in line without even looking, she was just minutes away from finishing her shift and exhaustion plus routine were taking a toll on her concentration, she just wanted to finish quickly and go home. The subject mumbled his destination as best as he could, Belgrade; she immediately noticed he was a foreigner, it didn't matter, after all, it was nothing new, many travelers of other nationalities bought their ticket there; the woman continued to watch the computer monitor, mechanically, she indicated the price and the departure time, in an hour, the individual, without a whimper, quickly handed over the sum in Serbian dinars, the woman gave him the change, the man extended his hand to take it, something caught his attention, she slightly raised her gaze and glanced at the tattoo on the hand, he swiftly withdrew it from the counter along with the ticket and turned around; a young woman was still in line, she was traveling to Leskovac, while managing the ticket sale, the lady glanced, somewhat impatiently, at the clock, there were still fifteen long minutes before her shift ended, after taking a breath she gave the price to the blonde teenager on the other side of the counter.

Back in London, Bernard Dumont rushed into the room accompanied by Rosamund Frost.

"Tom, your suspicions were correct, Valiente has already been spotted in Serbia."

"That's good news, Bernard. Where exactly?"

"In Subotica, in the north of the country, the man bought a ticket to Belgrade."

Cruz asked:

"When did this happen?"

Frost replied:

"The subject bought the train ticket to Belgrade just over twenty-four hours ago, Tom."

Dumont looked at the woman in astonishment, then said sarcastically:

"Tom? Did I miss something, Rosamund? Two days ago you called him Tomás."

"A lot can change in forty-eight hours, Bernard."

She stated, Cruz joked.

"Stop being jealous, friend. What were we discussing? Ah, yes, that Valiente has a day's advantage on us."

With a mischievous smile, Frost turned to Cruz, then the woman said:

"Where do you think he could be heading, Sherlock?

Eastman was the one who opened his eyes wide now.

"Sherlock? Definitely, you and I missed something, Bernard."

After a brief session of jokes, Cruz resumed the conversation about the course Valiente might take, for this, he looked at a map for a few minutes.

"I believe the man must already be in Turkey or about to enter the country."

Dumont shook his head doubtfully.

"What about Greece? Or Bulgaria?"

"Could be, Bernard, I insist, Turkey is just a possibility, but in this, you have to think as if you were Valiente, it's easier to cross Greece and make it to Turkey through the border, he's fleeing, he needs to get out quickly from countries where we can track him, and getting to Turkish territory makes things a lot easier for him."

"I see." —Dumont looked at Frost—, "then let's communicate our "Sherlock's" instincts to our bosses, so they can send the respective alerts."

A short series of jokes emerged again, Cruz tried to deflect them, he was in the middle of his friends' laughter when the words from his recent phone conversation with his friend Carole came back to him. "You know? My husband says you're like a hunting dog, you feel better in the field pursuing the prey, I think you should get out of that office and chase it on the ground, if you're as good as J.C. says, and I'm sure you are, that's the solution, think about it, my friend," Cruz, as if thinking out loud, said:

"My friends, I think we should go there."

Bernard asked intrigued:

"Where, Tom?"

"To Turkey. Could we do it?"

The man's cell phone vibrated, he looked at the screen, it was a WhatsApp message, he read, "The beasts are on the prowl, you should come to the stable and rest a bit, in Gümülcine the flock awaits you"; the man, who was sitting alone in the last row of the bus, looked thoughtfully out the window, he had just passed Lasmos, in a little less than twenty kilometers, he would arrive at the place; Valiente weighed his options, a little over a hundred kilometers separated him from the Turkish border. "Do I continue? If they are warning me, it's likely they have identified me and are waiting for me... —the man scratched his head a couple of times— . Damn it, I have no choice, I'll have to stay a couple of days in the stable."

Smiling faces with Russian flags, the state television of Russia showed a crowd of people gathered somewhere in Vilnius, the Lithuanian capital; many of them were shouting cheers for Vladimir Putin, the images also recorded celebrations in towns of Latvia and Estonia. There was a change on the screen; now one could observe how armored troop transport vehicles, followed by tanks carrying flags with white, blue, and red stripes of the Russian Federation, paraded through the main roads of the three Baltic capitals. The streets, though empty, showed isolated groups of sympathizers with flags who came out to greet; then the state television showed an exultant and smiling Russian president walking in the Kremlin with a martial step on an endless red carpet, the press conference guests applauded on either side of this carpet, after climbing some steps and reaching the white podium with the golden double-headed eagle, Putin raised his arms, a long and loud burst of applause followed, then Vladimir Putin began his speech saying, "The mistakes of history have been corrected; the treason has been finally avenged, Russia will bring back into its fold those territories and our brothers who were left in the lurch due to the disloyalty and weakness of those who turned their backs on the greatness of our motherland." Thousands of kilometers away, Ayman al-Zawahiri watched the Russian president's moment of glory; the man smiled, things were finally starting to take the shape he had envisioned, it was a matter of days before the conflict would take on more serious overtones. He muttered to himself, "The West will die by its own poison, for the glory of Allah."

CNN's news showed a series of powerful explosions in the darkness of the night; a headline just below the news anchor revealed breaking news, the Polish and Ukrainian borders were under Russian fire, the anchorwoman, with a stern face and blond hair tied in a bun, indicated that attacks on both border lines had started after nine o'clock at night, Central European Summer Time; two military analysts were aiding the journalist in analyzing the dramatic turn the events were taking. Onboard a Falcon 2000 of the French Air Force, Bernard Dumont and Tomás Cruz watched the news; circumstances had forced Eastman and Frost to stay in London, while Dumont accompanied Cruz to Turkey, the four reviewed the latest news through the satellite communications system of the French Armed Forces, SYRACUSE.

"How do you see it, Craig?" Dumont inquired.

On the other monitor, Eastman's tired face could be seen; he tilted his head, the gesture did not show much optimism.

"Based on the information shared with me so far, we have withstood the strong onslaught of the Russians, our forces are receiving air support and stopped the advance of their tanks; however, the Russians have committed more than twenty tank divisions to both war fronts. The question is how long our forces can withstand the pressure.

"How far have their forces penetrated?"

"In Poland, between fifteen and thirty-five kilometers, while in Ukraine, they have managed to advance more, ranging from thirty to forty-five kilometers. Specifically, there is a point where the Russians are concentrating their efforts to break through the NATO's defense line, in an area near a small town in Poland, Biala Podlaska, the area is called Lisy. If they manage to break through that part of the war front, we do not have enough reserve forces there to counter the breakthrough, the most worrying part is that we don't have troops or tanks to send there, which would give the tanks practically a free way to Siedlce; if I were in command of that group, I would carry out a double enveloping maneuver to the north and south of my position, which would face us with the terrible alternative of having many of our men caught in a couple of pockets."

Tomás Cruz thought aloud:

"Mmm..., like in World War II, I remember the Falaise Pocket*, shortly after D-Day."

Eastman's voice was heard on the monitor:

"With one difference, Tom, in Falaise the Germans managed to evade the encirclement set in the pocket, the bulk of their troops could escape, in our case we do not have a rear guard that allows us to avoid falling into the trap."

Dumont leaned back in the chair.

"And if these cursed pockets close, what happens, Craig?"

Silence dominated the atmosphere for several seconds.

"Consider Warsaw and all of north and central eastern Poland lost."

A warning sound came to Dumont's computer; it was an encrypted message, he read the content, then looked at Cruz.

"Gentlemen, Valiente is in Greece, apparently he's still there, a system of cameras at a bus station allowed his identification."

*Falaise Pocket: name of the encirclement that Allied forces subjected the Germans to in Normandy in August 1944.

XIV

Valiente got off the bus at the Komotiní bus station, checked the map on Google to find his way, and after locating the place he was going to, he crossed the street, preferring to take a taxi. He got into the first one available and showed the driver on the map the place he wanted to go to, which was Café Cukur, about ten blocks away. Once they arrived at the café, the man paid, left the taxi, and entered; after taking a seat, he ordered a coffee and a cake, made sure there were no security cameras, and thirty minutes later, he left the place and walked a block towards a mosque, where they were waiting for him. Despite having a street access door, he preferred a more discreet entrance, about fifteen meters away, a solid stone arch and a metal gate marked another entrance to the Yeni Mosque. The man walked the long path to another gated door, took off his shoes, placed them in the indicated spot, and entered. Several individuals were praying; at the back, he saw the man he was looking for, who immediately identified him, gestured for him to enter the small room to his left, and Valiente obeyed and took a seat on one of the plush cushions decorating it. A few minutes later, his host came in and closed the door. Valiente stood up.

"As-salamu alaykum," the man extended his hand.

"Wa alaykum as-salam, peace also be with you," he also extended his hand and they shook hands; both took a seat on the cushions, and the host said:

"You did well to come, the Greek police and the Turkish one on the other side of the border are waiting for you." The man paused, almost with resignation, he said to his guest: "It's ironic, you know? Your kind gesture with the woman at the restaurant in Brno had a cost, they identified you and now they are after you."

Valiente raised his hands towards the ceiling.

"Every good deed we perform in life will be taken into account by our Lord when we have to give an account in heaven." The man took a deep breath, then looked at him. "Thank you for sending me the warning signal. What do you think I should do now?"

The man stood up and pointed to a small room adjacent to the sitting area.

"Eat and rest here for a few hours, at nightfall everything is prepared for you to cross the Turkish border through a path. I got you a passport and other documents with a different identity, you cannot stay here for long under the current circumstances; constant movement is the best strategy."

The rough noise of the landing gear coming out indicated that it was almost time for the Falcon 2000 to land at the NATO air base, very close to Nea Anchialos, in Greece, from there a Black Hawk would take Dumont and Cruz to Komotiní, the last place where Valiente had been seen. Cruz looked through the window at the calm green and blue waters of the Pagasetic Gulf.

"Bernard, what is the identity of our elusive Valiente?"

Distracted watching the scenery, Dumont answered:

"Andrei Ivanovich Kurchatov."

Cruz shook his head from side to side several times.

"Mmm..., a devilishly Russian name."

Dumont's ironic gesture was followed by a comment:

"My friend, if the man speaks Russian, his name is Russian, and his nationality is Russian…"

"Damn…" Cruz lamented, "this undermines our theory of the Arab conspiracy."

The order from the President of the United States was peremptory; it was necessary to attack the Russian air base from which the attack on the USS Eisenhower had been carried out. Part of the high command was not convinced of the convenience of escalating the conflict; after all, according to some of their generals, the conflict was for now limited to the Baltic, Poland, and Ukraine. The prudent thing was to support Europe and its former NATO allies, without assuming a direct conflict with Russia; their fears pointed to reaching a phase where the alternative would be the use of atomic weapons, which, for now, was dangerous and unnecessary. Trump, visibly annoyed, dismissed that line of action; in his opinion, it indicated fear, and the enemy, according to him, is more determined when they smell it. "Gentlemen, in case you haven't noticed, we are at war; the Russians must know that we are willing to go to the utmost if they continue their irresponsible actions," he expressed. A few hours later, about a hundred Tomahawk missiles were launched from several U.S. Navy submarines and warships, at least twenty of them hit the Diagilevo air base and air defense battery systems near this base.

The lethal, yet subtle, Russian response did not take long. Minutes after the attack on their airbase, the United States Navy's submarine base in Kings Bay, Georgia, experienced a severe cyberattack that damaged radar and sonar equipment, early warning systems, and caused a severe electrical overload that ruined the electrical substation, computing systems, cooling, and refrigeration. Much of this base, which hosts the Atlantic fleet of nuclear ballistic missile submarines, would be out of commission for the following two weeks. To ensure clear evidence of the attack, the nearby small town of St. Marys experienced a blackout and cyber-outage for more than five days.

The United States Navy's Black Hawk gently landed on the airbase ramp in Alexandroupoli, from which Dumont and Cruz descended, crouched, escorted by a couple of soldiers. A few meters from the helicopter, the DGSE liaison officer with the Greek National Intelligence Service (EYP) was waiting for them; after the usual greetings to him and several Greek intelligence agents, Dumont asked the French agent:

"Do we have any news on the subject, Jean Pierre?"

They all spoke in English as they walked towards the black vans that would transport them, Jean Pierre Gallois replied:

"We could hardly locate him, we had to conduct an exhaustive analysis of video material from the public security system and commercial establishments, finally the trail led us to where we believe the man is."

Cruz asked with interest:

"Where?"

"In a mosque, right in the center of Komotini."

Dumont inquired bluntly:

"When do we go in?"

A Greek agent, who belonged to the Interpol, answered the question:

"We already have the judicial order, the operation is planned to happen in about four hours," the man glanced at his watch, "just after six in the evening."

"Understood," Dumont replied, "let's hope Valiente is still there."

The journey from Alexandroupoli to Komotini took about forty-five minutes. The convoy of vans stopped at the Police headquarters in this city, after entering the parking lot, the team discreetly entered a room where the local police chief was waiting for them, they immediately studied the operation on a map.

"The problem is that our streets are very narrow and the blocks in that area are quite irregular," Captain Nikos Manoudakis explained in fairly poor English, "although this also presents an advantage for us." The man opened his eyes, "once you enter, it will be very difficult for the subject to escape." Manoudakis paused, then pointed on the map, "Another important point, this street, whose name is Ermou, is pedestrian, we already have plainclothes officers stationed there, if the terrorist tries to exit through there, he'll fall into the trap."

Dumont approached the map.

"Captain, the street above that surrounds the mosque, is it one-way?"

"That's right, it goes north and then west."

"Even better, if the man tries to escape in a car, we'll be waiting for him at the intersection with this street," Manoudakis finished saying the name, "Loaminon, sir, that's the name, I already have our personnel there."

Cruz looked at the man from Interpol in Greece.

"I have a question. Who will enter the mosque?"

"A team from Interpol, a couple of men from Greek intelligence, and Captain Manoudakis's men, you will wait with some of our officers in a nearby small café."

Tomás Cruz nodded, the Greek Interpol agent looked at his watch, then glanced at the local police commander.

"Are we ready, Captain?"

Manoudakis frowned.

"We are prepared, friend, that murderous rat falls into our hands today."

XV

The subject, accompanied by a woman, walked silently through the long entrance hall of the European Parliament, in the background, the sound of incessantly clicking camera shutters could be heard, other media were filming the historic moment, it was midnight on January 31, 2020; the subject, with his somber face, took the flagpole bearing the United Kingdom's flag and moved it forward, then he tilted it towards the woman, who took the flag to fold it over her arm, he, meanwhile, placed the flagpole back in its place, then both walked slowly into the parliament building. Meanwhile, at the official residence of the British Prime Minister, the projection of an image with a countdown showed that there were less than five seconds left until eleven o'clock at night in London, a shrill sound was heard, as well as the cheers of the crowd present there, then a series of chimes marked the beginning of a night of celebrations by citizens who supported Brexit, while others, meanwhile, wept for the United Kingdom's exit from the European Union. Amid the contradictory images of this day, on CNN the news segment presenter covering this historic event displayed on the screen excerpts from a brief speech, made public hours earlier by the French President, Emmanuel Macron, who stated, with a bitterly premonitory tone, that "the departure of the United Kingdom from the European Union must signify a historic alarm signal that should resonate in all our countries, that must be heard throughout Europe and lead us to deep reflection." The image of Boris Johnson appeared on the monitor. "Many think that tonight is the end, they are mistaken, today is the beginning of great things for the United Kingdom." The events that marked the news unfolded with tremendous speed, the image with a deeply troubled face of Nicola Sturgeon could be seen, with a grave but firm voice, she expressed that "Scotland continues in the heart of Europe, we are a nation proud to be part of the unity of Europe, Scots deeply regret the decision of the United Kingdom to leave, today we may find ourselves on the sidelines of that unity, but we remain at heart in the European Union, I reiterated today that Scotland must decide its own future in a referendum about our independence, the best path forward is for Scotland to be an independent country within the European Union, alongside our European brothers and sisters." All those memories rushed at once to the mind of Craig Eastman, who, dismayed, watched the latest events in Scotland on television; a decision by the Supreme Court, the court which settles disputes among the members of the United Kingdom, declared null all acts carried out by Sturgeon to advance Scottish independence. The Scottish First Minister stated she would not comply with the ruling, therefore, from a legal perspective, she found herself in a state of rebellion, which triggered a series of legal actions aiming at her immediate arrest. The images showed an enraged crowd in St. Andrew Square, the flags with the white cross of Saint Andrew on a blue background were waved by thousands of Scots, the scene repeated in every corner of their territory; protests also extended to Northern Ireland, where the crowd declared they wanted independence from the United Kingdom. Eastman was immersed in his thoughts, swinging like a pendulum between his memories and the news, when the sound of his cell phone's ringtone brought him back to reality, he immediately answered:

"Craig?"

"Yes, speaking."

The voice on the other side sounded tired:

"Nick Fallon, good afternoon."

"Sir, good afternoon."

"Are you at Vauxhall?"

"Yes, sir."

"I'm sending for you, I need you here urgently."

"Of course, sir. What happened?"

"Did you hear about Poland?"

"Yes, bad news travels fast. Something related to that?"

"Something worse, Craig, something much more serious. I'll wait for you here."

Intrigued, Craig Eastman hung up, prepared his things, soon they would come for him, then he looked at the TV screen, the image on CNN showed several destroyed British Challenger 2 tanks, from their wreckage thin columns of smoke rose. Eastman saw on the lower edge of the monitor, the man couldn't help but put his hands on his head, the information said, "Russian advance, Goclaw, highway 2, on the outskirts of Warsaw."

Dumont, Cruz, and the three men from Greek intelligence entered Café Mustafa, right at the entrance of the place, Tomás slightly bumped into an individual who was leaving, he would remember that small incident later. Once inside, Cruz looked around, there were no tables to sit at, it was actually a small shop where, in addition to coffee packages, spices and some typical Greek sweets were sold. After exchanging a couple of glances with Dumont, they concluded that it was not the right place to wait, among other things because they had no line of sight with the mosque where the operation would take place. Cruz noticed that there was a restaurant at the corner, named Filippos, which had a perfect location to observe the movements of the operation. They decided to go there, ordered something light to eat, some drinks, and settled in to wait for the outcome of the operation aimed at capturing the elusive Valiente. Cruz checked his Victorinox; it was ten minutes to six in the evening. "The party will start in twenty minutes," he thought to himself.

The dark blue Jaguar XJ was speeding on its way to Whitehall. Eastman, absorbed, was sitting next to the driver, a Royal Air Force soldier in civilian clothes, in the front seat. He had refused to sit in the back, detesting being given an importance that, in his opinion, he did not have, and if he did have it, it was superfluous to him. After leaving Whitehall Court, the driver took Horse Guards Avenue, shortly after turned left to enter Whitehall Gardens, where one of the private access gates to the office of the English Defense Secretary, Nick Fallon, was located. A naval officer received him to escort him to the elevator exclusively used by the secretary; he accompanied him until leaving him in the office of his personal assistant, who indicated with advanced apologies that Fallon was in an off-schedule meeting, "The secretary begs you to wait a few minutes," said the colonel of the British Army; thirty minutes later, the voice of Nick Fallon was heard, the man walked the short corridor from his office to meet his visitor.

"Craig, I extend to you my most sincere apologies, the situation is crazy."

Eastman quickly stood up from the couch where he was sitting.

"Don't worry, Mr. Secretary, indeed things, minute by minute, seem more complicated."

After ordering tea and some cookies, the Defense Secretary showed Eastman the way to the office, which was spacious and finely decorated. At the end of it, a long board table monopolized the space; between this and the beautiful oak desk, where Fallon dealt with the kingdom's affairs, there was a spacious room with large and plush Chippendale-style furniture. After taking a seat, Fallon said:

"How's the situation with the Arabs going, Craig?"

Eastman gave him the latest details regarding the operation that was about to take place in Greece.

"Craig, the people from MI6 have informed me that the man with the alias Brave is actually Russian."

Eastman could sense where the conversation was heading, with a certain degree of resignation he replied:

"That's right, sir."

Fallon lightly slapped his right thigh.

"Well then, it's clear that our Russian friends prepared and cooked this stew, let's hope the subject is arrested and tells us how this tangle was planned and who ordered it."

Eastman raised his shoulders to respond:

"Indeed, Mr. Secretary, let's wait to see what Mr. Kurchatov tells us."

"Is that his name?" Fallon raised a hand. "It doesn't matter, although I notice you're not as convinced of my certainty on this matter. Am I right?"

Eastman kept silent for a moment, before responding he let out a light exhale.

"I believe so, Mr. Secretary."

"Come on, Craig, everything points to the Russians. Why wouldn't it be so? Can you bet on it?"

Eastman recalled the recent conversation he had with Cruz on the matter, then he had posed the same question to his friend, Cruz's words echoed in his memories, "In intelligence, my friend, we must suspect the cases in which all facts lead to a single responsible party, it is feasible that in a smart way the real authors want to take us off the path to blame the one who has nothing to do with the matter," Eastman was tempted to give Fallon the same answer, however, he refrained, as there is nothing worse than responding to a secretary of state with a mere hunch.

"No, Mr. Secretary, I wouldn't bet on it; however, it is prudent to wait and see what the Russian friend tells us." Eastman paused; "but... I believe you didn't call me to discuss this matter, did you?"

Fallon made a small gesture of displeasure.

"Certainly, Craig, a very serious issue is happening and I want your comments on it, it's worth emphasizing that this is absolutely confidential, understood?"

Eastman nodded, then said with evident curiosity:

"Don't worry. What is it about, Mr. Secretary?"

"Do you remember the W76-2 ballistic warhead?"

"Of course, it's a low-yield nuclear warhead..." Eastman's eyes widened. "You're not telling me that..."

Fallon interrupted him, shaking his head up and down several times.

"Exactly. The Americans are considering using it."

The individual entered hurriedly taking Kurchatov by surprise, who, uneasy, inquired:

"What's going on, my friend?"

Without preamble, the man replied:

"They are here, get dressed quickly, you have to leave this place immediately, take your documents." The individual handed him an envelope.

With a face of total uncertainty, Kurchatov said:

"And how will I leave?"

The man, hurried and nervous, replied:

"I'll take care of that, come on, get dressed quickly, time is of the essence."

A loud and deep noise was heard.

XVI

Rosamund Frost decided to leave her office that morning, the atmosphere was extremely tense and she needed a calmer space to review the most recent information received from al-Hamzi. She remembered there was a Starbucks nearby; she briefly reviewed the most sensitive information before storing the non-confidential information on her laptop. After walking a couple of blocks, she entered the most iconic coffee place in the world, its unmistakable smell immediately filled her nose, a brief memory of Tomás Cruz came to her, she was surprised, shook her head slightly, and immediately dismissed it, "it's just the coffee, he's addicted to this," she convinced herself. After ordering a coffee and a snack, she took a seat in the quietest part of the establishment. Frost opened her laptop and read the report while devouring the snack, then she replayed in her mind the information she had read in her office. The Mossad had finally identified the man in the shirt that Tomás had spotted, it was Ahmed al-Awlaki. Something caught the woman's attention in the report; the man was no longer working with Al Qaeda, he had been out of the terrorist organization for four years, since then there had been no news of al-Awlaki. "What the hell is this guy doing meeting with al-Hamzi?" Frost thought. Another aspect of this information aroused her curiosity; al-Hamzi had returned three days later to Mirpur Khas, the small town near Karachi, this time he was followed by a local CIA agent, who shared the effort to track the terrorist's activities. At one point, the man got on as a passenger on a motorcycle that abruptly came to pick him up. To avoid attracting attention, the agent decided to wait there to see what happened next. A little over an hour later, the subject returned and got off the motorcycle. He took a photo of the small plate of it; al-Hamzi took, almost at the same time, the bus that would take him back to the capital of Pakistan. The man on the motorcycle was not al-Awlaki, which further complicated the case. Who was it? The friends from Mossad and the CIA were working on it.

Frost thought that all that was left was to wait for the man to make another visit to Mirpur Khas; perhaps on that occasion, they could discover the cause of his frequent trips there. The exclamation of the woman at the next table woke her from her thoughts, the young woman watched, with a consternated face, the television screen. She decided to do the same; a CNN reporter reported, while in the background intense smoke could be seen, that Russian occupying forces were already in a suburb of Warsaw.

"Craig, the Russians are practically on the outskirts of Warsaw."

"It's a pity, Mr. Secretary, I saw it on the news. How serious is the situation?"

The Secretary of Defense tapped his stylus several times on his notebook.

"Very serious, we will have to pull our defense lines back at least five kilometers from Warsaw."

Eastman expressed distressed:

"Which means..."

"Giving up, in practice, half of Poland, and the Russians want more, everything seems to indicate it."

"My God..." —Eastman commented softly.

The Secretary of Defense nervously scratched his forehead several times, then looked at his interlocutor.

"Craig. What would be the consequences of using low-yield nuclear weapons?"

"Extremely worrisome, Mr. Secretary, it would lead us to a moment of greater probability of a nuclear conflict."

Fallon stood up and looked out his office at the Thames River, frowning.

"The Americans say that, on the contrary, it would reduce the probability, according to them, the mere suggestion of it would make the Russians back off."

Eastman shook his head from side to side, indicating his disagreement with the statement.

"That might have been possible in 2020 when the Americans launched the low-yield warhead, at that time the Russians did not have it; but today they do. If we add the hypersonic missile to that... the imbalance is evident, if the Americans use it, they will respond, there is no doubt."

"And... what would be the effects?"

"Low-yield warheads have a power of five to six kilotons, it's difficult to estimate the damage on a battlefield, no doubt less severe than in a populated area, everything within a hundred meters around will be destroyed, soldiers, civilians, weaponry, equipment... all, the real concern is the radioactivity, an effect that would multiply if there is an equivalent response from the Russians, and from there to..."

Fallon, still at the window, interrupted him, as if thinking out loud, said:

"To escalate to high-yield nuclear weapons there's only a small step, my God, Craig, this can end badly, very badly.

The mission to capture Valiente was postponed until after the Maghrib prayer, which is held once the sun has set. Manoudakis escorted the leader of the Greek Army's special forces group, Major Christos Metaxas; two squads from the first Greek raiding regiment had been assigned to the operation, to these were added four agents from Greek intelligence and ten members of the local police who were following them. The entry into the mosque would be made in four groups, six soldiers ahead, an intelligence agent and two police officers behind; outside, snipers from the special forces covered all possible exits, in the same way, everything within a block's radius was virtually sealed off by the police, nothing and no one, entered or left. Things happened in a matter of seconds, they raced through the mosque's garden, Metaxas gave the order to one of his subordinates to break down the main door, who without hesitation knocked it down, at a quick pace, without making noise, the group of men entered the mosque's large prayer hall, there was no one; Christos looked to his left at a closed door, with a sign, the Major indicated it to be broken down, the dry hit of the falling door was heard; in the dim light Christos turned on a flashlight, the place was uninhabited; the shrillness of a voice complaining in Greek reached the ears of those in the small room, it was the Imam, he vehemently rejected, with a loud cry, the violation of a holy place, dedicated only to reflection and prayer, Manoudakis and Metaxas went out to meet him, with bulging eyes the Imam was shouting, escorted by several soldiers.

"Who is in charge of this insult to the house of Allah and Islam? Who is it, I ask, this is unacceptable!"

Metaxas, with a firm voice, replied:

"Me. Have you prayed to your god? You're in trouble."

"What are you talking about?"

"Harboring terrorists leads to prison. You know that, right?"

"This, sir, is a place of peace, we in no way accept the use of violence."

Manoudakis looked at him intently, then asked:

"By the way. What is your name?"

The Imam's gaze radiated fury.

"Ahmet Kara, sir, and I am the Imam of this mosque."

Metaxas looked at a couple of his soldiers.

"Take Mr. Kara to his office, meanwhile, we will search for the terrorist you harbor in this holy place... Understood?"

The two soldiers grabbed, almost lifted from the ground rather, the Imam, his screams echoed in the huge prayer hall. After ordering a search in every nook of the building, Manoudakis communicated with one of his agents who was in Filippos, the restaurant, he told him to allow Dumont, Cruz, and Gallois to enter the mosque; once inside, they also assisted in the reconnaissance of the different spaces of the building. Tomás Cruz wandered through various places without finding anything, after a while, Dumont approached him for a moment.

"What do you think, Tom? The prey has eluded us, don't you think?

"Don't doubt it, Bernard, don't doubt it."

Cruz was facing Dumont, so when the Imam peeked through the door of the office where he was, Ahmet Kara could not see him, Tom noticed that he briefly looked towards a place, then sat down again, the Imam's movement caught his attention, Cruz turned around to focus his gaze on the site, it was either the mosque's exit door or the small door in the corridor, Cruz decided to snoop around a bit, then he said to Dumont, pointing with one of his hands:

"Bernard. Do you want to accompany me?"

XVII

Lieutenant Klaus Lange observed with his binoculars, shielded by the trunk of a tree and amidst a bush, in the background, the road 580 was visible, leading from Warsaw to the west of Poland, a small hill in the middle of the wooded area guaranteed him a perfect visual control of the zone, behind, camouflaged, were the Leopard 2 tanks of the second squadron of the 203rd Panzer Battalion of the German army. The last forty-eight hours had been crazy, the heavy onslaught of the Russian armored cavalry, supported by its powerful artillery and short-range missiles, had forced them the day before to retreat across the Vistula River at full speed, since then they had carried out three small retreats totaling sixteen kilometers, the NATO defense line was now about six kilometers from Warsaw, which had finally fallen into Russian hands twelve hours before. A tense calm was in the air; for two hours, a sepulchral silence had replaced the previous cacophony of explosions, bursts of gunfire, planes, and helicopters flying low; Lieutenant Lange's squad's mission was to cover the retreat of the NATO forces, the high command had determined a retreat line along highway 579, which runs from south to north through much of Poland, the group of tanks commanded by Lange was located about fourteen kilometers from it, from where the 579 ended, both north and south, an imaginary line was drawn, this marked the new line of defense, the reserve forces were now on the edge of the E75 highway, there NATO and the United States were moving all available troops and equipment; the general in charge of the defense plan, Wolfgang Heusinger, was at the command post, on the outskirts of Poznań, about one hundred ninety kilometers west of the E75. A voice interrupted Lieutenant Lange's observation:

"A bit of coffee, sir?"

"Thank you, Günther, I was indeed in need of something warm to drink."

Sergeant Günther Lang tilted the thermos to fill the cup.

"Too quiet, isn't it, sir?"

"That's right, the Russians are up to something."

"Where are they?"

"I estimate about two thousand five hundred meters away. Yes, do you see that white house?" —Lange pointed over the log, the sergeant took the binoculars to look—. "They must be there."

After observing for a moment without noticing any movement, the sergeant commented:

"We definitely got stuck with the worst part, sir, we could get trapped if we don't move to the west."

"Or what's left of our ashes if we can't contain their advance."

The sergeant seemed to sink his eyes into the binoculars.

"Something's approaching, sir."

Lange took the binoculars again.

"Damn it, sergeant, it's a drone, and it's a Russian one, coming from their position, if they see us, we're cooked."

Cruz entered the small cubicle, stopping just at the edge of the narrow door, the first glance didn't yield anything that caught his attention, then he took a couple of steps; Dumont, his friend, entered after him. Cruz now crouched down, looked from side to side of the small room, made an inventory of what was there, a sofa, flanked by several cushions on the ground, a rug, and a small table with a lamp. "Not much to see here," he thought, the man stood up and was about to leave when he suddenly stopped, Dumont, surprised, crashed into Tomás Cruz.

"Damn, Tomás. What's wrong with you?"

As if he were an automaton, Cruz turned back towards the sofa, picked up one of the cushions that served as a backrest, and lifted it, underneath there was something rolled up, next to it, a thin pillow, Tomás unrolled it, it was a mat one meter eighty long.

"This is what it's about, Bernard."

The look of bewilderment on Dumont's face was evident.

"How the hell did you notice that? Does it seem relevant to you?"

"The cushions weren't perfectly aligned, mon ami; besides, don't you find it odd to find a mat and a pillow? Why were they hidden under a cushion on a sofa? Right in the room where the imam was eagerly looking..."

Dumont shrugged and gestured with his hands, still unclear what it was about.

"Maybe the imam likes to take a nap here, or has a lover and enjoys her intimate visits here." —He let out a mocking laugh, then Dumont looked at him the same way a psychiatrist would a patient—. "Are you this paranoid about everything, Tom?"

"About almost everything, Bernard." —Cruz also let out a slight laugh, then knelt down to look under the sofa, stretched out his arm, after pulling it out, looked at what he had in hand, with the face of a TV series detective, looked at his friend, to express with a slight grimace on his lips:

"Do you find a train ticket from Subotica to Belgrade useful?"

Lange and the sergeant hid behind the log, motionless and silent for several minutes, waiting for the drone to leave, praying not to be detected; it, to their relief, changed course and returned to fly southeast, Lange watched it with binoculars until it was out of sight, then directed them southeast, at the white house, the figure of a 125 mm cannon emerged, gradually the silhouette of a T-90 tank advanced from the thick foliage serving as camouflage, Lange's eyes widened, simultaneously he could see a significant number of tanks of this model advancing.

"Damn it, Günther, the Russians are restarting the advance."

"Do we notify the command post in Poznań?"

"Yes, sergeant, and also request air support, we're going to need it. Ah! and have them reconfirm the instructions to follow."

The sergeant nodded, to sneak crouched down, on the horizon Lieutenant Lange observed the appearance of several squadrons of Russian Ka-50 attack helicopters, the only thing he managed to say in a low voice was, "Shit..., the party's started, the missing guests have arrived."

Dumont reported the news to the man from the Greek special forces and intelligence, as well as to Captain Nikos Manoudakis; the security perimeter was then expanded to fifteen blocks around, the exits from the city were also closed.

"The man apparently slept here, Bernard, but how did he leave? Did he slip away before or while the operation was being carried out?"

The Greek intelligence man entered the room, Dumont asked him about the imam:

"Has the man said anything?"

"Nothing, he insists that no one has been here, argues that many of the visitors to the mosque are foreigners, that ticket could belong to any of them."

"Ah! What a coincidence, he doesn't even believe that story himself."

Dumont indicated, playing nervously with his keychain, a small Victorinox knife, one of those with several functions, on one of the spins on his index finger, the keychain fell to the carpet, a hollow noise was heard, the three men looked at each other, Tomás immediately crouched down to move it, a wooden cover, with a rustic hemp handle, could be seen, Cruz lifted it; Dumont placed his cell phone flashlight, a narrow metal staircase descended a couple of meters, it was apparently a tunnel. Nikos Manoudakis was quite overweight, plus he was one meter ninety centimeters tall, he could run the risk of getting stuck in the entrance of the narrow tunnel of eighty by eighty centimeters, two smaller and thinner policemen were selected to inspect it and find where it led, a probe with a camera was conditioned for them to carry with them, seven minutes later, they came across a ladder similar to the entrance, a little over two meters above, a wooden cover awaited them; one of the agents climbed up to it, tried to open it, but it was not possible, something very heavy was on top of it. On the portable radio communicator, everyone heard, in the mosque room, the voice of one of them, all in Greek, Manoudakis translated in his very particular English:

"They cannot gain access to the other side, something very heavy is on top of them."

Another hoarse noise was heard on Nikos Manoudakis's radio, he listened carefully and with a look of annoyance he also replied in Greek, then the face of the corpulent captain showed surprise, then it seemed that he was asking something, Cruz, Gallois and Dumont observed and awaited the corresponding translation.

"Is something wrong, captain?" —Dumont anticipated asking.

Manoudakis replied:

"They tell me they want to return and get out of the tunnel, they are dizzy, it seems that..."

Dumont, annoyed, interrupted him:

"We have to know what's on the other side captain, they can't have gotten dizzy, they haven't been there more than fifteen minutes. Can we...?"

Cruz placed a hand on Dumont's shoulder.

"Bernard, calm down, the captain was about to tell us something else. Right, captain?"

Manoudakis, between puzzled and bored, expressed with a bulldog face:

"They are dizzy due to a penetrating smell... How strange!"

Cruz asked again:

"Smell of what, captain?"

Manoudakis glanced at him.

"Spices. How curious, isn't it?"

The memories of Tomás Cruz were activated immediately, he rewound the moment of entering Mustafá Café, he also remembered the incident with the man at the door of the place, he was behind other men who, as best as they could, carried a heavy and at the same time voluminous barrel, Tomás closed his eyes, in the image that came to his mind he saw how the man tilted his head down in a sign of apology, he raised his hands and shouted something in Greek, at that moment Cruz assumed it was about being careful with what they were carrying, then the man walked quickly to help load onto a truck, a few meters further, the huge barrel. Something else had caught Cruz's attention. What was it? He closed his eyes again... Then, the man felt an intense smell of spices in his nose.

XVIII

The Greek police and intelligence were questioning the imam and the owners and vendors of Mustafá Café, it had already been forty minutes since they entered this place and they had obtained little or nothing from them, Cruz was already starting to get impatient.

"Bernard, we're wasting time."

Dumont raised his eyebrows in a sign of helplessness.

"I know, Tom, our Greek friends aren't making much progress, I would have directed the interrogation in another way, but..."

Tomás looked at his watch.

"Bernard, Valiente eluded the security perimeters, these people wouldn't find their grandmother disguised as a terrorist, it's almost two hours since he left here, in the best of cases, he's a hundred kilometers away. Do we have a map?"

Dumont asked Gallois, who had a local connection from his cellphone to the internet, to check a map of the area. Looking at the screen, they measured the distance from there to the border via the available roads. Cruz expressed himself as if he were thinking out loud:

"OK..." —Cruz pointed with his index finger—, "there's only one border crossing with Turkey, we're a little more than one hundred kilometers from it, I don't think it'd be so naive to exit through there."

Gallois then pointed out:

"You're right, Tomas, it's not logical for him to exit through there. A bit further north maybe?"

Cruz, thoughtful, shook his head.

"No, I don't think so, time is running out for Kurchatov, he needs to leave Greece as soon as possible." —The man pointed at the screen—. "I'd bet that he attempts to cross the border through this sector." —A name appeared on it, "Perifereiaki Zoni Parkou."

Dumont asked, with a gesture of uncertainty:

"So, what do we do, Tom?"

Cruz looked up, observed the man from Greek intelligence who, at a short distance, was conversing with someone on his cellphone, then looked at Gallois.

"We need to convince your friend from the intelligence that there's nothing more to be done here, we must cover this area, which I estimate must have an extension of about twenty kilometers, if we're lucky, maybe we can prevent Kurchatov from crossing the border; and if he's already on the other side, my friends..., we can say goodbye to Valiente."

The ringtone of the cellphone sounded, waking up Bernard Dumont, who, on his way to the airbase to take the helicopter that would take them to the Turkish border, took the opportunity to nap, he, between surprised and drowsy, answered it, on the device's screen appeared an unknown number.

"Dumont speaking. Who's calling?"

"Bernard, hello, Craig Eastman."

"Salut, Craig. How are things over there?"

"Not so good, Bernard, not so good. Is Tom with you?"

"Yes. Shall I pass him to you?"

"Please."

Dumont, with a curious face, observed his companion, then passed him the cellphone, in a low voice expressed:

"Craig wants to talk to you, his voice seems to indicate that he doesn't have good news."

Cruz took the device.

"Hello, Craig."

"Tom, forgive me, there's not much time for formalities, things in Poland are going badly."

Cruz didn't understand the message at that moment, after a brief silence, he answered:

"I'm sorry, Craig, but I don't understand. What's happening?"

"I can't tell you much over the phone, friend, but, believe me, things are getting more complicated than we initially estimated."

"I still don't understand, Craig."

Another space of silence followed, Eastman was looking for a way to convey the message so Cruz would understand the seriousness of the matter related to low-yield nuclear warheads, the worried voice of Eastman returned:

"Tom. Have you ever seen the movie The Day After?"

Cruz, still not understanding what it was about, searched his memory, was he referring perhaps to The Day After Tomorrow? No, he thought, unless the crisis had triggered a new ice age, it wasn't that movie, then he remembered another from the eighties, in it, a conventional type war happened in Europe, the USSR sent tanks and troops from East Germany to the border with the Federal Republic of Germany, their purpose, that the United States would surrender West Berlin, when these did not yield, the conflict began and escalated to something bigger, Tomas then remembered the image of a huge luminous mushroom rising from the ground, his eyes closed, the man brought his other hand to his forehead.

"Yes, I remember it, Craig, it can't be... Is that what it's about?"

"Yes, Tom, don't speak of the topic with anyone, Bernard is going to receive the same call from Paris, things, as I mentioned to you, are not going well in Poland, the Russians are about to break through the NATO defense line, if they do, we can say goodbye to Poland."

"And why the alternative you mention?"

"I can't tell you much, but the Americans are considering it if we lose Poland."

"It's madness, Craig, we all know it."

"We'll talk later, Tom. How's the hunt going?"

Tomas briefed him on the state of things and where they were heading. Craig, after listening to him, indicated:

"Do whatever it takes to capture that bastard, Tom, it's the miracle we need to find out if the Russians weren't planning to stir up this mess and to convince our people and the Russians that this is just a plot to drag us into war; if we lose him, we are already warned of where we're heading."

Eastman hung up, Cruz returned the cell phone to Dumont, who, intrigued, asked:

"What's happening, Tom? You're as pale as if you had seen a ghost."

"Something like that, Bernard, something..."

Dumont's cellphone rang, almost simultaneously another ringtone was heard, it was a call for the Greek intelligence agent accompanying them If there was something that characterized Nikos Manoudakis, it was his lack of patience; the interrogation of the imam had been going on for more than two hours without any results, in a small interrogation room. The friends from Greek intelligence and the local police had designed a shift plan to interrogate him, a glass that concealed the compartment on the side allowed the others to see and record the details of it. It was the turn of the husky captain, he entered through the side door, lifted one of the chairs, turned it around, and sat down with the backrest of it against his voluptuous belly, the chair looked minuscule, the man, with the face of a grumpy ogre, observed the imam.

"Ahmet, save what's coming to you if you don't cooperate."

"I can say nothing if I know nothing."

"Stop the nonsense, Ahmet, you know a lot about your Russian friend."

The imam stared at Manoudakis.

"I demand the presence of a lawyer, my rights are being violated."

The captain nodded and then made a mocking grimace.

"I demand a lawyer... Boy, you've got guts, Ahmet, guts that lead to insolence. A lawyer? As long as you don't tell us anything, the next lawyer you'll have will be a professional interrogator in a special place, for those who threaten the security of Greece to sing like birds."

"Are you threatening me?"

"No, Ahmet, I'm not threatening, I'm just warning you that there they won't have the patience nor the preferential treatment we are giving you."

The imam crossed his arms.

"Well, Allah will surround me with courage to face the violence of those who hate Islam."

Then, the imam spat twice on the floor, Manoudakis's patience finally ran out, the man got up from the table and grabbed him by the neck, the captain's hand was so large that he had to squeeze hard for the interrogated to feel the pressure, then he lifted him, as if he were a doll, and slammed him against the wall.

"I'm sick of you, piece of garbage, either sing, Ahmet, or you won't even make it to the next interrogation!"

The imam, seized by terror, felt like he was running out of air.

"Confess, worm. Confess! Where is the Russian going? Tell me or you die!"

In the room next door, one of the intelligence officers opened the door to the corridor to interrupt the interrogation, but his boss stopped him.

"Let him be, give him a couple of minutes."

The imam, with a red face and about to burst, somehow managed to spit at him, the saliva landed on one of Manoudakis's cheeks, the captain pressed his thumb even harder on the neck, something cracked in the cramped neck of the interrogated.

"Where the hell is he headed, damn it! Tell me or you die now!"

Manoudakis lifted the poor man a bit higher, his feet no longer touching the floor, he began to kick, his face began to turn livid.

"Speak now! Where is it!"

The imam mumbled something, Manoudakis reduced the pressure and let the poor man down to the floor, then asked, bringing an ear close to his mouth:

"What are you trying to tell me, worm?"

The imam took a bit of air, then whispered something to him, Manoudakis then said:

"Repeat it, scum."

The man repeated the murmur. Manoudakis reduced the pressure on the neck and then looked at him smiling, then he told the imam:

"See how everything goes well if you behave well with your daddy?" —The captain changed the smile for a grimace of hatred in seconds—. "If you lied to me, I'll come back for you and I will have no mercy. Did you understand?"

The husky captain lifted the imam like a feather and gently sat him on the chair, then looked at the glass and raised the thumb of one of his hands.

XIX

Andrei Ivanovich Kurchátov peeked his head over the edge of the barrel, the truck they were traveling in would stop a few blocks later in a small warehouse, the Russian would put on an overalls with the logo of a company that fumigates homes and businesses to control rodents and other types of pests. Minutes later the white van with the logo of this fumigation company was leaving the place, two individuals were ahead, Kurchátov was behind; the van took a secondary road to the east, then, about ten kilometers, a truck with cows was waiting for them, there the Russian was camouflaged among them, he took a route that would take him to a small town, Sapes, two kilometers before, the truck took a secondary unpaved road that would take them to a farmhouse little more than a kilometer from the highway; a white and burgundy van, with the logo of a courier company, was waiting for them, again the corresponding overalls, the Russian behind and two individuals in front, from there they would leave to retake the highway and, after passing through another small town named Aúpa, enter highway number two towards Alexandroupolis, everything was fine until, just under a kilometer from the city, a checkpoint came into view, several cars and trucks were being searched, the driver reduced the speed, he and his companion in front looked at each other.

Rosamund Frost reviewed the new report received from the Mossad, which indicated that al-Hamzi had returned to Mirpur Khas. "That's good news," she thought. This time, he had met again with al-Awlaki at a café located in a different place from the first one. After about ten minutes of conversation, the latter left, and al-Hamzi stayed a while longer, then paid and walked to the bus station. The Mossad and CIA operatives assumed he was returning to Karachi, but a block away from the bus station, the motorcycle rider from the previous time was waiting for him. Together, they left heading north. This time they had a team to follow them, and a little over fifteen minutes later, they entered a large house on the outskirts of the town. The surveillance team waited discreetly for more than an hour, then al-Hamzi and his motorcyclist came out; the rest was routine. A block away from the bus station, al-Hamzi got off the motorcycle, walked to it and half an hour later he was taking the bus back to Karachi. "Who did al-Hamzi meet with?" she wondered. Both the Mossad and the CIA had coordinated a surveillance operation to get that answer. "I wish I could talk about this topic with...," she decided to dismiss the idea outright, yet she couldn't help but think, even if for a short moment, of Tomás Cruz.

"Sir, we have received news."

"What's happening?"

"Something related to Brave."

The calm voice of Ayman al-Zawahiri was heard:

"What has happened to our warrior?"

"He is being chased by our enemies in Greece, sir."

Ayman al-Zawahiri spoke again in a calm manner:

"Is the success of his mission in danger?"

"If Brave falls into their clutches, the enemy might learn of our plans from his lips, that is, if he doesn't withstand the interrogations."

"I am convinced that, if captured, Brave will endure any torture, he would rather die than reveal our operation." —Al-Zawahiri gently caressed his beard for a brief moment, then seemed to awaken from a lethargy—; "however, the operation has priority in this case, if it's necessary to eliminate him, give the order for it to be so. Understood?"

His assistant responded, Al-Zawahiri noticed that he did not leave the shadowy room where he was, then looked at him.

"Anything else?"

"Another development has emerged, sir."

"What?"

"Something related to that uncomfortable issue we have silenced and kept under wraps, sir."

Al-Qaeda's leader is known for his coldness, never showing the slightest emotion, this time was different, turning his face towards the person speaking to him, Al-Zawahiri's eyes widened in surprise.

"We don't have time, you must take the left path, Kemal."

The man obeyed and went down a narrow street, meanwhile, his companion placed on his cell phone Google Maps, looking at the screen, guided Kemal; an hour later, avoiding any main road or highway, they took highway number two, beyond three kilometers from Alexandroupoli, the men breathed a sigh of relief, then continued their way towards the Turkish border. The sound of a cell phone ringing surprised them, it was the cell phone of the one who had guided Kemal, the person answered in Greek, whispered something, then hung up.

"Any news?"

Kurchatov asked curiously, the man without looking at him responded:

"No, it was just a call to check how everything was going."

A cold shiver ran down Brave's back; normally, in an operation like this, where someone is being extracted from a territory, there is no further communication, this to avoid being located by their pursuers, unless it's not going well and the order is being changed to an... execution. Brave looked closely at the eyes of the person in the rearview mirror, this one, impassive, watched the road, in his mind the Russian wondered, "Is this the case?"

The Greek intelligence operative listened, in silence and with interest, to what his interlocutor was saying, then hung up and interrupted Dumont, who, with his consternated face, was still talking on his cell phone.

"Good news, Manoudakis, the police commander of Komotini managed to get the information from the imam about where the escape place would be."

The three men ran towards the Black Hawk that would take them to the Turkish border, Dumont and Cruz shouted in unison:

"Excellent!" —Dumont inquired—: "What place are we talking about?"

The man shouted back, they were already very close to the helicopter, the rotor noise was very loud, as was the air current it generated.

"I'll show you on a map once we're on board!"

The meeting room of the NATO Secretary General looked more like a gathering for a funeral, the worried faces denoted the critical moment the organization's forces were facing against the Russian attack in the Baltic countries, Poland, and Ukraine. George Carington observed General Klaus Steinhoff, chairman of the military committee of the organization.

"Klaus, please update us on the situation in Ukraine."

Steinhoff rose from his seat to explain using the huge map projected on the screen.

"Mr. Secretary, Defense Ministers, what started with the Russian capture of Luhansk and Kharkiv has now reached a point where the Russian forces are a little more than fifty kilometers from Kyiv, practically holding thirty percent of Ukrainian territory in their power."

The British Defense Secretary, Nick Fallon, asked:

"What troops are assigned to this operation, General? How many tanks and troops are we talking about?"

"Involved in this operation, which they call "Red Torch," are at least ten tank divisions, about a thousand in total, two thousand five hundred armored combat vehicles, two thousand artillery pieces, five hundred fifty aircraft, and four hundred helicopters. We are also talking about one hundred thousand soldiers already on Ukrainian territory, their rear line is ten kilometers inside their territory." —Steinhoff paused, then pointed with one of his hands on the map—. "Practically, the Sea of Azov is today under Russian naval control."

Gerard Debré, the French Defense Minister, expressed:

"What about Poland? Are we holding out?"

The general's face did not bear good news.

"Poznań fell, the defense line has now retreated about ninety kilometers from the border with Germany."

Debré asked again:

"How many tanks do they have in Poland right now?"

"They now have twelve divisions, about one thousand two hundred tanks, if we add their combat armored vehicles, we are talking about four thousand vehicles."

One of the meeting attendees, who had remained silent, threw a very uncomfortable question, several faces disapproved of the blunt manner in which it was asked.

"How long do you estimate the Russians will be at the German border?"

Steinhoff couldn't hide his annoyance in his response:

"Excuse me, sir, I think we are anticipating events. What makes you think the Russians will reach the border?"

The individual replied without showing any change:

"The facts speak for themselves and are, indeed, incontrovertible. The Russians will reach the German border in a maximum of forty-eight hours, general, you and everyone here knows it."

Carington tried to calm the mood:

"Gentlemen, this is not the time for discussions." —The NATO Secretary stared intently at the individual, Caspar Brown, he was the Deputy Defense Secretary of the United States—. "Caspar, let's not anticipate events, our forces, with your support, are making a superhuman effort to contain the Russians, and they will succeed in stopping their advance."

"George, it's not my intention to sour the meeting, but so far the Russian advance, despite our efforts, has been unstoppable." —The man paused, then looked at the Defense Secretaries and Ministers present—. "Practically, Poland is isolated from the east, with the Ukrainians losing a good portion of their territory plus the Russian alliance with the Belarusians and naval control of the Black Sea, the situation there is very complicated. I would suggest withdrawing our troops in Ukraine and Poland to Germany, the Czech Republic, and Romania."

A commotion broke out in the meeting room, again Carington intervened:

"Calm down, please, gentlemen." —The NATO Secretary General's annoyed gaze focused on Brown—. "Caspar, frankly what you suggest is unacceptable, it implies giving up on the defense of two NATO allies, it is, essentially, a defeatist stance that also gives us no guarantee that they won't decide to move forward in Germany, Romania, and the Czech Republic."

"It's actually a realistic stance, George, however, we believe there is another solution, we are sure that the Russians will immediately understand that they cannot continue advancing and doing whatever they want."

Debré intervened:

"Mr. Brown. What solution are we talking about?"

"It's inevitable, Mr. Debré, the time has come to use the W76-2."

The uproar stirred again in the room, Carington rose from his seat, his patience apparently worn out.

"What you propose is irresponsible, Caspar."

"I'm sorry, George, forty-eight hours, that's the deadline President Trump has given us. If the Russians reach the German border, we will use a package of low-yield nuclear warheads, both

Shtorm

in Poland and Ukraine, there is no other alternative to stop the Russians, and we will carry it out, make no mistake about it."

XX

"For more than seven years, America has occupied the most sacred lands of Islam..." "Plundering its riches, dictating to its rulers, humiliating its people, terrorizing the neighbors, and turning their bases on the peninsula into a spearhead to fight against the Muslim peoples nearby..." "Despite the horrendous devastation inflicted on the Iraqi people by the Crusader-Jewish alliance, and despite the astronomical number of deaths — which has exceeded one million — despite all this, the Americans attempt once again to repeat the horrendous massacres, as if the prolonged sanctions imposed after the brutal war, or the fragmentation and devastation, were not enough for them...". "Now, while the American purposes behind these wars are religious and economic, they also serve the petty state of the Jews, distracting attention from their occupation of Jerusalem and the murder of Muslims there...". "Allah, the Most High, said: 'Believers! What is the matter with you that when you are told to go forth in the cause of Allah, you cling heavily to the earth? Do

you prefer the life of this world to the Hereafter? But little is the comfort of this life, as compared with the Hereafter. If you do not go forth, He will punish you with a painful punishment and will replace you with another people, and you will not harm Him at all. For Allah has power over all things...". "Allah, the Most High, said: 'Do not falter or grieve, for you will be superior if you are true believers...'". Ayman al-Zawahiri was reminded of some phrases from the "Declaration of the Islamic Front for Jihad against Jews and Crusaders," published in 1998 and signed by Osama Bin Laden, himself, and other leaders of the so-called Islamic Jihad; this marked the beginning of Al Qaeda, from this declaration, there would be a change in strategy in the fight against the Western enemy, no longer against the "near enemy," but against the one who from afar incited, provoked, through conquest and exploitation, brothers to fight and annihilate each other. The United States and its allies, including Israel, should, as in the past were the ignoble crusaders, be defeated and annihilated. "The new field of Jihad must be Europe," declared al-Zawahiri in The Knights Under the Prophet's Banner. "Europe is and will be our new frontier, land of conquest," states al-Zawahiri in his book, published in 2001. The leader of Al Qaeda reflected sitting with his Kalashnikov by his side, his faithful companion he never parted from. "Europe will soon fall, and then, like a house of cards, the empire of evil, the one that has exported evil and apostasy, yes, the United States will be next, we will use their evil technology to inflict on them the same damage that through it the infidels have caused us," he whispered to himself, "soon will come that day, when a voice will decree its own destruction... that voice, theirs, one of their leaders will start the holocaust of their sick society, that voice will be of...," his assistant's call interrupted his thoughts.

"Sir, it's time to go, we must move from this place."

Al-Zawahiri could not stay in one place for more than three weeks, as he could be identified by American intelligence or that of its European and Israeli allies, who did not rest in determining his location, while also seeking to eliminate him; Al-Zawahiri nodded, rising with the energy of a young man, the Al Qaeda leader, walking firmly, exited the small compartment, then, without looking at his assistant, asked:

"One question, Fateh. Has the next phase of our plan started?"

"Our contact reported that it is close to beginning, sir."

Al-Zawahiri slung his Kalashnikov over his shoulder.

"When? Timing is important, it can't be delayed much."

"Within the next forty-eight hours, sir."

The light at the end of what seemed to be a labyrinth illuminated his face, Al-Zawahiri's lips revealed a smile loaded with wickedness, then he said:

"Magnificent. Do you know something, Fateh? A voice... that voice, the voice of the heretic, will be the beginning of their end."

The Black Hawk took off in the darkness of the military base in Alexandroupolis, through the intercom the man from Greek intelligence showed Cruz, Dumont, and Gallois the location that the imam had indicated to Nikos Manoudakis.

"You weren't so far off from the escape site, Tomás, it seems they plan to make it in this small lagoon further south, its name, 'Limni Ninfon', is located near a plain where a small river flows into the Aegean Sea and less than a kilometer from the Turkish border."

Cruz indicated with a stern face:

"I wouldn't neglect this area we identified to the north either, it could just be a false lure to distract us and facilitate their escape."

"Agreed," the man replied, "we have covered this and other potential escape routes."

As they flew low over the Aegean Sea, Cruz mulled over an idea that had been gnawing at his mind since he learned of Valiente's real name. Why could a Russian have ties with Al Qaeda? Besides capturing him, they would have to somehow prove his linkage to Russia And if they didn't find her? Or was it a trap to lead them to think about the responsibility of the Russians? In that case, the question arose again. Why would a Russian ally with Islamic terrorism? The man closed his eyes and remembered. What piece of the puzzle was missing in this case? His mind went back to the end of the Cold War, once the USSR shattered, the then Commonwealth of Independent States emerged, shortly after some former Soviet republics divorced from the CIS, among them Chechnya, predominantly Muslim, Azerbaijan continued in the CIS, but was also predominantly Muslim. What if Kurchatov was Muslim? It was worth investigating more about him; Tomás touched Dumont's shoulder and expressed through the helicopter intercom.

"Bernard. Could you do a favor for Rosamund?"

Dumont replied with a joke, then smiled:

"Should I send your regards? Order some flowers for her?"

Cruz squinted his eyes in a sign of sarcasm.

"Very funny, good that you're in a good mood tonight, mon ami, no, it's about something not so romantic. Could you ask her to find out Kurchatov's second surname and investigate more about his family?"

Dumont placed his right hand horizontally on one side of his forehead, then said:

"It will be a pleasure, mon colonel, although the flowers for the girl wouldn't be a bad idea."

Dumont burst into laughter. The Black Hawk's pilot gave a notice through the headsets, they had to get ready to disembark, they would soon touch ground.

Karachi is a megalopolis of more than fifteen million inhabitants, a financial and commercial center, it also brings together industries and centers for medical and computer research; with two ports on the Arabian Sea, this city is a hub of business development and the most populated city in Pakistan.

Karachi is also the operation center for the most radical Islamic terrorist groups, there and in the north of Pakistan operate these groups, which mainly intend to turn this country into a fundamentalist state; north of the city is a huge complex called North Nazimabad Town, built at the end of the fifties to house the Muslim refugees arriving from India after the independence from the United Kingdom and the subsequent partition into two countries, India and Pakistan, there, in this huge suburb, in block G, in Samar Garden, a apartment building, Rashad Sharif was working focused on his laptop; Sharif was a systems engineer graduate from the Federal Urdu University, he, a moderate Islamist, had suffered the pain of losing his father in an anti-terrorist operation carried out at the end of 2018 to search for those responsible for an attack on the Chinese consulate and a marketplace in Karachi; by mistake, his father was taken down for being considered as part of the leaders of a faction of the TTP, Tehreek-e-Taliban Pakistan, since then, the young Rashad, now approaching thirty years, had sworn, next to his grave, to avenge his death, he then began to attend a madrassa close to his home, there he learned everything he needed to know about Islam and all the necessary to hate the West and the Government of President Mamnoon Hussain even more, ally and accomplice of the United States in the extermination of the Islamic faith. The man was working on his computer when the sound of a received message on Telegram caught his attention, he read it, "You must be aware of the news, soon the word must be heard," Sharif scratched his chin, then decided to turn on the television, he tuned into CNN, Nick Robertson reported from a small town in Poland, Rzepin, that the Russian attack front was now less than thirty kilometers from there, which put the Russian army just forty kilometers from the German border; Sharif turned off the TV, he needed to make some last adjustments, he clicked on the screen of his computer with his wireless mouse, Sharif smiled, the image of the software he had designed recently and that had a lot to do with what was happening in Poland was that of Donald Duck.

Rosamund Frost observed the decrypted message on her computer, made a gesture of strangeness, however, she proceeded to check in Kurchatov's file, only a surname appeared, she then checked the rest of the information about him, there was nothing about him in the CIA, DGSE, or Mossad archives; Frost looked at her watch, "there could still be someone in the Mossad offices, I'm going to send them a message asking for more details about the Russian's family and his second surname," she thought, typed the message, and sent it through the encryption program, decided to go to the cafeteria to look for something to eat and a hot tea to drink, while walking down the corridor to it, the woman smiled remembering the last part of the message received from Dumont, "Tom sends you many warm hugs," this message, which Cruz was unaware of, as well as a smile, caused Rosamund an unexpected joy; while she was serving the tea and gobbling down a sandwich, she questioned herself about the reason for the sudden sensation of enthusiasm that engulfed her when she read that part of the message. "We will have to find out when Tom returns," she told herself, however, her heart, in opposition to her rational side, told her that it was valid to give herself a chance with Cruz. "Should I trust you?" she wondered, shrugged her shoulders, and left the small cafeteria carrying the tea cup. "Bah! What the hell. Why not try it?" Back at her cubicle, she noticed that her computer screen was flickering, a message had arrived, she took a seat and opened it, it was the response from her friends at the Mossad, she read it carefully, it said, "Full name of the subject: Andrei Ivanovich Kurchatov Tsarnaev, our apologies, an inadvertent error from our agent, he thought Ivanovich was the first surname, his father is of Russian origin, born in Sim, Chelyabinsk; his mother was born in Argun, Chechnya." The woman brought one of her hands to her mouth in a gesture of astonishment. "Chechnya? I must inform this novelty immediately." She drafted the report and ran off to the elevator.

XXI

Kurchatov got out of the car, they had left the highway for an unpaved path, which they traveled for about ten minutes, now it was necessary for him and his escorts to walk a couple of kilometers to the point where they would meet with two Turkish guides who would take Valiente to Turkish territory; in the middle of a bush, they parked the car and covered it with some branches to prevent it from being detected from a short distance, then, in the dark night, he and his companions put on their night vision goggles, the walk to the meeting point took half an hour, the three men positioned themselves behind some bushes about fifty meters away to wait for the signal from the companions with whom they would meet. Eight minutes later, a series of short light signals could be seen, in Morse code it meant they were in the agreed place, this meant they would travel just under five hundred meters to the north bank of a river, its name, Maritsa; once they were on the other side of it, just over two kilometers would separate Kurchatov from Turkish soil. The three men met with one of the guides, once at the riverbank, the four individuals swam the fifty meters to reach the opposite shore, after taking a small break, the second Turkish guide joined them, then they all started the journey towards the border, they had not walked a hundred meters when they saw a faint light heading straight in their direction, one of them whispered for them to immediately lie down on the ground.

Tomás Cruz and a member of Greek intelligence observed the dark landscape through their night vision goggles, once on land, they decided to divide into four groups of two to better cover the extensive territory, the best place to wait for them was on the south side of Maritsa River, it had two branches, they would be waiting for Valiente at the south branch of this river, the Black Hawk had touched the ground about four kilometers southwest of Limni Nimfon lagoon, just three hundred meters from the border, Cruz indicated on the map the place where they should patrol in hopes of being able to find the Russian, after walking for more than an hour and a half, they decided to take a break, Cruz and his companion checked the map to locate the place, for this, they turned on a small flashlight, Tomás, through some signs, indicated that they should walk about fifty meters to the north, they were about to do so when at that moment the noise of something falling to the ground was heard, the men immediately turned off the light, decided to put on their night vision goggles again; Tomás Cruz took the weapon he had been given upon descending from the helicopter.

Kurchatov muttered something resembling the word damn. Their Quran book and Tasbih, contained in a plastic bag, fell right onto a stone on the ground, causing a brief but loud noise. The five individuals, lying on the ground, looked at each other. Valiente looked forward, the dim light was no longer there, the man whispered:

"What do we do now?"

One of the Turkish guides replied softly:

"The best thing is to split into two groups, you, Kemal, and I will go to our left."

The man pointed to the east of where they were.

"You." —The individual looked at the other escort from Kurchátov—, "go with Onur to the right. That would take them to the southwest of their position."

The man asked quietly:

—Understood?

All nodded, crouching in the darkness, they set off.

Tomás Cruz and his companion from Greek intelligence were still lying on the ground. Through the night vision goggles, Tomás thought he saw a movement, he moved the goggles slightly to his right, out of the corner of his eye he looked at his companion, who seemed not to have noticed it; he unsecured the weapon, as always, his mind, which at that moment was working at full speed, was about to coordinate the movements of his body with his instincts. "If what moved is Valiente, he's a short distance from the border, it's now or never," he thought, in a fraction of seconds his legs, like a spring, leaped forward propelling his body in the direction of the movement.

Kurchátov ran hunched behind the Turk, flanked by Kemal, the snap of a branch was heard, Kemal whispered a curse in Greek, drew his pistol, and aimed toward the noise, the guide violently grabbed his arm and said softly:

"Are you stupid, Kemal? Keep running, damn it."

The three men continued their course towards the border, at that moment, just over a kilometer separated them from Turkish soil, then the powerful and dry noise of a shot was heard, Kurchátov watched in horror as the Turkish guide fell to the ground, he let out a moan of pain.

Tomás Cruz observed through the goggles three indistinct shapes moving, the noise of a branch he accidentally stepped on made a huge noise in the midst of the night's silence, without thinking he shot at the first shape, Cruz must have been just over ten meters away from where they were, he crouched behind a bush, he looked a few meters ahead, the green colored digital image of a bush was right in front, if he took that direction, he would arrive right behind where he saw the shapes moving, almost lying on the ground he headed there, what he saw... chilled his blood.

The Turkish guide received the shot on the right side of his back, the trajectory of the bullet, which was inclined from below upwards, penetrated one of his lungs, the intense pain, coupled with the lack of air, left the man lying on the ground in the middle of a growing pool of blood. Kemal looked through the scope, no one was approaching; to his agitated brain came the memory of the instruction received hours before, "If there's danger, the passenger must be eliminated," without thinking he took his gun, glanced sideways and did not see the Russian, a shiver ran through his body, he was about to turn his head to the right when he saw the man kneeling, Kurchátov, with a low but firm voice, expressed:

"Shoot, Kemal, all is lost."

Kemal nodded slowly, unsecured the revolver and placed it near his forehead, he slowly squeezed the trigger and said:

"I'm very sorry."

The shot was heard, powerful and loud, several hundred meters around, Kurchátov heard it, but if death was like this, it didn't hurt; incredulously, he raised his eyes to look at his executioner, Kemal was grimacing in pain, slowly he collapsed to the ground, the Russian then heard behind him, a voice in English:

"Hello, Valiente."

Kurchátov, without turning around, replied in Arabic:

"Allah is great."

Cruz was in a position perpendicular to the Russian, he approached and lightly kicked Kemal's body to see if he was alive, he did not move, with a foot he moved several meters the weapon from him, then he crouched down and took his pulse, he was lifeless; pointing at him with his weapon, intrigued, he asked:

"Allah is great? Aren't you Russian, Andrei Ivanovich?"

Cruz noticed through the scope a slight tremor in the Russian's body, however, he did not respond. Tomás spoke again, there was no time to lose.

"What's the purpose of all this, Andrei Ivanovich? If you help us, you might save yourself from a firing squad, or... from Guantanamo, I think the wall is a better option, they won't treat you very well in Guantanamo."

Kurchátov decided to reply in English, while imperceptibly and slowly, he searched for the pistol on his belt, visually Cruz could not see this movement.

"Allah always brings us unexpected surprises. Is it not so, infidel?"

"Come on, Andrei, tell me what all this is about, the alternative of a world at war is not good for anyone, including your people."

"The alternative of a world at war was chosen by the West, not us; children and the elderly, our women and our finest men have died due to the violence of the bombs that have been dropped on our land." —The man paused—, "our houses, the fields filled with crops, the animals that gave us milk and meat, destroyed because of your missiles and bombers, we have suffered persecution and war for decades, don't come to talk to me about war..., infidel."

As he spoke, Valiente touched the rough butt of the pistol, ran over it to look for the safety, found it, then slowly slid it with his index finger.

"So should the children and women of the West pay for it? Should one madness follow another? It makes no sense, Andrei Ivanovich."

"We must all pay the cost of war, infidel, everyone..."

Kurchátov tilted his body and threw himself to the ground, the noise of the gunshot was heard.

XXII

"Is Kurchátov's mother Chechen?"

"One hundred percent sure of it, sir, and she practices Islam."

The director of MI6 scratched the bottom of his chin, looked at Frost, beside him stood Craig Eastman.

"My God. How is the hunt for Kurchátov going in Greece?"

"The last information we received indicates that he was on the ground and very close to where he would presumably flee to Turkish territory."

For a couple of seconds, John Mansfield's hand stayed on his mouth, hiding it, then he rubbed, uncomfortably, his right cheek.

"Do you know something? The news about Kurchátov gives us an indication that all this could be part of a plot hatched by the people from Al Qaeda; however, this is still not conclusive, after all, the man is Russian. Isn't that right?"

Eastman replied:

"It is clear, sir, that we need Kurchátov to tell us his connection with the people from Al Qaeda and give us details of their plans."

Mansfield, with a stern face, looked out the window of the office, after a short silence, he expressed with his lost gaze, it seemed he was thinking aloud:

"We need him, gentlemen, if we want to avoid the worst that is already coming our way, and we need him alive, dead or... escaped does us no good."

Tomás Cruz could barely see Kurchátov's rapid movement, a flash left him momentarily without vision, the night vision goggles turned entirely green, he felt a slight pinch in his right arm, instinctively threw himself to the ground and took off the goggles. In the darkness, he heard Bernard Dumont:

"Are you okay, Tom?"

Cruz complained in French:

"Why the hell did you take so long?"

"You have to add drama to life, Tom."

Dumont expressed after a small chuckle, two of the Greek intelligence men, who accompanied the Frenchman, approached the Russian, signaled with a thumb up, the man was alive and conscious, immediately they put handcuffs on him; Dumont breathed a sigh of relief, helped Cruz up to then approach Kurchátov.

"Excellent, thank goodness, we didn't have to kill you, ruskie." —Dumont then observed with a flashlight his friend's arm, made a gesture of relief—. "That bullet passed close, Tom."

A slight wound bled on the upper right arm of Cruz, he took out his handkerchief and placed it on top, pressing lightly, that hurt a bit, Cruz held his breath for a moment, then looked at his friend.

"Fortunately, weeds never die. And now? What do we do with the Russian?"

Dumont looked at him for a moment, seemed not to understand Cruz's comment about the weeds, let it go, things were not to waste time on conversations.

"We have to have a Q&A session with our dear Valiente."

The afternoon, though sunny, was cool in London, Craig Eastman was having a coffee on one of the terraces of MI6 headquarters, took a brief moment of rest to drink a cup. "It's unbelievable, Tom created in me an addiction heretofore unknown. Coffee," he smiled, while thinking about it, the memory of an old Russian friend came to mind, he had taught him to drink vodka and had gotten him into the universe of this drink; now at least once a week, he drank a shot of Russian Standard Imperia or Absolut Premium with his wife. Once, at a defense conference in Helsinki, they had carried out a tasting of several brands, "good thing we were at the hotel bar, in the end, we had to be escorted to our rooms by one of the bellboys." That memory caused a laugh in Eastman. Anatoli Kolesnikov "How is Anatoli doing?" he thought;

months ago, he had written to congratulate him on his appointment as advisor to the Ministry of Defense of his country. Kolesnikov was highly esteemed in the Russian government, both President Putin and the current minister continuously sought his advice on matters of defense and strategy. Kolesnikov, like Eastman, had written several books on military history and defense, and was also a professor at the General Staff Military Academy, the Frunze Military Academy, and other think tanks on these subjects. A phrase came to Eastman's mind, it had been mentioned in one of his favorite movies, The Sum of All Fears, based on a novel by Tom Clancy, in it, CIA Director William Cabot, played by Morgan Freeman, says, "To keep the back channels open, in hopes of staving off a disaster." Eastman wondered, "Could talking to Anatoli be a way to stop this absurd conflict? How would I do it? Would he listen to me? To be able to do that," he thought, "we would first have to resolve the question posed by Valiant and Al Qaeda's role in all this mess"; the man drank the last sip of his coffee, stood up from his seat, and prepared to enter the building, before leaving the disposable cup in the trash, then he said softly, "Damn, Tom, we need Bernard and you to make this guy talk."

The interrogation was not going well, Kurchatov either remained silent or answered evasively. Dawn was approaching, and the long hours of questioning and intimidation yielded no fruits. Dumont, with pronounced dark circles under his eyes, approached Tomás Cruz, who, as usual, was drinking a cup of coffee.

"This idiot is not cooperating, Tom."

Another individual from Greek intelligence entered the room where the Russian was, after twenty minutes, he came out and shook his head side to side in a sign of helplessness; Dumont, sitting in the long corridor next to Cruz, said:

"What if we use truth serum?"

Cruz looked at him skeptically.

"That only happens in the movies, Bernard..., it's useless."

"So, what on earth do you suggest? We have to do something!"

Cruz rubbed his head for a moment, then looked at his friend.

"Bernard. What's the name of the police chief in Alexandroupolis?"

"Hmm..., let me remember. Makukakis maybe?"

Cruz smiled.

"I remembered, Nikos Manoudakis. What if we try it with our friend the police chief? It worked with the imam."

Forty minutes later, the burly police chief was giving a thumbs up and a slight smile before entering the room; that face automatically changed to that of a furious Rottweiler when he opened the door.

The tension in the crisis room located in the basement of the west wing of the White House was evident, on the large screen, satellite images of the Russian army's movements, already just ten kilometers from the Polish border with Germany, could be seen. President Trump inquired with a furrowed brow:

"How long will it be before the Russians are at the border?"

The acting Secretary of Defense, Mark Esper, indicated:

"Less than twenty-four hours, Mr. President."

Donald Trump grumbled:

"There's no alternative, we have to use the low-yield nuclear warheads."

Mike Pompeo, the Secretary of State, replied to the president:

"Mr. President. Wouldn't it be too hasty to do so? This could lead us to the escalation of a nuclear conflict with long-range missiles of greater destructive power."

"Tell that to the Russians, Mike, they are the ones who started this party."

Pompeo insisted:

"Mr. President, if this ends in a nuclear escalation, it will be the American citizens who pay the price for Russian madness."

Trump made the typical grimace of annoyance, pursed his lips, and looked towards the ceiling.

"And if we do nothing, Europe, and then America, will be at the mercy of Russian ambition. No, this is not the time to show weakness in front of Putin, Mike."

The president looked again at his Secretary of Defense.

"Mark, where are our short-range missiles located?"

"Germany, United Kingdom, and Italy."

"Very well, Mark, order them to be installed in our planes and have them, from now on, on maximum alert."

XXIII

A series of thunderous noises were heard in the interrogation room, followed by short periods of silence, then the sounds of banging and screeching returned; screams, followed by long moans, continued to be heard for several more minutes, after that, a succession of hits preceded a prolonged scream and several words in a tone of evident suffering, then silence once again took over the room; Dumont, Cruz, and the intelligence people exchanged looks, one of the Greek subjects accompanying them rose to open the door and take a look when the burly Nikos Manoudakis got ahead of him, his face of frustration said it all.

"The damn guy won't cooperate, I need something to motivate him to talk. Do you have photos of his family? Children, wife. Is his mother still alive?"

Dumont and Cruz looked at each other, the former replied:

"Let me check with our people."

Bernard Dumont contacted Frost, who immediately set about gathering more information about Kurchátov. Forty minutes later, it arrived, and the Frenchman handed it to the Greek, who smiled upon seeing it, and immediately entered the room where the terrorist was dozing after the last session of painful interrogation. Manoudakis took the pitcher of water and poured a glass, then emptied its contents onto the face of the interrogated man.

"Wake up, angel, I have more questions for you."

Kurchátov, groggy, replied:

"I will not answer anything, you can kill me now if you wish, I'm not afraid of death."

The Greek policeman took a chair and moved it close to where the terrorist was, then he took a seat.

"Aren't you afraid of death, you little vermin? Who then can be afraid of death? Would the death of someone scare you? For example, that of your mother?"

The terrorist's face turned to one of infinite rage. Manoudakis noticed it immediately; he had to take advantage of his moment of emotional vulnerability.

"Aimani Kurchátov Tsarnaev..., age, sixty-seven, mmm... do you want more data about your dear little mommy? I have her address in Chelyabinsk, ah, I want to show you something else."

Manoudakis, with a satisfied face, slowly pulled out a sheet, on it, in its upper right corner, could be seen a photograph, the eyes of the interrogated filled with rage, tears began to descend down his cheeks.

"Your mommy still looks good..., she could live a few more years if you cooperate."

Kurchátov, his face about to explode, replied:

"If you touch a single finger on her and I'll kill you, damn son of a bitch."

Manoudakis did not let him finish, he gave him a strong slap.

"We are going to touch more than a finger, piece of trash, either you tell me what you know, or I take the phone; the Russians already know about your shenanigans, filthy worm, a few Federal Security Service agents are a block away from your lovely mommy's house." - In horribly pronounced Russian, the Greek leaned in to whisper very slowly: "Lyunblinskaya Ulitsa and Plastkaya Ulitsa, house number twenty-three... that's the address of our dear Aimani. What could she be doing at this time? Preparing what could be her last dinner? Tell me everything you know or your mom dies in a matter of minutes!"

"Go to hell, shitty cop."

Manoudakis pursed his lips and nodded several times, then took the cellphone and dialed a number, on the other side, an agent at the Komotini station answered, this one, surprised, listened to his boss say:

"Mikhail, eliminate her."

The policeman managed to hear another voice yelling:

"Wait, let's talk!"

A few thumps and screams were heard; sitting in the uncomfortable chairs on the side of the building corridor, Cruz,

Dumont, and the intelligence people were waiting; Manoudakis came out, his expression of delight indicated that now the interrogation had been successful.

"All of them, my friends, all without exception end up singing like tender little birds with me."

Dumont let out a sigh of relief.

"C'est magnifique, monsieur! What did he tell you?"

"He works for Al-Qaeda, there's no doubt about it, he confessed that his contact with the group was a certain Buazaui."

Cruz then said:

"What about the Russians? Are they involved in this?"

Manoudakis looked over his glasses.

"That cost a little more for him to tell me, in the end, he yelled..., sorry, he indicated to me, that they were not involved."

"Did he say anything about Koslov? Why meet with him then?"

"The redhead couldn't resist my charms, he confessed it was a maneuver to make it appear they were in the game."

"Redhead? Goodness, this Greek is quite something," thought Dumont, then he pressed on:

"Did the man say anything else?"

"No, the little bird was very exhausted from the interrogation, he sleeps the sleep of the just." The giant tidied up his black tie halfway and heavily stood up to shake everyone's hand, then headed down the long corridor towards the exit, before leaving he turned around to loudly say:

"Hey, my friends, you should name me the chief of CIA interrogations! See ya!"

"Sir, something unexpected has occurred just outside Warsaw."

General Valeri Karpov was enjoying his lunch, a succulent pelmeni which reminded him of lunches at his grandmother's house, accompanied by a glass of white wine produced in Stavropol; things were going well, the campaign couldn't be more successful, in less than a week, the forces under his command had advanced from the Belarusian border to practically ten kilometers from Germany, "Berlin is within our sights, just over seventy kilometers away, it's time to take what was ours," thought Karpov while taking a sip of wine, the senior officer looked disdainfully at his aide, Colonel Mikhail Bromkovski.

"What's happening, Mikhail Eduardovich?"

"Sir, a German tank brigade is attacking our rear."

Karpov, worried, put his glass on the table.

"Do we have casualties?"

"Numerous, sir."

"When did they start the attack?"

"Just over half an hour ago, sir."

"This is undoubtedly an unexpected event, Mikhail."

Karpov stood up from the dining table to check the map in the huge attached campaign tent, where the command room was located.

"Sir, this attack is accompanied by artillery and anti-tank weapons."

After looking at the map, Karpov asked:

"But where did the scoundrels come from?"

A call came into the Russian Twentieth Army command communications team, Bromkovski took the handset, after listening, he looked at his superior.

"Sir, the German tank brigade is receiving NATO air support, our rear line is in danger."

General Karpov, with a face of annoyance, shook his head from side to side, then ordered:

"Damn it, Mikhail Eduardovich, order our forces to stop advancing towards Germany and let's take care of finishing off these inconvenient Germans. Inform them that our planes eliminate the air attack."

"What is now the distance to the German border of the Russian troops?"

President Trump inquired with annoyance, it was clear he detested this kind of meetings, they were long and exhausting for him, requiring a patience he did not possess; Trump felt comfortable in scenarios where he was in control of what was happening and things came to him quickly; in this, as in other moments of his presidency, events didn't seem to adhere to his plans. The Secretary of Defense responded:

"Less than ten kilometers, sir."

Donald Trump thought for a moment about the consequences of his decision. Was this what he was looking for when he opted for the presidency? Would this be his legacy? A world at war? Not any war, a nuclear one, "it is quite different to determine the profitability level of a real estate project in New York than this mess of a nuclear escalation," he said to himself, a comforting thought came to his mind, he was the right person for this moment, "history placed me here precisely because of it, I am the only one who has the balls to make a decision as critical as this, it requires character, Obama wouldn't have the nerve I have to make a decision of this kind," he reflected, then looked at his Secretary of Defense and said:

"The time has come, Mark, history demands our leadership, it calls us to teach the Russians a lesson through a nuclear weapon, may God help us in this mission."

"Does that mean we deploy our bombers with nuclear weapons, Mr. President?"

Trump looked at the map on the giant screen in front of him.

"That's right, Mark, I authorize the deployment of our bombers from the United Kingdom and support from our bases in Germany and Italy, let them be in position and wait for my order to strike the designated targets."

The five F35A fighter jets waited for the order to take off, above, at twenty-five thousand feet, two squadrons of F16Es were waiting for them; the Lightning IIs gave full power to their engines to take off from the runway of Spangdahlem Air Base, in the west of Germany. Minutes later, three F35s took off from Aviano Air

Base, in the northeast of Italy; similarly, a squadron of F16Es would escort them to the place where they should await orders to fire at the assigned targets; their mission was to create a distracting operation that would allow the two B52H bombers, from different altitudes and geographical positions and escorted by several F16s, to attack points not yet identified in Polish territory. The crews of the two B52 Stratofortresses awaited the takeoff order and reviewed the last details of the mission in the operations room at the Royal Air Force base in Fairford, Gloucestershire, in the southwest of the United Kingdom.

The French Air Force's Falcon 2000 LX flew at a height of forty-nine thousand feet; upon boarding, the aircraft's pilot had informed Dumont and Cruz of a change in plans – they would land in Paris, where they would meet with Eastman and Frost. A sort of mini-summit would take place between the directors of the DGSE and MI6, commissioned by the governments of both countries due to the critical conditions of the German border with Poland. Dumont rose from his seat to fetch some packets of peanuts and something to drink.

"Jean Claude was right, Tom, the bastards from Al Qaeda were involved in this mess, he did well in telling you."

"Why did J.C. do well?"

Cruz asked curiously, as Dumont brought over the water bottles and several packets of peanuts.

"You know how bureaucratic we can be sometimes in intelligence agencies, with J.C. in the clinic, this would surely have been lost in a file as a possible cause and it would have stayed there, in the darkness of a metallic drawer full of folders. Fortunately, you took care of moving the matter."

Cruz opened one of the peanut packets and began to eat some, then squinted his eyes to say:

"Thanks, Bernard, however, there's something that worries me, verifying the theory of Al Qaeda's plan to lead us into a war is all well and good, but how do we tell the Russians? How can we convince them of it?"

Dumont looked at him with a reproachful look.

"Tom, we've just traveled half of Greece to chase and capture Valiente, thanks to our bulky Greek policeman, we got the information we were looking for, enjoy the moment."

Cruz reclined in the comfortable chair of the executive plane.

"The world is about to go into nuclear war, Bernard, there's no moment to enjoy."

Dumont opened the water bottle and took a sip, seemed to remember something, then smiled, looking at the ceiling of the plane.

"You know something, Tom? Jean Claude, who as you know is an avid reader of spy and war novels, always says that the cases we get involved in are like those novels, each chapter has a part of the path to its conclusion."—The man paused, took another sip, then said—:"If you ask me now, I have no idea where we are going or how we will solve it, at the moment we don't know how the hell this damn mess will end, but, perhaps, in the next chapter, we will find the answers that allow us to reach its solution."

Dumont looked out the window at the orange hue of the sky, which was accompanied at the top by a blue that varied from deep, almost black, to a light blue, before merging with the elongated orange strip, he turned his face to mention to Tomás Cruz the beautiful sunrise that was hinted at, Cruz slept deeply and

Shtorm

peacefully; "it's time to sleep a bit," he said to himself, "the awaited chapter may not end well."

XXIV

Lieutenant Klaus Lange was overwhelmed, in the small forest, fleeing the Russian onslaught, a second battalion of tanks had been gathered, this added to small groups of motorized infantry, artillery, and infantry troops with anti-tank weapons, in practice, it was a complete brigade; he was the senior officer, so all the present officers and the rest of the troops looked at him to follow the next actions to develop. Lange tried to disguise his nervousness, however, he couldn't help but swallow hard, then asked for a map to observe the terrain, while thinking about how to lead the difficult moment. The voice of a sergeant was heard in the distance:

"Sir, we have a couple of small drones, we could take a look. Don't you think?"

Lange looked into the distance to see who it was, after locating the non-commissioned officer, he answered:

"Good idea, sergeant, let's send the two drones to have a better perspective of the Russian movements."

The drones returned half an hour later, Lange and the other officers had a clearer idea of where the Russians were and what their movements were about, in a short meeting, before starting the counterattack, the lieutenant addressed his men:

"Does anyone remember or know who Michael Wittmann was?"

A respectful silence was heard, the voice of a soldier interrupted:

"The best tank commander of all times, sir! He destroyed more than twenty British tanks during the D-Day landings in Normandy."
"Very well, soldier, Captain Michael Wittmann was a brave war hero in World War II. He masterfully combined, with his courage, the three factors that a man of armored cavalry must know how to handle: armor, mobility, and armament, plus a decisive element in tank warfare, eliminating as many anti-tank weapons as possible. Gentlemen, we will have to put these four skills into practice today; without a doubt, the Russians outnumber us, but today, with our bravery and expertise, we will show them that we are better

fighters than they are and we will make sure to kick their butts. Do we agree?"

A barrage of cheers was heard, the actions on the battlefield that Lange and his group of brave fighters would carry out could well change the course of the battle for the control of Poland.

Once the Falcon 2000 touched down at Le Bourget Airport, northwest of Paris, a helicopter was waiting for Dumont and Cruz to take them to the DGSE offices; once aboard, the Super Puma immediately took off. Ten minutes later, it landed on the helipad of the General Directorate for External Security, where a sergeant from the French army was waiting for them and guided them to the office of Pierre Cousseran, its director, who came out to greet them at the door of the meeting room.

"Welcome, good work, gentlemen."

Cousseran showed them where to sit. Also present in the room were the director of MI6, the French Minister of Defense, as well as the Secretary of Defense of the United Kingdom, and the rest of the team. Cruz managed to exchange a greeting glance with

Rosamund Frost; without even sitting down, the DGSE director stated:

"Life is very complex, and ironic. Now that we have managed to untangle the enigma of Valiant, we find ourselves in the midst of a case that places the Russians in control of all of Poland, just ten kilometers from the German border, with more than forty percent of Ukrainian territory, not to mention the Baltic countries." Cousseran made a brief pause, "to make matters worse."

John Mansfield, the director of MI6, finished Cousseran's sentence:

"We were warned, what we did not think is that they would actually do it, despite our objections, the Americans are deploying B52 bombers to launch low-yield nuclear warheads in Poland, with which they believe they will deter the Russians from advancing into German territory."

"Which is undoubtedly a mistake."

Expressed with a look of concern, Craig Eastman, Tomás Cruz then suggested:

"In complex situations, equally difficult solutions, we have to talk to the Russians then."

The French Minister of Defense, Gerard Debré, raised his eyebrows.

"Good point, Monsieur Cruz. How do we do it? We practically have all communication channels with them closed."

Nick Fallon tapped his fingers on the table.

"It would have to be someone with access to the Ministry of Defense or Putin himself, we don't have time to waste on failed contacts."

Eastman barely heard the phrase "communication channels" and thought of Anatoli Kolesnikov. Could he be the way to effectively communicate with the Russians? The man, somewhat undecided, decided to indicate:

"Gentlemen, I believe I may have the person to contact in Russia."

Anatoli Kolesnikov was born in Moscow on January 21, 1962, the son of a prominent military man, whose family in turn had a long history of service to the Rodina's Army, both for the Red Army and for the new Russian Federation Army. Kolesnikov obtained, in 1983, the rank of second lieutenant at one of the Suvorov military academies; then he simultaneously studied business administration at Moscow University, where he graduated as an administrator in 1987. With his father's help, he entered, in 1988, still without the rank of captain, the military strategy and defense course at the university, where he would later become a professor, the Russian General Staff Military Academy. One of his professors would be then Lieutenant Colonel Sergei Serdiukov, today the Defense Minister, with whom he established a relationship similar to that of a father to his son. In December 1999, when Vladimir Putin took over the reins of the Russian government as interim president, Kolesnikov was a recently promoted general. Putin had already taken a great liking and respect for Colonel Kolesnikov, as he had played a leading and successful role in the Second Chechen War; his mentor, General Serdiukov, with Putin's approval, appointed Major General Anatoli Kolesnikov as commander of the RVSN RF (Strategic Missile Troops of the Russian Federation), something unprecedented since this position was normally held by a Colonel General, two ranks higher than him. As the commander of the strategic missile forces, which included not only medium and long-range land missiles but also bombers and submarines with nuclear strategic and tactical weapon deployment, Kolesnikov developed, despite significant budget restrictions, an ambitious modernization plan that allowed the Russian Federation to maintain a deterrent power against its main rival, the United States. In 2005, Lieutenant General Kolesnikov was appointed by Putin as the director of the FSB (Federal Security Service of the Russian Federation), which replaced the KGB of the former USSR, a position he held until 2008, when he resigned due to personal reasons from the military career and from the FSB leadership; Putin, and Serdiukov, appointed him as an advisor to the powerful Security Council of the Russian Federation. If there was a man in Russia close to power and with extensive knowledge of the security and defense of his country, it was Anatoly Kolesnikov, a member of the select group of people close to Vladimir Putin and of his mentor, the current Minister of Defense; Kolesnikov was also considered a moderate, one of those who could afford to refute and present, with solid arguments, proposals for a less conflictive policy with Europe and the West, despite sometimes not convincing the Russian president, this was one of the reasons Kolesnikov enjoyed his trust; "It's always good to listen to another point of view, even if afterwards I do exactly the opposite," Putin would sometimes say, half jokingly, half seriously. Late at night, during a break from the

Security Council, which did not rest in these days of conflict, Kolesnikov's phone emitted a sound, he, who was taking a tea and tasting a cookie, checked the screen, it was a message on his WhatsApp, he clicked on it, Kolesnikov squinted and brought the phone closer to him in surprise, it was a message from his great friend, Craig Eastman.

"Do you think the man will answer, Craig?"

Tomás Cruz asked with pessimism, the meeting that had just ended had not been free from a strong discussion regarding contacting Kolesnikov, some, like the French Minister of Defense, considered it a mistake, for him, Kolesnikov was the brain that had convinced Putin to carry out the whole invasion operation of the Baltic countries, Poland, and Ukraine; "Gentlemen, you will remember me," Debré said with irritation, "it is, no more no less, like making a call to the devil." Eastman exhaled strongly.

"I don't know, Tom. Do you know? I am sure that Anatoly will want to answer me, but sometimes, no matter how convinced we are to do something, the circumstances around us force us to do the opposite of what we wish."

"Is it true that he was the man behind all this Russian madness?"

Eastman made an uncertain grimace.

"Yes and no, I know him well, I think, and I know that he has always considered it a mistake to lose the Baltic countries, they should never have, in his opinion, isolated Kaliningrad, from that perspective I am convinced that he designed the strategy and everything that allowed the operation there to develop, I also consider that he had a lot to do with Ukraine." The man took a breath and then released it strongly. "As for Poland... Hmm, I'm not so sure that Anatoly agrees with its benefits."

Both were having coffee at a table located in a corner of a café specially opened for everyone present at the meeting; Cousseran, Mansfield, and the two defense officials from France and the United Kingdom had momentarily suspended it due to some important news they were yet unaware of. Tomás Cruz threw another question:

"If your friend doesn't answer us, what do you think will happen, Craig?"

Eastman raised his eyebrows, then nervously scratched his forehead.

Shtorm

"The apocalypse, Tom, nothing less than the beginning of the end of everything we have known and believed to have until now."

XXV

Lange, who had ordered complete silence until then, devised a crafty way to order the anti-tank artillery batteries hidden in the forest to start the attack; over the radio, two brief sounds were heard, or two dots in Morse code, which meant the I. Immediately a baptism of fire fell upon the Russian tanks that were covering the rearguard line a few kilometers from Warsaw. An hour and a half earlier, Lieutenant Lange had ordered a cryptic message to be sent to his communications officer through the emergency communications system. It requested aerial support at the start of the operation at specified coordinates. The officer complied, and in the early dawn of that morning, NATO's high command received an unexpected communication from within Poland.

Several Russian artillery positions and tanks exploded into pieces; taken by surprise, they began trying to locate the source of the attack. A scattered group of ADIM—Automated Direct or Indirect Fire Mortar—which changed location after firing, launched a second volley. The Russians suffered human and equipment losses from the impacts. For fifteen minutes, the Russians received an intense baptism of fire without knowing precisely where the attack was coming from.

The element of surprise was essential. Lange and the rest of the two tank battalions watched through their binoculars from their Leopard 2s; their tank, like the others, was buried on the slope of a small hill, all the 120mm guns of the Leopards aimed at a previously determined specific target; after the first attack, the Morse code signal of two dots was then heard again, a deep roar, that of all the German tanks' guns roaring fire, followed five seconds later by a series of LAHAT anti-tank missiles swiftly heading towards their targets, located more than five kilometers away. Once the barrage was completed, the tank group surged forward to move out of their hiding place.

The communications operator at the advanced command post couldn't believe the message he was reading, which was located on the outskirts of Storkow, Germany, just over fifty kilometers from the Polish border. The message came with an authentication code. The man quickly verified it; indeed, the message was authentic. He raced out of the campaign tent to deliver it minutes later to the aide of Major General Marc Rendront; this officer, holding the rank of major, read it surprised, immediately entered the command tent, and made it known to his superior. Rendront, astonished, expressed:

"An unexpected surprise, no doubt. Is this information reliable?"

"Yes, sir, the message is authentic. However, it's a suicidal act; they are surrounded by Russians. Have they lost their minds?"

Rendront replied:

"Never underestimate the qualities of a warrior, major. A certain dose of madness is required to perform acts of bravery. Do we have news from the Russians?"

"The most recent information from the front indicates they are slowing down their advance towards our border, sir."

"Wonderful, they must be as surprised as we are, gentlemen, we must do something and soon. What help can we send them, Gerhardt?"

Rendront was referring to Colonel Gerhardt Kammhuber of the Luftwaffe, now under the orders of the Belgian general. Without a second thought, Kammhuber responded:

"Sir, we can send a staggered attack with a couple of A10 squadrons and some Tornado IDS for ground attack, we can also send them a squadron of Typhoons as escort."

The general nodded, then asked again:

"Anything more we can do for them? Some missiles, perhaps? They're sending us coordinates. What do you think, Philippe?"

Colonel Philippe Forissier, from the French Army, replied:

"Sir, we can use the M270 multiple rocket launchers, they have the range to send a few gifts to the Russians."

General Rendront gave a light tap on the meeting table in the command tent.

"Say no more, gentlemen, let's send them everything we can, let's help those brave warriors. Major, notify the high command in Brussels immediately."

Craig Eastman:

Anatoli, I know this message is unexpected for you. Can we talk?

Kolesnikov, surprised by the message on WhatsApp, scratched his chin, then after a moment, decided to reply, then typed on his cell phone. Eastman heard the notification sound of an incoming message, immediately read it:

Anatoli Kolesnikov:

Hello, Craig. Don't you think it's a bad time for us to talk?

Eastman grimaced with concern, showed the message to Tomás Cruz, who suggested a reply. Eastman nodded in agreement, then wrote the message and sent it. In Moscow, 2,400 kilometers away, the notification sound was heard on Kolesnikov's cellphone, who smiled upon reading it.

Craig Eastman:

On the contrary, dear friend, this is the best time to talk, I need to communicate with you.

Kolesnikov replied:

Anatoli Kolesnikov:

You're going to get me hanged for talking to you, call me in fifteen minutes at this number.

Eastman and Cruz read the message, Eastman let out a slight chuckle, the latter expressed:

"Very well, Mr. Eastman, time to break the news to our bosses."

They were heading to the boardroom when Bernard Dumont approached them, the man was pale, Tomás Cruz asked him:

"What's wrong, Bernard?"

"Friends, something very serious is happening in Poland."

Rashad Sharif finished reviewing the package of programs on his computer, the instructions were clear, he needed to send it once the Russian troops reached the German border with Poland, the man checked on the TV monitor, the CNN news reported that the Russian troops were now just over ten kilometers from the border, NATO forces were fiercely resisting the Russian advance along the entire frontline of attack. The woman was about to say something else, but the man turned off the TV, he decided to check the official Russian news system on the internet on his computer, the TV presenter reported with a smile of satisfaction that the Russian Federation forces had reached the German border at two points, in Kostrzyn and Slubice, the armored cavalry and infantry forces were consolidating the front and expelling the rest of the NATO forces. "Damn bastards at CNN, they are hiding the news!" he exclaimed, clutching his head, then Rashid Sharif made a decision that would further complicate things, he programmed "Arshad", as he called it, to activate after midnight, New York time.

The first squadron of A10C Thunderbolts took off from Rostock-Laage Air Base, northeast of Germany, they had departed from the United States Air Force base in Spangdahlem and made a stopover in Rostock to refuel, the A10s carried two external fuel tanks under their wings, the mission involved flying almost to

Warsaw and they had to be assured of not having autonomy issues for this reason. The combat aircraft, five minutes after takeoff, switched to low-altitude flight mode to avoid Russian radar and early warning systems. With a ten-minute interval, the second squadron of Wharthogs, as the A10s were also known, took off from Rostock-Laage; above, at just over thirty thousand feet, twelve Eurofighter Typhoon fighter jets escorted them to ensure their protection from attacks by Russian aviation. Further north, at the Luftwaffe air base in Schleswig, a squadron of Tornado IDS combat aircraft took off, in support of ground forces, this would split into two groups upon entering Polish territory, their mission, also in low-altitude flight, consisted of attacking the Russian front lines further north, in order to relieve pressure on Lieutenant Lang's tank group; shortly after, a group of six Tornado ECRs took off, their target, to eliminate Russian anti-aircraft defense and radar systems in the operation zone. Between Frankfurt and Cottbus, just ten kilometers from the Polish border, the M270 NATO multiple rocket launcher systems received the order to saturate with fire an area twenty kilometers in length by ten in depth according to the coordinates sent by Lange, phase two of the baptism by fire was about to arrive for the Russians stationed in that area corresponding to their rear lines.

XXVI

"Hello, Craig."

The dry and distant voice of Anatoli Kolesnikov was heard on the cellphone after a couple of ring tones.

"Anatoli, glad to hear from you." A brief pause was heard on Kolesnikov's cellphone, "we need to talk."

"We are talking, Craig. What's the reason for your call?"

"Anatoli, it's better to discuss this in person. Can we meet?"

"I don't think that's possible given the circumstances, Craig."

"On the contrary, given the circumstances, we must meet, that's why we need to see each other."

"Craig, I insist. What's the reason for your call?"

A brief silence, which actually seemed longer, took over the conversation, Kolesnikov heard something like a sigh from the other side of the line.

"Anatoli..., we have confirmed information that Russia did not perpetrate the acts that led to this madness."

Kolesnikov let out a comment filled with irony:

"How good that you have confirmed something that we already knew."

"Save the sarcasm for another day, Anatoli, we know who's behind all of this."

"We don't need to meet for that, Craig, you could tell me now."

"There's another very sensitive matter, Anatoli, believe me, we need to meet."

"All topics are sensitive these days, Craig, frankly, I don't see the utility in meeting."

Eastman cleared his throat a couple of times.

"For the sake of our families, of our children, it's imperative we meet, Anatoli, give me the chance to talk to you, even if it's just for ten minutes, I'm not asking for more." A new silence took over the phone call, after a couple of minutes, Anatoli Kolesnikov's voice was heard:

"Give me a few minutes, I'll confirm via WhatsApp."

"I saw on CNN some good news, they were reporting that some crazy German tank commanders, supported by anti-tank artillery, are giving the Russians a beating in Poland."

Dumont had a grin from ear to ear; while Eastman was talking to Kolesnikov, he, Frost, and Cruz were having coffee; Frost asked:

"Where did they come from? Supposedly, they had wiped out any resistance from us in Poland."

"It's not very clear, but it all seems to indicate that they waited hidden in a medium-sized forest very close to Warsaw."

The woman commented, somewhat surprised:

"How did they not discover them? With all the blessed technology available now? You can detect even a couple of mosquitoes making love."

Dumont replied sarcastically:

"I think that's fine, Rosamund, we should all make love and not war, besides, in these days of combat and shooting..., sadly, what is most lacking is sex."

Frost gave him a scorching look, Cruz chuckled, then added:

"In a conflict, you can do everything right and, yet, one mistake, just one, can cost you the war; besides, overconfidence leads us to make mistakes, the Russians perhaps assumed they had already eliminated any potential threat in Poland." -The man paused-; "As for the other thing, about sex, I fully agree with you, Bernard, regardless of whether it's good or bad..."

Dumont raised his hand to the air and let out a sigh:

"Aaahhh, my friend, in times of scarcity, quality is the least of concerns."

Frost called them back to order again:

"You men are too basic, your neuron actually shapes like a sperm, you say so much nonsense... Let's get back to the point, I don't think this group of crazy, or brave Germans can last long without help."

Dumont, with a gesture of jubilation, mentioned:

"I understand that help is already on its way, plus, since this rear attack took them by total surprise, it practically paralyzed the Russians' advance towards the German border, which has given more time to prepare our counteroffensive, which I understand is about to begin."

Rosamund Frost let out a sigh of relief:

"That is good news, hopefully, the counteroffensive is successful, this considering that the Americans were thinking of the option..." -The woman refrained from saying the word she was thinking of, then finished the sentence-; "I mean, the other alternative."

Anatoli Kolesnikov:

"Let's meet in Prague today, ten at night, however, before that I need a favor from you, you have to ensure that my plane will not be shot down, these are not good times for a Russian plane to travel through the center of Europe, if you manage it, see you at the Carlo IV hotel, I'll see you in the lobby."

Eastman showed the message to everyone present, Nick Fallon directed his gaze at Cousseran.

"Well, it's a step forward without a doubt, we don't know where this will lead us, but at least we now have a communication channel with the Russians, tell him to send us the registration number, we will make sure he arrives safely in Prague."

Craig Eastman wrote to him about the issue of the plane's registration number, as well as the arrival and departure times at the Prague airport, the response came minutes later. Having coordinated this thorny issue, Pierre Cousseran indicated by looking at his watch:

"Very well, gentlemen, you have to go now. Mr. Eastman, it's mid-morning and you must be ready for the meeting."

Fallon inquired:

"Must? Who will go with him?"

"Mr. Secretary, I'm referring to our three musketeers, they will accompany Mr. Eastman, John and I discussed it and agreed, they make a good team, he may well need them."

Cruz took the opportunity on the way to the airport to call Carole, he wanted to ask about the health of his friend.

"Carole, hi, it's Tom. How are you?"

His friend's voice sounded very happy:

"I wouldn't change places with anyone, Tom. Jean Claude woke up from the coma! He's doing very well!"

"Congratulations, Carole! Tell J.C. I'm as happy as you are, this gives us all peace of mind, it's undoubtedly the best news these days."

"I will tell him. You know? He asked a lot about you."

"Give him a big hug from me, there will be time to have champagne together to celebrate."

"Understood, I will give it with pleasure. And you, how are you doing?"

Cruz didn't want to give her too many details, things were not looking good, and it was not the time to worry his friends, especially Jean Claude, after an evasive answer, he said goodbye, she before hanging up told him:

"Tom, do what you have to do so that J.C., you, and I can have that blessed champagne. Understand?"

The NATO counteroffensive began shortly after the Falcon 2000, with Cruz, Eastman, and their friends on board, took off from Paris destined for Prague. Two armored divisions, of which one had recently arrived from the United States, entered Polish territory from Germany after a powerful softening exercise by the anti-tank artillery and NATO aviation; surprised, the Russian forces soon found themselves temporarily in a sort of sandwich, the brave group of Lieutenant Lange attacking cleverly in the east of Poland at their rear, efficiently supported by aviation which for a time managed to isolate the Russian invasion forces from Belarusian territory, while, from the west, a violent charge of armored vehicles, artillery, and NATO aviation forced them to yield ground. Meanwhile, Putin ordered the Russian forces in Ukraine to be reinforced, an additional tank division refreshed the tired forces at the front, it entered from the north, in Belarus, the Ukrainian and NATO forces soon found themselves in a desperate situation, every minute of this attack placed them at the risk of being encircled, very soon the NATO high command realized that the only way out was to escape south towards Romania, immediately, troops and equipment were in full retreat crossing the narrow border bridge over the Tisza River. Ukraine was, in practice, totally lost by NATO.

The trojan activated at the scheduled time, surreptitiously, as is its style, it installed itself in the main computer of NORAD (North American Aerospace Defense Command), seconds later it accessed two more computers, the first, that of one of the assistants to the Secretary of Defense, at the Pentagon; the second, on the computer of the White House press chief, in Washington. The worm virus, which waited for the trojan to do its job, now had the doors open to carry out its sinister task.

XXVII

The Falcon 2000 flew at forty-five thousand feet, if one looked out the windows of the executive jet, the sun was already beginning to set, it had taken off from Paris just over half an hour ago. While Bernard Dumont spoke on the phone at the back of the plane, Eastman, Frost, and Cruz were talking; Cruz decided to ask the former:

"Craig, your friend Kolesnikov sounded somewhat distant, besides being arrogant, in the conversation you had. Don't you think?"

"When you're surrounded by people full of fanaticism or simple flatterers who out of convenience would give their life for Vladimir Putin or the motherland, you must be very careful with what you say or how you say it; that, especially, in a country like Russia."

Frost intervened:

"I agree with Tom, the guy sounded pedantic. So, do you think your friend was watching his back?"

"Without a doubt, Rosamund, being an advisor on defense issues in our countries, whether it's the United Kingdom, France, or Germany, is very different from being one in Russia; here our directors expect a different vision of the problem being analyzed, a viewpoint that enriches the path to its solution; things are very different in Moscow; if you are an advisor you must be careful in subtly presenting both the problem and the solution, the leaders in the Rodina, not just now, have always been very sensitive to dissent. Anatoly has not reached the place he has today in the Russian Government without being careful to express in public what in private he can express to Putin or to his mentor, the Minister of Defense."

From the back of the aircraft, it was heard:

"Ukraine fell."

Dumont hung up his phone, Eastman, with a furrowed brow, said:

!Damn it. When, Bernard?"

"A couple of hours ago, our forces were ordered to retreat south, into Romania, the Russians are breathing down our necks, our rearguard is less than two kilometers from them."

"How many men are we talking about?"

Eastman answered that question:

"All members of their armed forces must total about one hundred and eighty thousand men, plus about thirty thousand we sent to reinforce the defense of the Ukrainians, I think in the best-case scenario we'll manage to evacuate half, maybe one or another tank or armored vehicle and some birds that must already be at some Romanian or Hungarian airport."

"Do Hungary, Slovakia, and Romania run the risk of falling? Are the Russians willing to continue towards them?"

Eastman looked at Frost, who had asked the question.

"In my opinion, they won't do it, at least for now, although... as things stand, anything can happen.

Cruz rose from his seat to serve himself coffee, offering to bring drinks to his companions, everyone accepted, on his way to the small cafeteria he asked:

"For now? What do you mean by that, Craig."

"I think that for the Russians the loot acquired for the moment is more than enough, which does not mean they do not want to do it again in the future with the rest of the countries of the former Iron Curtain."

Dumont intervened:

"Do you really believe that? If Poland falls, they'll have the buffer of territory that prevents them, in their insane distrust, from an invasion into properly Russian territory.2

"Remember that, for them, Poland, Ukraine, the Baltic countries, even Finland, are historically Russian territory, until now they have done nothing but recover part of what was theirs."

Dumont disagreed, and then a discussion broke out between him and Eastman. As they talked, Frost approached Cruz to help him bring the drinks, the woman took the opportunity to reproach Cruz:

"Is it my impression or are you avoiding me, Tom?"

Cruz, surprised, replied:

"Sorry? Why would I do that?"

"Because you are doing it."

"I don't understand, Ross, you, the model of a woman with independence and self-control, are you upset because I'm ignoring you?"

The woman, blushing, realized that she had let herself be carried away, for the first time in a long time, by her emotions.

"No, you're wrong, alpha male, I'm not upset at all, I was just asking."

Cruz realized it then decided to reduce the tension of the moment:

"Forgive me, you're right, it's not that I'm ignoring you, it's the pressure of everything that's happening."

She smiled at him, with a mischievous gesture she looked at him intently to tell him:

"Are you a man of your word, Tomás Cruz?"

"Of course, Rosamund Frost. Why do you ask?"

"Remember that you and I have a talk, with wine and pasta, about Ross MacDonald and Raymond Chandler novels."

"A debt that will be gladly paid as soon as possible."

Both resumed their seats with the drinks, five minutes later the pilot signaled that they were about to land in Prague, a long and difficult meeting awaited them with Anatoli Kolesnikov.

Anatoli Kolesnikov was a tall man, over one meter ninety centimeters, in good shape, the man wore a blue jacket, white shirt, and dark gray pants; sitting in the elegant hotel lobby, he raised his hand as soon as he saw his friend Craig Eastman, the greeting was more cordial than in the phone call; Kolesnikov stood up from the sofa and walked towards his friend extending his arms to hug him and greet him in perfect English:

"Craig, what a pleasure to see you after not speaking for so long. How are you? Diane? The kids?"

"Everyone is very well, fortunately, Anatoli, thanks for asking. And yours? Yekaterina?"

"All very well too. Did you know I'm going to be a grandfather? Svetlana, my daughter, gave us the good news, she's already four months pregnant."

"What great news, my friend! Congratulations!"

"It certainly is news that has us very happy, hey, if we survive this debacle, you will be one of the godfathers, Craig." Kolesnikov paused. "But, well, we are not here to talk about our families, right? From what I see, you came well escorted."

Eastman smiled and introduced his companions, Kolesnikov indicated that he had requested a private room, he apologized to them, preferring to first talk alone with his good friend.

"I must apologize to you, Craig, although I think you already sensed it when we talked, my tone sounded sharp, as you can imagine a few from the Russian intelligence service were by my side, or listening to the call properly intercepted, I had to be prudently distant with you."

"Don't worry, Anatoli, I knew it from the beginning."

"Good, to our matter, Craig. What did you want to tell me that brought us to this beautiful hotel in Prague in the middle of a war?"

"I'll be honest with you, Anatoli, you know there have never been secrets between us, one topic has us very worried, besides the Russian aspirations to conquer territory."

Kolesnikov interrupted him:

"You know well that we didn't start this."

"True, Islamic terrorism, specifically Al Qaeda, put us in this mess. Did you guys know?"

Kolesnikov made a gesture of mischief.

"No, but we suspected it."

"An unexpected gift. Isn't it?"

Kolesnikov let a smile filled with sarcasm show.

"I insist on the question, Anatoli. How far do Russian intentions go in this conflict?"

"You know my stance on it."

"Yes, I do, you have always been in favor of recovering the Baltic countries and Ukraine, the idea of Poland never crossed your mind."

"That's right, I won't tell you more about it."

The man made a sign, meaning that there could be microphones in the small room; Eastman said:

"I understand, Anatoli, I will ask you a direct question. Does Russia intend to cross the border and invade Germany?"

"No, not for now."

"Not for now?"

"You know, there are some who have delusions of the past, of the German Democratic Republic, even within Germany itself."

"Well, we know that, but from there to invade Germany, there's a long way."

"You know my position on that, but tell your people that for now they can be calm, we do not plan to cross that border." — Understood, that for now is the one that does not reassure me.

Kolesnikov interrupted him with a gesture, raised his right index finger, and shook it several times in the air.

"But... you did not have me come here just to ask me that. Or did you?"

"No, there's another matter as I was saying, and one that greatly concerns Europe."

"Which one?"

"This is a confidential matter, Anatoli, the Americans are thinking of using their low-yield nuclear warheads if you cross the border between Poland and Germany."

Kolesnikov squinted his eyes.

"Do you think it's just a threat? What, as they say, are they bluffing?"

"No, Anatoli, they're not bluffing, this is serious. Can we be reassured regarding what you just told me? I mean, Russia wouldn't cross the border. Is that so?"

"That's right, Craig, besides, take into account that your counteroffensive seems to be working."

"True, but things can change, Anatoli, if there are some in the power circle of the Russian Government who dream of recovering the old territory of the GDR, then we are in trouble."

"You know, I can't promise you, at this moment, more than a mere for now."

The ring of Anatoli Kolesnikov's cell phone interrupted the conversation, he answered immediately.

Shtorm

XXVIII

Klaus Lange knew that his mission was, in essence, suicide. Under normal conditions, the tanks, which lie buried from their attack position, would move to another previously dug position, thus maintaining their stealth to mislead the enemy; this was not the case, he didn't have enough people or time, and the terrain was filled with Russian tanks and troops; all he had was the expertise and bravery of his team, until now, the aerial and artillery support from NATO, combined with the rapid movements and accuracy of tank fire, plus the anti-tank support from his troops had helped; nevertheless, this initial advantage would soon end. The sudden attack by NATO troops caused confusion in the Russian rear and high command, but once they recovered from the surprise, they gradually began to retake control of the terrain amid temporary chaos; at least twenty anti-tank rockets fell in the area where Lange's group of tanks was moving, despite the sixty tons of weight of his Leopard, it shook violently, the sound of pieces of rock or earth hitting the armor certainly instilled fear. Through the visor, he observed how several anti-tank missiles fell within the perimeter where several T90s were located, he saw one of them explode, the powerful roar of a Wharthog's engines was heard, another powerful explosion made the tank vibrate, the driver stopped and immediately backed up a bit, then observed through the visor, decided, in a fraction of seconds, to turn left, meanwhile, the gunner detected in the modern system a Russian tank less than two kilometers away, the system calculated and turned the turret in seconds, the shot made the tank wobble, Lange observed satisfied through the visor, a T90's turret flew through the air, this was the sixth T90 that his crew had taken down that day, not bad; Lieutenant Lange ordered to reload, a Russian helicopter then appeared on the scene, the Ka-52 Alligator launched a pair of anti-tank missiles, one of them hit the Leopard 2 that was one hundred fifty meters to his right, it exploded, some parts of the tank hit the armor of Lange's tank, the man saw three Spike LR missiles pass by seeking their Russian targets, two T90 tanks soared through the air as they were hit. Lange and his crew scored three more targets, the sound of the Alligator's rotors was heard again, it passed behind his tank, a Stinger, launched by a German soldier from the shoulder, hit the tail of the Alligator, which fell to the ground spinning out of control. The gunner, who was distracted for a couple of seconds while the crew celebrated the fall of the Russian helicopter, returned to observe in the visor, a T90 was pointing straight ahead with its 125 mm cannon.

"Russian tank in front!"

The turret was forty-five degrees to his right, the gunner turned it, immediately Lange ordered:

"Fire now!"

The turning time of the Leopard 2's turret was not enough, the shot from the T90 hit the lower part of it causing it to fly through the air, fortunately, the fire protection and the upper armor of the tank kept the crew unharmed, minutes later the four men came out of what was left of the armored vehicle, the battle for Lange and his crew had ended, fortunately, with their lives.

The nuclear protocol was activated at the missile launch base in Bangor, Washington state, a dozen ICBMs began their launch process; meanwhile, in Detroit, where President Trump was visiting a car plant, "The Nuclear Football", the briefcase that controls the missile launch system by the President of the United States, which was guarded by an Air Force major in one of the cars of the presidential convoy and which has a couple of small lights, suddenly changed from red to green, the noise alerted the officer, who, between surprised and terrified, called his superior to report the news.

At the Pentagon, the order was received to make the B52s take off from the Royal Air Force base in Fairford, Gloucestershire, it was initially an order that did not yet imply a missile launch, when consulted, the Secretary of Defense preferred to call President Trump, who answered on the reserved line, he replied that their takeoff was authorized as a preventive measure pending the development of the Russian advance towards the German border, a few minutes later the two U.S. Air Force superbombers took off from the base; Mark Esper took the opportunity to reconfirm an order that came from the nuclear briefcase accompanying President Trump.

"Mr. President, did you also order the deployment of twelve ballistic missiles?"

"That's right, Mark, we will soon start the launch protocol with the codes, we cannot allow the Russians to take Europe."

A call was received by the major guarding "The Nuclear Football", it was from the Chairman of the Joint Chiefs of Staff, General Michael Dunford.

"Major, the Secretary of Defense needs to urgently speak with the President."

The officer quickly approached President Trump, who took the phone.

"What's happening, Mark?"

"Mr. President, the Russians have already crossed the German border, they are also crossing the border between Ukraine and Hungary, the same thing is happening at the border with Romania."

"My God, Mark! Is that confirmed?"

"Yes, sir, I am sending you the latest NATO report."

"Thank you, I'll check it later, we can't wait any longer, Mark, start the protocol to launch the low-yield missiles from the B52s."

"The protocol is being initiated, sir."

The major said nothing of the previous incident, assuming, amid the moment's tension, that it had been activated from the Pentagon as part of the protocol.

"Craig, the Americans have initiated the nuclear launch protocol."

"What the hell? And you?"

"Obviously, we are doing the same."

Eastman asked, dismayed:

"How much time do we have?"

"No more than twenty-five minutes. What the hell is happening, Craig?"

"Damn it, I don't know, let me call our Secretary of Defense, my God, Anatoli, this can't be happening."

"It's happening, Craig, and in less than half an hour we'll be in a nuclear war."

Bernard Dumont's phone rang, the man answered, the paleness of his face made it obvious that it was not good news, he hung up.

"What's happening, Bernard?"

"Disaster, my friends, disaster... sources from our intelligence inform us that the United States plans to launch a nuclear attack against the Russians in Poland."

Cruz stood up from the seat in the hotel's café.

"What the hell? We have to inform Craig about this!"

Nick Fallon's cell phone rang, he, who had just fallen asleep, answered with a sleepy voice:

"Hello?"

"Mr. Secretary, Craig Eastman, my apologies for calling so late."

"Don't worry about it. What's happening? How did it go with your Russian friend?"

"We'll have more time to talk about that later, Mr. Secretary, the issue now is that the Americans activated the nuclear launch protocol."

"Damn it. Who told you that?"

"Anatoli, he confirmed to me that the Russians are proceeding in reciprocity to activate their launch protocols."

Fallon leaped out of bed.

"But I don't understand. Why would they do that? Did the Russians cross the German border?"

"No, sir, in fact, we've pushed the Russian front back more than sixty kilometers from the border."

"Then? Have they lost their minds in the United States?"

"We need to do something, sir, we don't have time."

"Damn it, Craig, what a way to wake me up! I'm going to talk to Esper, see what he says. Are we sure that the Russians haven't crossed the German border? Maybe somewhere else?"

"Totally sure, Mr. Secretary."

"I understand, I'll call Esper and get back to you."

Trump was back in the presidential limousine on his way to Air Force One, on a secure line conference call with the Secretary of Defense and the Chairman of the Joint Chiefs of Staff, targets were chosen on Polish territory; now it was necessary to prepare the Gold Codes, or authentication codes, for the launch. The president broke the case that protected the card where the codes were, Trump recalled which numbers were among the random assortment of numbers and letters on the card, he indicated them aloud; now it was Esper's turn, he mentioned the ones on his card, General Dunford completed the last checks, then nodded to Esper, everything was authenticated and ready to proceed with the launch order. The general asked over the line:

"Mr. President, do you order the launch of four missiles from our B52s that are already in position?"

Donald Trump heard the question, for the first time in a long while, his hands were sweating given the enormous pressure he felt at that moment; a few seconds of silence preceded the answer:

"Yes, General, I authorize the launch of four missiles at the designated targets."

XXIX

Nick Fallon was walking in circles, he tried to communicate several times with his American counterpart, his cellphone gave a busy tone or rang for a while without any answer, after a couple of minutes of persistence without results, the man in the robe sat down on the sofa in his living room. What to do? The minutes slowly peeled away and time, in a dangerously way, was running out; Fallon, with visible excitement, took the cellular phone, as if an idea had reached his worried mind, he looked up the number and dialed it. On the other side of the line, a sleepy voice responded, it was the British Prime Minister.

"Hello?"

"Mr. Prime Minister, Nick Fallon, my apologies, I know it's very early, but I need to talk to you."

Harold Callaghan responded still drowsy:

"Nick? What time is it? No... no problem, tell me what's happening."

"Prime Minister, the Americans are initiating the nuclear launch protocol."

Silence was the response on the other side of the line.

"Mr. Prime Minister?"

"Good Lord, Nick. Is this confirmed news?"

"Yes, Prime Minister."

"And why on earth are they doing that? It's irresponsible. Have the Russians reached the German border yet?"

Fallon explained that no, according to NATO information, the Russian lines had already retracted more than sixty kilometers, as discussed with Eastman, something he had already verified.

"For the love of God, Nick. What do we do? Have you spoken to the Americans?"

"I've been trying to reach Mark Esper for several minutes without success, sir, I think you should call President Trump."

"Good idea, Nick, stay on the line."

Callaghan had Trump's personal number, he looked for it then dialed, after a few seconds, the Prime Minister's voice was heard again:

"It's useless, Nick, Trump isn't answering, his lines must be blocked due to the protocol itself."

Fallon, sitting on the sofa, closed his eyes and nervously rubbed his forehead, then looked at the clock, six minutes had passed, time was pressing, he clicked his fingers with his other hand.

"And what about the Vice President? Could we talk to Pence?"

"Of course! I have Mike's phone, I have a good relationship with him, in fact, I get along better with him than with Trump, I'll call him now, wait."

Callaghan dialed the number, there was no answer, he hung up.

"He's not answering either, Nick."

Fallon, desperate, scratched his head with both hands, the tense but under control voice of Callaghan was heard again:

"Wait, I think I have the number of his secretary."

A brief silence was heard again, Fallon heard the Prime Minister say:

"Nick?"

"Yes, sir."

"Let's hang up, I'm going to call this number to see what happens, I'll get in touch with you again."

Callaghan dialed the cell phone number, it rang several times.

"James?"

"Yes, speaking. Who's calling?"

"Harold Callaghan, James."

"Sorry. Who?"

"The British Prime Minister, James, a favor, I need to urgently speak with Vice President Pence. Is he near you?"

Static noise took over the conversation, Callaghan insisted again, the voice was heard again on the other side:

"The Vice President is currently giving a speech, excuse me, but I can't interrupt him. Can you call him in an hour?"

Callaghan muttered a curse under his breath, took a deep breath, then said:

"James. Are you married? Do you have children?"

"Yes, sir."

"Where do they live?"

The subject's voice sounded surprised, he replied:

"In Washington, sir." —James, if you do not interrupt the Vice President, your children and your wife, as well as many Americans in Washington and perhaps other cities in your country, will receive the terrible explosion of a Russian nuclear missile in ten minutes. I believe it is advisable, for the sake of your loved ones and many of your fellow citizens, that you interrupt him immediately.

A brief moment of silence followed Callaghan's voice; the sound of hurried footsteps could now be heard, a brief low-voiced conversation was heard, then someone spoke:

"Hello?"

"Mike?"

At the Pentagon, the Secretary of Defense, Mark Esper, waited for a conference call between President Trump, the Strategic Command headquarters in Nebraska, and himself to be made, for which they used the secure line, commonly referred to in the defense environment as the golden phone. This line is impossible to hack; at Offutt Air Force Base, Lieutenant General Daniel Burnette received and confirmed the attack order, which were actually two, one for the missile base in Bangor, Washington State, and another for the B52 bombers already in the air. Unbeknownst to them, an encrypted message of one hundred fifty characters was sent to both bases, as well as to the rest of the strategic defense system bases for informational purposes and as part of the priority defense condition they were in. The respective commanders at the two military facilities verified the authenticity of the codes; the two messages, according to the codes, were authentic, so they proceeded.

On board one of the B52s, the attack order arrived, and its commander initiated the launch process. Another similar instruction arrived at the commander of the strategic missile base in Bangor, after verifying its authenticity, he entered the targets' coordinates into the computer, then the colonel, alongside his senior officer, took the keys to insert them into the computer.

"Mr. President, people very close to NATO assure me that this is an induced error to make the Americans launch a nuclear attack."

"Anatoli. Who designed in our war games all the possible deception alternatives from NATO and the Americans?"

"I understand the message, Mr. President, except that this time the information comes from NATO itself, the Americans are being manipulated by someone."

The icy voice, on the brink of indifference, of Vladimir Putin was heard:

"That, if I am not mistaken, was alternative number two. No, Anatoli, we must assume, no, we must understand that it is a delaying maneuver of our enemies so that we can not react to the American nuclear attack, the countdown continues and New York, Washington, and Boston are in our sights.

"Mr. President..."

The dreadful sound of the call concluded by the Russian president reached Kolesnikov and Craig Eastman's ears, followed by a loud and intense knocking on the door of the private room, both looked towards it, then, helplessly, they looked at each other horrified; the planet was minutes away from nuclear holocaust.

XXX

Back in Washington on Air Force One, Trump, who was in a video conference with his Secretary of Defense, communicated with Vice President Pence:

"Hello, Mike, it's Donald Trump."

"Mr. President, a pleasure to greet you."

"Mike, the protocol indicates that you should know that we are in the phase of launching two low-yield nuclear missiles on Polish territory."

"Did the Russians force us to it, Mr. President?"

"That's correct, Mike."

"Mr. President, you have my full support in this matter, we cannot allow the Russians to invade Europe."

"Thank you, Mike, you must return quickly to Washington, things are going to get very ugly here."

"I'll return immediately, Mr. President, see you soon."

"Craig, the United States plans..."

"I know already, Bernard, come on, let's enter."

With a resigned face, Eastman signaled them to enter the private room, everyone took a seat, Dumont inquired with a puzzled face:

"And now, what the hell is going to happen?"

Cruz replied:

"Mutually Assured Destruction."

"That's right, Tom, the infamous MAD..."

Added Eastman, Kolesnikov added:

"Ensuring we have enough nuclear weapons arsenal to eliminate each other, either to avoid conflict or to gain something in return for avoiding it."

Frost, as incisive as was her demeanor, slid a caustic comment:

"Who or those came up with that theory? Two unsatisfied males, I guess, now, because of Islamic fundamentalism, Allah and who knows what other god, the lunatics from Al Qaeda are about to achieve that, in the name of those stupid enough to concoct it, we all go to hell."

Eastman mocked as he introduced his Russian friend:

"Dear Rosamund, it is a pleasure to introduce you to one of those men..."

Blushing with a mixture of rage and embarrassment, the woman managed to say, staring at him:

"Again, a pleasure to meet you, Mr. Kolesnikov..."

Kolesnikov could only respond with laughter, joined by the others, when the sound of Craig Eastman's cellphone interrupted them; he hurriedly took the call.

"Yes, Mike Pence speaking. Harold?"

"Mike, it's great to talk to you, I urgently need you to listen to me, the nuclear attack must be stopped, it's all a vile setup by Islamic terrorism."

A burst of static returned, Pence's choppy voice came through:

"What are you talking about, Harold?"

"My God. Aren't you aware, Mike?"

"Obviously not, Harold, we're not remotely developing the launch protocol. Where on Earth did you get that story?"

"Mike, two B52s took off a few minutes ago from Fairford Air Force Base, the Russians also detected activity in their strategic missile base in Bangor, you're preparing to launch several of them."

Mike Pence frowned.

"Have you all lost your minds, Harold? I insist, we're not developing any nuclear protocols, I would know."

"Then, please, call President Trump and clear up this misunderstanding, the Russians are activating their protocol in response."

Pence shook his head in frustration and surprise.

"I don't understand, Harold. Is this a joke? If it is, it's in very poor taste."

"Mike, I must insist, call Trump, clear up the misunderstanding or stop this madness, we have less than ten minutes, I'll call you again in three."

Mike Pence hung up, looking absent for a few seconds, thinking about the madness the British Prime Minister had just mentioned to him, he looked at his private secretary.

"James, get me through to President Trump."

After insisting for a few seconds, Pence's secretary approached him.

"Mr. Vice President, the President is not responding."

"Then call the White House."

Mike Pence's pale face showed concern.

"Are you alright, Mr. Vice President?"

"The British Prime Minister just informed me that we're about to start a nuclear war, no, I don't feel well, James, I want to believe it's just a joke."

The private secretary managed to contact the assistant to the private secretary to the President, after a few minutes of waiting, he got on the phone.

"Gary, Mike Pence, please, I need to speak with President Trump, I'm trying to reach him on his cell phone and can't contact him."

Gary Harris, the private secretary to the President, replied with a tone of surprise,

"I'm sorry, Mr. Vice President, that seems strange, you've just finished a telephone conference with him."

Pence's forehead wrinkled, confused, he replied:

"I don't understand anything, Gary, I haven't spoken with President Trump since yesterday."

"Mr. Vice President, now I'm the one who doesn't understand anything, before you spoke with the President, I contacted his cell phone and you spoke to me."

"What the hell are you talking about, Gary? I repeat, I haven't spoken to you or the President, something very strange is happening, Gary. Is it true that we've initiated the nuclear launch protocol?"

"I'm sorry, Mr. Vice President, that's a topic I cannot confirm or deny over the phone."

"Damn it, Gary! Then I need you to put me through to President Trump immediately!"

Gary Harris's voice, now nervous, responded:

"Wait, Mr. Vice President, he's on Air Force One, I'll put him through."

*MAD: Multiple Wavelength Anomalous Dispersion, a system for solving crystal structures.

XXXI

The process of launching Russian strategic ballistic missiles also continued, in his Kremlin bunker, President Putin and his Defense Minister activated the protocol, the former ordered to select targets, the cities of New York, Los Angeles, and Boston, then gave instructions to prepare the launch of two missiles from the Plesetsk aerospace base, located in northwest Russia, and one from a 955A-class Borey submarine, a fourth-generation Russian nuclear submarine, the latter targeting the capital of California; all, including the commander of the Prince Vladimir, awaited authorization from the President of the Russian Federation to launch the new Sarmat intercontinental ballistic missile.

"Mike?"

"Yes, Mr. President, we need to talk, I understand that the protocol for the launch of nuclear weapons has been activated."

"Mike, I don't understand, we talked just a few minutes ago about this." "Now you're telling me you don't know that the protocol was activated? Have you gone mad? Are you suffering from short-term amnesia?

"Mr. President, you and I have not spoken, someone has impersonated my voice in that case. The truth is, just a few minutes ago, I received a call from the UK Prime Minister, who has been trying to get in touch with you. He told me that we are preparing..."

Trump interrupted him:

"Mike, stop, we already know what's happening in Poland, we must react immediately."

"Mr. President, regarding Poland, the Russians haven't reached the German border."

"Mike. Are you insane? Of course, they haven't reached the German border, they crossed it! Haven't you read the damn NATO report?"

"Mr. President, I can assure you that hasn't happened, the English Prime Minister told me that the Russian front has retreated more than sixty kilometers."

"Nonsense, Mike! That's false! It's part of the Russian plan to make us hesitate to launch the attack. Don't you understand?

"Mr. President, the plan, I don't know whose, is to drag us into this so we launch nuclear weapons from our B52s and from Bangor, the Russians will respond and that will be the end of everything, whoever benefits from this madness..."

Trump again interrupted Pence:

"Look, Mike. Where the hell did you get that we're going to launch missiles from Bangor? No one has given that damn order!"

"Mr. President, then please verify it, the Russians detected missile launch activity in Bangor."

The president then reluctantly ordered his Secretary of Defense:

"Mark, call Bangor, reconfirm that everything is normal there. Mike, if this isn't true, someone is playing with us. Are you sure that you and I didn't speak less than ten minutes ago?"

"Absolutely sure, Mr. President, and indeed, someone is playing with us."

Esper then interrupted Trump:

"Excuse me, Mr. President, you also ordered the missile launch from Bangor."

Trump picked up the phone handset.

"Mark..., I never gave such an order."

Esper and the Joint Chiefs of Staff Chairman looked at each other in surprise.

"But... Mr. President, we spoke with you about this five minutes ago."

"Damn it, Mark, call Bangor and cancel that order!"

Mark Esper ordered General Dunford to immediately call the Bangor missile launch base, who promptly got in touch with Lieutenant General Burnette.

"Daniel, good evening."

"Sir, good evening, everything is ready for the missile launch to the assigned targets."

"Abort that launch, Daniel! That wasn't authorized by the president!"

"Sir, I can no longer abort the launch, it can only be done from the president's or vice-president's briefcase."

"Damn it! How much time do we have, Daniel?"

"Right now, three minutes and fifty seconds, sir."

Esper rubbed his forehead, petrified with surprise, General Dunford addressed the Secretary of Defense:

"Mr. Secretary, the only option to abort the missile launch is with the president!"

Esper then looked towards the camera.

"Mr. President, abort the launch from the briefcase!"

The Major turned the briefcase so Trump could see it, the officer pointed at a red button marked Cancel, the president immediately pressed it. General Dunford, holding the phone handset close to his right ear, asked:

"Was the launch aborted, Daniel?"

Lieutenant General Daniel Burnette did not respond immediately, Dunford insisted:

"Daniel?"

"No, sir, the order is still active."

Dunford and Esper shook their heads in disbelief, the former practically shouted at President Trump.

"Mr. President, have the vice president abort the launches from his briefcase!"

Trump indicated over the speaker to his vice-president:

"Mike, cancel the launch from your briefcase. Now!"

An Army lieutenant colonel, who, as always, stood three meters from him, quickly approached, they opened it, Dunford asked General Burnette:

"How much time do we have left, Daniel?"

"Two minutes and forty seconds."

The briefcase, which was a twin to the one accompanying President Trump, displayed the red Cancel button at its bottom right corner, Pence immediately pressed it, with a somewhat sweaty face, the vice-president said:

"I pressed the button, Mr. President."

"General, Mike has aborted the launches from his briefcase, verify with Bangor." Dunford sighed and then asked:

"What happened, Daniel? Was the launch canceled?"

Silence was, for now, the answer. Esper seemed to remember something, then shouted:

"Damn it, Michael, we need to also confirm that the B52s have canceled their launches!"

XXXII

"What would a nuclear war look like, Craig?"

Tomás Cruz inquired. Eastman and Kolesnikov glanced at each other, a smile full of worry followed that exchange of looks, Eastman made a skeptical grimace, then took a breath and replied:

"Our Russian friends see the missiles leaving from the United States, minutes earlier two low-yield nuclear bombs explode in Poland, then, from Russian strategic bases, the same amount of missiles head towards the United States, later from their bombers, Russia sends two low-yield nuclear devices to the United Kingdom, from where the low-power ones carried by the B52s were launched."

Kolesnikov added:

"It will have taken less than an hour, and there will already be at least one million dead."

Eastman continued:

"Then the United States launches a hundred warheads toward Russia, they do the same, meanwhile NATO launches another hundred in retaliation, Russia responds by launching at least three hundred warheads towards Europe and the United States, another two hours have passed."

"By then, three million more lives will have been lost."

Kolesnikov lamented, Rosamund Frost joked:

"Will there be anything left to destroy after this?"

"Believe it or not, yes, at this point what comes next is making sure on each side that the opponent can't recover from the first blow, then they attack the thirty most populated cities on both sides."

Kolesnikov scratched his chin.

"Eighty-five million people will have died an hour later."

Eastman indicated:

"In just over five hours, ninety million people will have ceased to exist."

Dumont inquired:

"And how many more will die later from the effects of radiation?"

Kolesnikov answered that question:

"Another similar number in the following weeks."

"Keep in mind that there will be at least between thirty and forty million injured once the exchange of missiles and bombs is over, what remains of hospitals and clinics will collapse."

Frost inclined her head and nervously grasped her hair.

"And this is going to happen in less than two minutes..."

The noise of a cellphone interrupted the conversation:

"Sir, the launch order was canceled."

A general sigh was heard on the communication, Esper confirmed the news to President Trump and his vice president; Trump then inquired:

"And the B52s?"

On the launch control screen of one of the two strategic bombers, the green light went off, automatically disabling the launch of the missile with the low-yield warhead. The agitated voice of the Secretary of Defense was heard:

"Mr. President, one of the B52s is still going ahead with the launch order!"

Trump asked:

"Can we give a direct deactivation order to the commander of the bomber?"

"No, Mr. President, it's part of the protocol, our communications could be interfered with and a false order issued using your voice."

Trump joked:

"Isn't that exactly what they just tried to do to provoke a nuclear war with the Russians?"

Esper asked his Chief of Staff.

"Michael, how much time do we have?"

"Less than fifty seconds, sir."

Esper rubbed the back of his neck with visible nervousness.

"Damn, Michael. What can we do?"

"We only have to try to deactivate the warhead once the missile is launched."

From the air base in England, a message arrived, confirming that the missile had been launched from the B52, General Dunford's agitated voice was heard:

"Mr. President, the missile is on its way to Poland!"

Esper complained:

"Damn, we have to deactivate the warhead!"

Trump inquired:

"And how do we do that?"

Dunford shouted:

"Mr. President, try doing it from your briefcase!"

The president, with the guidance of the officer guarding the briefcase, pressed another button, one of light grey color, which indicated Disarm.

"Damn it, it didn't work!"

Trump yelled through the intercom, time was running out, less than twenty seconds remained for the missile to hit its assigned target in Polish territory.

"Mike, press the grey button in your briefcase that says Disarm!"

With ten seconds left until the missile hit, Pence followed the president's instruction, pressed the grey button, then closed his eyes.

XXXIII

"Craig?"

"Yes, Mr. Secretary."

"The American missile hit Poland."

Eastman, with his elbows on the meeting table, closed his eyes and interrupted Fallon.

"My God. How many casualties are we talking about?"

"Relax, Craig, don't go worrying your Russian friend, they might launch a missile in response; although in reality, we were saved by a hair, the warhead was disarmed five seconds before the missile carrying it fell." Do you know how the Russians are regarding this issue?

Eastman sat relieved in the chair, watching Kolesnikov talk on the phone; he gave him a thumbs-up and winked.

"Sir, I believe they are as happy as we are that the warhead did not explode."

President Trump got out of the limousine at the bottom of the stairs, decorated with a fine red carpet with golden trim, where a smiling Vladimir Putin awaited him; Trump climbed the stairs with a determined stride and, returning the wide smile, gave his Russian counterpart a firm handshake. Both walked down the long corridor to the impressive golden door where two honor guard soldiers stood at attention, saluting both heads of state. They then moved towards a spot where the enormous flags of the two countries awaited them; the military band, accompanied by the Kremlin honor guard, began the welcoming ceremony for the visiting dignitary. After the United States anthem, both walked on the carpet and bowed their heads from a distance in direction of the two flags. A day of meetings and signing of trade and military agreements followed the ceremony, then the two heads of state gave a press conference.

"Mr. President, count on the Russian Federation for the defense of peace and the joint struggle for its consolidation. Once Boris Yeltsin, speaking of freedom in democracy, said 'we do not appreciate it until it is gone'. I think the same should be said about peace; it is a precious asset that we do not value until it is lost. That is why we must defend, promote, and protect it, as well as being relentless with those who want to snatch it away from us. We must ensure, you and us, that it is always so, for the sake of humanity"; President Putin finished his speech amid moved applause. Then President Trump, after listening to the last part of the translation and thanking and hugging the Russian president fiercely, began his speech expressing: "After what we've experienced these last weeks, the world has never before needed a deep reflection on the fight against terrorism, the West has never before needed to think about the common defense of the principles and values that govern us, and the civilized world has never before required that Europe, Russia, and the United States leave behind differences marked by history. It's time that we begin to work on these pressing issues, our people would not forgive us for falling into the darkness of war and its harmful consequences, among them the harmful consequences of a nuclear holocaust. My successor, who will soon arrive at the White House, will have a tough task in this regard," Trump continued his speech, which ended twenty minutes later with a call to Putin to "work without renouncing the search for our interests, in the preservation of what's most precious for our societies, the supreme values of life, freedom, and the well-being of our democracies." A burst of applause followed the speech of the President of the United States, both embraced each other tightly once more. Christiane Amanpour, who was covering this historic meeting from Moscow for CNN, began analyzing its results with a guest political analyst, Bernard Dumont turned down the volume of the television, then commented:

"After the storm comes the calm."

Tomás Cruz, who was in Paris these days and had gone to greet his French friends, replied:

"A different calm, there have indeed been many changes, Bernard, Europe, and the world in general, are no longer the same."

Tomás Cruz was right, things had changed, among them the map of Europe, which today showed the Baltic countries and Ukraine under Russian power and influence. After intense and complex negotiations in which the Russians even threatened to continue to Berlin, a peace treaty between the European Union and Russia had sealed the end of a short but bloody war that had cost the lives of more than a hundred thousand soldiers and at least thirty thousand civilians, not to mention the wounded and the enormous losses of buildings and infrastructure. On their part, the United States, the nuclear powers of Europe, plus India, Pakistan, China, and Russia had agreed to negotiate jointly a mechanism to reduce and control the nuclear arms race and prevent terrorist acts, such as those carried out by Al Qaeda, from happening again. On the TV screen, images of the signing of agreements in Moscow were shown. Cruz, who was watching the images, took the opportunity to ask Dumont:

"What happened with Valiente, Bernard?"

"The man ended up in a cell in Guantanamo, the United States requested his extradition, he is currently undergoing trial there, presided over by a military judge and jury."

"Mmm..., the man faces quite a few years of prison."

A familiar voice was heard behind Tomas Cruz:

"Yes, and very likely, Tom, the death penalty."

Cruz turned around excitedly.

"Mon ami! You told me this morning that you would stay at home."

Jean Claude Lebel, elegantly dressed, inclined slightly.

"From today, I am again at the service of La France, dear friend, I just wanted to surprise you."

Forty-eight hours before the meeting in Moscow between Trump and Putin, thanks to information collected months before during an interrogation of Valiente in his Guantanamo prison, which led to the execution of a sophisticated intelligence operation using, among other elements, Artificial Intelligence, two GBU-57 bunker buster bombs were launched from a B52 bomber, a couple of minutes apart, targeting a refuge in the mountains of Pakistan located a few kilometers from the Afghan border; shortly after, a verification operation of the results of this bombing, carried out jointly by British, Russian, and United States special forces, confirmed the death of Al-Qaeda leader, Ayman al-Zawahiri and a part of his personal guard; other operations carried out in the following hours allowed the capture of part of the leadership that made up the terrorist group's networks operating autonomously in Pakistan, Afghanistan, Egypt, and Turkey; similar operations in Paris, London, Madrid, Amsterdam, and Rome led to the elimination, in some cases, and capture, in others, of cells of this terrorist group. Amanpour was now interviewing Secretary of State, Mike Pompeo; Cruz took a sip of coffee, Bernard Dumont asked him:

"Do you think this will eliminate Al Qaeda?"

"It's hard to tell, Bernard, the problem with terrorism is that you never know how, when, and where it's going to strike again."

Lebel added:

"Besides, there are the sleeper cells of ISIS."

"That's right, in terms of terrorism, at least for now, the war isn't won, we can only celebrate having won some battles."

Dumont asked:

"Do you think the death of Al-Zawahiri will generate a strong reaction from these madmen? Well, from those who remain?"

"Bernard, in relation to Islamic fanaticism, we must always assume that an attack is just around the corner."

Lebel frowned.

"Terrorism is a thousand-headed monster, we've cut off a hundred, it could attack us sometime in a market square in Madrid, in the Paris metro, or in a shopping center in London."

Cruz added:

"That's not the worst part, J.C., they already know there are other means, even cybernetic ones, to generate chaos greater than that derived from the explosion of a bomb, they have become more sophisticated, we will have to devise new equally creative ways to track their plans."

Late at night, when the MI6 offices were almost empty, Rosamund Frost read the Mossad report; she preferred, in cases that required all her analytical capacity, to print it, placed the paper on her desk and leaned slightly forward to read it.

Case: Tracking Said al-Hamzi.

The subject left Pakistan, left Karachi two days ago. Positive identification of the subject at Hamid Karzai International Airport in Kabul. Activity so far normal, no contacts. Target tracking in progress.

A development has emerged regarding Vasiliy Koslov, his whereabouts are unknown.

Frost leaned back in her chair after reading the document, after thinking for a few minutes, decided to make a call.

"Tom?"

"Ross? So nice to hear you! Don't you sleep?"

"You see, always thinking about how to defend the United Kingdom."

A slight laugh was heard.

"What makes you call me at this hour? Well, besides missing me."

Now a nervous laugh was heard on the other side of the line.

"What makes you think I've missed you?"

"Admit it, you miss me, you have good memories of our last dinner."

Another laugh was heard.

"OK, Tomas Cruz, if that makes you happy, I've missed you. Now, moving on to our business, I'm sending you an email with a report I received recently from the Mossad. Al-Hamzi is no longer in Karachi... and Koslov has disappeared."

The tone of Cruz's voice changed.

"Where is Al-Hamzi now?"

"He traveled to Kabul two days ago."

"And Koslov?"

"Nothing is known about him for seventy-two hours, he just vanished."

"This is not to my liking, Ross, our suspicions are confirmed, Koslov and the Iranian issue seem like they will bring complications." "Me too, I want you to help me with this case, Tom."

"See? I knew you missed me, but I see it as complicated, I'm already out of the group, the assignment to the DGSE is over, as you well know, I am in Paris for other reasons."

The sound of a sarcastic laugh was heard.

"Don't you know? MI6 and DGSE have requested your reassignment for this case."

Cruz, surprised, responded:

"But who has done it? Neither the army's intelligence directorate in Colombia nor I knew about it."

The woman replied with a playful tone:

"Me."

Just over two kilometers from Orgun, a small Afghan village, located a few kilometers from the border with Pakistan, a couple of hundred meters off the road, a rustic and small peasant house dedicated to shepherding can be seen. From afar, it is nothing more than a peasant's house dedicated to fieldwork, and indeed, if one gets closer, that is the case; however, the house hides a basement, in which at that moment a meeting between two men is taking place. The first, younger, questioned the other subject, who was approaching fifty years old.

"Is everything ready, Yasir?"

"That's right, my lord. Is it time to do it?"

"Not yet, like the jackal, we must wait for the right moment to attack our prey, it will come, Yasir, and very soon."

The image of Fareed Zakaria, against the blue background of the set where he conducted his program Fareed Zakaria GPS, could be seen on the monitor, while he introduced his guest of the day to the interview. Images of President Putin, Trump, and leaders of Europe were shown, as well as videos of recent fighting on European soil, before finishing the introduction about the guest, an image of Ayman al-Zawahiri could be seen, then the image of the set expanded, Zakaria welcomed his interlocutor.

"Craig, it's a pleasure to have you back on our program."

"The pleasure is mine, Fareed."

"I have an initial question, Craig, after all that has happened in these last months and taking into account our last conversation on the matter, was your book premonitory?"

Eastman leaned back in his chair.

"It would sound arrogant on my part to answer affirmatively, Fareed, however, I believe that many elements of the book coincided in their occurrence and played a decisive role in the course of things we have experienced in recent times."

"Which of those factors you mention would you highlight, Craig?"

"The first, nationalism, division is the breeding ground for those who want to see Europe, and the West in general, falling into the clutches of chaos."

"Those nationalisms are more alive than ever today."

"That's true, nationalism was a topic that was frozen due to the Baltic and Ukraine conflict, however, it can resurge like weed if not cut; although regarding this, I want to be optimistic, Fareed, look at my country, a movement is growing regarding rejoining the European Union, if this can be achieved, I am confident that the pendulum will return to the side of integration, after what happened, we should have already learned the lesson."

"Let's hope that's true, Craig. What other factor would you consider?"

"Deterrence."

Zakaria made a curious gesture.

"What would this element consist of?"

"Experience tells us that we must strengthen NATO and additionally create a European defense system that deters our enemies from starting a conflict."

"What should be the main steps of this strengthening?"

"The Americans must return to NATO, have air bases, more planes, and tanks in Europe; the same for us. In addition, we must create at least three rapid reaction divisions while strengthening intelligence systems. We need a community organization that feeds on all the information handled by MI6, DGSE, and the other intelligence departments of the EU member countries."

"Doesn't it already exist? The EU INTCEN*?"

"It needs to be reformed, essentially the national intelligence bodies continue to set the pace for information collection and analysis, this makes these two actions carried out in a dispersed manner, it's like trying to have a clear view at night wearing sunglasses."

"I understand. So, would it be something similar to what the United States did after September 11?"

"That's right, I would add one last factor."

"Which one, Craig?"

"Terrorism."

"Wow, the importance that this element has gained. How to confront it from now on? It's clear that they can already cause even a nuclear holocaust." "Intelligence, Fareed, much intelligence, working better in the detection of possible attacks, cyber or through explosives, and developing better cooperation with our partners in Asia and America to determine where they are and eliminate them, both their leaders and the perpetrators of threats. For this, the new community entity that coordinates intelligence activities is also fundamental.

Zakaria checked his notes, then asked a question:

"I have one final question, Craig. And Russia? How do you analyze their actions in these recent events?"

Eastman allowed a slight smile to show.

"The Russians simply took advantage of an unexpected event.

"I don't understand, Craig. How is that?"

"Do you remember the attack in mid-1914 on Archduke Franz Ferdinand and his wife in Sarajevo?

"Of course, but what does that have to do with what happened now?"

"Wars are like viruses, Fareed, they need a host to live on, that attack was essentially an act of terrorism, one that occurred in the midst of the most propitious moment to detonate a conflict, and it certainly did. What happened in these last months is similar, Europe was a patient with low defenses in the midst of the fracture of its members, Russia just took part and took a good slice.

"And terrorism? Can it attack us again?"

"Yes, just like Russia, and both can do it in increasingly sophisticated ways, an Al-Qaeda cyberterrorist in Pakistan managed to duplicate the voice of the president and vice president of the United States, was able, through artificial intelligence, to have both hold a conversation in which random words and answers related to the conversation were used to an interlocutor, it is frankly amazing as well as worrying.

"Will Russia attack us again?"

"If it suits their strategic interests, they will undoubtedly do so."

"Wow, Craig, that's not the majority thinking now."

"I know, nor was I part of the majority when I wrote my book."

"Tell me something, Craig, will we be prepared for next time?"

Craig Eastman looked firmly at Zakaria.

"Returning to the example of the virus, we can prevent and take vitamins to improve our defenses, take care in washing our hands well, not greeting by hand, etc., but if the strain of the virus attacks us by air, or if it mutates, it will infect us indefinitely. We will prepare, we will surely be better organized than before, but no doubt terrorism and the territorial ambitions of some will attack us again.

"By the way. Will you write a book on this topic, Craig?"

Eastman smiled.

"In fact, I've already started working on a novel, I think it's the best way to share those decisive days we all lived through.

"Very interesting. Can you tell us what it will be called?"

"Not yet, but undoubtedly its name will have a lot to do with the tumultuous times we suffered through.

The world seemed to breathe easier after weeks that were very critical, loaded with destruction and violence, in addition to months of hard negotiation to build a world less vulnerable to war and more prone to diplomacy; terrorism now seemed to be in retreat, a series of additional hard blows were dealt in the weeks following to Al-Qaeda and ISIS; however, the lurking beast patiently awaited the right moment to disrupt that peaceful moment reached. Only the future would reveal if it could achieve its purpose.

*EU INTCEN – EU Intelligence and Situation Centre.

EPILOGUE

Now promoted to major for his heroic acts of war, Klaus Lange took a martial step forward when he heard his rank and name from the German Minister of Defense, then walked with a firm step to stop just in front of the German Chancellor, then he stood at attention with his gaze forward; she took from the fine leather box that contained it, a huge medal hanging from an elegant red ribbon with thin gold and black bands on its edges, it was the Grand Cross of Merit with Star and Band, awarded to those who demonstrated bravery and daring in the defense of Germany; previously, Lange had been awarded the NATO medal in its meritorious services class and the European Union with the Service for the Common Security and Defence Policy. The chancellor, smiling, hung the medal around his neck and subsequently handed him the order of the chancellery where such honor was granted for the services rendered to the country; all the officers, non-commissioned officers, and soldiers who survived the heroic act of war on the outskirts of Warsaw were awarded that sunny spring afternoon with lower-ranking decorations; the chancellor approached Major Lange to express with enormous gratitude, "Thanks to the bravery of you and your men, Europe, Poland, and Germany can breathe easily under the skies of freedom and democracy, we will never have a way to repay you and your brave warriors for your sacrifice in the defense of our values, the values that make the West great—the woman paused; from the bottom of my heart, major, I express to you, in the name of the German people, our eternal admiration and gratitude," tears fell from the chancellor's eyes, Major Lange, with his eyes also about to shed some, smiled as he bowed his head and with a cracking voice thanked her. The noise of a formation of Typhoon fighter jets from the Luftwaffe flying close to the ground in honor of him and his brave soldiers accompanied the ceremony; Lange, visibly moved, watched them with joy.

Tomás Cruz saw the woman enter the room; her silhouette, elegant and attractive, monopolized the last rays of sun, which, submissive, settled on her; moments after her stunning entrance, on the speakers, Gregory Porter began to sing the popular Nat

King Cole song, L-O-V-E, "L is for the way you look at me", the woman's deep green-blue eyes met Cruz's astonished gaze, Porter continued, "O is for the only one I see", Carole, smiling, came from behind him, tapped his shoulder and lifted her arm for Rosamund Frost to come closer, "V is very, very extraordinary", the lips of the beautiful woman sketched a delightful gesture of joy, she approached with a firm step, gracefully swaying her curvaceous figure, "E is even more than anyone that you adore can", Jean Claude, joining his wife, accompanied by Bernard Dumont and Craig Eastman, then pronounced his name:

"Salut, Ross, welcome!"

Cruz heard Frost's melodic voice respond to the affectionate greeting; Carole, after giving him an effusive couple of kisses, looked complicitly at her husband and friends, they immediately understood, leaving them alone; a surprised Cruz, somewhat clumsily, managed to return the greeting. The woman's voice, confident and sweet at the same time, was heard:

"For nothing in the world would I miss accompanying you today, Mr. Cruz."

"I was afraid that it would happen, Madame Frost..., you mentioned that a mission awaited us in London."

Porter, conspiratorially, sang, "Take my heart and please don't break it", she, resolved, took the initiative and gave a tender kiss on the cheek to the pale robot in front of her. After years of loneliness and nostalgia, of living imprisoned by resignation because of unrequited love, a light of hope arose for Tomás Cruz that warm evening. Could it be the end of so many winters alone? Only time would tell, however, for the first time in many years, Tomás felt relaxed, decided to let the future mark his path without fearing, or calculating, what its outcome would be. Gregory Porter's tune continued with a "Two in love can make it", Cruz let out a light laugh, raised his glass and, staring at Rosamund Frost, toasted with the beautiful woman who might return his faith in love. That evening, finally, Tomás Cruz suspected he was happy.

END

Printed and bound in the United Kingdom
30/10/2025
01988605-0002